# CAPTURED

# CAPTURED

## FROM THE FRONTIER DIARY OF
## INFANT DANNY DULY

# GREGORY J. LALIRE

**FIVE STAR**
*A part of Gale, Cengage Learning*

GALE
CENGAGE Learning·

Farmington Hills, Mich • San Francisco • New York • Waterville, Maine
Meriden, Conn • Mason, Ohio • Chicago

**LIBRARY OF CONGRESS CATALOGING-IN-PUBLICATION DATA**

Lalire, Gregory.
    Captured : from the frontier diary of infant Danny Duly / by Gregory J. Lalire. — First edition.
      pages cm
    ISBN 978-1-4328-2875-2 (hardcover) — ISBN 1-4328-2875-4 (hardcover)
    [1. Wagon trains—Fiction. 2. Frontier and pioneer life—Fiction. 3. Mormons—Fiction. 4. Indian captivities—Fiction. 5. Oglala Indians—Fiction. 6. Indians of North America—Great Plains—Fiction. 7. West (U.S.)—History—1860–1890—Fiction.] I. Title.
PZ7.L1595Cap 2014
[Fic]—dc23
          2014006871

First Edition. First Printing: July 2014
Find us on Facebook– https://www.facebook.com/FiveStarCengage
Visit our website– http://www.gale.cengage.com/fivestar/
Contact Five Star™ Publishing at FiveStar@cengage.com

Printed in the United States of America
1 2 3 4 5 6 7 18 17 16 15 14

*For my mother and father*

# DIARY ENTRIES

**PART I: THE WESTERING WOMB** . . . . . . . . 9

May 3, 1866: Post–Civil War Womb . . . . . . 11

June 13, 1866: Womb and the Wagon Bed . . . . 28

June 28, 1866: Womb and Worry . . . . . . 43

July 4, 1866: Womb and Independence Day . . . . 57

**PART II: THE WESTERING GLOOM** . . . . . . . 83

August 1, 1866: Parting of Ways Gloom . . . . . 85

August 18, 1866: Waiting Around Gloom . . . . 109

September 4, 1866: The Gloom of Two Phils . . . 136

November 3, 1866: More Gloom and Another Story . . 172

**PART III: THE WESTERING TOMB** . . . . . . 207

December 6, 1866: Tombs and the Other Side of the

Story . . . . . . . . . . . . . 209

December 25, 1866: Tombs of Captain

   Fetterman's Command . . . . . . . . 259

February 4, 1867: Anticipating More Tombs . . . 289

March 16, 1867: Putting Tombs on Hold . . . . 342

★ ★ ★ ★ ★

# PART I: THE WESTERING WOMB

★ ★ ★ ★ ★

# MAY 3, 1866: POST–CIVIL WAR WOMB

Inside Mum's tummy I feel safe. I'm not sure why, knowing what I know and *not* knowing everything else. A brother died in here in '62, a sister in '63. In '64 twins (one boy, one girl) came out alive and then succumbed to summer complaints before they learned how to say "Mum" or "Mama" or "Mammy" or "What in tarnation we doing out here anyhow?" Actually, they were all half-brothers and half-sisters to me. Or you might say they were nothing to me, since I wasn't born yet. Anyway, all that birthing and dying happened in the city of Chicago, in our tenement house by the stockyards and slaughterhouses. Papa Duly was at war to free Southern Negroes during those years, always far, far from home. Mum did what she had to do without him. It wasn't easy, what with Grandpa and Grandma Duly and Mum's younger sister, Maggie, sharing our three and a half third-story rooms and hardly able to fend for themselves on account of age, illness, and general sloth. Nothing much has changed in that regard. None of them has gone anywhere. Right now I hear Grandpa Duly grunting in his sleep like a hog, Grandma Duly beside him coughing up phlegm, and unlucky Maggie shooing a black ally cat out the kitchen window while Mum is bent over in her brown calico dress scrubbing the kitchen floor with a broken brush she once used to comb her long straight yellow hair.

Mum has always been pretty, but also pretty desperate. Not having a steady income will do that to you. But she never let poverty and the absence of her husband eat away at her during the Civil War, and the men who stayed behind for one reason or another came to her as if her hair were a field of gold and her lips two powerful red magnets. Most of them she turned away, but not all of them. She never wrote Papa Duly about her four dead babies, two inside her, two out. No reason to. He had enough already on his tin plate. Besides, he didn't know the daddies, except for one—the burly silver-haired Negro Leon P. Flowers, who lives in the dank basement of our building for free because he fixes things and who has done the Duly family many favors over the years.

Anyway, Papa Duly, who was not anybody's father at the time, never wrote Mum about the terrible things he saw on Virginia's battlefields or whether he was even alive or not. And he was capable of writing, 'cause Grandma Duly insisted she taught reading and writing to her entire brood early on. "Land sakes! None of 'em done nuthin' with it," she often complained to Grandpa Duly, who was mostly bedridden and had to listen. Then she would review the children's learning history as if they weren't his children, too. "Cholera got Bub and Sis and they never seen a schoolroom. No-account Timothy done quit school early like his father and the grippe got him. Rebecca aimed to be a teacher, God bless her soul, but she got in the family way at fourteen and died in childbirth along with her little one. Willie, as bullheaded as his father, become a fisherman and forgot everything I learned him before he sailed into a squall and got drowned in Lake Michigan. That left only my beanpole baby, Abraham. Smart as a whip he was even before I learned him a single thing! Talked like a book at age two. So what'd he do when he grow'd up? Butchered cows for a living, then went to war for dying. That's nuthin'. That's what a *dummkopf* would do." After hearing each review of their children, Grandpa Duly would simply grunt.

On the evening before an 1864 battle in the Virginia wilderness, Private Abraham Duly told a fellow bluecoat, "Sure I miss Elizabeth—the way she cocked her head when she combed her hair in front of the mirror with the cracked glass, and the way she moved when she walked up the stairs ahead of me. But I swear I can't remember the color of her eyes no more, and there ain't nuthin' good to write home about." That other bluecoat, who was a corporal with more book learning than Abe, got most of both legs and his entire right arm blown off by artillery shells shortly after dawn. But he still had his writing arm, and a week later he wrote Mum what Abe had said (leaving out the "can't remember the color of her eyes" part), because he truly believed Abe had been shot dead by the Rebs. In fact, Papa Duly had skedaddled, not died, in the middle of all those flying shells and musket balls. He would come back to fight again when he got hold of some whiskey and got his grit back, but by then most of the men in his company, including the corporal, were dead. When there was finally something good for Papa Duly to write home about, namely the end of the Civil War, he wasn't talking, let alone writing. He resembled a tall, pale ghost that possessed only enough spirit to haunt himself. Mum, who had received the corporal's letter of sincerest regret, and everyone else Papa Duly knew back in Chicago assumed he had died in action. In fact, he was not officially a war casualty at all, although still a shell of the man who had marched in a shiny blue uniform out of Camp Douglas, Illinois, like he was going to conquer the world, at least the southern world. Mum and Aunt Maggie, Grandpa and Grandma Duly, and Mr. Leon P. Flowers were in for the shock of their lives. You see, Abraham Duly made it back to his Chicago home in October 1865, half a year after General Ulysses S. Grant accepted General Robert E. Lee's surrender. His only explanation was that he took the wrong train and got lost.

My Aunt Maggie is howling. Oh, how that young lady can howl. The black ally cat has scratched her already-pitted cheek and bitten her on the point of her prominent nose. Seems like just this morning Maggie was howling because she woke up to find that Grandpa Duly and Mum had eaten the last buttermilk biscuits. Mum interrupts her floor scrubbing to administer ammonia water and old rye whiskey to her sister's wound. But Maggie howls on anyway.

"Why, oh why, must you do that, Elizabeth?" Maggie asks, tears in her eyes.

"Who else will administer to your wounds, Mags?" says Mum.

"The Lord shall. Ouch! That stings."

"I'm only trying to help."

"You're hurting me as much as that wretched cat did. My poor nose."

"It will survive."

"I hope not. That wretched cat deserves to die."

"I meant your nose. I've stopped the bleeding."

"Why does it have to be so painful, Elizabeth?"

"Your nose?"

"Life! I think you enjoy to see me suffer!"

"Pshaw, nonsense. Will nothing satisfy you, gal? I'm only trying to make it better—that is your poor nose."

"I know I am suffering for a purpose. The Lord wants my attention. It says so in the Bible. I must put my faith in the Lord. Leave me now, Elizabeth. I need to go pray."

Mum returns to her floor scrubbing. She knows she can't compete with the Lord in Maggie's eyes. I wonder if Maggie can pray and howl at the same time. She is nineteen, just four years younger than Mum, but Mum is as much a mother to her as an older sister. A nearly fatal bout with the pock three years ago left Maggie's flesh badly pitted, and she wraps her face in a wool scarf the rare times she steps foot out of our building. She believes no man will ever have her, and she spends much of her time reading from the family (that is the Hotchkiss family) Bible, the one their God-fearing mother, Sarah Hotchkiss, was carrying in 1859 when she was thrown from a runaway wagon and crushed her skull against a whiskey barrel that had also been thrown from the wagon. The Rush Street Runaway, as the newspapers dubbed the fatal Chicago accident, had occurred because "Whiskey Man Dan" Hotchkiss, an employee of a neighborhood saloon and also Sarah's whiskey-fueled husband, had been in the driver's seat and going too fast when his heart gave out. The Rush Street Runaway made orphans of the Hotchkiss girls: Maggie, twelve, Elizabeth, sixteen, and Cornelia, eighteen.

It might seem peculiar that I'm thinking about such things now. But it isn't really. You see, most of what I know about happened before my time. Mum often talks about the past to Mr. Flowers and Mags and also to herself and me (that's pretty much the same thing right now). There is very little I can do at this point in my life except think, so naturally I think about many things—past, present, and future. And I feel I am definitely family oriented, or will be after I'm born. Anyway, back to the Hotchkiss girls. To support the family of three after the tragic accident, Cornelia went to work serving drinks at their late father's saloon (no, he didn't actually own it but he drank like he did) and took a room above because she was working all the time and kept such late hours. Elizabeth stayed home being a substitute mother to Maggie and entertaining a handsome older man, Abe Duly, who she soon married. She popped the question to him, because he was tall with shy eyes and an interesting double-dimpled chin, older but not too old, extremely thoughtful, kind to his elderly parents, unattached to anyone else, and steadily employed at the slaughterhouse just around the corner. He said yes, because Elizabeth was not only a poor orphan but also the prettiest gal in the neighborhood with her perfect yellow hair, catlike green eyes, and high, wide cheekbones with apple cheeks that gave the impression she was always smiling at him. When Papa Duly moved into the tenement house to live with Mum and Maggie, he brought those elderly parents with him.

It was *not* a marriage made in heaven, more like a marriage made in the slums of Chicago. Papa Duly's job was steady but also unnerving. He tried not to think about it, but you couldn't keep your eyes closed when you were stunning or killing livestock. For the stunning of cattle he used a poleax, a fourteen-pound tool with a rounded hammer face opposite the ax blade. With almighty force, he brought down the rounded head of the poleax onto the cow's head, just below the horns. An accurate blow sent the cow to the floor, but sometimes it took another two or three blows to bring about unconsciousness. Other workers would take it from there in rapid fashion—chaining the cow's back legs, dragging it off to be hung upside down, slitting its throat with a sharp instrument, gutting and skinning it. The blood and gore surrounded Papa Duly, but at least he wasn't doing the actual throat slitting, which drenched a fellow with a stream of blood. On occasion, though, he worked with the hogs, which was worse because the poleax step was bypassed. After the squealing pig's back legs were chained, it was hooked to a wheel, hoisted into the air, and transported by overhead rail to the place where the throat cutter stood waiting like a medieval executioner. The blood that was drained out from the hogs didn't go to waste—it was collected and used as fertilizer. The hogs would no longer be able to squeal at this point, but they often were still squirming when they were dropped into a vat of boiling water. Mum heard about this systematic slaughter every day for three weeks and then she stopped asking her husband how his workday went. He didn't want to hear about her days in the tenement house, either. The days were all too hot or too cold, overcrowded, overwhelming, financially overextended, and full of scrubbing (floors, walls, clothes, underclothes, sheets), sickness, seizures, scrap soup, and stench. At least blood was absent, except when poor Grandpa Duly had blood in his stools or poor Grandma Duly coughed up blood or unlucky Maggie Hotchkiss accidentally gave herself cuts with kitchen knives, sewing scissors, and even sheets of paper. It was not long before Elizabeth and Abraham stopped speaking to each other except out of necessity.

Then came the war. Abe didn't necessarily want to fight or kill, but he wanted to preserve the Union. He also wanted to free the slaves and himself. Out of his acquaintance with two hardworking free Negroes (one of whom was building handyman Mr. Flowers) and his hatred for both the slaughterhouse where he worked six days a week and the tenement house where he slept most nights, he joined up in Illinois and went east to teach the Confederates a lesson. The next year, Cornelia Hotchkiss, the oldest and most peart of the three sisters, went in the opposite direction when she finally met the right man.

In the saloon business Cornelia listened to and rubbed elbows with men from all walks of life. Most of the patrons had sad stories to share and demanded she show them great sympathy, either for one night or forever. The well-to-do patrons were usually married and told lies about their marital status, their pasts, their futures, and her wide-eyed beauty. With her dirty brown hair, the large Hotchkiss nose (which Mum managed to avoid), square jaw, and too-thick neck, she knew she wasn't beautiful and that the size of her eyes was due to wide-eyed skepticism. Drunk men would say or do anything. Maybe drunk women, too. But she always stayed under control. When men bought her drinks, the bartenders watered them down for her and, in any case, most of her hard liquor ended up on the sawdust floor or inside spittoons. Cornelia spoke of these tricks of the trade and related her saloon stories during her daytime visits to the tenement house. Mum was a good listener but didn't need drinks or tricks to draw men to her like houseflies. Of course I was not even conceived of when Aunt Cornelia and Mum were having their lively discussions, but since my creation, so to speak, I've picked up this information from Mum's candid conversations with open-minded Mr. Flowers and her sometimes uncomfortable talks with unlucky, biblically focused, perpetually peaked Aunt Maggie.

Getting into the subject of Mum with men (even my own father, whose voice I've never heard) is a bit unsettling. Most of them have come and gone. But I must say that Mr. Flowers is a pleasant, gentle sort, even though he is larger than anyone in the building. His size and darkness scare some folks around here, but Mum and I know different. Sometimes they hug each other when they don't think anyone is looking, and he never squeezes her too hard. And the time he put his hand on her growing belly, he was worried he might somehow damage the little guy inside—me! Although his hair is mostly silver and he has large crow's feet next to his eyes, he is robust. He can fix anything we got from damaged kerosene lamps to broken chair legs and he hauls water and wood and anything else Mum needs to carry up three flights of stairs.

Not sure how I got to talking about Leon P. Flowers. I guess it's because I was talking about men and I hardly know any men except Leon P. Flowers and Grandpa Duly, who is Mr. Flowers' complete opposite—small, weak, pale, sickly, grouchy, uncommunicative, and unappreciative of Mum (never thanking her for feeding him soup and other things he doesn't have to chew). That's right, I was about to mention the man Aunt Cornelia found one night at the saloon—a night when all the talk was about General Robert E. Lee and how that Virginia gentleman had given the Yankees a thrashing for the second time in two years at a place called Bull Run. His name was Wheelwright. She told Mum he was different. He was a gambler, not a drinker. He didn't have much money in his pockets and was almost twice her age, but he wasn't full of alcohol, lies, or self-pity. He was intent on *not* doing three things—*not* fighting in a war he didn't care a lick about, *not* being a bachelor his whole dang life, and *not* being poor in a country that was bursting with golden opportunities. He had missed the gold rushes to California, Nevada, and Colorado, but now he aimed to get rich somewhere up in the Northwest, and if he didn't have to do it alone, so much the better.

"You proposin' holy matrimony?" Cornelia asked him after knowing him two nights and one day.

"Nope," he said. "However, I am proposing to propose later in the month if my luck holds out. Now, Corny dear, I'll have to ask you to excuse me for a few days while I engage in the holy game of poker."

It took a two-week winning streak at five-card stud to get Mr. Wheelwright a traveling stake and a suitable wedding ring for Cornelia. It took Cornelia two seconds to accept his marriage proposal. He didn't have to ask anyone for her hand in marriage since she was an orphan, and anyway he had won her hand the first night they met. Two days after visiting the justice of the peace, they left Chicago by rail. Her two sisters were teary-eyed and not just because Cornelia would no longer be giving them part of her saloon salary. They also looked up to her. She wasn't afraid to go out into the world and work or to go after what she wanted. She was a risk taker. She could just up and leave the tenement house, the saloon, and all the rest of the city behind. That was something that Mum only dreamed about sometimes at night and that Maggie couldn't bear to imagine anytime. Cornelia did leave her sisters with a good sum of her new husband's bankroll and told Mum, "There'll be more of the same coming your way, Elizabeth, just as soon as Wheely finds his gold mine!" Cornelia never used the word "if." She knew what she and her man wanted and didn't have any doubts that they would get it.

The newlyweds went by steamboat to Fort Benton on the barely navigable Upper Missouri and then continued by pack mule to the Grasshopper Creek diggings at Bannack in what would later become Montana Territory. It was slim pickings for newcomers and only Mr. Wheelwright's dexterity with cards prevented Cornelia from having to take a job at one of the fledgling Bannack saloons. But they both made important friends and connections, and with their assistance in 1863, Mr. Wheelwright discovered or bought a series of claims seventy-five miles away at Alder Gulch. He hit pay dirt, as the couple had expected all along, and they moved to the boomtown of Virginia City to live and prosper. Road agents, who stopped gold shipments to line their pockets, plagued the area. But Mr. Wheelwright, who was so opposed to the Civil War, proved he could fight for a cause—namely, his own money—by becoming a leader in the vigilante movement. Accumulating gold and hanging thieves—life is good for Wheely. His wife isn't complaining either. I know. Mum reads all of Cornelia's letters out loud.

Today, the Wheelwrights live in style inside a flush Virginia City home, with flowerpots in every window, innerspring mattresses on every bed, and the grandest piano in all of Montana Territory. True to her word, Cornelia has tried to send money to her sisters in Chicago, but there is no easy way. More gushing letters than treasure has gotten through to us at the tenement house. Her last letter was for Mum's eyes only.

"I saw something I adored in Wheely's eyes way back in Chicago and now I know absolutely what it was," Cornelia wrote. "I saw flashes of gold! He hasn't disappointed me one single bit. You'd adore him, Elizabeth. Sure he came up high and dry in Bannack, but he's game as a banty rooster. What a marvelous provider! He doesn't bother with cards anymore. He has taken more gold from the Gulch than you can imagine. The saloon life is over forever, my dear. We don't have to take a back seat to anybody. Wheely is a pillar of Virginia City society, and I am the pillar right next to him in the loveliest silk and velvet dress you've ever seen, imported from San Francisco by way of Salt Lake. We're really not so terribly remote here—at least not in the warmer months! Our wealth and good fortune is boundless now that Wheely and the vigilantes have taken care of the road agents and other riffraff!! Wish you were here.—Your everloving and always faithful big sister, Cornelia Hotchkiss Wheelwright. P.S. Will send money soon. Have you found a man, a white man, who can provide for you? It can't be that difficult. You are too lovely, Elizabeth, to suffer any longer in that dreadful place. If I could do it, so can you! Is Maggie pulling her weight or being her usual bother? Dear God, I love Mags awfully much but she can be such a lump! And one more thing, and allow me to be perfectly blunt with you, dear Elizabeth, as only sisters can be: Are the Dulys dead yet? What a burden they have been for you! So much like their demented son!!!"

Theoretically, letters from an admired older sister living so far away should be cherished and saved. That's what I heard Mum mumble after she reread that particular letter and agonized over it for the tenth time. The letter was shocking for its candor—too close to the truth to be cherished. Mum did save the letter, but only because she twice withdrew the pages from a stove burner at the last second. Cornelia's words hit Mum so hard that they knocked her off her feet and she couldn't do her chores or anything else for two days. "I'm as useless to the world as Grandpa Duly," she moaned, sounding a lot like

Maggie. But at least Maggie can usually find something in the Bible to lift her own spirits. Not even the sympathetic words of Mr. Flowers (the only one she had allowed to read the letter) could snap Mum out of her paralysis. I was worried about her, and about me, too, since she was barely eating anything and that kind of thing can affect the both of us. Finally, a bone-rattling coughing seizure by Grandma Duly did the trick.

"Cornelia gets her husband's gold and I get my husband's mother's phlegm," Mum said to Mr. Flowers. "Well, never mind. I will not whine again about it. Life must go on."

Mum has every reason to be jealous of her older sister. Despite all her beauty, intelligence, and generosity, Mum has nothing to show for it—at least until I show myself. She married Abraham Duly, but he could not handle peacetime in Chicago or war in Virginia. She must care for Abe's difficult and sick parents. On the other hand, the not particularly attractive Cornelia found love in a saloon, deserted her sisters in Chicago, and obtained vast wealth in Virginia City. When Mum finally got around to replying to Cornelia's letter, though, she wrote nothing to suggest she was green with envy or prematurely bitter by life's unfairness.

"I could easily write mean-spirited things to her—how she is only interested in gold and does not care enough about poor Maggie," she said while staring hard into her broken hand mirror. "But I won't. I want to be bigger than that."

Nobody else was in the room at the time, unless you count me inside her tummy. I gave a little kick to show I was listening.

Mum composed a simple short letter in which she congratulated Cornelia on her good fortune, admitted that the only man in her life providing anything was a man of color, and mentioned that Grandpa and Grandma Duly, even with their lives hanging by a thread, were ornery enough to outlive her. As an afterthought, Mum added that she was trying to teach homebody

Maggie some nursing skills because Mum did not intend to be the sole Duly caretaker forever. She made no mention of her "demented" husband or for that matter me.

But I guess I should say something here about Papa Duly. He is my father after all, whether I like it or not. He is alive and in the Chicago area, though quite out of touch. Normally a grown son like him would have been expected to take some responsibility for his parents, but Papa Duly is neither normal nor able to help anyone, not even himself. He is what you might call a broken man. That's what I call him anyway instead of using words like "demented, "buggy," or "mad." Those words sound ugly. Not that I'm trying to deny the truth, but who really knows the truth about anyone? It was the Civil War that broke him more than anything else. Poor Papa Duly. He hates war, and who can blame him for that? I hate war, too, even though I admit I have never been an actual eyewitness to battle. Papa Duly, the broken man, is in a confined place. Sort of like me. But the places are as different as Heaven and Hell. That is to say I love where I am—in Mum's tummy—and I can't imagine he can stand being where he is. Nothing can be done about it though, not by him and certainly not by me. Anyway, I'm not going to cry about it like a baby.

Maybe Papa Duly should never have returned to Chicago after the war. Home, our tenement house, could not make him whole again. What am I saying! If he hadn't come home, I'd be out of luck. That is to say I wouldn't be where I am right now, in Mum's tummy. You see . . . never mind. Sometimes it's better not to see too much. Is my face ever red! Of course I can't see it with my own two eyes any more than anyone else can. But I can feel the redness—instinctively, you might say. I am kind of glad I won't be showing my red face to the world for another two or three months.

Allow me to get back to Papa Duly. He not only came home

but also returned to the old job he never liked in the first place. Working in a place where you walk around all day ankle-deep in the blood of cows and pigs can drive a man to drink. But the drinking didn't help Papa Duly. Neither did the thinking. With or without whiskey, his cogitations left him in a stupor. The slaughterhouse boss threatened to fire him for thinking too much on the job and for missing too many days of work. Papa Duly acted first. One day at noon he walked out without a word, taking with him his poleax so that no poor beast would ever again be stunned by it.

He might have found another job, but he didn't try. He mostly stayed in bed, like his sick old father. Abe, though, was able bodied. His mind just wasn't working right. He barely said a word to Mum, let alone to Grandpa Duly, Grandma Duly, or Maggie. Sometimes he treated them like strangers. He became a stranger to them. When he wasn't lying in bed he would stand in a corner of the bedroom staring at the walls as he waited for Mum to lead him somewhere—just like he was one of those unfortunate animals at the slaughterhouse. He was already dead on the inside—well, almost. He didn't even last two months with Mum before two men in dark overcoats hauled him off to Dunning, an overcrowded and somewhat terrifying combination poorhouse and asylum for the insane northwest of the city. Papa Duly, being in a stupor, hadn't done anything dangerously crazy in Chicago until the day he tried to strangle poor Mr. Leon Flowers.

It wasn't for anything Mr. Flowers had done. In fact, it was a case of mistaken identity. One morning when Mum was out getting Grandma Duly's cough medicine, the old Negro came up from the basement to share a humpback whitefish he had caught in Lake Michigan. Papa Duly immediately jumped on the burly man's back and began choking him. "Your evil plan to assassinate me won't work, John Wilkes Booth!" Papa Duly cried out, at least according to a short newspaper account that Mum read out loud to Maggie, who had slept through the whole choking incident. Grandma Duly screamed during the attack, though, somehow getting the idea that an intruder named Mr. Booth was trying to murder her son with a poisonous fish. Her screaming woke up Grandpa Duly and brought other residents of the tenement house scurrying to the third floor. Then a panting Chicago policeman arrived.

Mr. Flowers was really in no danger, since he had a thick neck and outweighed Papa Duly by fifty pounds. He probably wouldn't have even pressed charges. But Papa Duly, believing the officer was a Booth accomplice, bit him on the shoulder and upper arm. Amazingly, the newspaper article has one quote and it is from Grandpa Duly, who hardly even says two words to his own wife: "My boy don't see things the way you and I see things. He's different and he possesses good sharp teeth. That don't make him a mad dog!" Upon being arrested, Papa Duly told the authorities he was Abraham Lincoln and was only trying to protect himself. Unfortunately, he stuck with that story in front of the judge.

Papa Duly, being both poor and crazy, is in the right place now, everyone says, including Mum—although I can't help but feel sorry for him. Mum has only visited the place once and she didn't even get in to see Papa Duly because he insisted to the doctors that she was John Wilkes Booth's mistress. I'm not sure whether or not he now realizes he is Abraham Duly, not Abraham Lincoln. Mum doesn't make inquiries. I guess she is glad to be rid of him, at least most of the time. He did leave something behind, namely me. Of course there wasn't much of me yet when he departed and he couldn't see me in any case. He probably doesn't even know I exist. I've grown considerably in the months since then. If you could peek inside at this exact moment, you might even be able to tell that I'm a boy.

Like I said, I'm feeling real safe in here right now—as snug as a bug in a rug. And I have this ability to see pictures in my mind's eye of things outside the womb, to know things without knowing how I know things, to hear human voices, snorts, coughs, and howls, and to feel the energy of the people who are around me—and not just Mum. Is it any wonder that I'm in no blamed hurry to be on the outside experiencing things directly without the safety net of my current warm and cozy environment? But it's already May and I instinctively know I'll have to get out of here long about July. Considering Mum's previous bad luck in this area, I am not real confident how it will all turn out—that is to say, how I'll turn out. That's why I'm writing so furiously right now. Of course, it helps that writing comes so naturally to me. Mum, full name Elizabeth Hotchkiss Duly, doesn't help me one lick. It takes her two weeks just to compose a letter to her well-to-do sister Cornelia Hotchkiss Wheelwright in remote Virginia City, Montana Territory—and Lord knows how long it takes until Cornelia's long-nailed, grabby fingers can actually clutch the letter. Of course, if I don't die prematurely, I aim to write, write, and write some more on the outside. *That* and breastfeed. Maybe I'll even learn to speak and walk and use the privy out back, if I can find the time. You see, with apologies to poor Papa Duly at the Dunning asylum, I have so much stuff I *need* to write about already, and I haven't lived to see my first sunrise or sunset or anything that comes in between.

I'm done writing* for now. And, at last, Aunt Maggie is done howling. Good job, Mum. I hope one day you can heal my inevitable wounds, too. Now if only Grandpa Duly will stop snorting in his sleep and Grandma Duly will halt her coughing fit. Why don't you stop scrubbing the floor for now, Mum, and get a load off your feet. We both could use the rest.

(*Dear Reader. I don't literally have pen and paper in hand in here; I'm not a particularly large fetus, but, still, there's barely enough room for me. I am etching these words firmly into my skull so that they can be recalled exactly and transferred to *my* diary, the Lord willing, at a later date.)

# June 13, 1866: Womb and the Wagon Bed

Sometimes things happen so fast that it's hard to get your bearings. And even though you don't move more than a few inches forward or backward yourself, you get on a roll. That's how things are right now for me. I've been a bit overwhelmed by the changes taking place, and I don't mean in my personal development. I best etch it out in my skull right now before I am too buried in change to remember what happened before. Buried in change before I'm even born? Makes me wonder how often that has happened to others. I have no way of knowing. Are there others like me? Of course physically there are, but I mean mentally. Or am I unique? Maybe I'm just thinking too much about it all. Life rolls on, even inside the womb.

Yes, that's right. I am still inside Mum, who is flat on her back inside three-time widower George W. Gunderson's covered wagon that is in a terrible rut along the Oregon Trail. She hasn't been feeling too well lately, and though she doesn't eat much, she vomited twice this morning. We're countless miles from the hustle and bustle, the dirt and the stench of Chicago. Not that the trail lacks activity, both of the migratory human and animal kind. Not that there is any shortage of dirt no matter which direction we look. Not that the pulling oxen don't sometimes smell as bad as the cows and hogs back in the stockyards. Way out here, as a rule, the skies and beasts are bigger and the air and water are cleaner. Every creek we've come to, Mum has compared it to Bubbly Creek, also known as the South Fork of the Chicago River's South Branch. Bubbly Creek, more or less a sewer for the Union Stockyards, is filled with so much manure and so many carcasses that it sometimes catches fire. Still, the worries and dangers are greater out here for Mum, mainly because she is dealing with the unknown, an honest but hardheaded man with ideas, and one particularly restless, hard-kicking fetus—me.

Our jumping-off point was Independence, Missouri, even though most everyone else has been jumping off fifty miles to the north at St. Joseph. Seems the Burlesons, who are running this small wagon train, as well as Mr. Gunderson had friends and relatives living in Independence who could give them good deals on covered wagons and all the accessories and supplies. And we didn't so much "jump off" onto the emigrant road as crawl away from Independence like a diapered babe leaving its mother's lap for the first time. Not that I've reached that stage yet, of course.

Driving the lead wagon is our wagon master, Monroe Burleson, who has more hair on his upper lip and eyebrows than on the top of his head and thus keeps his well-worn flat-brimmed straw hat pulled down tight over his ears and tied under his chin. He was raised in a place called Ohio City, since annexed by Cleveland, but calls himself a farmer. He takes pride in keeping his nose and his mind clean and his hands dirty. Like the rest of us, he has never previously gone west by an overland route, and when it comes to understanding most things about this foreign terrain he is dreadfully at sea. But he is a devout Methodist with the most hard cash, the most bulk about his middle, the most oxen, the most audacity, and the most conspicuous wife in unusually tall Amanda, whose fine long dresses are made for sitting not walking and whose bonnets are loaded with lace and feathers to accentuate her fair face more than shield it from the sun.

Mr. Gunderson, who must be on the downhill side of fifty, befriended Mum in Independence. She refers to him as her benefactor rather than a friend while he clearly wants to be something more than a benefactor or a friend to her. He's the kind of man who needs to be married, not like Mr. Flowers or some of the other men Mum has known—maybe not even like Papa Duly. A robust Mormon widower, Old Man Gunderson looks like a formidable pirate with the red bandana he wears over his head instead of a hat, his thick black beard, and his swarthy face with a patch over the right eye. Looks can be deceiving. He is definitely a family man—he has half a dozen sons with him. He hails from the northeastern Ohio shores of Lake Erie like the Burlesons and is Monroe Burleson's only Mormon friend, or at least was before the wagons started rolling. There is some tension on the trail.

Occupying the other seven wagons in our party are families who apparently couldn't leave the Midwest until the Civil War was over. All the men have wives and they all seem content taking orders, which is perfect for Mr. Burleson, who loves to give orders even though he calls himself a "farmer" and was once an Ohio bank clerk who paid someone to serve for him in the late war. There are only a few children, and none under the age of ten, making this arduous trip—not that I could play with other children right now even if I had a mind to do so.

The sluggish start from Independence of our nine-wagon party was due to a number of factors—waiting in vain for more wagons to join up there; obtaining the wrong or shoddy supplies; disagreements on whether to bring along rocking chairs, violins, and chamber pots along with flour, sugar, and salt; Amanda Burleson's long goodbyes to friends and relatives and dealing with several dress and hat makers; a twister and a thunderstorm; Mr. Gunderson's instant infatuation with my Mum; and Mum's difficult pregnancy. While Monroe and

Amanda Burleson, who never had any children of their own, didn't much want Mum to join the traveling party, George Gunderson wouldn't have it any other way—even though he already has six boys and the oldest is *nearly* Mum's age.

When Mum mentioned to Old Man Gunderson that she was heavy with child and had left her younger sister behind to fend for herself, with whatever assistance the Lord could provide, he was non-judgmental. She thought it prudent not to tell him about leaving Grandpa Duly and Grandma Duly with Maggie at the tenement house or husband Abraham Duly at the asylum. It might cause some misunderstanding. Actually, Mum has no reason to feel guilty. She had been training Maggie to be a decent caretaker and a responsible adult and had asked Mr. Flowers to come up from the basement to check on her twice a day. Plus, Cornelia had been able to send gold from Virginia City to Salt Lake City, have it converted into greenbacks, and then transferred to a new account for Mum at the First National Bank of Chicago. In short order Mum had gone to the bank and put the account in Maggie's name after taking out only a modest amount of traveling money.

Mum had spent her last dime making the trip by spring wagon and railroad car from Chicago to western Missouri, and she feared she would be stranded there. But then she dropped her black shawl on the main street in Independence, and Mr. Gunderson, being a pirate-like white knight, retrieved it. He gawked at her flowing yellow hair, comparing it to waving grains of golden wheat, and then apologized for his forwardness. She accepted his apology so graciously that he asked her to sit with him in Old Temple Lot. Back in the 1830s the Latter-day Saints, or Mormons, had planned to build a temple on that spot before gentile persecutors drove them out of the county and then the state. He told her all about his people's exodus from Missouri to Illinois and about how a decade later Brigham Young brought the Church of Jesus Christ of Latter-day Saints west as far as the Great Salt Lake and declared, "This is the place." Mum listened so well that Mr. Gunderson declared, "That is the place for me." And then he took her hand in his oversized paw and added, "And I believe for you, too."

To prove how serious he was, he took out a letter he was writing to a cousin in Salt Lake City and quickly scribbled a P.S.: "Met a Perfect Angel. Hope to bring her along. Keep your fingers crossed." He read to Mum what he wrote and when she acted surprised, he told her that her worries were over and that she was free to travel west in his covered wagon. I was so startled I nearly turned over in the womb. But Mum didn't even bat an eye. He took her with him to mail the letter at the Overland Stage Station, which was making a run to Salt Lake at the end of the week. Afterward he and Mum went to the best eating establishment in town and sat at a semiprivate corner table sharing a rare porterhouse steak. Eating meat doesn't repulse Mum the way it does Papa Duly, but she only picked at her slice of fancy steak. She had cravings for pickles and pig's feet, which happened to be on the menu, so Mr. Gunderson bought her both of those items, no questions asked. He didn't talk with his mouth full, which was lucky, because when he opened up to her about himself, his mouth was like a gulch during a gully washer. She in turn told him things about herself, but only the things she wanted him to know. Again, no mention of Papa Duly or his parents. She did mention that no matter how much she talked to me or hummed to me, I would still kick like a mule when she stopped.

"I reckon he'll be a boy," Old Man Gunderson said. "Boys can be like that—real rambunctious. I should know. I sired six of 'em."

"And the boys won't mind me riding in your wagon, Mr. Gunderson?" Mum asked as she wiped pickle juice off her chin.

"Not my boys. And please call me George. The lads may be rambunctious, but they know who is boss. Besides, how could any male of the species object to such a prime example of femininity?"

Mum flashed her apple-cheek smile. "I'm getting awfully big," she said, patting her belly. Then she ate the last bit of pickle.

"Which makes you even more prime, Libbie."

"You make me blush, Mr. Gunderson" she said, without blushing. "I'm afraid I might not be of much use to you on the trip. I find myself getting awfully tired, and the journey hasn't even begun."

"Never you mind, Libbie. The boys and I shall handle everything. Two of them happen to be right good cooks."

"Wonderful. But, you see, sir, I have no money. And you'll be expecting something of me in return."

"Hogwash! All I would wish in my heart is for you in due time to please give serious consideration to becoming my bride. I have no other wife at this time."

"Yes, you told me. But I've only known you for several hours."

"The best hours of my life, Libbie. And I do not say this lightly. I am not as a rule a rash man."

Mum continued to polish her apple-cheek smile, but thankfully she did not commit to anything.

The next day on the main street, while Mr. Burleson was shouting out last-minute instructions and orders and Mrs. Burleson was wrapping up her long goodbyes, Mr. Gunderson broke the news to them. "The little lady shall ride in my wagon," he announced, as Mum stood there hunched over, trying not to look so plump.

"This is a family wagon train, George," Mr. Burleson replied.

"She'll be my worry, Monroe."

"Being in the family way doesn't count."

"She counts to me."

"Every passenger is the worry of the wagon master."

"You master the wagons, Monroe. Don't try to be my master."

"Be reasonable, George. We're already late as it is."

"Don't let us stop you. Libbie and I are ready to roll."

Mr. Burleson scratched the top of his straw hat, pinched his nose, twisted his mustache, rubbed his double chin, and then finally turned to his wife. Mrs. Burleson was looking Mum up and down as if Mum were merchandise at the general store. Then the wind blew one of Mrs. Burleson's bonnet feathers down over her eyes and she turned away to make adjustments. Mr. Burleson waited patiently.

At last, Mrs. Burleson faced Mum again. "You look absolutely wretched, missy," she said. "Shame on the cad who did this to you."

"Her name is Elizabeth—Libbie," said Old Man Gunderson. "And she is beautiful."

"Does she have a last name?" Mrs. Burleson asked.

"Of course," Mr. Gunderson said, although Mum had never told it to him.

Mrs. Burleson did not bother asking what it was. Something made her sneeze. She produced a linen handkerchief with fancy stitching around the hem and kind of waved it in front of her nose. Another question came to her mind. "Have you nowhere else to go, missy?" she asked.

Mum lowered her head and bit her tongue.

"Does she talk?" asked Mrs. Burleson. "Never mind. It doesn't matter. We can't leave her in the street. Let's get this show on the road."

"She may come along with us, George, and ride in your wagon," Mr. Burleson said, "as long as you understand that I am fully in charge of this wagon train."

"Of course," said Mr. Gunderson.

"I thank you, sir, from the bottom of my heart," Mum said to the wagon master as she put a hand over her heart. Then she patted her belly. "We thank you," she added.

Mr. Burleson kept his eyes fastened on her. "George tells me you had run out of track, Miss," he said. "We can't expect you to wait for those Irishmen to finish the transcontinental railroad. They've started to lay track parallel to the overland road, but there's no telling when they'll get the job done."

She smiled at him. "Yes, we'd run out of track, Mr. Burleson, and nearly out of hope. You are all so kind."

Amanda Burleson cleared her throat and it sounded like a frog croaking. "My joints are aching again, Burly," she said to her husband. "I need to sit."

Mr. Burleson did not respond immediately.

"Monroe Burleson!" she shouted, actually looking down at the big man. "Help me up onto the wagon seat."

"Yes, Mandy," he said.

But then Mum's knees buckled and she started to collapse right there on the main street of Independence. The wagon master had no choice but to catch her. She had become as limp as a doll. Old Man Gunderson borrowed Mrs. Burleson's fan to bring the color back in Mum's face and after several minutes took her off Mr. Burleson's hands. When Mr. Gunderson carried Mum to his wagon, second in line, the wagon master followed. And as Mr. Gunderson got Mum settled on a patchwork quilt made by one of his late wives, the wagon master closely studied the shape of the pregnant passenger.

Amanda Burleson, despite her aching joints, marched right up to the back of the wagon bed and shouted to everyone inside, "None of us got time to wait for the railroad!"

Mum (and me, too, of course) later learned from Old Man Gunderson that the Burlesons were headed not to Salt Lake City like Gunderson and sons or even for Oregon's Willamette

Valley like the other families in the wagon train. Instead, they were bound for the Indian Springs Hotel and Resort, owned by Amanda Burleson's uncle, because it was the belief of her and her uncle that only daily soothing baths taken in Oregon mud could make her joints stop aching. It didn't matter what Monroe Burleson believed. His wife was going west for the cure, with or without him.

"They bicker more than I did with any of my wives," Mr. Gunderson said. "But each time they have a squabble, they patch things up faster than you can say 'Jack Robinson.' He'll call her 'Mandy' and she'll call him 'Burly' and they'll go rail at some storekeeper or town drunk. Monroe wants to be a farmer and Amanda wants to be the belle of the ball, but their differences don't keep them apart. Wherever one goes, the other goes, including Indian Springs Hotel and Resort."

Mr. Gunderson added that they were good to him even when he was one of the only Mormons in their Methodist community in Ohio and that they had brought elaborate flower bouquets to the caskets of all his wives. They knew he had been dreaming for decades of one day living in Brigham Young's Zion by the Great Salt Lake and that only his wives had been holding him back. When Amanda Burleson's aching joints drove the couple west, he was the second person they asked to come along— right after Hanna, the Burlesons' longtime colored maidservant.

That's why George W. Gunderson's covered wagon is almost always second in line to the Burlesons' wagon—including right now as we negotiate these nasty ruts in the Oregon Trail. Old Man Gunderson has done hardly any driving himself, and he's not holding the reins now. One of his sons is—George the youngest from his third marriage. All six sons are "Georges." It's downright confusing to Mum, the other emigrants, and even the Gundersons themselves. But, we've been westbound on this beaten path for a month now, including time spent waiting for high waters to recede on nameless creeks, and I can tell (call it instinct if you like) all the Georges apart. I also know when it's George VI driving without even seeing him. He's barely fourteen and by far the worst driver of the bunch, making bumps where there aren't any, hitting every mud hole, sometimes straying into the wrong ruts, sometimes getting out of line from the other eight wagons in our party.

No matter what, George VI blames the four dumb oxen that are, in my humble opinion, smarter than him with a superior sense of direction. He constantly curses the poor beasts for traveling at just two or three miles an hour and tells them that one day he'll be astride a thoroughbred like Cincinnati, the handsome seventeen-hands horse that Ulysses S. Grant rode to Appomattox Court House to accept Lee's surrender. In short, George VI should really focus more on the job at hand—getting Mum and me to Fort Laramie in one piece. They all seem plenty rambunctious, though, even the oldest, George I, who turned twenty the other day on the trail. He says about three-dozen Methodist girls are pining for him every day back in Ohio but that it is high time to give the Mormon girls in Utah Territory a break. His openly stated birthday wish is to one day have more wives than Brigham Young. Apparently, his father is half-brother to one of Brigham Young's seventeen wives. This Brigham Young fellow, whom Old Man Gunderson calls "the Prophet" and "Lion of the Lord," rules the Utah desert and is said to have sired thirty-one daughters and twenty-five sons. Talk about your extended families!

George I has a lot of catching up to do in the wife department since he never married one of those Methodist girls. But I'm happy to report that he has shown no interest at all in Mum. Maybe he fears the wrath of his father or is looking for younger females who don't have anything in their wombs yet. It doesn't really matter, as long as he keeps his rambunctious hands off her. Actually, Mum knows how to handle his type. She is more concerned about her pirate benefactor, Old Man Gunderson. It turns out that Mr. Gunderson is just eight years younger than the Prophet and has no intention of collecting such an unmanageable number of wives. But he has hinted that after Mum becomes his bride, he wouldn't mind taking on two or three more wives to do the housework and help with Mum's newborn baby and all the other babies that come along in the years ahead in Zion. That notion doesn't sit well with Mum. She doesn't say anything of course, but I can tell that it causes as much turmoil inside her as my inadvertent kicking and her overly sensitive internal organs. Lying around like she does in the back of *his* wagon, she is in no position to shrink in aversion when he comes near, but I do think some of her vomiting can be attributed as much to him as to her pregnancy or to the secretive fact she has a husband institutionalized back in a Chicago loony bin. George W. Gunderson calls himself a "Saint" but I say he ain't—for one thing, when he's around Mum he breathes too heavy on her and his beard accidentally tickles her face far too frequently. For another, he produces great gray clouds from an exceptionally large clay pipe, even in mixed company. And I've distinctly heard George II tell one of his younger brothers that their father was violating the Word of Wisdom revelation that forbids the human ingestion of tobacco.

Still, I shouldn't be too down on Old Man Gunderson. He is hard on his boys, but they truly are rambunctious and sometimes go off at half-cock. With Mum, he is a perfect gentleman. That is to say he doesn't touch Mum's belly unless she asks him to do so. And the fact is that Mr. Gunderson has never actually had more than one wife at any one time . . . so far. His three wives had all been sickly, and all had died on him, but there had always been at least two months between wives. Burying his stick-in-the-mud gentile third wife last March in God's Acre

Cemetery in west Cleveland had opened the door not only for a fourth wife but also for travel to Mormon Country. "Paw's a man on a mission," his sons often say when they can't quite understand his hardness toward them or his softness for Mum.

Mum, of course, does not have a religious bone in her body. While Maggie was constantly reading and quoting from the Hotchkiss family Bible back at the tenement house, Mum only picked it up when she was dusting or needed a solid doorstop. And I don't think too much can be made of the fact that she has been increasingly crying "For God's sake!" and "Lord have mercy!" while bouncing around in pain in Old Man Gunderson's wagon bed. No matter how much kindness Mr. Gunderson extends to her, she is too strong-willed to be won over by a man more than twice her age who looks like a pirate. She has no intention of ever becoming a Mormon wife. She has other plans for *our* final destination that involve branching off the old Oregon Trail onto the relatively new Bozeman Trail. Because that means parting ways with the Burleson wagon train at or near Fort Laramie and hitching a ride with someone bound for the Montana gold fields, she hasn't said a word about it to the Georges or anyone else. But I know all this because Mum has a tendency to talk in her sleep about not only her poor sister Maggie, who must be struggling mightily to keep up with Papa Duly's decrepit parents, but also her rich big sister Cornelia, who said in her last flowery letter that the streets of Virginia City are paved in gold and that she is treated like the queen of England by the largely male populace.

Ouch! I think I just felt that last bump as much as Mum did. As far as our ride in the wagon bed, this is the worst part of the trip so far. Passage was difficult through the heavy mud we experienced down in the "bottoms," so we detoured to higher ground. But now, suddenly, things are worse. From what I have gathered from bits of conversation here and there, we are on a stretch of rocky terrain on the dry divide between the Little Blue River valley and the Platte River valley. And from what I am experiencing firsthand, George VI is hitting every big rock. Here comes one now. Lordy! There must have been six inches of daylight between Mum's back and the wagon bed on that one! Mum is groaning and holding her whale belly as if the force of one of these jolts might jar me clear out of the womb. Oh, no! Here we go through a rocky cut. Bumpty-bump-bump! Things go bump every minute on the trail but these last few bumps beat all!

Sorry, Mum. I didn't mean to kick you like that, but . . . George VI! Stop this thing. You're cutting it too close on that side. Ouch! Old Man Gunderson is off on his plow horse scanning the countryside for game to shoot. But one of your older brothers can drive us through. Any one will do. You aren't ready for this rocky cut. It's too long, too rocky. Those George brothers of yours are just walking behind, throwing pebbles and sniggering at our predicament. Lordy! You misjudged the width of this prairie schooner, George VI. On the right side we're completely out of the rut and on a ridge! We're riding on just two wooden wheels and oh my God! Lordy! Lordy! You're going to bust an axle or something! You've got to give more than a lick and a promise, kid. If you keep this up I'll become as religious as Aunt Maggie. I swear to God: there can't be a worse driver than you in all creation! We're going to capsize, *dummkopf*! That's one of Grandma Duly's favorite words. It means dummy, dummy. Mum has forgotten about the Lord. She is now hollering like a wild Indian, though we have not heard from any wild Indians yet. And I'm kicking like a mule, though I'm far more familiar with four oxen not kicking much and one plow horse that probably forgot how to kick.

Those rambunctious brothers of yours are spilling their guts. What's so all-fired funny, boys! If Mum splits her whale belly open and I end up sprawled naked and dead on the wagon bed like one of those fishes Mr. Flowers used to catch in Lake Michigan, your daddy won't like it one bit. Haven't you seen that twinkle in his one good eye? George W. Gunderson might not think much of me, but he adores Mum. He didn't let Mum and me join up in Independence and ride in the back of his wagon with all his worldly goods strictly out of the kindness of his heart. Your Daddy, that old Mormon devil, has an eye on the future. You can bet the holey soles of your dusty boots, boys, that he has plans, with a little help from Mum, to make another George or two. Ouch! At least in here I have some padding and such. Poor Mum. What you have to go through to realize your dream! I don't know what feels farther away, Maggie and the tenement house or Cornelia and the fields of gold.

Could a bucking horse be any worse than this wagon ride? It won't be easy when it comes time for Mum and me to part ways with that one-eyed Mormon pirate George W. Gunderson. But that time is far down the Oregon Trail. And the way George VI is driving, that time might never come. Lordy! Does this rocky cut never end! My biggest worry right now is whether or not George VI can get the other two wheels of this tilting wagon back down on the ground and in the right rut. Poor Mum! Poor me! We are in this together. We are tilting more than ever now. George VI is swearing at the oxen. How did a fourteen-year-old Mormon boy ever acquire so many curse words? But never mind him. I can't help but think of the 1859 Rush Street Runaway that took the lives of Mum's parents, Sarah and "Whiskey Man Dan" Hotchkiss. Are Mum and I fated to die in another crash—the Oregon Trail Overturn? I wonder if Mum breathes her last, does that absolutely mean I am doomed, too? The truth is—and I do want to tell the truth here—is that I'm gravely concerned for Mum but even more so for myself. Call me selfish or self-centered if you wish, but nobody is perfect.

And keep in mind my background—I was conceived by a wild-eyed Civil War veteran trying to return to society (such as it was in our part of Chicago) and a desperately poor Chicago woman looking for a way out. Furthermore, I'm not even born yet. Lordy! I just want to get out of this rocky cut alive.

# June 28, 1866: Womb and Worry

For me, and everyone else in the Burleson wagon party, everything has been new. We had no conception of the country over which we would pass or what we might encounter from weather, sickness, or the native people. We're at Fort Kearny, Nebraska, at last. It was named two decades ago for a General Stephen Watts Kearny, who they say conquered California before the California Gold Rush. I guess he must have stopped in Nebraska along the way. This was a planned stop for the Burleson wagon train, but we would have had to stop here in any case. All is not well with Mum. She is out of the wagon bed and on a medical cot, not on account of any accident or sickness but because of me. I feel rotten about it. She's in pain and I'm hardly kicking anymore. Everyone is worried, including the fort surgeon, who keeps examining her with a hairy hand lubricated with unsalted lard, and George W. Gunderson, who paces around her cot with the Book of Mormon under his arm and holding his large clay pipe that he can't keep lit.

Well, not everyone is *that* worried—certainly not his two oldest sons. George I and George II, against their father's commandments, have been hanging out in the nearby settlement of Dobytown, where there is gambling, liquor, and disreputable men and women. "None of its principal attractions is right even for a bad Saint," Old Gunderson told his sons. "Besides, your future mother needs you by her side, boys. If she passes on to her reward like your mothers did . . ." He did not need to finish his sentence. His message was clear to his selfish young Georges—if Mum died, there would be hell to pay. In the meantime he was paying too much attention to Mum to bother with them.

The two oldest set up camp at the livery stable in Dobytown anyway. The next three didn't go there, but they never appear at Mum's bedside either. They spend as much time as they can buying, trading, and just looking at the sutler's store or else imitating cavalrymen in and around the overcrowded, two-story-high soldiers' barracks. Some of those bluecoats are not much older than them. As for the youngest, George VI, he mostly sits on the steps outside the fort hospital. He is whittling his own pipe out of a piece of cottonwood, but it looks more like a whistle and he keeps cutting his hands and cursing his bad luck. Occasionally he pokes his head inside to ask for a bandage or just to see if Mum is still breathing. He is basically a good boy and feels as rotten as I do. You see he is full of guilt that if the most recent apple of his father's eye dies, it would be because of him—that is to say, his reckless driving on the trail. He's even harder on himself than his father is, which is saying a lot.

Actually, George VI answered my silent prayers by correcting his error in that rocky cutoff and making it clear through without tipping the wagon over. So there was no fatal crash, not any kind of crash at all. But Mum hollered so loudly from the jarring experience that Old Man Gunderson relieved his youngest of the reins permanently and made him walk in the wagon's dust next to the tied-in-back plow horse. The ride smoothed out after that, in part because the other Georges did the driving but also because we traveled over endless miles of flat bluestem prairie. "We are getting pretty well out to sea," commented one of the other travelers who had once sailed the oceans. "Looks to me more like some neglected garden," said his wife. We saw nary a tree, and woody vegetation was scarce because of prairie fires caused by lightning (which sometimes flashed in the horizon) and Indians (who we didn't see at all). Some of the men in our party said the Indians set fires because they were destructive savages. But Old Man Gunderson, a hunter at heart who had lost sight in his right eye long ago from an accident with a muzzleloader, argued that the natives were promoting the growth of the grass to attract deer and other game. It all makes me wonder about the character of the Indians we will inevitably meet down the trail, or road, whatever you want to call it. In any case, the Georges who were on foot spent much of their time filling bags with buffalo chips and cow chips for our cook fires.

As for the buffalo themselves, we have encountered two massive herds of the top-heavy furry beasts. With their large heads and humps, wiry hair, curved horns, and narrow hips, they seem like creatures only my imagination could conjure up. But I have indeed felt their energy and seen them kick up clouds of dust in my mind's eye, and I have heard Mr. Gunderson describe them as ferocious free-roaming beasts that see humans as mere dots on the endless prairie. Even Amanda Burleson was left speechless by the sight of a two-thousand-pound bull barreling toward our lead wagon until diverted by some force of its own nature. Nobody from our party has yet shot one for food or sport. Only Mr. Gunderson actually tried, but he said that his Henry repeater was not any kind of buffalo rifle and anyway that Mum told him she craved sour pickles and coffee grounds rather than buffalo meat.

Yes, there are domestic cows out here, too. Homesteading has started in the area, because land can be had for free if you improve it with houses, corrals, and crops. It isn't the Great American Desert like some folks back in Chicago still think, but seeing a few plowed fields and soddies (homes made from the sod of thickly rooted prairie grass) didn't make any of our party want to stop and put down roots. The Gundersons are bound for Salt Lake City, and it doesn't matter to them whether the Great Salt Lake Desert is really a desert or not. The other eight families have their hearts set on Oregon—seven on the fertile Willamette Valley and of course one on the mud baths of Indian Springs. Only Mum has an earlier place in mind. Even in pain, she has not lost sight of her dream. As for me, I suppose I could go most anywhere since I have not lived anywhere on the outside yet. But I must confess, I am partial to emerging at some location where no Indians are on the prowl.

All the while we were in view of the Little Blue, and afterward too, the younger Georges were asking about Indians who might want their fine scalps. The older men of our party obliged by spreading rumors they had heard back in civilization about outrages committed by "hostiles." Thing is, it was more than just rumors. We passed powerful close to some shallow unmarked graves, with the soil trampled by livestock and wagons to keep the wolves from digging up the remains. Old Man Gunderson knew the whole true story from old-timers back in Independence. Less than two years earlier, in August 1864, a Cheyenne and Arapaho war party attacked a freight train of eight wagons (just one less wagon than we have in our party), killed five of the men, mortally wounded a sixth, and burned every wagon. A couple out for a Sunday buggy ride found the bodies after seeing the smoking wagons. The one wounded teamster lived long enough to tell the tale. On Monday morning, employees from the Thirty-Two Mile Creek station of the Overland Stage Line showed up to bury the dead. The station was called that because it was thirty-two miles from Fort Kearny, which was built to protect travelers on the Oregon Trail, and I swear I would have jumped clear out of Mum's womb if that meant getting to the fort any faster.

Instead, when we neared Thirty-Two Mile Creek, things

almost ground to a frightening halt. We came to a steep descent, and the weight of the Burlesons' lead wagon pushed hard on the oxen, as the brake wasn't strong enough. "I told you so," said Monroe Burleson, speaking to the other men, though it had been his wife's idea to "just go for it." The wagon made it to the bottom but with a wobbly front wheel and minus the water barrel, two lanterns, and three of Mrs. Burleson's hatboxes. Amanda Burleson's joints had been badly shaken, but she was more concerned about her belongings. She ordered Hanna, her maidservant, to fetch her hatboxes, while the men fixed the wheel and the three youngest Georges threw handfuls of sod and cow patties into the creek.

Much deliberation followed on how to proceed with our group's descent, with Mr. Burleson, who strutted about as if he had invented the wagon wheel, shooting down everybody else's ideas. A few of the men wanted to toss things out of their wagons to lighten the loads, but they were overruled because their wives, more protective of cherished belongings, insisted on voting. Finally, with her hatboxes back in the lead wagon, Amanda Burleson stepped forward.

"No call for you gentlemen to surrender until you at least see the enemy," she said, looking every man, one by one, directly in the eye. Only three of them were as tall as her. "Other wagon trains don't do this kind of thing until they're caught in the Rockies in a snowstorm. Isn't that right, Burly?"

Her husband raised his bushy eyebrows, bit his lip, hitched up his britches, and smashed his flat-brimmed straw hat even further down on his bald head. But when his response came out, it came gentle. "You are quite correct, Mandy."

The other men nodded sheepishly. For the wagons that followed (and this was *not* wagon master Burleson's idea), they ran poles through the rear wheels for additional braking, but only after Old Man Gunderson had transported Mum to the valley below on a handheld litter. Mum had to be reloaded in the wagon bed for the difficult creek crossing. Because the water was so high, the men had to spend time re-digging the ramps on both banks and then double up the oxen teams. I kept thinking about something—rather worrying myself into a tighter fetal ball. But it wasn't about the possibility of Mum drowning (which wouldn't do me any good either). Instead, I was thinking that this would be the perfect spot for those hostile Cheyennes and Arapahos to attack. But there really wasn't a bad spot for them, not when we had such limited manpower and were so far from any fort.

During the creek crossing and afterward, Mum, despite her discomfort and outright pain, had the decency to keep reassuring me. "Don't fret, Angel Lamb," she said over and over, patting her whale belly. "We'll be at Fort Kearny before you know it. Indians have never attacked the fort. And anyway, the Indians can't even see you. So, you see, there is no reason to kick. Everything will be just fine." That worked for a while until I overheard one of the Oregon-bound men confess to Old Man Gunderson the real reason he was traveling to the far coast to put down new roots.

"I hear the savages aren't as savage out there as they are here on the Plains," the man said. "I once had a little girl cousin as fine as cream gravy who moved with her family to Kansas two springs ago. That very summer, she saw the savages fill her daddy with arrows, scalp him, strip him clean, and cut off his privates. Then she saw those same savages rip open her expecting mother and tear the baby right out of her womb. Finally the savages took turns savagely ravishing the little girl before setting her on fire. Nope. I got my sights set on a place where the savages have been tamed."

Old Man Gunderson, who didn't ordinarily swear like his sons, told the fellow to lower his damned voice. Luckily, Mum was sleeping at the time. But I heard every gruesome word, and I didn't forget. I thought to myself, maybe Papa Duly back in that three-story Dunning insane asylum wasn't really so bad off.

I sighed like a baby when we reached the south bank of the Platte River without having seen a single hostile native or, as George III put it to sound clever, even a non-hostile native couple. But my sigh only elicited a terrible groan from Mum. Her pains had worsened, and I was in no position to do anything about it.

"So that's the Platte, eh," said Monroe Burleson, grinning. "Looks too thin to drink and too thick to plow." He paused for a moment and then issued a belly laugh to encourage others to appreciate his wit.

Old Man Gunderson, for one, did not bite. "Folks have been saying that since the days of the Forty-niners," he said.

Mr. Burleson tugged down on the brim of his straw hat and turned away from the river.

A few miles upstream, we rolled into Fort Kearny, but Mum had finally fallen asleep and didn't even open her eyes. So I had to fret alone. The first thing I noticed—I guess you understand by now I don't need eyes on the outside to see—was that the fort had no fortifications to keep out those savages I had heard so much about on the trail. But there are plenty of soldiers milling about, and all around the parade grounds, intermixed with young trees that the soldiers planted, are sixteen blockhouse guns, two field pieces, and two howitzers. Best of all, for Mum's sake, there is a hospital here, which is made of wood, like the officers' quarters and the sutler's store. In all directions beyond those structures are two dozen broken-backed, falling-down mud buildings of various sizes, none of which looks any more inviting than the soddies we passed on the prairie.

When we first arrived at the fort, I did some kicking but

Mum wouldn't wake up. I was kind of in a panic. I guess I tried to yell, but of course nobody on the outside could hear me. Mum needed to get to the fort hospital but the others all had their minds on other things. For some it was food. For others rest. For Amanda Burleson it was the seemingly inadequate way the U.S. Army had put together Fort Kearny.

"It just doesn't look substantial," she complained to her husband, but loud enough for all of us to hear. "Isn't a fort supposed to be substantial?"

A sergeant, wearing a too small sack coat and with only one of his pant legs tucked into his unpolished boots, shuffled out to greet us. He proved to be surprisingly jolly.

"It's as substantial as yours truly, ma'am," the sergeant said, patting his belly almost the same way that Mum did. "Ain't nothin' to fear here as long as you stay a civilian. I don't want none of you folks to worry about Injuns. We got some snakes passing through our sod walls but not one of those slithering scoundrels wears a red skin, and they don't kill nothin' around here but our mice and rats."

Some of our party smiled back at him and nodded their heads. But Amanda Burleson just glared at the sergeant as if he were a snake himself. Maybe she expected we would be greeted by a twenty-one-gun salute or at least a brass band. And of course, her husband spoke up, being the wagon master.

"I know you're just trying to reassure the womenfolk, sergeant," Monroe Burleson said. "But sakes alive! All through the territory on the way here, we saw many crude, hastily dug gravesites along the trail."

"I assure you, sir, they weren't snake bit," the sergeant said, trying to maintain a smile in the face of the Burleson scowls.

"There have been no cholera epidemics lately that we are aware of. And not that many people fall under wagon wheels or accidentally shoot themselves."

"Accidents do happen on the trail, sir," the sergeant said. "I'm just glad all you folks made it."

"This far," said Mrs. Burleson.

"We have a woman who is with child and in much pain," interrupted George W. Gunderson, and I would have clapped my hands if I was able.

Mr. Burleson didn't hear his old friend or just ignored him. "We have far to go, sergeant, and I'd just like a little reassurance from the Army for the sake of my wife and the people I'm in charge of that *no* Indians are stalking the Platte Road."

"That's right," said George Gunderson IV, the most studious of the rambunctious brothers. "I found arrowheads."

"The honest to God truth is, ten thousand of you folks have passed through already this year and they all had their scalps intact."

"What about the Snake Indians?" asked George V, the second youngest and the biggest worrier of the bunch. "They sound mean."

"The Snake are far, far to the west, young man. Hereabouts we have mostly the Cheyenne, the Arapaho, and the Sioux. Don't you fret none. They stirred things up plenty in '64 and '65, but this year they ain't been on the warpath. Why they've been as quiet as church mice."

"So far," said Mrs. Burleson.

"Only things certain in life, ma'am, are death, stampeding buffalo, and late Army payrolls."

"Don't try to humor us, sergeant."

"Sorry, ma'am. The fact of the matter is this: you folks got here to Kearny mighty late. I'm gonna be honest Injun with you. In case nobody told you, the mountain snows will be falling long before you get to Snake Country. The passes figure to be near impassable . . . at least for wagons. I'd say your biggest fret ain't Injuns but the plumb lateness of the season for reachin'

Oregon Country."

"No need to scare us half to death, either," said Mrs. Burleson.

"Beg your pardon, ma'am. Hate to be the one to tell you what you're in for on the road ahead. But somebody should do it."

A dark shadow seemed to fall across our entire little wagon train. Some of the men hung their weary heads and began muttering prayers as their wives clutched their shirtsleeves. Mr. Burleson took out his Swiss pocket watch and studied it as if it was a crystal ball that could divine our party's fate. "I knew it, I knew it!" he declared. "We should have left Independence earlier. We should have . . ."

"Shut your bazoo!" Mrs. Burleson snapped. "No more *should haves!*"

Heads jerked up, all down the line. Many mouths were agape. Not even Mr. Gunderson had ever talked to their wagon master that way. Mr. Burleson crossed his arms and bit his lip, then just stared blankly off into space like a red-faced statue.

"Some of us are only going as far as Salt Lake," said George III, breaking the stunned silence.

"We're safe, right?" said George V.

"Well, sonny, not exactly," the sergeant said, no longer even trying to smile. "You'll still run into the Rockies."

"Have you even been to the Rocky Mountains, sergeant?" Mrs. Burleson asked.

"Well, not exactly, ma'am. But I've heard . . ."

"I thought not. If you please, sergeant, show us to your commanding officer."

"Wait," shouted Old Man Gunderson, bless his heart. "First fetch a doctor on the double. We can worry about all the rest later."

"Somebody sick?" the sergeant asked, looking one by one at

the emigrant faces. "Hope it ain't nothing *too* contagious."

"I told you, sergeant. We have a woman with child . . . in the back of my wagon."

"Is that right?" The sergeant took a peek in the second wagon. "So you do," he said, grinning again. "Won't Doc be surprised!" He saluted Mr. Gunderson and then pointed out the post hospital.

And so Mum finally got to see a doctor after all those unsettling days on the trail, and the doctor is still seeing her. He says he is the post surgeon and an officer, but just about everyone here calls him "Doc." While Doc is definitely the twitchy nervous type and Mum groans every time he touches her, the medical instruments on the side table seem clean and the medical books on his shelf aren't dusty. I'm sure I could be in worse hands. Not that I feel all that safe at the moment—certainly not as safe as I did before Mum carried me off in a westbound covered wagon.

When you come right down to it, though, my state of apprehensive would exist anywhere. It just so happens we are stuck way out in Nebraska Territory. It will be the same no matter where Mum is when she has me. You see I know there is nothing out there, whether in Chicago or in Nebraska Territory or anywhere in between, as warm and as cozy as my current home. I also know I can't continue to loiter. I just want, the Good Lord willing (Lordy! I have gotten religion), to be born alive. Please stop groaning, Mum! I realize I've been a heap of trouble so far, but it doesn't exactly fill me with confidence to hear you carry on so. Like it or not, my nine-month residency is just about up. It's a tough situation. I suppose we both have to grin and bear it. And now here to remind me of my pending emergence into the outside world is Doc, more specifically his probing lard-saturated fingers. Mum groans louder. Ouch. I can feel your pain, Mum. The things we—that is to say a woman and her unborn child—must go through. Not that I blame Doc. This isn't what he wants, either. I'm sure he'd reach in and yank me right out if his freckled arms were long enough.

"Do you have to do that?" Old Man Gunderson says, biting on the stem of his clay pipe. "She is a lady."

"I am a doctor." His probing continues unabated. As clean as all those tools on the side table look, I'm glad he's not using any of them.

"I know, Doc, but Libbie, uh Elizabeth . . ."

"I'm sure your wife is worried more about a healthy birth than her modesty."

"Is it time then, Doc? Is it time?"

"No. Why not step outside and get some fresh air, Mr. Gunderson. I've seen your son outside. You and your wife have been through this before."

"Not exactly. Before it was always wives and midwives."

"I don't follow you, Mr. Gunderson."

"It's like this, Doc: Libbie is my wife-to-be and, as far as I know, this is her first."

"I would say otherwise, but no matter. I assumed you were her husband."

"Not yet. Can't you see how young she is! I plan on having Brigham Young himself marry us in Salt Lake . . . that is, in the city, perhaps even in the temple I hear he's building. She told me her husband died in the Civil War."

"But you *are* the father?"

"No, Doc. Being as honest as the day is long, I can't rightly say that."

"Well this child obviously was conceived *after* the Civil War."

"Look, Doc. Maybe the man was only mortally wounded in the Civil War. Maybe he came home to die and did just that—during or after conception. I don't know. It's no matter to me and should not get you all unbalanced. You strike me as dreadfully nervous for a doctor, Doc. The midwives who handled things with my wives never fussed over details. They just did the job and got paid for their trouble. If you're worried about getting paid, don't. I'll pay your standard price for infant delivery."

"I don't have a standard price. Out here I'm used to dealing with arrow wounds and gunshot wounds and soldiers' bellyaches."

"I figured as much." Mr. Gunderson snaps his eye patch and peers closer with his good eye. "You *really* got to do all that with your fingers?"

"I am doing what I can for her. I don't mean to sound like an old croaker, but I'm considering chloroform and forceps. You spoke of wives. You have more than one?"

"They're all dead."

"Well, thank goodness for that. I mean . . ."

"Forget it, Doc. It's all water under the bridge." Mr. Gunderson's pipe has finally stayed lit. He puffs long and hard in celebration and then blows smoke rings that make Mum squirm on the examining table. "And rest assured, Doc, my little Libbie here will be my one and only living wife . . . at least for a while."

"That's fine, but right now there is nothing to be done, by you or me, Mr. Gunderson. She has had several false alarms. I'll just have to keep her under observation."

"Me, too."

The doctor exhales like a gush of west wind and steps back from the table. "I'm going to wash my hands now and let her fall asleep. Your smoke seems to be bothering her."

Mr. Gunderson shrugs, turns his head, sticks out his bearded chin, and blows his next smoke rings in the doctor's face.

"If you don't mind . . ."

"How soon will it be, Doc?"

"Days, maybe a week. I don't know. Look, since you admit to being neither her husband nor the father, I'll have to ask you to

take your pipe outside, Mr. Gunderson. You can wait there with
. . ."

"The hell I will. She's been riding in my covered wagon for a
month and a half now. She wouldn't be here today without me.
She's my concern, and I'm not going to pass the buck."

"But . . ."

"I'm not letting her out of sight. I was there when my six
Georges came into this world, and I'm going to be here this
time for George VII, Georgina, or whatever my future wife
chooses to call her newborn."

"And you are sure the father is *not* living?"

"Of course, I'm sure. Mormon women have only one
husband, and she's a Mormon woman . . . or will be soon. Like
I already told you, we're going to get married with no questions
asked about the late father. So just get on with it, Doc."

"There's nothing to get on with."

"Why the hell not!"

"Don't shout, Mr. Gunderson. It's not helping anyone. Like
I told you before, this woman is *not* ready yet."

# July 4, 1866: Womb and Independence Day

Ready or not, Mum, I'll be coming out soon and without the help of the post surgeon or any other frontier doctor. Our party didn't dare wait for me any longer at Fort Kearny. If the sergeant's words about our tardiness didn't sink into the heads of the Burlesons and the other westbound families, the warning of the post commander on our second to last day there sure did. "You were ill-advised to start out on the trail so late in the spring," he said, enunciating each word carefully as if speaking to ignorant children. "You can not continue to dawdle. Wagon trains that don't reach Independence Rock by July 4 know they are behind schedule and are likely to face a fall snowstorm in the mountains."

Well, today's the Fourth and we're *not* at Independence Rock. We're at a place called Ash Hollow, which has the first genuine trees we've seen since leaving Kearny 100 miles ago but is still 250 miles short of that granite landmark, which, like our jumping-off point in Missouri, was named for our country's major summer holiday. *Independence* to me is a scary word. And *rock* sounds like a hard place. But Independence Rock is the least of my worries. I will never see it even if I do get out of the good old womb in fine shape. The fact is that Mum isn't planning on being at Independence Rock or Devil's Gate or any of those other places that are on the Sweetwater River *beyond* the North Platte. Her big secret, unknown to everyone in our party but me, is to turn off at some earlier point onto the Bozeman

Trail, the shortest and supposedly easiest land route to Virginia City. Of course before the turn off is possible she must leave Old Man Gunderson and find a Montana-bound wagon party willing to take her—and me. That is, if I make it out alive.

I keep mentioning that, don't I? Well, that's because that's what I'm always thinking about, at least in the back of my mind. I am trying to have a positive attitude about the whole thing, but to pretend I'm not frightened would be like pretending I'm not helpless. Fear and helplessness just go with the territory. I don't want all this writing (i.e., etching on my skull) to be for naught. If you are reading this, then of course it wasn't for naught. But how can I be sure? I worry that my early internal etchings might wear away in time like the soles of the Gunderson boys' shoes. Or, if the etchings stay put and I get out alive, grow up, and learn how to write for real, I might no longer be able to translate the etchings into words. In other words, I might grow up to be too normal, that is to say average. My experiences as a fetus might be typical, but I've not heard of anyone who has ever taken the plunge into the outside world and been able to record a pre-birth diary. I'd like to be the first. I mean somebody has to be the first. Why not me? On the other hand, I also ask: "Why me?" George Washington, Lewis and Clark, John C. Frémont, and John M. Bozeman—those were genuine trailblazers. I don't even have a name yet. And you already know about my parents and my grandparents. They are or were nothing special (except Papa Duly, but he is considered abnormal). I mean Mum is loving, supportive, and kind, but to be perfectly objective, she is special *only* to me and, to a lesser extent, Old Man Gunderson. What I must do right now is to just stop thinking about it. What happens happens. And no matter what happens, Lord, no matter if anyone is reading this or not, I just want to thank you for allowing me to enjoy my full dependency for the past nine months.

I can't tell you what the future holds for my etchings and me (you being the dear readers, along with the Lord, of course), but I can tell you about where I've been. And so I shall. Allow me to go back to my etching.

Since leaving Kearny, I have felt so much negativity in our party, none thankfully from Mum, who I know in her heart really wants to have a healthy baby. I'm sure Mum has felt that negativity herself, and it can't help! Amanda Burleson, among others, blames our continual dawdling on Mum and Old Man Gunderson's "babying" her just because she is pregnant. Mrs. Burleson will be of no help when it's Mum's time—which will also be my time—because the refined woman with more hats than heart does not like to bend over (those aching joints, you know) or get her hands dirty, especially not over a whale-bellied woman she considers indecent. As far as she is concerned—I overheard her whispering this to other ladies and so did my poor mother—Mum was raised on the wrong side of the railroad tracks in Chicago and possesses neither morals nor a husband. "It's commonplace of women in her station to cook, clean, and take care of family up until the moment of giving birth," Mrs. Burleson said. "Instead, she just lies in there like a fat deadbeat, adding unnecessary weight to George's wagon." Mum has not felt up to defending herself, though she of course has had a disabling pregnancy (I really am sorry, Mum!) and does have a husband, albeit one lodged in an insane asylum. And while two other anonymous white men (I have no wish to learn their identities) and the kindly old man of color Leon Flowers got Mum in the family way when Papa Duly was away earlier, that was war time. Strange things happened on the home front as well as the battlefield during the Civil War.

In their lucid moments during the first three years of the war, Grandpa and Grandma Duly expressed moral outrage at Mum, even though they would have been out on the street if not for the help of Mr. Flowers and other of Mum's men friends. Then in 1864 when that corporal wrote the bad-news letter to Mum and everyone thought Papa Duly had died in battle, the old Dulys stopped speaking to Mum all together. That wouldn't have been so bad, but Maggie Hotchkiss took their side against her own sister, declaring, "Thank the Good Lord that Abraham is lying cold somewhere and does not have to come home to a wife carrying on like a common harlot." Poor Maggie just couldn't stand the fact that even though she was younger and unmarried, none of those men gave her pockmarked face and scrawny body a second look. But Mum let Maggie have her say. It was only after Papa Duly showed up unexpectedly on our fire escape with his powerful mental scars that Mum finally stuck up for herself, telling Maggie, "I bet all those fancy-laced Southern belles weren't as pure as driven cotton either!" It isn't certain whether it was Maggie or one of the old Dulys who told Papa Duly what Mum had been up to during the war, but it's hard to hate any of them right now. They are all so far away and will be even farther away soon. I may never see any of them ever again.

The Lord says—and I'm starting to find out you can hear the Lord pretty good from the womb—that it is bad to hate anybody, since He created *all* people. Not that the Lord will hate you for hating some people, because the Lord hates sin and wickedness and the world He created is full of sinners and wicked people. Actually, it's pretty darn confusing, even for a fetus, to understand exactly what the Lord is saying at any given time. Mostly, I think our doings here on Earth leave him pretty much speechless. Lord knows there are few people I actually hate, so far anyway, but I hate Amanda Burleson. She don't care beans for Mum, let alone me. I do believe she is more attached to her half-dozen hatboxes.

When our train was a few miles west of Fort Kearny, we had

to stop at the hellhole Dobytown for a few "dirty minutes," as Mrs. Burleson put it, because George I was still carousing there. While Old Man Gunderson was dragging his oldest boy away from an adobe saloon by his britches (which George I was carrying, not wearing), Mrs. Burleson was telling everyone that we should leave Mum in that dubious place so that she could have her bastard child among the besotted stale humanity. It was all Mr. Gunderson could do to keep from reducing Mrs. Burleson a hat size or two by smashing her head repeatedly with the butt of his Henry repeating rifle. Well, perhaps I exaggerate—if I was on the outside and had a gun, that's what I would have wanted to do. But Old Man Gunderson did say: "You'd better control your wife's wicked tongue, Monroe Burleson, or you are going to lose all the Gundersons before Salt Lake. And you need us more than we need you. It would be small potatoes for us to take our wagon across the river to another train right now and follow the Mormon ruts to our chosen land." Mr. Burleson apologized, even if his wife didn't, and offered to lend us Hanna, their Negro maidservant, if and when Mum finally went into labor. Meanwhile, Old Man Gunderson made George I walk shirtless (to display the red slashes on his back caused by three cracks of the paternal bullwhip) behind the wagon for a week to cure the twenty-year-old of the desire to sow any more wild oats before the Gundersons all settled down near Brigham Young and his seventeen wives.

We had only traveled about thirty miles west of Fort Kearny when everyone temporarily forgot about how late we were running and went back to worrying about Indians. At a place called Plum Creek (where we found no wild plums much to the disappointment of Mum, who had a sudden craving for them), our emigrant party made camp for the night and received a visit from six men driving a half-dozen freight wagons from Denver to Fort Kearny. The leather-faced, calloused teamsters had known hard times, close calls, and shooting scrapes or had at least heard about these things. Some were talkers, some weren't, but they were all hungry for our Arbuckles' pre-roasted coffee. One of the emigrant wives had a pot going at a cook fire in the middle of our circle of wagons and the guests huddled around, accepting refill after refill in their tin cups as they told a gruesome story to our gawking party.

No, it hadn't happened to them personally. But they had been acquainted with some members of the unfortunate party involved, fellow teamsters they were. It happened two summers ago, when the red men were on a rampage and murdered 200 white people, including women and children. On the night of August 7, 1864, at this exact spot, the thirteen teamsters made camp. Two wives had come along, pregnant nineteen-year-old Nancy Morton (four years younger than Mum) and a Mrs. Smith, as well as a teamster's twelve-year-old son, Danny Marble. The next morning 100 Cheyenne raiders, many of them the particularly fierce Dog Soldiers, descended from the bluffs and overwhelmed the small wagon train. Nancy, who had recently lost two young children to measles (Mum cringed upon hearing that sad fact), suffered two arrow wounds in the side and then witnessed the deaths, stripping, scalping, and mutilation of her husband and all the other men. Two Cheyenne warriors put her on a pony and led her into captivity along with young Danny. Mrs. Smith had managed to escape into the reeds by the creek, and that night, soldiers found her in a state of shock hiding in a field. The next day, soldiers buried the dead men.

"Some had their eyes gouged out," commented a teamster who the others called Plug because of his fondness for tobacco. Plug simulated the hideous act with his dirty, jagged fingernails. "Some had their tongues gouged out," said another, called Red (though his hair was white), sticking fingers from both his hands into his surprisingly small mouth. "And some," added a sawed-off teamster named Stumpy, before he paused for dramatic effect and stared up from his campfire seat into Amanda Burleson's narrow but widening eyes. "And some," he repeated, "had their genitals cut off and stuffed into their mouths." Stumpy started to make a gesture below his waist. Mrs. Burleson didn't flinch, but Monroe Burleson bulled his way between his wife and the gesturer, blocking everyone's view (except mine of course). We all had heard that kind of thing before along the trail, but nevertheless, Mr. Burleson did what he thought a gentleman must do. He excused his Amanda and the other wives in our party, except of course for poor Mum, who was in a sweat under covers in the Gunderson covered wagon bed—forgotten by most of the men and assumed by the rest to be too out of it to hear this true horror tale of the Great Plains. But she heard and I heard, as Stumpy asked for a fourth cup of belly-wash and then continued the story, leaving the dead men buried and concentrating on the two captives.

When the raiders stopped for a noonday meal and some rest, Stumpy related, young Danny ran to Nancy, and she held him to her bosom as she stroked his intact hair. Danny suddenly popped his head up and said, "Let's do what they want, Mrs. Morton, and then they won't kill us." Just as quickly he lowered his head and burst into tears. And the Indians did whatever they wanted, including beating the pair. One of the tormentors held up the scalp of Nancy's brother and then rubbed it in her face. The sight of it made Danny sick. The second night out, the warriors did a war dance around a pole decorated from top to bottom with scalps. Danny tried to stay close to Nancy's side. He knew his father was dead and he might never see his real mother again. When drunken warriors threw spears and arrows in Danny's direction, Nancy stood up for him, shouting: "Leave him alone! He is my papoose." The Indians seemed to listen.

But they did not leave her alone. She suffered terribly. They whipped her and abused her.

Stumpy paused in his storytelling to slurp his no longer steaming coffee. Plug jumped right in and uttered words that must have been on the tip of his tongue: "She went blind for a spell and lost the wee one inside her, the child of her late husband. I tell you good folks, it's a sin to Moses what they done to her." Plug wiped tears that had formed in puddles in his dark, sunken sockets—yes, the same guy who earlier had simulated the gouging of eyes. Hearing about Nancy Morton's stress-induced miscarriage caused Mum to roll over onto her whale belly and pound her fists against her temples. I didn't feel so hot myself.

The captivity story continued with Stumpy doing most of the telling, but with Plug and Red filling in now and then. The trio worked well as a team, while the other three teamsters just stared into the flickering flames and drank Arbuckles' as if they had no bottoms to their bellies. Mum tried to cover her ears. I had no choice but to listen.

Nancy Morton, the teamsters said, kept trying to comfort Danny. But she couldn't forget her poor *third* child, who, unlike the first two, didn't even have the chance to be born and breathe a little bit before disaster struck. And sometimes visions of her scalped, mutilated husband crept into Nancy's head in the middle of the night. "I want to die!" she cried out one day when she didn't jump to a warrior's command and he threatened to impale her with his spear. "No!" screamed Danny. "Then I will be left all alone!" And so Nancy decided to live, even though she was experiencing what the three silent teamsters as well as the three talkative teamsters agreed was a fate worse than death.

"We don't have to know everything," Monroe Burleson snapped. He wiped his brow and looked all around as if he expected somebody might be sneaking up on him. "I have a mind to go to bed."

"A bit squeamish, mister?" said Red. "Imagine how Nancy felt."

Mr. Burleson glanced at his wagon. "I ask you gents to keep your voices down. And just tell us plain and simple what happened to Nancy and the boy."

Red tugged on long strands of white hair that hung to below his shoulders. He looked hurt, as if Mr. Burleson had done him an injustice. Plug set down his tin cup and put a wad of tobacco between his cheek and his gum and began chewing like a cow with a mouth full of manure. "Ain't nothing simple about their story," Stumpy said. "We got to do it justice."

"Justice?" said Mr. Burleson, scratching one of his bushy eyebrows. "Fine. But it's getting late and we need to push off bright and early . . ."

Red nodded sadly. Plug turned his head and spit a brown stream, not too far from Mr. Burleson's feet.

"All right, mister," said Stumpy. "I'll skip ahead to September 1864."

And so he did.

"This major, name of Ned Wynkoop, met in council with the Injun chiefs out in the Smoky Hills, and he got them to release a few captives," Stumpy continued. "One of them was Danny Marble. The soldiers found the ragamuffin talkative and in surprisingly good shape. They took up a collection and bought him new clothes in Denver. The boy had all his marbles—you know, he was good in the head. But maybe he wasn't as strong in the body as the soldiers thought. Anyway, Danny caught typhoid fever after he was returned to his widowed mother and died in November."

"The kid had no luck," commented George II, who, with his brothers, was listening with as much interest as their father and the other men. "I once was laid up in bed with typhoid for four weeks, but I didn't die."

"Me, too," said George III.

"You boys were luckier than Danny boy," Stumpy said, finally putting down his cup of coffee to wipe liquid from his chin whiskers. "And your mother was luckier than Ann Marble, Danny's mother."

"We had three mothers between the six of us Gunderson boys," said George I. "And all three are dead."

"Sorry to hear that," Stumpy said. "You can bet Ann Marble must have wished she was dead. At the very least she was more forlorn than a starving, three-legged mutt trying to find a bone. First the Injuns mutilate her husband and take away her boy, then she gets her boy back from the Injuns only to have God Almighty take him away forever. Comforting clergymen and friends told Ann Marble she should keep her spirits up because she was bound to meet her Danny again in heaven. It's hard to keep your spirits up, though, when all your spirits are wrathy. Her only wish, they say, is for those demon redskins to be all to pieces extinguished."

"Most interesting, I'm sure, but what about Nancy Morton?" Old Man Gunderson said, while biting on the stem of his unlit clay pipe. "Isn't that who your story is about?" He must have been thinking of Mum lying there in his wagon bed.

"Yes, what about that Morton woman," echoed Mr. Burleson. "Did the savages extinguish her?"

"Nope," said Stumpy. He stretched his arms toward the sky and stretched his legs toward the pot of coffee but still didn't look any more sizable. He had a good, strong voice, though, one that must have commanded much attention from his oxen.

"Well?" said Mr. Burleson. "Are you going to tell us more or should we go to bed?"

Stumpy smiled so big his tight round face could barely contain it. He poured himself another cup of coffee. He knew he had a captive audience all to himself. Plug was busy chewing and spitting. Red, despite all the coffee, had about run out of steam.

"Yes, Nancy," Stumpy finally said, as if recalling an old sweetheart. "One of the sons of a Cheyenne chief wanted to marry her, but she turned him down flat, even though half the Cheyenne Nation threatened to kill her if she said no. Luckily, another chief, too old for courting and such, declared that no marriage would take place. This chief, Black Crane I believe, sheltered Nancy in his tepee till the younger chief set his sights on one of his own kind. But that wasn't the end of it, not yet. Come October, some of her captors gathered firewood to burn her at the stake. They expected her to scream bloody murder or get down on her hands and knees to beg for mercy. But that gal had plenty of gumption. She told them that she would gladly die and go to the happy hunting ground so that she didn't have to be tormented by them another Injun minute. Her Cheyenne capturers appreciated her grit. They called her their 'brave white squaw' and held a dance instead of a roast."

"She danced with them?" George II asked. "Those wild Indians?"

"Those gals in Dobytown danced with you didn't they, number two?" said George I.

"Actually, fellas, it wasn't that kind of dance," said Stumpy. "I reckon it was more like one of them war dances or sun dances. Injuns don't dance like us."

"They set her free?" asked George VI, who hadn't stayed up this late since we left Independence.

"Not right then, sonny," Stumpy replied. "I don't want to give you nightmares now."

George VI reached into one of the pockets of his overalls and pulled out the primitive wooden pipe he'd carved. He bit on the stem and blew imaginary smoke, on account of his father didn't want him using real tobacco. "Don't worry about me, mister," he said. "I've heard plenty worse from my brothers. Ouch!" He had a splinter in his lip.

Stumpy slapped one of his unsubstantial thighs and cackled so long that George VI's face turned a bright red and Mr. Burleson stamped his feet impatiently.

"Back to Nancy," Stumpy said at last. "The Indians were too busy stealing and killing to concern themselves much with their captive. Food was scarce that winter, and Nancy was ailing after falling out of the saddle one cold day. A warrior got hold of some white man's medicine during a raid, and he told Nancy to try a bottle of strychnine. Now, Nancy wasn't born yesterday. She knew that a little of that stuff could cure a case of indigestion, but that too big a dose would kill you for sure. Nancy pretended to take a swallow and then passed the bottle over to a chief who was feeling out of sorts. Well, that old ignorant chief guzzled the potion right down and died on the spot."

"Sake's alive, fella!" shouted Mr. Burleson. "I've heard enough. We're all ready to snore here. No more coffee now. Enough is enough."

"I'll excuse you, mister, if you want to call it a night."

"I'm the wagon master! I'm calling it a night for everybody."

"As soon as he tells us what happened to Nancy," said Old Man Gunderson. "All right, Monroe?"

"All right, George. But shorty here better make it in twenty words or less."

"The name's Stumpy, mister. And I'm done talking." He buttoned his lip and then crossed his little arms.

Plug spit his biggest brown stream yet. He was done talking, too. But Red suppressed a yawn, swept a hand through his thick white hair, and stood up. He had his second wind.

"I'll tell you," Red said. "Nancy Morton tried to escape. Old Chief Crane whipped her and starved her. She couldn't take it no more. She hung herself from a tepee pole. But . . . is that more than twenty words, mister wagon master?"

"Yes," said Mr. Gunderson. "But never mind. Is that the end?"

"Well, it wasn't the end of Nancy Morton."

"Go on. Go on."

Red beamed as if he had outwrestled a bear. "One of the Cheyenne cut her down before her neck snapped. Several times after that, the starving tribe tried to trade their captive for coffee, flour, sugar, tobacco, you name it. But the soldiers never offered enough food or supplies in return. 'No deal,' Black Crane said. 'She make good granddaughter. You cheap. You no hornswoggle chief.' Finally in mid-January '65 two traders heard enough scuttlebutt to travel more than 200 miles in the snow to negotiate for Mrs. Morton. The old chief held out until the traders were willing to fork over $2,154 worth of goods. The next morning, the traders pulled out of camp before breakfast with Mrs. Morton in tow. They were afraid the old chief would change his demon mind, so they cut a hurried path in the snow to Platte Bridge Station, which is where the Indians killed Lieutenant Caspar Collins last July—but that's another story. From Platte Bridge Station, Nancy traveled east in an army ambulance to Fort Laramie, where she told the *very* story I'm telling you now."

"End of story, then," Monroe Burleson said. "Let's call it a night, gentlemen."

"You bet," Red agreed, but he managed a few more words: "So it was that after one hundred seventy-six days of torment, Nancy Morton was free at last, though no doubt Black Crane and the other red demons were still heavy on her mind. At the fort, she recognized this Cheyenne named Big Crow who had taken part in the massacre of her husband and the others at Plum Creek. They hung the red demon by the neck until he was buzzard meat."

All the George Gunderson sons cheered, as did some of the men in our party. Red smiled, but the other teamsters just sat there by the dying fire. They were all too familiar with the story.

"Justice is served," declared Monroe Burleson.

"Sweet revenge," said his wife, who suddenly appeared from behind the first wagon. Amanda Burleson had obviously stayed hidden but close enough to the campfire to hear the entire captivity story. "But didn't they hang Black Crane, too?"

"Only got the one redskin, Mrs. Wagon Master," Red said. "We can't shoot or hang them all."

"Yeah," said Plug, before making his last spit of the night. "But we gave the rest of 'em smallpox."

"I love a happy ending," shouted George III.

"Who says Mrs. Nancy Morton will live happily ever after?" said the never satisfied Amanda Burleson, cracking her knuckles, which made Mr. Burleson jump.

"So far, so good, ma'am," replied Red. "She got back home to her folks' place, in Sidney, Iowa, I believe. Everybody there is jumping for joy, as you can imagine."

"And are you imagining that, Mr. Teamster, to humor us?"

"No, ma'am. Read about it in the newspapers—I can read real good, ma'am. Nancy Morton told how she felt. 'It felt like I had arose from the dead and had awakened and found myself in Paradise.' That's what she said, ma'am, when she got home. What's more, last November that brave little lady went up and got hitched to this George Stevens fellow, and they was planning on having a passel of youngins. She's Nancy Stevens now. It's been in the papers and the talk all along the trail."

"Children are *not* for everyone," said Mrs. Burleson.

There was nothing more to be said. The men in our party, as well as Amanda Burleson, left the campfire and retired to their respective covered wagons. They were all too tuckered out to think about posting a guard or two in this dangerous country. The six teamsters poured what coffee remained onto the flames, extinguishing them, and made their way to the nearby freight wagons. I could have done without their tale of horror and captivity, but I was glad they were so close that night. They were all well-armed, seasoned travelers, unlike our men. Not that teamsters necessarily fare any better than emigrants when it comes to hostile Indian attacks. I could practically see the terrified faces and mutilated bodies of those thirteen teamsters killed near Plum Creek two years ago. I could see Danny Marble's face, too. He had premature worry lines, like George V. Worst of all I could see the face of Nancy Morton. She looked too much like Mum, except her hair was pitch-black instead of yellow.

Mum surprised me by falling straight to sleep and then having one of her most restful nights since we left Independence. No doubt the ending of the Nancy Morton tale had pleased her as much as it had the men, maybe more so, because Mum is a sucker for poor, unfortunate folks who overcame adversity. I've often heard Mum read aloud from her prized copy of *Oliver Twist,* that Charles Dickens tale in which his favorite orphan lad ultimately escapes the London slums (even worse than where we lived in Chicago) and lives happily with his savior, Mr. Brownlow. The teamsters' tale didn't have the same effect on me, I'm afraid. I was squirming the whole night at Plum Creek, trying desperately not to kick Mum. I was seeing things from a slightly different point of view. Mum maybe didn't consider all the details closely enough. After all, while Nancy Morton lived through her ordeal, the mistreatment by the Indians caused her to lose the baby she'd been carrying when captured. It wasn't so long ago that Mum herself had experienced a couple of those miscarriages. That was back in Chicago where there aren't any wild Indians and very few tame ones. Yes, even though we were at Plum Creek, I knew I had far more to worry about than just a hostile Indian attack if I wanted to make a safe, healthy passage into the outside world.

There was no repeat massacre at Plum Creek. If the Indians were out there, they were hiding with the wild plums, and they let us pass in peace. Maybe we had too many oxen and not enough horses for them. Maybe we had too many armed teamsters and not enough pipe tobacco. Maybe we had too much coffee and not enough whiskey. Maybe Amanda Burleson seemed like a tougher female to crack than even Nancy Morton. Maybe they didn't know about Mum and me, so vulnerable to attack, in the back of Old Man Gunderson's wagon. Maybe we just got lucky.

We parted ways with the teamsters in the morning and continued to push west. At mid-morning we got a scare from a hard-riding scout carrying a dispatch from Fort Kearny to Fort Cottonwood. Just the pounding of his horse's hooves was enough to create a near panic in our party. He apologized for frightening us and assured us no hostiles were on our tail. Still, the scout was in an awful hurry and his buckskins seemed ruffled, so the Burlesons and some of the others expressed nervous skepticism.

"It ain't redskins running up my backside," the scout insisted over a quick cup of coffee, strong and black. "I got me a fine plump Arapaho squaw in Cottonwood Springs." Mr. Burleson was about to excuse the womenfolk again, but changed his mind when the scout didn't elaborate on his uncivilized love life. "These unsettled times can't last long, friends," the scout continued, talking as fast as he rode. "Soon none of us will have reason to be back on this good old trail—not sitting in the saddle or sitting on a wagon. The railroad is a coming lickety-split through the territory, which will be a state soon, and before you know it, friends, one of them steam-belching iron horses will bring straight to my Cottonwood doorstep that red-haired gal I thought I left behind in Kentucky." The scout spit out the last of his coffee. "I'll miss these unsettled times, that's for damn sure." As he tightened the cinches on his saddle, the scout mentioned that the Union Pacific rail lines were only about four months work behind us. The UP hadn't begun to lay track out of Omaha until last summer and only forty miles of track were in place by the end of last year. But the scout said that Jack Casement, the new construction boss hired this past January, was one of those "driven men," and that the UP was now laying sixty miles of track every danged month. "And I'm a driven man myself," the scout confessed as he mounted up and gave his rested stead a pat on the neck. "A plump Arapaho squaw can do that to a man."

The buckskin-clad scout raced on to Fort Cottonwood, beating us there by a day and a half. The fort, built out of cedar logs on the south side of the Platte three years ago, was originally called Cantonment McKean and its official name was now Fort McPherson. But Cottonwood was what the soldiers called it, and we did, too. It was there for our protection—that is to say for the protection of everyone who ventured on the Oregon Trail—but we didn't linger long enough to even look up *our* scout, although some of the Georges thought they saw his buckskins hanging out to dry next to a tepee west of the fort.

We continued following the south side of the Platte River for only about ten more miles before our party came to a dividing point in the trail and had to make a decision in the rain. We could keep going straight along the south bank of the South Platte and cross later on at Julesburg in Colorado Territory or we could take a branch of the trail that crossed right here to the south bank of the North Platte. Monroe Burleson tested the waters by rolling up his trouser legs and stepping into the muddy river. The water barely reached his knees.

"It isn't particularly deep right here," he announced, "but it might be deeper further out. One never knows for sure. By my reckoning the river's two-mile wide at this spot. Everyone agree? Good. I don't feel like getting any wetter right now. The trail on this side looks good, free of mud. We best keep going straight."

Even as he spoke, a couple of the young Georges, II and III I believe, splashed in after him as if they were schoolboys who couldn't resist jumping into a mud puddle. One man, the willowy but often overlooked Orval Needmyer, removed his slouch hat and swiped at the rain puddle on the brim. "We're already plenty wet, Mr. Burleson," he said with a slight stutter. "I. . . . I say, that is I suggest, we cross here." But the others didn't even look at Mr. Needmyer, not even his own wife, who I had never heard speak and was trying to be inconspicuous under a steel-ribbed black umbrella. Mr. Needmyer restored his hat so it practically covered his droopy eyes. Then he slouched and stepped backward. He wasn't the type of man to press an issue, and he looked as if he wanted to share his wife's umbrella. Maybe he was the one who made decisions back home, but not out here on the trail.

Monroe Burleson scurried back to dry land to get the oozing mud out of his shoes. "Everyone with me, then," he said. It wasn't really a question, but Mr. Needmyer and other nodded their heads while a few shrugged their weary, wet shoulders and Mrs. Needmyer tipped her umbrella ever so slightly. It was a wonder to me that couples like the Needmyers could muster enough courage to leave their homes in the Midwest for the westward trails. Maybe it was because all their neighbors were doing the same or else they possessed a quiet strength that I wasn't able to detect without any worldly experience.

Old Man Gunderson cleared his throat and adjusted the soaked red bandana that he wore over his head. He peered across the river with his one good eye, his beard pointing toward the opposite bank. I could sense everyone holding their breath, because Mr. Gunderson not only looked like a pirate but also sounded like one at times. Certainly, he was the only man in our party who dared challenge a decision by the wagon master.

"You thinking otherwise, George?" said Mr. Burleson, beating his old friend to the punch. "You with Orval on this?"

Mr. Needmyer dared to stand up a little straighter and perk up his long ears.

"Julesburg is on this side, right?" Mr. Gunderson said. "Well, then this is the right side to be on. Julesburg is a town and towns have doctors. Libbie needs a doctor. That's become clear to me. And I want it to be clear to all of you. So let's not just stand around here thinking about it. You two boys out there, get the hell out of the water. We're going straight, like Mr. B. says."

Mr. Burleson grinned. He and his old friend hadn't been agreeing on much lately. He finally had both shoes on again. "Let's move out," he shouted.

The Needmyers and the others responded well, heading for their wagons on the double.

"Hold it!" The commanding voice of Amanda Burleson stopped everyone in their tracks. "Not so fast," she added, but nobody was even moving. Her spoon bonnet was tilted to the left, but it was repelling water well. The decorations on it—ribbons, lace, and flowers made of organdy and silk—looked none the worse for wear. She flashed her fiery eyes at Mr. Gunderson and then at her husband. I half expected to see smoke coming out of her animated nostrils. "Julesburg also has Indians!"

In silence, all the frozen travelers let her words sink in for half a minute. Then one finally spoke.

"What's that—Indians in a town?" It was tiny, shy Mrs. Needmyer finally saying something. Her umbrella was lowered, trembling in her small hand, and her surprisingly loud voice was also trembling. "Did you hear that, Orval?"

Mr. Needmyer, slouching again, just shuffled his feet in place and opened his mouth like a thirsty man trying to catch the rain. Like everyone else he was clearly stunned to hear his wife speaking up in public.

"I don't wanna go to that town," called out George V. "I wanna go where there ain't no Injuns. I wanna go to Salt Lake."

"Stop whining, you baby," his slightly older brother George IV told him, slugging him on the shoulder to drive home his point. "Mrs. Burleson is talking."

Amanda Burleson put her hands on her hips and reminded everyone that in January of last year a great force of Lakotas and Cheyennes had attacked Julesburg's stage station and sacked the town, and then, less than a month later, another mighty Indian raiding party had hit the town again. "With our rotten luck, just when we get there, the savages will unleash a third attack," she said, finishing off her sentence with a slashing motion across her throat.

Many in our party gasped. Mrs. Needmyer accidentally poked Mr. Needmyer in the belly with the pointed end of her umbrella, and he screamed. Nobody was surprised. They figured Orval Needmyer was deathly afraid of Indians.

Mr. Burleson was tugging at his mustache, trying to make sense of what his wife was saying, in front of his followers no less.

"Both events made the papers back in Cleveland," Mrs. Burleson continued, quite calmly now, as if she were remembering some society news. "You read them out loud to me, Burly. Don't you remember?"

"Of course I remember, Mandy," said Mr. Burleson. "But . . . but that's old news, more than a year old."

"Who knows what the savages are thinking or if they are thinking at all," his wife said. "They don't tell time the way we do. They just do what they please whenever they feel like it. Do you want to have my scalp on your conscience?"

He didn't. Neither did Old Man Gunderson, although he no doubt was thinking more about Mum's scalp.

"I withdraw what I said before," Mr. Gunderson said. "Julesburg's only doctor might be a horse doctor, and for all we know he may have already had his scalp lifted. Libbie is a fighter. She will persevere."

Nobody waited for Mr. Burleson to withdraw his previous order to go straight. And so we crossed right there, where the Platte was two miles wide but never did get any deeper than two feet. Our crossing was surprisingly quick with no mishaps. Mum slept right through it. We followed the trail along the North Platte for a few miles when we came to a greater obstacle—the steep slope of Windlass Hill. Below it was a hollow, named for the ash trees that grew there, where plenty of firewood and fresh water awaited us. How to get down in one piece was the question. Even Amanda Burleson didn't dare suggest that we "just go for it." And a brief test demonstrated that sticks in the back-wheel spokes would not work this time. One of the other women came up with the idea of using all the men to hold on to each wagon as "human brakes," but the men all agreed that there were not enough of them to make it work. And Mrs. Burleson concurred wholeheartedly.

It looked like we would be stuck atop the hill for some time because not even Monroe Burleson pretended to know how to proceed. But George III, who had read enough books to know there were cowboys as well as Indians in the Wild West, took the opportunity to practice his lassoing on a tree stump and on the three younger Georges. While watching this display, it dawned on George I that since there were so many trees to latch onto and we had no shortage of hemp, we could lower the wagons into the hollow with a system of ropes. It worked, too, which almost restored George I to the good graces of his father, who could not completely forget his oldest son's disgraceful display at Dobytown.

So here we are, safe and sound for now, in Ash Hollow, where we are resting, refitting, and commemorating the Fourth. Our party's negativity and fretting over Indians and time has seemingly taken a rest, too. This place is a four-mile-wide draw between high white cliffs, an oasis really. Besides the ash trees, our party is reveling in the flowers—primarily roses and jasmine, Mrs. Burleson says, and she knows flowers almost as well as she knows hats. We have also discovered currant bushes and grape vines, plus the freshest, cleanest spring water we've tasted since leaving western Missouri. A mountain man of advanced years named "Beaver Dan" Eastlick hangs out in the hollow, sometimes sleeping in an abandoned trappers' cabin that has become an unofficial trailside post office. We can deposit letters here that will be carried to the States by eastbound travelers. The rest and spring water has done Mum so much good that this morning she managed to sit up and scribble out a couple of surprisingly long letters.

One was written to poor Maggie at the tenement house. Mum wished her younger sister, Papa Duly's ancient parents, and the kindly man of color Leon P. Flowers good health and enough of the Lord's bounty to sustain them. She threw in the Lord's name for Maggie's sake, although, like me, Mum admits that the ordeals on the trail have seemingly brought us closer to our maker. Mum asked Maggie to wish Mr. Flowers good luck on getting his U.S. citizenship, which would happen if the Congress ever passes a recently proposed fourteenth Amendment to the Constitution (which we had heard about at Fort Kearny), and to tell her old black friend that her favorite person on the wagon train was a maidservant named Hanna, who had been a slave before escaping to Ohio on the Underground Railroad. "Poor

Hanna," Mum wrote. "Working for Mrs. Amanda Burleson and our wagon master, Mr. Monroe Burleson, is no picnic. They are so bossy and thoughtless. It just might make Hanna long for the good old days in Mississippi." She went on to tell Maggie just how rough things had been so far on the Oregon Trail but that she was *not* complaining. She added in large cheerful script: "In a land noteworthy for its nothingness, we have found a green spot to marvel at, and it is here that I fully expect to bring into this world a fat, healthy baby girl who I shall call Sarah after our dear late mother or possibly Hanna."

I'm sure it would have disappointed Old Man Gunderson had he been allowed to read this letter to Maggie since it made not a single mention of him or his six sons. Not that I wasn't a wee bit disappointed myself. In my self-absorption and worries about the outside world, I had simply never imagined that Mum was expecting and wishing for a daughter. Frankly, I had assumed that she was not only aware of my sex but also positively joyous over it. Her second letter, which would have upset Mr. Gunderson even more, was addressed to Abe Duly, in care of the Dunning asylum on the outskirts of Chicago. It said simply, "I hope all is well in your world. If you ever get well enough to reenter the outside world, my husband, I trust that you will find your way back to the slaughterhouse district and understand why it was necessary for me to leave that place forever. Do NOT worry about me. Forget me. Take care of yourself, my husband." She did not mention the Lord in that letter. Mum trusted Hanna to deposit the letters without letting the Burlesons or any of the Gundersons know what she was doing. As for Beaver Dan Eastlick, he never learned how to read.

Now Hanna is back in Old Man Gunderson's wagon bed with Mum and me. Oh, boy! Something is happening here. Mum is getting so near her time that I can almost feel it (Lord, may she get through this—and me, too!). There is no doctor, but Hanna has some practical experience from the days when dark-skinned working girls dropped their young right in those white cotton fields of home. Half of those black babies might have died during their first year of life, according to honest Hanna, but she also says they at least all got out alive and had a fighting change in the Southern world of slavery. I figure if anybody can get me outside safely it is Hanna.

She is directing Mum's pushing and breathing in the most, calm, reassuring singsong voice. I don't need any directing myself—I know which way I'm going. Nobody else is in the immediate area. They are all over by the largest of the Ash Hollow springs, feasting, fiddling, fancy stepping, and firing off firearms to commemorate the birth of our nation. But that's fine with me. I don't need Monroe Burleson or Amanda Burleson telling Mum what to do or George VI nearby trying to whittle something out of a piece of ash or George W. Gunderson hovering over us with his one good eye and clay pipe like he's Mum's husband or my Daddy—he *ain't* neither.

I know it must be funny being on your hands and knees like this, Mum, and I have no idea why, but Hanna knows what's best. Let's not argue with her. No need for you to say anything. This is it, Mum. Oh, Lordy, I'm starting to slide. Push, Mum, push. Don't hold your breath too long now. Let it all out. That's it. You *can't* make too much noise. Listen to Hanna. She keeps saying, "You can do it, Miss Elizabeth, you can do it, Miss Elizabeth," even though you keep telling her to call you Libbie. Well, you're doing it, Mum. Keep going. I'm not holding back now, either. I'm sliding fast as I can, feet first. I know you were hoping to see my head first, but I guess I'm a little scared, not quite ready to go head-first into the wild frontier. Like the lady says, keep a-pushin', Mum. That's it! Lordy, I do believe you've got the hang of it.

Hey, my tiny little toes are wiggling free. Hanna has enough sense not to pull on them. Good, Hanna. Now, she's welcoming my chubby little legs . . . my body . . . my arms. Hanna's letting it all happen naturally, no pulling, no force. That's the way we like it. Thank you, Hanna. Of course there's still the head. My head feels so big and heavy, what with all these words etched onto my brain. But I say, "Let's go for it!" I'm lighting a shuck for the outside. Now, if my head doesn't get hung up, I'll be . . . yes, yes, it's going on through. My head's not *too* big. So long, womb. It's been a pleasure. I'll always think of you as home. Happy Independence Day, Mum. You, too, Hanna. I'm so happy I could shout, laugh, and cry all at the same time. By God, it has come down to this at last: I AM BORN.

★ ★ ★ ★ ★

# PART II: THE WESTERING GLOOM

★ ★ ★ ★ ★

# August 1, 1866: Parting
## of Ways Gloom

We are temporarily but comfortably lodged just above the confluence of the Laramie and North Platte rivers at Fort Laramie. Most everyone here is talking about teaching Red Cloud, war chief of the Oglala Sioux, a lesson and running around like headless chickens while I'm mostly sucking my thumb, a habit I picked up in the womb. I am nestled in a cradle in one of the rooms of the framed duplex officers' quarters. I can smell Mum's breast milk but she is not within reach at the moment, having settled into a crudely made rocking chair that is slightly off its rocker. I believe a lieutenant's wife and baby once occupied this place before cholera struck. Something is always striking down somebody here in the West. Mum has been overprotective—even taking me to the outhouse with her—but I'm not complaining. Fort Laramie has been a military post for sixteen years but has no walls around it. That makes me edgy. I'm used to being surrounded by comforting walls. I could make a fuss and cry about it, but Mum has dozed off protecting me, and she needs her sleep. Soon she must deal with parting ways with George W. Gunderson and sons. (The "W" by the way stands for "Wolfe," the family name of Old Man Gunderson's mother.)

George VI, the youngest of the brood, was in here a little while ago playing wild Indian—shaking a rattlesnake's rattle over his head, chanting gibberish and dancing around my crib like a warrior without rhythm. Mum told him to stop, that babies couldn't focus on anything so far away or recognize the sounds he was making. That only convinced George VI to pause in his dancing to dangle the snake tail in my face and rattle it in my left ear. I just stared at him blankly, not wanting to encourage him, yet not wanting to let on that I knew how foolish he looked.

"Look at him pretending not to notice," George VI said. "What a fake! He sees *everything*. He hears *everything*."

For a supposedly dumb kid, George VI was acting a bit too perceptive, but luckily Mum told him to go take his rattlesnake dance act to Red Cloud's village.

And he did run off like a not-so-brave warrior a moment later when his daddy barged into the room as if it and everything inside it belonged to him. First thing Old Man Gunderson did after adjusting his eye patch was joke that his youngest son would likely be the only "untamed Indian" anybody ever saw around the fort. Mum made no response, except to stop rocking. Mr. Gunderson then crossed his beefy arms and walked over to the rocking chair, his head held high so that his black beard was pointed at Mum's back. Next thing I knew Mum was rocking again, but much too fast. Mr. Gunderson had accidentally put the chair in motion while clumsily trying to put his hands on Mum's neck and shoulders.

"Not now," Mum said. "The baby . . ."

"Bosh," Mr. Gunderson said. "Your cub can't see all the way over here, and even if he could, he wouldn't know what he was seeing."

"Just the same. It's no time for romance."

"I've been very patient, Libbie."

"You're a good man. Don't ever change."

"All I want is a little kiss, a little display of affection. Is that too much to ask?"

"I'm . . . I'm worried."

"I told you, there's nothing to worry about. My previous wives are all dead. And I have no woman in line for matrimony except you."

"Not that. You know, Red Cloud."

"I believe the red devil already has a wife."

"Be serious. He's on the loose."

"Look. This is Fort Laramie, and the commanding officer himself told Amanda Burleson that the fort has never been attacked. He did admit to her under persistent questioning that once in 1864 about thirty Indians raced through the parade ground making off with horses. That was embarrassing for sure, but that was two years ago and nobody was injured. Rest assured that since then only peaceable Indians have showed up at Fort Laramie, to trade or beg or to talk peace. There's even a name for them—the 'Laramie Loafers.' "

"Red Cloud is not loafing."

"True, but he's a long way from here."

Mum nodded, even as she bit a wayward strand of yellow hair. "I'm still worried . . . about other things." She bowed her head; she could not look at the good man she *needed* to abandon.

"I know—we're running later than we should be. You have the snow in the mountains on your mind. Well, don't you fret your pretty, little head, Libbie. Your future husband will get you through to Salt Lake in one piece." His hands, which he must have believed were reassuring, went to work on Mum's shoulders again, rubbing, rubbing, rubbing so innocently. Then, suddenly, a few of his calloused fingers slipped below her shoulders, where only I belonged.

"What are you doing, Mr. Gunderson?" Mum asked.

"Nothing, nothing." He jerked his hands away. "At least call me George."

"I'm tired, George," Mum insisted.

Mr. Gunderson gripped the back of the rocker so hard that it stopped rocking. But then he backed off and began the long process of lighting his clay pipe. No matter how much turmoil was around him or agitation was in his heart, he could always fall back to that pipe—as comforting as my green blankie (a "birthday" gift from Hanna), I suppose. For Mum's benefit, he marched over to the cradle, patted me almost gently on the head with his tobacco-stained fingers, and told me I was a good little soldier for weathering the trip just fine after first seeing the light of day in Ash Hollow. As he turned his back on me to return his attention to Mum, I raised my head as high as I could and stuck my tongue out at him. He spun around suddenly as if he could feel somebody behind him pointing a weapon. I quickly let my head fall back on the blankie and closed my eyes, breathing hard, drooling hard. He looked even more like a pirate when he appeared in my mind's eye. I could still see him glaring at me with his one good orb.

"I don't mean to flog a dead horse, Libbie girl," Mr. Gunderson said, finally showing his back to me again. "But that cub of yours is a mite peculiar."

"What's that you say?" Mum said, leaning forward in her rocker. "My Angel Lamb is perfectly normal and perfectly healthy."

"No offense now, my dear. He isn't even a month old, and when it comes to size he couldn't hold a candle to any of my Georges as newborns. Yet I swear your cub was lifting up his head just now and, well, trying to spit or something."

"That's impossible. Babies drool; they don't spit."

"His head was up. I saw it."

"OK, what of it? I've seen it, too—so what."

"It struck me as a tad unusual, that's all. None of my cubs ever . . ."

"Not all cubs . . . babies . . . are the same." Mum seemed flustered. She glanced at my crib and sighed. "The minute my

Angel Lamb was born he was able to raise his head as if he wanted to sniff the roses and jasmine in Ash Hollow. I attribute that to his being inquisitive and developing a strong neck during all that jarring around in the wagon bed, especially when George VI was driving. Having a strong neck doesn't make him strange, you know. Pudding is still just a normal baby."

"Sure he is."

"As normal as that boy of yours who thinks he's a wild Indian."

"Look. Boys will be boys. And I'll treat him just like he was one of my own." Mr. Gunderson patted Mum on the head even more gently than he had patted me. He struck a match, still trying to light his pipe. "You named him yet? I mean he isn't going to be *Angel Lamb,* is he?"

Mum started to speak, hesitated, and then shook her head so hard that a strand of her yellow hair whipped against her nose. "It wouldn't be fair to call him by a name like that out in public. It's more of a private name. A Mum's name for her baby."

"So, you have an alternative?"

"Well, yes. Yes. I have already come up with another name."

It was true. She was now sometimes calling me "Pudding" in honor of her own mother. On the Christmas before her fatal fall from the runaway whiskey wagon, Sarah Hotchkiss had revealed to her daughter (who was not yet a Mum of any kind) the family's favorite dessert recipe—for boiled plum pudding. And during the Civil War, Mum had called her twin toddlers "Puddin' Plums" before the pair succumbed to summer complaints and for some time after that as well.

"And what might that name be?" Old Man Gunderson asked.

"If you must know, it's Pudding."

"Pudding?" Mr. Gunderson was too much of a gentleman to start laughing. He worked with both hands on his pipe so you couldn't see his mouth at all.

"I would have called him Sarah, after my mother, but he wasn't a girl. My mother loved pudding."

"To eat or as a name?"

"All right, Mr. Gunderson. I admit 'Pudding' isn't a good public name either."

"I favor George VII, as I might have mentioned a time or two," Mr. Gunderson said, clicking his tongue. "I'd feel honored if you would name him that."

"I know. I know. But he isn't a George."

"What is he then?"

"I don't know. I just haven't decided." She stared at the ceiling.

Nobody asked me—not that I could tell anyone what I wanted. I certainly didn't want to be another George. On the other hand, Pudding was about as ridiculous as Angel Lamb, especially on the wild and woolly frontier. I thought of some good frontier names—the teamster names. Stumpy wouldn't do, though. I planned to be tall like my father. Plug was worse. I didn't like the smell of tobacco, let alone want to taste it. I liked Red, except my hair wasn't red or white. I had some light brown hair when I was born but it has all but disappeared. I hoped she wouldn't call me Baldy; I was confident my hair would come back. Abraham Duly Jr. might have been all right with me, but it didn't even cross Mum's mind.

"Why rush things?" she said. "He'll have the name I give him for a whole lifetime."

"That's right. He's no Indian boy. From what I've heard, an Indian child will often have three or four names in his lifetime. If your cub was a Plains Indian papoose, you could call him 'One Who Raises His Head' or 'Drooler' or 'Little Spitter.' "

For the first time since he barged into the room, Mum stared hard into Mr. Gunderson's one good eye. "I appreciate all you've done for me, Mr. Gunderson, but *not* your attempts at humor."

"My apologies, Libbie. I have never been known for my sense of humor. I'm trying to develop it."

"No, I apologize. Perhaps I've been too serious."

"No, no. You've been just right, Libbie. And I can say in all seriousness that no matter what you call your cub, his last name shall be Gunderson. That's a solemn promise."

Mum said nothing, but her face tightened like a hangman's noose and her body reacted so violently that she nearly tipped over her unbalanced rocker.

"Careful now," Mr. Gunderson said, striking another match on the back of Mum's rocker. "Don't get too excited . . . yet."

"I'm very tired."

"Yes, you get your rest. Resting now is a good thing. We'll be pulling out in a day or two. And when we do, they'll be no riding behind in the wagon bed anymore. You're done wearing the bustle wrong, Libbie girl. You'll be pulling your own weight . . . like a good, well, like a good Latter-day Saint wife."

I could hear Mum's gasp all the way from the cradle, but Mr. Gunderson didn't seem to notice. And he didn't go away. He fiddled with his pipe until it was finally lit. Then he took two long puffs, blowing the smoke out in Mum's direction as if he wanted to leave his scent on her. Suddenly, he spun to the side and looked in my direction, no doubt hoping to catch me with my head up or at least with my eyes open. But I feigned sleep, and he finally walked out of the room in a puff of smoke

That was about fifteen minutes ago. Nobody has come in to bother us since, although I keep hearing officers' wives whispering on the porch—about Mum and Mr. Gunderson instead of Red Cloud. The chair rocking, as uneven as it might be, has done Mum some good. She has dozed off and isn't so much snoring as purring through her nose.

I suppose I should get some shut-eye myself, but the truth is, I have a lot on my mind and, though less than a month out of the womb, I don't sleep like a baby anymore. I once did, really, even when worried beyond my weeks. After Ash Hollow I couldn't stay awake for the life of me. If you want to know the truth, I was afraid to be awake because I was an infant and it was summertime and the heat and indigestion were giving me diarrhea. I thought I might get a fatal case of the summer complaints, like Mum's Puddin' Plums during the war. And if not that then the cholera that took the lives of Bub and Sis, two of Grandma Duly's children, or the measles that felled Nancy Morton's first two children. And that wasn't all. I'd heard tell, mostly from the womenfolk in our party, of ague, bilious fever, consumption, croup, diphtheria, dropsy, dysentery, inflamma-tion of the bowels, inflammation of the head, inflammation of the lungs, scarlet fever, scurvy, and whooping cough. During the first three weeks of my life, the only time I didn't think of those awful things was when I was asleep, because my dreams were usually of the womb and thus warm and comforting. And even when the dreams got a little scary—like me falling into the muddy Platte or into the painted arms of wild Indians—they were at least disease free. I figured if I was going to die young of some horrible disease, it was better to die in my sleep when I was dreaming of something else.

Disease, of course, is still lurking out there, crouched behind a wall or hiding behind a bush, ready to ambush me. But now that I'm approaching a month old, it is no longer constantly on my mind. What's mostly on my mind now are two things that make sleep difficult—how Old Man Gunderson will react (and I can't imagine it being remotely pleasant) to Mum's decision to go to Gold Country instead of Mormon Country and how exactly we will get there through Indian Country. Mum has been secretly (secretly from the Gundersons and the Burlesons and the others in our party, not from me) arranging meetings with young and bold, or foolish, young single men who have plans to take the Bozeman Trail to the Montana gold fields after they gather enough supplies and courage. Mum takes me to these meetings, not only because she can't bear to be out of my sight but also because she wants to find a young, strong single man who can at least tolerate having a baby along. Mum still doesn't have money, of course. But even after the ordeal of having me, she still has her looks, including those breasts and that long yellow hair that practically demands to be touched. Like Old Man Gunderson, these young single men will expect something in return for our passage to the gold fields, but not necessarily marriage. Enough said on that unpleasant subject.

Between Ash Hollow and Fort Laramie, my sleep kept me from seeing the Oregon Trail landmark known as Courthouse Rock and its smaller companion, Jailhouse Rock. Mum said I didn't miss much. She said that the pair of rock formations looked nothing like the Chicago courthouse and jail on Hubbard Street where Papa Duly had spent some time for trying to strangle the kind old man of color Leon P. Flowers. About twelve miles further west I woke up. At Old Man Gunderson's insistence, Mum had reluctantly taken the reins of the wagon for the first time and had handed me off to him for the first time. His pipe smoke had agitated my tiny but sensitive nostrils. That was as close as I had been to the land pirate's eye patch, and his rough beard was tickling my nose. I felt like I wanted to giggle out loud, but Mum hadn't even seen me smile yet, so I began bawling my head off instead. I didn't stop until Mum turned over the reins, took me back in her arms, and pointed out a natural curiosity up ahead. On the naked plain before me lay a conical mound with a pinnacle rising out of the middle of it.

"We've found the needle in the haystack at last," Mum said,

securing me in one arm and pointing as eagerly as a bird dog at the rock formation. "See, Pudding. It's sticking right out."

"I'd hate to be pricked by a needle that big and fat," Mr. Gunderson said. "It's more chimney-like."

"Chimney Rock!" shouted Monroe Burleson from the lead wagon, which had come to a halt. "That's Chimney Rock, folks!"

"Church steeple!" declared Amanda Burleson, her voice as loud as his.

"But they call it Chimney Rock, Mandy," Mr. Burleson insisted.

"I don't care, Burly. "Who is *they* anyway?"

"I don't know. All the emigrants who passed this way before us, I reckon."

"To see such a singular phenomenon after all that flatness we've gone through, it can only be God's will. It *must be* a church steeple!"

"A Methodist church steeple no doubt," Mr. Gunderson whispered to Mum, still trying to develop his sense of humor, I suppose.

"Let's move in for a closer look!" yelled Mrs. Burleson.

"We're moving in for a closer look!" yelled Mr. Burleson.

As the wagons began rolling again, I raised my head slightly and took a good look at the formation that had caused such a sensation. To me, it resembled a milk-filled breast with one incredibly large and dangerous looking nipple—something for the male child of a God or perhaps a baby dragon to suckle. Next thing I knew, I was smiling. And Mum saw it. She beamed and announced my great accomplishment.

"Pudding smiled!" she cried. "Did you see that? Pudding smiled!"

Mr. Gunderson groaned and took a puff from his pipe before he turned away from the chimney-steeple-nipple to look at my face. By then I had stopped smiling. Nevertheless, I soon had more reason to smile. Mum was giving me the necessary hip, trunk, and neck support to make me feel relaxed, comfortable, and ready to feed. My nose floated over the nipple and after some sniffing and some pressing of my chin against the fleshy mound, I became stimulated and extended my upper lip up and over the nipple to grasp a mouthful and begin to suckle. Old Man Gunderson snorted like a pig, yelled something at the oxen, bit on his pipe stem, and went back to looking at his Chimney.

Most of our party did more than just look at the spectacular three-hundred-foot-high shaft. We circled up next to the conical base of the formation and made camp. A nearby spring quenched everyone's thirst, and when Monroe Burleson clambered up the cone, most of the other men followed. They took a steep, winding path to the spire and, like many who came before them, carved inscriptions in the sandstone. Mum sat by the spring, and I fell asleep in her arms. I didn't even wake up when Amanda Burleson picked up her husband's Henry rifle and fired a shot in the air—perhaps to celebrate reaching Chimney Rock in a manner less trying on her joints than climbing or maybe just to hear the great echo. I heard about it later from Mr. Burleson, who complained that his wife had almost given him a seizure with that shot. He thought that while the men were communing with the chimney/steeple high off the ground, sneaky savages were attacking the womenfolk below.

The Chimney Rock climb turned out to be a mixed blessing. It marked the end of the prairie lands and the beginning of more treacherous terrain. That meant a lot more climbing ahead, but *with* the wagons and often more challenging—"The beginning of phase two of our journey" is the way Monroe Burleson described it. "The hard part," Amanda Burleson added.

I slept through our breaking camp commotion and didn't

wake up again until we were next to a detached butte known as Scotts Bluff. According to Mrs. Burleson, the bluff got its name from a fur trader named Hiram Scott before any wagons passed this way. She had read about him in Washington Irving's *The Adventures of Captain Bonneville*. Apparently this Scott was with a party of hungry trappers on the North Platte in 1828 when he took sick and could not walk. His companions went out in search of food, but did not come back. The abandoned Scott, perhaps motivated by revenge, managed to crawl sixty miles before he died at the base of a bluff. The story didn't seem to have any moral. Scott was dead and his companions got off scot-free. I figured it must be a true tale, because if it was fiction then author Irving would have provided his readers a lesson like in those Aesop's Fables. Amanda confirmed its factualness by concluding with the fact that fur trader William Sublette found Scott's bones the next summer. The way I figure it, Scott must have crawled right past the startling spire that came to be known as Chimney Rock. If he had died there, it would have been known as Scotts Monument, and believe me it did look as much like a tall monument as a dirty chimney. Of course then somebody would have had to come up with another name for Scotts Bluff. I thought about calling it George VI's Bluff anyway because the youngest of the George boys had worked himself into a huff by the time we got there. He threatened to climb it and jump off it if his father didn't agree to let him drive the wagon again.

"You even let that stupid woman drive," George VI complained before his father belted him across the mouth and threatened to use the bullwhip.

George VI's Bluff would have had a double meaning, you see, since George VI had no intention of climbing and jumping—he was only bluffing. Never mind. Nobody in our party, not even Mum, cares a lick about word play. And it's a fact that everything out here already has a name, except me.

It was Old Man Gunderson himself who drove the second wagon across a gap (yes, it already had a name, too—Mitchell Pass) on the south side of Scotts Bluff to avoid the badlands between the north end and the river. George VI walked behind with his five older brothers. Every time he grumbled something out of his sore mouth, one of the other Georges would kick him in the seat of the pants. I guess it isn't easy being the youngest. Mum and I got to ride in the back of the wagon during that stretch, with her holding me just a little too tight. I'm her one and only child right now, and though I would never encourage her to have any more, it's comforting to know that if she does, I will always be the oldest (the earlier dead ones don't count). All the way across Mitchell Pass, Mum kept staring at me real close, right into my baby blue eyes. I thought she was thinking how cute I was until she suddenly blurted out: "Your pupils are so narrow, Pudding. Your father's pupils used to do that every time he had some painful memory or crazy thought. But what memories could you possibly have? As for crazy thoughts . . ." Mum rolled her eyes to the underside of the cover on the wagon. "Well, I'm not exactly a religious woman but I pray to the Almighty that you won't be cursed with those, too."

Anyway, here I am in this officer room at Fort Laramie listening to Mum purr in her sleep while I lie awake in my cradle trying to have as many normal thoughts as possible. At this point, I have convinced myself that even if I grow up normal in appearance and in my thinking, I will still be able one day to take the etchings from the inside of my skull and scribble my pre-birth and post-birth diaries. Lordy! I hope I am not deluding myself.

I can no longer hear the officers' wives gabbing out on the porch, but I can still see them in some parlor, sipping tea and waving their arms. I believe they are boasting which one of their husbands will permanently tame Red Cloud, but I don't find their talk very stimulating and am tuning them out. I wish I had a mirror so I could see if my eyes are dilating or not. While I can't see my own face, I can see things I shouldn't be able to see. For instance, right now I see two buckskin-clad brothers passing a jug of whiskey back and forth as they stagger across the parade ground toward these officers' quarters. It isn't the first time.

Their names are Philip and Luther Kittridge, and though they were born in St. Louis four years apart, they look like identical twins when drunk. Mum had met earlier with Philip, the older but shorter and bolder of the two, after learning that he had gone to the gold fields with trailblazer John Bozeman himself in 1864 and had returned successfully to Missouri the following year to buy a farm for his parents. Now his parents were dead and the farm sold, and he was determined to head back to Montana with his restless younger brother to make enough money so they never had to farm again. Philip told Mum that he would never risk bringing along a woman, let alone a woman with a baby, but he was sober at the time. Later, liquored-up Luther showed up at Mum's bedside and made a dozen different proposals, one of which was to transport mother and child in the back of the Kittridge spring wagon, but hidden under a bearskin blanket for at least seventy-two hours to keep his older brother from noticing them and turning back.

Now, the brothers enter without knocking, taking as much for granted as Old Man Gunderson but without his history with Mum. I'm not surprised. They fall as one to the floor and then raise onto their knees and flail away at each other. Their coonskin caps take off like flying squirrels. Each brother is aiming for the face, sometimes with open fist, sometimes not. A surprising number of punches land on their chins and noses without noticeable effect. Blood whips around their faces like a red dust storm. Mum wakes up and screams, "Watch out for the baby!"

I'm on the edge of the cradle watching, not so much out of fear as curiosity. I heard about brother vs. brother during the Civil War, but *that* war is over. These Kittridges fight each other for fun. Interlocked, they roll close enough to rock my cradle. Mum springs out of her rocking chair and jumps on the pile, pounding her fists against hardened male backsides. Go, Mum, go. Give it to this unbrotherly pair! I am so proud of her. Sometimes a mother has to act unladylike for her child to appreciate her.

Mum looks like she's riding a two-headed bucking bronco, not that I've seen a bucking bronco with one head yet. Whoops! She's bucked off and flying in my direction. Watch it, Mum. But being a virtually helpless baby I can't really get any words out. I close my eyes and try to scrunch up in a ball. Nothing like this ever happened in the womb. Once I was inside Mum and now Mum is right on top of me.

The cradle overturns. Boom. A miss by inches! Mum is no heavyweight, but I could have been crushed just the same. Luckily, I am able to keep my head up, which keeps it from banging against the hard wood floor. Mum is lying on the floor, holding her back with one hand and reaching out for me with the other. She is bawling. The Kittridges are now separated, sprawled out on their backs, laughing. Old Man Gunderson runs into the room waving his Henry rifle. Amanda Burleson is right behind him holding down her feathered bonnet, but she stops in the doorway to stare. Now Monroe Burleson arrives, trying to see into the room around his wife's blue-gray feathers and lofty shoulders.

"Great Scott!" Mr. Gunderson shouts. He steps over the brothers to get to Mum. She moans and cries for Pudding and Angel Lamb, one in the same. Old Man Gunderson finally gets the message and puts down his rifle so he can hand me to her. She nearly crushes me with a mother bear hug.

"I told you it wasn't Red Cloud attacking," Mrs. Burleson says from the doorway. "He isn't *this* noisy."

"Yes, Mandy," Mr. Burleson replies.

"What happened here?" Mr. Gunderson asks, turning away from Mum to glare at the bloody men on the floor. "Who are you? What are you doing here? You aren't even officers."

The Kittridges don't answer. They are back to rolling on the floor, still laughing, still bleeding. In disgust, Mr. Gunderson looks like he is going to kick the noisiest brother, Luther, in the ribs.

"They aren't even soldiers," Mrs. Burleson says in greater disgust. "They're the two drunken desperadoes who bumped into me on the parade ground and didn't even apologize." She turns to her husband behind her, "And *you* let them get away with it."

"I reported them to the commanding officer, didn't I?' Mr. Burleson protests. "What more could I do?"

"If you have to ask, never mind," his wife snaps.

Mr. Burleson, almost on tiptoes, enters the room and stands over the fallen brutes. He seems to be breathing harder than they are. Mrs. Burleson seems to be holding her breath as she shakes her head. She cracks her knuckles, and it's like a gun going off.

"What are they doing in your room?" Mr. Gunderson says to Mum. Actually his voice is raised, which is rare for him. Does he think she is to blame?

"A minute ago they were fighting," Mum says. She keeps hold of me while picking herself off the floor without any help. "Now they are laughing."

"What were they fighting about?"

Mum now is back in the rocking chair, rocking me like a

baby—you know, like a normal baby. "What do drunk men fight over?"

"I wouldn't know," says Old Man Gunderson and you can tell he isn't lying.

"Mostly women, a certain kind of woman," says Amanda Burleson, as usual looking down her considerable nose at Mum. Mrs. Burleson adjusts a feather in her hat and does an about-face like a well-trained soldier. Clearly, she does not want to gaze upon an indecent woman with two indecent men in her room. How I hate Amanda Burleson.

And just like that both Kittridges stop laughing, restore the coonskin caps to each other's heads, and raise themselves off the floor. Monroe Burleson quickly backs away toward the door as if his wife has awakened twin giants. The brothers push back their caps, sweep long strands of curly hair out of their eyes, and look as if they want to punch someone. But they are not so drunk that they would take a swing at a lady or even smack her in the backside. Mr. Gunderson walks over to the brothers as if he intends to give them a piece of his mind. But he stops and just stares.

"If you all must know, we was having a parley about doing what was right but both of us can't do what's right so we started fighting over which one of us would do what's right," says Philip Kittridge while untying his dark red kerchief. He uses it to wipe the blood trickling from his brother's broken nose. The blood doesn't show at all on the kerchief, so Phil turns it over and wipes away the pool of blood that has formed in the cleft that dents Luther's square chin. They don't look so much like twins anymore. Philip's chin is small and knob-like, his hair less curly than his brother's and already turning silver at the temples, his shoulders are broader, his waist thicker, and his eyes darker without Luther's sparkle.

"Make sense, man!" Mr. Gunderson shouts. "Or are you too drunk!"

"Not too drunk to see why Lib wants to say adios to you."

"You must be plum crazy. What's your name?"

"Philip Kittridge. And that's my little brother, Luther."

"Actually taller and much handsomer," says Luther. "Right, Lib?"

"Lib? Her name is Libbie. Mrs. Elizabeth . . ." Mr. Gunderson pauses. Mum still hasn't told him her last name.

"And you're obviously Old Man Gunderson," says Philip.

"Oh, yes, the one-eyed Mormon that *Lib* mentioned in passing," says Luther. He uses his brother's already bloody handkerchief to treat a cut over Philip's left eyebrow. Philip then puts the kerchief inside his buckskin shirt, right over his heart.

"What right have you scoundrels to call her Lib or to call me an old man? If my sons showed such impertinence, I'd give them a whipping. Consuming a jug full is no excuse. It is my privilege and mine alone to call her Libbie. She is the future Mrs. Gunderson to the likes of you two."

"Not likely, Pops," says Luther, tugging an earlobe with his left hand while licking the swollen knuckles of his right.

"That's right, old man," says Philip, flipping the tail of his coonskin cap. "You're heading to Salt Lake, where even the lake is dry, not to mention as salty as a deer lick. She's headed to Virginia City, where there's gold. Me and my younger brother here happen to be headed that way ourselves, so we want to do what's right."

"What's right? You aren't taking my Libbie anywhere."

"We'll marry her first, Pops," says Luther, his eyes sparkling like fool's gold.

"That is one of us will," explains Philip. "They got a chaplain here at the fort who can do the honors before we go. It's the right thing to do. And that's why we got to clawing and gnawing at each other. Only *one of us* can do the right thing."

"Me," Luther insists, "I asked her to marry me first. I got first rights."

"You'll get last rites if you don't watch it," says Philip, while grinning no less. "She asked me to go to the gold fields because she knows I've been there before and got the full experience and can be trusted to do the right thing."

"You turned her down."

"Well, brother, I thought on it. I thought on it a lot, her silky blond hair, her . . . well, gold is where you find it, brother. A body has a right to change his mind. Respect your elders, Luther."

"The hell I will, Phil. You thought of me having her, so you had to have her instead."

"Luther, Luther, you are so confused. You're not cut out to be a family man just yet—not like me. She has a youngin' and you're practically a youngin' yourself. But I'm sure you'll make a right decent brother-in-law to Lib."

"By thunder, you got it all wrong. And I'll show you just how wrong!"

Luther, having sobered up some, throws his most powerful, accurate punch yet. The tight fist lands on Philip's chin, knocking the older Kittridge clear off his feet. But Philip brushes off the blow by wiping his chin with the back of his hand. Now he rises with blood in his eyes. Luther waits like a wooden Indian. Philip connects with an uppercut to the jaw. Luther goes down. And he isn't getting up. I think he's out cold. Score one for the older Kittridge. But Mum isn't keeping score. She's rocking me in the chair like there's no tomorrow while trying to shield my blue eyes from the violence. There is a kind of innocence in her gesture. She has no clue how much I can see with my mind's eye. None of them do.

"You'd be wise to keep away from my wife to be," Old Man Gunderson says to the standing Kittridge. "She's not interested in gold. She's interested in . . ."

"Me," interrupts Philip. "Better me and the gold, than you and a salty farm or whatever they got in Salt Lick."

"Salt Lake, you . . . you . . ." Mr. Gunderson's face is now blood red behind his black beard, which I now see has some distinct gray in it. I'm not sure if he can't think of the right name to call Phil Kittridge or just doesn't want to use that kind of language in front of Mum and Amanda Burleson.

"I'm afraid, old man, that you are no longer in the picture as far as Lib is concerned. She deserves a younger, more capable man headed in the right direction."

"Me," says Luther, though still flat on his back on the floor.

"If I only had my bullwhip," mutters Mr. Gunderson.

Monroe Burleson steps over to his old friend and pats him on the back. He tells him not to worry. He whispers to him: "Mandy," he says, "is certain that the commanding officer would never allow Elizabeth to go with the drunken Kittridge brothers into Red Cloud's Powder River Country." I'm not sure if anyone but me hears him. Mrs. Burleson isn't saying anything for a change. She is rubbing her aching knee joints, the ones that can only be healed in special Oregon mud. I don't think she would have cared if Mum ran off to become Red Cloud's squaw.

Philip Kittridge is now kneeling on the floor, gently slapping Luther's cheeks, to get the cobwebs out of his brother's head.

"Brotherly love," Mr. Burleson mumbles to nobody in particular.

Old Man Gunderson sidesteps the brothers, brushes past Mrs. Burleson, and edges back over to the rocking chair. He glares down at Mum like a vulture wondering about its next meal. She rocks on as if he isn't even there. She begins humming to me. I'm not sure if it is to comfort me or to annoy him. He is annoyed! He grabs the chair and holds it still.

"What is going on, Libbie?" he asks too loudly.

"I'm trying to rock my baby," she says, "if you don't mind."

"Tell me you aren't interested in either of those two rough-necks." Mr. Gunderson's voice is now a strained whisper. "Tell me, it's just their whiskey talking!"

"I am not going to marry either one of them, if that's what you mean," Mum says.

"Good." Mr. Gunderson relaxes his hand on the chair, and Mum goes back to rocking. "Now tell me you aren't interested in gold."

"What gold?"

"Like those scoundrels said—the gold in Virginia City."

"I can't say that."

"Why not?"

"I've been poor all my life."

"I'm not poor, Libbie. I am a generous man."

"I know you are, Mr. Gunderson."

"George! Call me George! Is that so blessed hard?"

"I'm sorry, Mr. Gunderson. I'm sorry, George."

"Tell me you'll call the little one George, too. George VII."

"No . . . I can't do that."

"Why not?"

"His name is . . . his name is Daniel."

"What?"

"Daniel. D-a-n-i-e-l."

Holy oxen! I suddenly have a name—I mean something besides Angel Lamb and Pudding. A decision made under pressure for sure, but I don't think Mum will change it. *Daniel. Dan. Danny.* I can live with any of those. It's not a total surprise. I knew Mum couldn't call me Pudding forever and would never stick me with the "George" label. She has been kicking around those "D" names since I left her womb in Ash Hollow. That old mountain man who sometimes stays there at the makeshift "post office" is known across the Rockies as "Beaver Dan Eastlick." I wouldn't mind being named for an old mountain man, even if he can't read or write. But he is *Dan*. I am *Daniel*. And Chicagoans from all walks of life knew Mum's father, who got the fatal heart attack while driving that whiskey wagon in Chicago, as "Whiskey Man Dan." Nobody called him Mr. Hotchkiss. For that matter, nobody called him Daniel. Then there was Danny Marble, the twelve-year-old kid the Indians held in captivity along with the pregnant Mrs. Nancy Morton. Danny survived his ordeal and was delivered to his free white mother, only to die of disease that same year. I don't want Danny's kind of luck. But he was *Danny*. I am *Daniel*.

I know Mum knows a Daniel from the Hotchkiss family Bible. Heck, he has his own book. She and I used to listen to her sister Maggie read aloud from the Book of Daniel—Chapter Six, I believe. For praying to his God three times a day instead of to Persian King Darius, Daniel gets tossed into a lion's den. But he survives, because God sends an angel down to the den to shut the mouths of the lions. I'm not sure what the moral might be—maybe that it's OK to pray to the Lord. Anyway, it can't hurt. The important thing is that Daniel survives. I'm all for survival. No lions out west, but the soldiers say there are *mountain lions* everywhere, not just in dens, and that they have fierce yellow eyes that glow like phosphorous. They are so dangerous that settlers have put bounties on their heads. Makes me wonder which would be scarier: To come face-to-face with a wild Indian or a wild cat?

But right now all I see is Mr. Gunderson's dazed face. He keeps forming my name on his lips without saying it. He is not one to curse, but I'm hearing a few questionable mutterings coming from his mouth and filtering through his beard, which seems to be graying before my eyes. His clay pipe is lying on the floor at his feet and he doesn't know it or else is just too confused in his head to bend down. I wonder if that is a tear I see in his one good eye, and I wonder if he is capable of producing tears behind that black patch.

"And so, Elizabeth," he says, and then he gets all choked up. He has been calling her "Libbie" as if she were his little pet dog totally dependent on him. "Is it your intention to throw away your happiness and risk your scalp by traveling with those two scoundrels to Montana to find gold?" He points toward the Kittridge brothers, who are now both standing but too busy straightening out each other's buckskin shirts to pay Old Man Gunderson or Mum any mind.

"And to find my older sister, Cornelia Wheelwright," Mum says. "She has already found gold in Virginia City—rather her husband has."

"An older sister who is rich, huh?" Mr. Gunderson twists his beard, making several small knots in it. "You never even mentioned her, just the younger one who you left behind."

"I am sorry, George. I was poor, pregnant, and desperate."

"And now you are poor and desperate with a baby in your arms."

"Yes—my little Pudding . . . Daniel. It would be nice if Daniel and I find gold at the end of the Bozeman Trail. But even if we don't, we will be taken care of. Corny and Wheely will see to that. They have flowerpots in every window and a grand piano."

"And no doubt a spare bedroom."

"Yes, with an innerspring mattress."

"Great Scott!" Old Man Gunderson spins around in a frantic circle as if he has lost his bearings. He doesn't want to face Mum or me or the Kittridges or the Burlesons. He stares at the floor where the bowl of his pipe, like some horrible one-eyed monster, seems to be looking up at his one eye with disdain rather than pity. I can tell what he is thinking, that he will now enter Mormon Country with six sons named George and not even one wife. It's written all over his gloomy face from the wrinkles on his brow to the dark bag under his non-patched left eye to that knotted graying beard.

"There is nothing more I can do or say?" he asks. His knees are buckling. I fear he might collapse.

Mum shakes her head. And I manage a little shake myself.

"You and . . . eh . . . Daniel are taking the Bozeman Trail?"

"I'm sorry, George."

"It is written on the wall then," he adds, needlessly.

# AUGUST 18, 1866: WAITING AROUND GLOOM

I wish I were somewhere else right now. I've been wishing that since we left Fort Laramie one hundred sixty-six miles down the trail earlier this month. That somewhere else could be Aunt Cornelia Wheelwright's fine house in the Montana gold fields (the rainbow at the end of the dangerous Bozeman Trail), our rundown tenement building in Chicago, the comfortable officers' quarters at Fort Laramie, or even the back of the No. 2 wagon in the Burlesons' wagon train—anywhere but in the company of Philip and Luther Kittridge. Somebody needs to teach those blowhards to keep their hands to themselves, not for my sake (they do a good job of ignoring me) but for the well-being of poor Mum. Compared to them, Old Man Gunderson, who I almost miss at times, was a saint.

My hands are clenched—nothing new about that. The only time my hands aren't clenched in fists of rage or despair is when I'm sound asleep and dreaming of sweet milk, sweet water, and sweet people I haven't met yet. Mum is still sweet, of course, but she has lots to do besides tending to my needs. Sometimes I have to cry my little lungs out just to get a bit of milk. It wasn't quite so bad on the trail when we mostly rode on the Kittridges' spring wagon, Mum on the seat next to one of the brothers and me tucked in a sling on her lap. But we're at Fort Reno now, waiting for permission to continue our journey, which all the soldiers say will be treacherous if not suicidal. Red Cloud and his followers have created a "red scare" in Powder

River Country. I have *too much* alone time. Mum makes meals for the Kittridge brothers, who are enormous, selfish appetites with legs, and sometimes for other men who have also been delayed in their quest to reach gold country. On top of that she washes soldier uniforms in the fort laundry to earn eating money for her and me. The Kittridges are anything but generous. What money they have, they spend on whiskey, which isn't even supposed to be on this post. Back at Fort Laramie Mr. Gunderson gave Mum a silver necklace that had belonged to one of his late wives, and he didn't even want it back when Mum decided not to continue on to Salt Lake City with him. He insisted that she keep it to remember him by, but the Kittridges seized it and sold it to the Laramie sutler, because they insisted Mum had to pay her way—and my way—one way or another. Mum says she does what she has to do and is just thankful that she is not pregnant again.

Right now I'm sitting in an open basket in the middle of a dingy room with a dirt floor and a sod roof. A large flying, buzzing green insect came out of that roof ten minutes ago and I have been following its dips and turns fairly well thanks to my recently improved eye coordination. I fear the insect will land on my face and I'm *not* certain I have enough hand-eye coordination to unclench my fists and swipe it away before it bites my nose. I know Mum is in the next room scrubbing blue uniforms, but I am resisting the urge to cry out to her. Yes, the horrible buzzing insect scares me at the moment even more than Red Cloud. What's more, I am hungry as a horse and my cloth diaper is soiled. But I will grin and bear it. She needs to keep working so she can feed herself and keep feeding me. Anyway, it might be OK to be a high-need baby if you are living in Chicago or New York, but out here on the wild frontier, you have to be more self-reliant.

Since I'm just lying here like a cottonwood log, I may as well etch in my tired skull what has happened since my last entry. My plan is still to transfer my mental diary to paper whenever I develop the necessary hand coordination for the task . . . that is if Mum can somehow get some paper. I doubt she will ever be able to afford such a non-necessity . . . that is to say a non-necessity to her. She's a reader, not a writer. For me, nothing has changed since I was in the womb. I was born to write even before I was born. Not that Mum has detected or suspected that trait. Of course I haven't given her much reason yet to believe that I am anything but an average baby. In her presence, I believe I display the usual amount of gurgling and cooing expected of one my age. And when I'm just lying here quietly, she has no idea I am having all these advanced thoughts. Things will change when I learn to speak I reckon, although I don't want to shock her and others, except maybe the Kittridges if they are still around (heaven forbid!), by bombarding them with my full vocabulary. I'll be careful about making my first spoken word "Mum" or "yum-yum" instead of "malcontent" or "miserable." The big change for Mum, when she can no longer remain ignorant about her innocent Daniel, will inevitably come when I start to write down all these thoughts and memories. I am NOT so smart at six weeks, however, to predict exactly when that will be.

I do know that I have grown up considerably in the last two weeks. When last I made a diary entry, Old Man Gunderson seemed resigned to Mum leaving his wagon and the Oregon Trail while the Kittridge brothers were fighting over which one of them would hitch up with Mum before taking her with them on the Bozeman Trail. Well, there were plenty of complications. Mum may have told Mr. Gunderson some whoppers about her ultimate plans all the way from Missouri to Fort Laramie, but she was not lying when she told him in the officers' quarters on August 4 that she would not marry either of the Kittridges.

That night Luther Kittridge tried to pull a fast one on his older brother. He did some more drinking before he ordered Mum to leave me with Hanna, the Gunderson's maidservant, and hauled Mum off to see the post chaplain. Luther explained the urgency of the marriage this way: "It'll keep Phil off your back on the trail and those lonely Montana miners off your back when we get to Virginia City." The chaplain, who was wearing his nightshirt and holding his copy of the Bible upside down, protested until Luther pointed a pistol in his belly. I saw the scene in my mind's eye from clear across the parade ground where Hanna was holding me in her fleshy arms while singing to me what she called a "pickaninny lullaby." A buck private, wearing long johns, volunteered to serve as the witness to the ceremony in exchange for a bottle of whiskey. But as soon as the chaplain spoke, Mum grabbed his Bible and hit Luther over the head with it. The younger Kittridge stumbled but did not fall. Mum half expected Luther to shoot her in self-defense, but when he didn't, she ran off to retrieve her baby—me.

The next morning, Philip Kittridge showed up at Mum's bedside at dawn. He wore his finest buckskins and a ridiculously large high-crowned, wide-brimmed white hat that he had purchased with his share of the silver necklace money. He said he didn't want to get married in some smelly old coonskin cap and, besides, it was what the cowpunchers were wearing down in Texas, never mind that he didn't own a single cow and had never been to the Lone Star State. He had dragged with him the frightened chaplain, who still wore his rumpled nightshirt. Philip hadn't brought along a witness; maybe it was supposed to be me. But Mum turned Phil down as flat as a Kansas bluegrass prairie. From my comfy cradle, which unfortunately would have to be left behind at Fort Laramie, I thought it might just be a nice dream but couldn't hide my enthusiasm. *You tell him, Mum!* I shouted. It came out of my mouth as a few drops of burped-up milk.

"But you turned down Luther last night," Philip said. "I figured it was all settled."

"How did you know?"

"My brother can't keep a blamed secret, not from me. He didn't know what he was doing anyhow. He was booze blind when he asked you, couldn't have hit the ground with his hat in three throws."

"Now I've turned you both down."

"Hey, I'm asking you nice and sober, Lib." Philip's face, though, was splotchy red, and he was clutching the front of the chaplain's nightshirt.

"I'm sorry, George . . . I mean, Philip."

"Man alive! You're confusing me with that Goddamned one-eyed ancient Mormon?"

"Just a slip of the tongue. I turned down George, too, remember?"

"Yeah, well that I can *comprende*. But look at me? I'm a man, not a fossil like George or a boy like Luther."

"I never said you weren't a man, Philip. Just not my man."

"You're making a big mistake, Lib. This means you won't be riding with us to the gold fields. Luther and I are planning to hit the Oregon Trail by early afternoon. After that it's only a matter of hours before we turn north on the Bozeman."

"I'd like to come along. Really I would. Just not as Mrs. Kittridge. And with Daniel, of course."

"A bitch and her bastard!" Philip yelled. He pushed back his cowboy hat and wiped his brow as if he had already spent a long day on the lonesome range.

"Your language, sir!" the chaplain said.

"What about my Goddamned language?" Philip yanked down on the brim of his hat with one hand and with the other shook the poor chaplain by the nightshirt collar.

Gregory J. Lalire

The chaplain cringed, seeming to sink inside his nightshirt like a rag doll.

"Let him go, Philip," Mum said. "He's half your size and you aren't so big yourself."

Amazingly, Philip did so. He didn't apologize, but he straightened the chaplain's collar and even picked up a button that had fallen from the man of the cloth. He then removed his cowboy hat and held it over his heart. "You want politeness, Lib, all right, you got it. I'm asking you again with my hat off. Will you marry me, purty please?"

"I must politely decline your offer."

"I'll put it to you plain then. You'll get a reputation. Most of the gals in Virginia City have reputations, and those reputations have been well earned in the honky-tonks and whatnot. Let me put it to you plainer. You'll be arriving in Virginia City with two men who you traveled with many days on the Bozeman Trail. Everybody will think you're a soiled dove, a sportin' woman, a dance-hall girl, a horizontal worker, a frail sister, a nymph du prairie, a . . ."

"Stop that! I get the idea."

"Sure you do. Now wouldn't it be better to arrive as a respectable woman—Mrs. Philip Kittridge?"

"Respectable or not, I plan to arrive there my own woman."

"And play the gold fields?"

"Look, Philip, perhaps if you, or even Luther, courts me when we get to Virginia City, I might change my mind and decide to marry . . ."

"Balls!"

"You're right, of course. I should be honest with you. I really can't marry either you or your brother. You see, I . . ."

"Nothing you say, Lib, is worth a fart in a whirlwind. You're nothing but a . . ."

"No more of those names. Not in front of Daniel!"

114

"A cussed adventuress," Philip finally blurted out. "That's the nicest way I can say it." He turned to the chaplain, who was now shaking almost violently at the knees. "That polite enough for you, Archbishop?"

The petite chaplain shrugged only his left shoulder or maybe it was just a nervous tick. He seemed to be eying the Colt revolver in Philip Kittridge's belt, perhaps remembering Luther Kittridge's pistol from the night before. Maybe his position as a man of God at an Army post was not his calling.

Philip cried out "Git!" and slapped his cowboy hat against the chaplain's right flank. On cue the chaplain bolted, running for his life. Philip then put his hat back on and pulled it down tight with both hands. He hitched up his britches and fingered the handle of his Colt.

"Now that he's gone . . ." He didn't finish his sentence. He jumped on Mum's bed and covered her in buckskins. He must not have been trying to kiss her, because his hat didn't get knocked askew. But what he was doing seemed worse. This isn't easy to record, even though I'm naturally worldly, far more than anyone can imagine. It looked to me as if he had a couple extra hands. The best I could do was raise my arms over my head and shake my little fists at the cad—a first for me, but unfortunately a development in my physiological growth that went unnoticed by Mum.

I did not even try to see if I was capable of shielding my eyes. Like most babies, I am naturally curious. I took in all the sights, sounds, and smells coming from the bed. I admit it was a bit of overstimulation. After I had seen a certain amount of thrashing around (and the ridiculously large hat finally did come off, as did the Colt), I turned away and closed my eyes. But I could still picture what was happening in my mind's eye—such an innate ability is not always a blessing—and I began to fret.

The thrashing finally stopped, but the turmoil continued all morning. When Hanna came in to try to convince Mum to stay with the Burleson wagon train, Philip was naked from the waist up and sitting on the bed struggling to get his boots on. As soon as he saw the maidservant, Philip restored his cowboy hat on his head, as if that made everything all right. Hanna put one and one together and called the dirty white hard case names usually reserved for men of color. Her loud cursing drew a crowd of soldiers. But Mum kept her mouth shut and I couldn't talk, so it was just the word of a white man against a woman of color who hadn't really seen anything and didn't want to part company with the one white woman who had befriended her on the trail west. The soldiers accepted Philip's story that Mum had asked for everything she got. Philip winked at a sergeant and went off to look for some contraband whiskey.

But that wasn't the end of it. Hanna voiced her suspicions to her employers, the Burlesons. Amanda Burleson had never thought much of Mum, but she still went to the post commander, because, as she told her husband, "Even a bad woman isn't half as bad as a bad man." Meanwhile, Monroe Burleson, out of a sense of friendship, relayed the horrible story to Old Man Gunderson, who rushed to Mum's side so quickly he forgot to bring his pipe. When Mum told him that nothing had happened and nothing had changed, he insisted that he could not allow her to go off with a cockeyed ravisher and his equally wicked brother.

"I'm afraid you have no say in the matter, George," Mum said. "I am committed to going."

"After . . . after this?" Mr. Gunderson reached in his pocket for his pipe, which was not there. He pressed his hands together as if trying to squeeze the juice out of an apple.

"It was nothing. Don't worry, no matter what, I *still* won't marry Philip or Luther."

116

"Go with them, Libbie, and you might as well be married to both."

"I suppose it depends on your point of view. A Mormon man can have two or more wives, so why can't a Mormon woman be allowed to have two husbands?"

"I know you don't mean that. Not *them*. And besides, none of you are saints. You could be, though, if you go with me to Salt Lake."

"Look, George, to be perfectly honest, I can't marry them and I can't marry you."

"Don't lump me in with those scoundrels. I'm not like them."

"That's absolutely true, but it doesn't change the situation. I should have told you this long before, but my last name is Duly and . . ."

"Duly? Duly noted. But it doesn't sound right. No matter, Libbie girl. Libbie Gunderson will sound so much better."

"Stop that, George Gunderson. It can't be. I am, how should I put this, *not* available. I tried to tell Philip Kittridge, but he was *not* in a listening mood. I am already a married woman."

Mr. Gunderson went pale. He poked an index finger in each ear like he was trying to dig out wax. He mouthed the word "what" without actually saying it. Mum saw no reason to repeat herself.

"I'm sorry, George," she said.

"Great . . . !" he said, unable to finish it off with "Scott." He kept gawking at Mum as if she had horns or was about to grow them. I actually felt sorry for him and would have gone off and fetched his pipe if I was capable of walking, or even crawling.

Finally, Mr. Gunderson rubbed his one good eye and asked, "Why?"

"I'm not sure," Mum said, but she didn't look him in the eye. "I thought I knew him. We were from the same neighborhood in Chicago. I liked his blue eyes and his unusual chin. He was tall but he never looked down on me. He barely looked at me. He was very shy. I asked him."

"I mean—why didn't you tell me?"

"Well, I liked you and . . ."

"You liked my wagon bed."

"Yes. And I had a baby inside me. We needed your wagon bed. I'll never forget what you did for me . . . for us."

Old Man Gunderson began to pepper Mum with questions about her alleged husband. She wasn't about to tell him about Papa Duly back at the Chicago insane asylum. She provided no more informative answers, except to emphasis that her husband, Abe, was not dead, at least not when she last saw him.

"I can't believe it," Mr. Gunderson said, pinching himself through his beard. "His name is Abe, like the late president?"

Mum nodded. "They don't have much in common, except they are both tall."

"Where's your wedding ring?"

"Abe couldn't afford one. That's the truth, George, honest."

"And you say his name is Abe Duly. Really and truly?"

"That's right."

"Thinking back on it, I believe you once let it slip out that your last name was Hotchkins . . . no Hotchkiss."

"Only until the wedding kiss. My younger sister is still a Hotchkiss. My older sister is a Wheelwright."

"Who happens to own a gold mine. But isn't marriage more important than gold?"

"I don't want to talk about it anymore, George. Can you just let it rest?"

"Can you at least tell me why he didn't come west with you?"

"I have nothing more to say about Abraham."

"All right. All right. But you don't have a wedding ring. You should have something. Where's the silver necklace I gave you?"

"Why? You want it back?"

"Of course not. But I want you to *wear* it."

"Forget about the necklace, George. Forget about me."

"And about your husband?"

"Yes. I mean, no. Don't forget that I *am* married."

"Whether you are married or not, Libbie, this going off with those two scoundrels doesn't sit right with me. It's an outrage!"

Old Man Gunderson left the room, soon came back to look for his pipe that wasn't even there, and then left again. Without much difficulty he worked himself into a righteous furor and sought out the scoundrel Philip Kittridge to teach him a lesson. Well, the finding part didn't take long. Amid a circle of shouting soldiers, Philip and Luther were again reeking of whiskey and throwing wild punches and clawing at each other's scarred faces. They were fighting over Mum but not over her honor.

Mr. Gunderson wasn't sure what to do, so he just joined the soldiers, crossed his arms, and watched the fierce brotherly combat. Finally the major who was commanding the post showed up on the double, with long-striding Amanda Burleson right on his heels. Nobody paid him any attention at first, so the major ordered a sergeant to shoot the next man to throw a punch. That ended the fight. Then the major threatened to throw the Kittridges into the stone jail at the new guardhouse. Philip protested, saying he and his brother were not Army and anyway were heading out on the trail that very day. The major obliged by banishing both ruffians from Fort Laramie forever.

The Kittridges loaded up their spring wagon with supplies—more ammunition than food. Along with two .44-caliber Colt Army revolvers apiece, they each proudly carried—and showed off to all the Fort Laramie non-officers—a shiny new breechloading Remington rifle that fired .50-70 brass cartridges. The rolling-block system, they explained, made for smooth reloading of these powerful, accurate weapons. The brothers boasted of being natural born fighters (and not just with each other) who were not afraid of whatever Indians were lurking about the Bozeman Trail. "Red Cloud has never seen the likes of us and our Remington rolling blocks," Luther insisted, even though he had sobered up. "We'll shoot our way right through the Sioux Nation if the redskins act ornery."

"You two and what two regiments?" a corporal asked, with a wad of tobacco bulging inside his left cheek. "If Red Cloud is really on the warpath, you'll be lucky to make it to Fort Reno, let alone the new Fort Phil Kearny. As for reaching the Montana gold fields, mister, you don't have a fighting chance."

Luther, wearing new shimmering black boots he bought with his share of the silver necklace money, stood toe to toe with the corporal. "You looking for a black eye, soldier boy?"

"I ain't looking for nothing." The corporal turned his head and spit a stream of tobacco at the boots of a nervous private. "You've already been banished from here for fighting. You'd best save your energy. You're going to need it. Heading up the Bozeman Trail, just the two of you, is like buying a pair of cheap tickets to Hades."

"My brother, Phil, has done it before, even without me."

"Yeah, before Red Cloud got riled."

"To hell with him and the rest of them feather heads."

The corporal whistled through his missing front teeth, then looked Luther up and down with something that might have passed for amusement. "You obviously have never met the man, sonny."

The corporal explained that he and a few of the other bluecoats *had* met or at least had seen Red Cloud when Sioux and Northern Cheyenne Indians came to Fort Laramie the previous spring for a council. U.S. peace commissioners talked treaty, wanting a guarantee that the Indians would not harass emigrants on the Bozeman Trail in exchange for annuities that would keep the squaws and papooses of the Powder River Country from starving. While the talks were underway, Colonel Henry B. Carrington arrived at the fort with some 1,300 men and orders to build more forts on the Bozeman Trail. Red Cloud noticed and was outraged that the Army was trying to pull a fast one on his people. The corporal claimed to have heard the chief tell one of his followers: "White man lies and steals. My lodges were many, but now they are few. The white man wants all. The white man must fight, and the Indian will die where his fathers died." So while many other Sioux leaders and the Cheyenne chiefs signed peace documents, Red Cloud stormed off without signing but with a solemn promise: He and his many Sioux followers would resist the fort builders as well as any paleface who tried to use the road that disrupted the buffalo paths in the last of the Sioux hunting grounds.

The banished but fearless Kittridges rode out of the fort in their two-horse spring wagon, with two other horses tied to the back, while most of the soldiers were still eating their noon meal. The brothers made no attempt to say goodbye to Mum, let alone me. More than ten miles down the trail, Luther suddenly wondered why instead of heading north they were still traveling west along the North Platte in the deep ruts of the Oregon Trail. Philip was confused himself, even though he had been on the Bozeman Trail before. Finally, at Bitter Cottonwood Creek, about twenty miles from Fort Laramie, he pulled the spring wagon over and they made camp. Too much alcohol had made Philip's head fuzzy since last he traveled the Bozeman, and he finally conceded that they must wait for directions on how to proceed. Wouldn't you know it, but the first party to appear at the creek was the Burleson train, now expanded from nine to a somewhat healthier thirteen wagons. It was an awkward situation to say the least, with Amanda Burleson and her maidservant, Hanna, hurling insults at the Kittridges, and Monroe Burleson trying to politely hush them up since the brothers were well armed and possibly dangerous. Then Old Man Gunderson appeared from wagon No. 2. He wasn't toting his Henry repeating rifle, but he did have his three oldest sons— George I, George II, and George III—backing him up. He told the Kittridges they better be treating Libbie right, and then he demanded to see her.

"What the hell you talking about, Pops?" Luther said. "We left *that* woman back at the fort."

"Don't lie to me," Mr. Gunderson said. "She wasn't there when we departed."

"Why would we lie?" said Philip, tipping back his cowboy hat. "We was contemplating just now that she was with you."

"Great Scott!"

"We figured she'd go back to you. She didn't have much choice after we decided she and the crybaby were excess baggage to take along in Indian country."

"Could be she found *another* man on another wagon train," Luther suggested. "Maybe one heading back east."

"No," said Mr. Gunderson. "I would have known. Anyway she wouldn't turn back. She was dead set on reaching her sister in Virginia City."

"You think she was fool enough to try to walk there with the crybaby on her back?" Philip asked, but then he immediately answered his own question: "Nobody's that damn dumb."

Hanna boldly stepped forward with her hands on her broad hips. "It ain't my position to say nothing to you two outstanding gentlemen," she said, "but that ain't gonna stop me. No, sir. That little lady gots to be somewheres. And you all are to blame more than the devil hisself if any misfortune come upon her or that precious babe in the wilderness."

That was sure nice of Hanna to speak up that way. Mum and I heard the whole conversation from the back of the spring wagon, where we were wedged in between burlap bags full of hardtack and flour and boxes of ammunition. A huge buffalo blanket kept us under cover and also kept us dripping in sweat. Mum had brought along a canteen of Fort Laramie water for drinking and cooling our foreheads and my green blankie for extra security. She had kept feeding me a nipple to keep me quiet as we rolled along the North Platte. A few times we were certain one of the Kittridges heard us back there—like when I accidentally sucked too hard and Mum yelped a bit or when I got a bad case of the hiccups. But the buckskin brothers were arguing so much with each other about how to get to the Bozeman Trail that they couldn't hear much else besides their own miserable voices. Of course, Mum knew that eventually, when she got hungry enough, she would have to reveal our presence. Well, she was plenty hungry now and also in the presence of her biggest supporter since we left Missouri (not counting me, of course). God bless you, Hanna.

"Nothing's happened to us," Mum shouted. She suddenly cast off the buffalo blanket and exposed us. I was only slightly annoyed for having had my meal interrupted. I clung to her tightly as she closed up her dress and carried me down from the spring wagon. "We're right here."

Mum and Hanna acted like they were long-lost kin reunited. They hugged each other so vigorously that I about got crushed between them. Then, they separated just enough for Hanna to smother me with kisses. Not that I wasn't glad to see her, too. I mean it sure beat seeing any of the others, who all gawked for five minutes. For once, Amanda Burleson, Old Man Gunderson, and the Kittridge brothers were speechless. And when the speaking resumed, nobody raised his voice or threw a fist. The Kittridges swore on their mother's grave that they hadn't known Mum and me were hiding in the back of their spring wagon. But Luther sheepishly admitted that he might have given Mum the idea back at Fort Laramie when he was drunk and not thinking straight. All three men who had proposed to Mum and been rejected seemed relieved to find her there in one piece. They acted civil to her and to one another.

A man driving one of the new wagons in the Burleson train knew this stretch of the Oregon Trail like the back of his hand because he had worked at both Fort Laramie and Platte Bridge Station since the days of the Pony Express. It was this fellow who let the Kittridges know the best place to turn north onto the Bozeman Trail—which happened to be another fifty miles farther along the trail at a spot he called "Three Crossings." That seemed to relax both brothers. Philip Kittridge removed his cowboy hat and playfully slapped himself in the knee with it.

"Oh, yeah, I knew that," he said. "I just forgot for a while."

Luther Kittridge played along, dancing a jig and asking if anyone had brought along a jug. Old Man Gunderson ignored them. He walked up close to Mum once Amanda Burleson had called Hanna away to fetch something from the lead wagon. You could tell he wanted to squeeze Mum to death, but when his chance came he just stiffened up like a soldier at attention and stared at Mum's tangled yellow hair, rumpled dress front, and bare neck. He started to ask her again about the silver necklace he had given her, but he thought better of it. After all, he was a gentleman and she was married to a man named Duly.

When we all moved on together, Mum and I were back in the spring wagon but atop the buffalo blanket instead of under it. The fresh air was hot, but the occasional breeze was welcome. Old Man Gunderson rode right behind us on his plow horse, leaving his own wagon in the hands of his six sons. George VI's driving had improved considerably with practice, and the other Georges would take turns resting in the wagon bed that Mum and I once occupied. Mr. Gunderson didn't want to let us out of his sight. I felt relaxed enough myself to get some shut-eye. The ammunition boxes were no longer digging into my back, and Hanna had acquired another pair of diapers for yours truly. My green blankie made a great pillow. I figured we would have fifty miles of peace and quiet before more hell broke loose.

I woke up in time to see us crossing the North Platte, but that turned out to be just the second crossing. Three Crossings was just eight miles up the trail, so there was no going back to sleep for me. Thoughts were rolling through my brain as noisily as wagon wheels. I knew Mum still wanted to go to Virginia City, but the Kittridge brothers had already left her behind once after she rejected their marriage proposals. Nothing had really changed, had it? Not that I could see. The prospect of seeing Aunt Cornelia didn't interest me much since I didn't know her. And gold didn't interest me much since I had not yet learned to become greedy, except when it came to breast milk, and gold couldn't buy a body that. I usually try to be supportive of Mum, but I was hoping the Kittridges would go off without us again. I knew we would be all right. Mr. Gunderson might look more like a pirate than a knight in shining armor, but he wouldn't just leave us on the trail. He would transfer us from the spring wagon to good old covered wagon No. 2 and keep us safe . . . if only Mum would let him.

Based on what I had heard about Red Cloud, never mind the wild cats and stampeding buffalo, Mum and I had a far better chance of reaching Salt Lake City with the George group than Virginia City with the two ruffians. Without even realizing it, I dug my knuckles into my eye sockets so deeply that tears flowed. Mum took hold of my tiny wrists and firmly but carefully pulled my arms away from my wet face. She squeezed me to her bosom and folded her hands behind my bottom to pray. Back in Chicago, she had left most of the praying—at least the noticeable praying—to sister Maggie. Losing those earlier babies had only hardened Mum's general disregard for the Almighty. The hardships on the trail, her difficult pregnancy (with me), her relationship with the Kittridge brothers, and her natural fear of the Sioux had not made her look up to the heavens for any favors. So you can imagine how stunned I was—maybe even to the point of speechless had I been able to talk—to hear her sudden prayer from this unorthodox praying position. "Please, Lord," she whispered almost fiercely. "I know you have a lot of emigrants to worry about down here. But if you can see it in your heart to deliver Daniel and me safely to Cornelia's front porch, I'd be eternally grateful."

Philip Kittridge recognized the turn-off place when we came to it, shortly after our third crossing of the North Platte. At the foot of a big hill, he swerved the spring wagon toward the north without even waving goodbye. The covered wagons continued to roll parallel to the river on the north side. Old Man Gunderson brought his plow horse to a halt and watched his six sons go in one direction and Mum go in the other. Finally he screamed. "Halt!" five times at the top of his lungs. He was ready to fire his Henry repeater in the air, but the Burlesons and Kittridges both finally heard him and both halted. Mr. Gunderson then rode to the spring wagon to make one final appeal to Mum's common sense. "I still got some of your clothes in my wagon and you left most of the rest back at Fort Laramie," he called out as he approached. Luther was already in the back with Mum and me, letting her know that she was welcome to stay with him and his brother without marriage or any other conditions if she was *that* determined to reach her rich sister in Virginia City. "We can still have fun en route," he insisted.

"Hey," said Mr. Gunderson. "That's a married lady."

"Get lost, Pops," Luther said.

"Over there is the road to Fort Caspar," Mr. Gunderson said to Mum, as he pointed a shaky finger at where the covered wagons had halted. "This scalawag and his brother are taking you on the Road to Ruin!"

Luther didn't get mad; he just laughed. "It's a hell of a lot more fun than the Road to Righteousness," he said. "Go on to Salt Lick, Pops, and find yourself a purebred Mormon virgin or two to marry. We're headed to Virginia City, where there ain't none of that breed at all."

Mr. Gunderson acted as if he didn't even hear Luther. With his one good eye he looked Mum up and down with such intensity I wondered if he could see her skin, bones, and internal organs under her tattered yellow dress. "Your clothes!" he said in desperation. "What about your clothes?"

"We'll pick up something more high quality for her to wear at Fort Reno. Don't you torment yourself now, Pops. We won't let her go naked, 'less she gets a hankering."

Mr. Gunderson tried a different angle, stressing the safety of going straight west to Fort Caspar, instead of north to Fort Reno. I felt like he was beating a dead horse, but I still would have provided him a whip if I could. Amanda Burleson and Hanna walked over from wagon No. 1 to investigate the situation. Hanna checked on Mum's condition and boldly reminded her that no man had the right to touch her if she didn't want to be touched. "I sure don't want you to go, but you got to go with what your heart tells you," said Hanna. Mum nodded, tears forming in at least one eye. Then Hannah apologized for not having had time to fetch any more of Mum's clothes from the Gunderson wagon. She did, however, give Mum a plain brown dress, apologizing for it being a colored woman's dress and oversized at that. Mum wiped her eyes as she thanked the ex-slave and told her she didn't have to apologize for anything. Then they hugged each other again.

"It ain't too late to change your mind," Hanna insisted. "You can always give me back that ugly old dress."

"I think the dress is perfect," Mum said.

"Never mind, Hanna," Amanda said. "Her mind is made up."

That didn't stop Hanna from voicing her support for Mr. Gunderson's position on the safety issue—safety from the Indians and from the Kittridge brothers. Old Man Gunderson looked at Hanna with something bordering on admiration. Amanda scowled. So did Luther.

Before Luther could protest or strangle the outspoken woman of color, Amanda nudged Hanna aside and stepped in front of Mr. Gunderson. Amanda said that she had learned from one of the new members of their party that the road to Fort Caspar might also be lined with red savages. Fort Caspar, according to this fellow, was actually the old Platte Bridge Station, renamed by the Army after the hostiles killed Second Lieutenant Caspar Collins there last year during a fierce battle. "Instead of worrying about pale-faced Queen Elizabeth here, you should be worried about your own dark skin!" Amanda lectured her maidservant.

Then Philip Kittridge, his cowboy hat resting on his head at a jaunty angle, climbed out of the driver's seat and came around to the back of the spring wagon. Without saying a word, he brought the discussion to a stop by pulling out one of his matching Colt Army six-shooters and spinning the cylinder as if it was a child's toy. Next he stuck a finger in the trigger guard and twirled the gun forward and backward. That was just showing off, but then he handed the Colt to Mum and put on an impromptu marksmanship show with his Remington rolling-block rifle, splintering a branch of a cottonwood with one shot and then breaking off a twig with a second shot. I didn't want to be impressed but I was. Maybe boy babies, especially those like me who first see the light of life on the frontier, are just natural-born firearm lovers. I found myself making cooing sounds: *Ah-ah-ah. Ooh-ooh-ooh. Gu-gu-gu-gun.* When Philip was done with his show, Mum tried to hand him back the Colt, butt first, but he motioned for her to hang on to it and patted his other holstered six-shooter.

"You and the colored lady want to talk about safety?" Philip said to Mr. Gunderson. "Anyone in your party able to shoot like I do? And Luther is nearly as good as me. I taught him all I know. And I'll teach Lib how to . . ."

Mum started to protest, but then she tucked the Colt somewhere in the folds of her dress. It was mostly for show as well, for she never had handled a gun of any kind back in Chicago.

"That's a good girl," said Philip.

"She's liable to shoot herself," said Mr. Gunderson. "Careful with that thing, Libbie."

"Only time to shoot yourself, Lib, is in the unlikely event that Red Cloud's redskins get Luther and me," Philip said, almost cheerfully. "You'll want to save the last bullet for yourself. That's what the veteran soldiers say to do. Beats falling into the hands of the savages! Ain't that right, Mrs. Burleson?"

Amanda Burleson wasn't afraid to look him right in the eye. "I imagine so," she said. "But if it comes down to it, Mr. Kittridge, I'd advise her to save the last bullet for you."

Philip Kittridge laughed and stroked the barrel of his Remington rolling-block rifle. Luther produced his own Remington and fondled the gun butt.

"Great Scott!" said Mr. Gunderson. "Giving Libbie a gun to shoot herself with is part of your grand Powder River protection program."

"It would be an absolutely last resort traveling on the Bozeman Trail with my brother and me," said Philip. "If she had to travel any further on the Oregon Trail with you, she might elect to blow her brains out right this instant."

Old Man Gunderson wasn't laughing. He stepped past Philip

and addressed Mum close up. "I need to hear it from you, Libbie. Tell me you want to carry that gun. Tell me you want to go shoot it out with Red Cloud."

"I'll do what is necessary to get to Virginia City," Mum said, focusing on his eye patch instead of his one good eye.

"I underestimated you, Lib," Philip admitted. "You'll do just fine."

Old Man Gunderson had one last argument. He said that Mum could go to Salt Lake City with him and if things didn't work out for whatever reason, she could always join one of the freight trains that carried supplies from Salt Lake to the Montana gold fields. But Mum said that she couldn't possibly wait that long to see sister Cornelia and that she didn't want to give him any false hope or give Brigham Young the chance to indoctrinate her.

And still Mr. Gunderson did not give up. "Never mind yourself, Libbie. Think of little George . . . I mean little Daniel, your Angel Lamb and Pudding. What are his chances in Red Cloud Country? And even if he makes it through, what are his chances in lawless, sinful Montana?"

"I must tell you, George, I like both our chances better there than in Mormon Country, where we could never be free."

"Amen, sister," said Hanna. "A woman's got to do what a woman's got to do."

"Yup," added Luther Kittridge. "The Road to Ruin is lined with gold nuggets."

It was all settled except for one last goodbye hug between Mum and Hanna. But Old Man Gunderson still trailed the spring wagon by horseback eleven miles up the Bozeman Trail. When Mum didn't wise up at a place called Sage Creek, Mr. Gunderson removed his red bandana from his head and wiped his brow. Then he closed his eyes and folded his arms, but remained standing, to utter a Latter-day Saint prayer in which he asked the Lord to protect *this fallen woman who does not want to be saved and her misbegotten child.* It's hard to say whether or not he believed her story about having a living husband somewhere back in Chicago or that I was the legitimate son of Abe Duly. It didn't matter. Husband or no husband, she was not going with him. George Gunderson kissed Mum on the cheek, patted me on my raised head, and galloped (or as close as his plow horse could come to a gallop) back to the Oregon Trail like a man fleeing the devil.

The rest of the way to Fort Reno Mum had to protect herself, not against any Indians, for we saw none of those, but against the advances of the Kittridge brothers. They did not buy the husband story or else considered it insignificant since the husband was clearly a lily-livered Easterner who could not hold on to his woman. While camped on the Middle Fork of the Cheyenne River, first Phil and then Luther tried to get to Mum's head with words of passion and then to Mum's middle with bodies of lust. The same thing when we reached Buffalo Springs, seventeen miles south of the fort. Lust like greed is quite foreign to me and unpleasant, so enough said about that.

Fortunately, Mum never lost her head. Twice she got them to fight each other over which one of them could please her most, and two other times she shoved the Colt six-shooter into their buckskin bellies. Philip said he regretted ever giving her the damned gun and fetched a bottle of whiskey he had tucked behind the ammunition boxes. The brothers shared the bottle instead of fighting over it and then hauled out a second bottle to celebrate the good feelings brought on by the first. It didn't bother them that Mum didn't put liquor to her lips. Soon enough they were too drunk to do any harm to her, but also in no condition to fight off Red Cloud should he pay us a surprise visit.

Red Cloud's scouts must have missed seeing such a small

party as ours, though the ever-boastful Kittridges contended that the savages were afraid to attack two well-armed fearless frontiersmen such as they. When we arrived at Fort Reno safe and reasonably sound (Mum had only a few bruises on her arms and legs and I had a killer headache), the soldiers told us that gold seekers had been passing by in great numbers all June and July. There had been some trouble from those chiefs who had not signed the spring treaty at Fort Laramie. At the end of June, seven Indians had run off thirty-five of the post sutler's mules and horses. On the same day in early July the Sioux had launched two separate attacks nearby, including one on a wagon train at Buffalo Springs in which one man was killed and another wounded.

"Land sakes!" Mum said. "That's where we made camp last night and where . . ."

"Where there would have been a heap of dead Injuns if Red Cloud had tried anything," said Luther Kittridge.

"I couldn't have said it any better little brother," said Philip Kittridge.

We've been at Fort Reno four, maybe five, days now. It's on a plateau overlooking the banks of the Powder River, near the mouth of the Dry Fork. The words "powder" and "dry" have special meaning to me, because Mum uses a mysterious baby powder given to her by Hanna that keeps me from getting a rash under my diapers and what baby doesn't like to stay dry! When originally built a year ago during Brigadier General Patrick Connor's Powder River Expedition, this place, predictably enough, was called "Fort Connor." Three months later the Army, also predictably, renamed it after a dead general—this time after a Major General Jesse L. Reno, killed back east during the Civil War at a place called South Mountain. There's a stockade with rough, eight-foot log walls that surrounds a warehouse and stables and such, but most of the buildings, including our quarters, are outside the stockade. I can't say I feel as safe as I did back at Fort Laramie, but at least I see soldiers marching around the grounds and some of them aren't even grumbling.

The bluster of the Kittridges does not impress the officers at Fort Reno, who have received many reports of hostiles skulking outside the garrison. They are intent on regulating emigrant travel north, even though Colonel Carrington recently established Fort Phil Kearny sixty miles up the Bozeman Trail. "The present status is one of war," Carrington declared. His General Order No. 4 requires that all emigrant parties must check in at Fort Reno and rarely are they allowed to proceed unless they include at least thirty armed men. We have two armed men, one armed woman, and me, a baby who cannot do much more than lift his arms over his head. We have no choice but to wait for more gold seekers to arrive from the south.

It is gloomy here at the fort. We have a small room in a barracks of unhewn cottonwood logs, chinked and mud plastered. The floor is dirt, the roof made of sod. The small post hospital was overloaded all winter with men suffering from scurvy. One soldier died from an accidental gunshot wound. More than a few soldiers deserted. The post commander himself died of illness last April. Now, many of the men still around are suffering from heat prostration and stomach ailments. Temperatures are still reaching eighty-five degrees every day. There is a shortage of canned fruits and fresh poultry because of the dangers and cost of freighting. In the storerooms, mice keep tunneling through the flour and the suspicious-looking old bacon. The Kittridges mostly complain about the lack of available whiskey, and while they don't fight as much with each other when sober, this unusually dry condition does not keep them from pestering Mum. Unlike Mr. Gunderson, Philip and Luther Kittridge have little decency and even less guilt. They no longer argue the fact that Mum has a husband back in Chicago, but they constantly disparage him for being a coward and a weakling. I imagine it would be even worse if they knew Papa Duly had been declared mentally incompetent and a danger to society and possibly himself. Captain George M. Bailey, the current post commander, seems to have a low opinion of the Kittridges, not to mention of Mum for being with them and me for having an "unknown" father. Not that Captain Bailey plans to banish the brothers the way the Fort Laramie commander did, because that would be like sentencing them to death, what with all the merciless hostiles lurking about the area.

Too bad. The overstimulated Kittridges have caused me to become overstimulated. Their voices make me fret and kick, twist and turn, moan and cry. I apparently put a small tear in one edge of my green blankie. Maybe I don't know my own strength. My headache won't go away. My hands seem to be constantly in fists, my legs are always curling up on me, and my belly swells. How I would love to flail out at those two lecherous men. They make me sick. The August heat doesn't help. Neither does the waiting. At some point the wait will be over and there will be enough other traveling men available so that we can proceed, but until then the gloom hangs over me. Mum blames my nightly fussing and crying on overfeeding, discomfort from intestinal gas, and my inability to belch easily. It's frustrating that I don't have the words to let Mum know exactly how I feel . . . and why. Not that it's the end of the world or anything. I'm not so sick I will die. Last night I had this fantasy of Mum pulling the trigger of the Colt revolver, not once but six times— three bullets for Philip, three bullets for Luther, all shots hitting them in the belly, well actually slightly below the belly. Maybe a six-week-old boy should not be having such evil thoughts. But something keeps reminding me I'm not your average six-week-old frontier baby. As for how I will turn out in the long run, there's no telling. I'll just have to wait and see.

# September 4, 1866: The Gloom of Two Phils

Today, I am two months old. No celebration planned. You don't get to officially celebrate your first birthday until you have been on the outside a whole year. Boy does that ever seem a long way off! It's not such an easy accomplishment. And then you get just one candle, and I suppose one wish, too. Of course even at age one, most babies reportedly have trouble blowing out a candle or making a wish. My only wish at two months is to still be alive at age three months and some place far from here. We are practically under siege at Fort Phil Kearny, recently built by Colonel Carrington in the heart of Indian hunting grounds, some seventy miles north of Fort Reno. Philip Kearny was another dead Civil War general, killed in September 1862 just like Jesse Reno, but in a different battle. Philip happens to be the nephew of Stephen W. Kearny, an earlier general whose name was used for Fort Kearny in Nebraska Territory (yes, it confused me when I first got here).

It seems like ages ago that Mum and I were at *that* Fort Kearny—heck it was even before I was born! Life in the womb had its own problems, but I'm certain things weren't as gloomy back then. Fort Phil Kearny is gloom personified. I've learned here that Colonel Carrington has also built a third Bozeman Trail fort ninety-one miles to the northwest, this one actually in Montana Territory but still two hundred eighty-one miles from our destination—Virginia City. And, yes, you guessed it, that third post is also named for a Civil War general, Charles Ferguson Smith, who died in 1862 (in the spring, though, not the late summer like Jesse Reno and Philip Kearny). I figure things are pretty gloomy up at Fort C.F. Smith as well, although time will only tell if I ever get to find that out for myself.

On the dangerous journey between Fort Reno and Fort Phil Kearny, Mum and I saw violent death up close and personal. When back in Chicago, Mum lost her twins to summer complaints when they weren't much older than me now, but that was different, as was the wagon accident that took the lives of Whiskey Man Dan and Sarah Hotchkiss, and the passing of very young or old-before-their-time acquaintances in the tenement house and the surrounding slaughterhouse district. Most everyone around here calls what Mum and I saw awhile back on the trail "cold-blooded murder" or "acts of savagery." To be perfectly objective, which isn't easy for me since I am in the middle of the whole mess and essentially helpless, you might also call them "acts of war." For it seems clear to me, even if Colonel Carrington has waffled on this point, that Red Cloud is at war already or at least on the brink. And what a scary brink it is. Makes me better able to appreciate what Papa Duly—let alone Generals Reno, Kearny, and Smith—went through on the bloody battlefields of the Civil War. It's a wonder to me that war doesn't make *everybody* crazy.

The violence we witnessed on the trail has affected Mum. How could it not! She sobs more when awake, screams more in the middle of the night, squeezes me more tightly to her bosom (not necessarily a bad thing), seeks out sympathy and reassurances from men in blue coats, and actually encourages close physical contact with Phil Kittridge, the very man who in my book (not yet written of course) violated her in her bed back in Fort Laramie. And, yes, Mum calls him "Phil" now instead of "Philip," at least in part because this fort is "Phil" not "Philip."

The trail violence, and Mum's reaction to it, has also affected me as well—not that she or anyone else has any idea. How can they? At most, they only know how an average two-month-old ticks. When they see me cry they simply attribute it to basic stuff like hunger, sleepiness, and dirty diapers. Well, I do cry over those things. But I also cry over death—the possibility of my own death *at any time* but also the deaths of others. Are there any other babies out there who do the same? It's impossible to say since I haven't met but one or two other babies my age, and none of us are great communicators.

So call me a crybaby if you will. But right now there just seems to be a lot to cry about. The Indians are all around us, and the eight-foot-high log walls are not all around us yet. Ground was broken less than two months ago on this fortification, and Fort Kearny is still under continuous construction. Mum and I are in a tent pitched between the post hospital and the officers' quarters. We are sharing the tent with Grace Pennington and her chubby-cheeked five-year-old son, Toby, who also were on their way to Virginia City. Grace, all tuckered-out in body and head, is lying face down on her own bunk. Her hair is all bunched up in back so that it looks like she has a black cat sitting on her shoulders. Toby also has black hair, but it's untamed and sticks straight out from his ears like the wings of a bat. He is relieving himself in a chamber pot. He recently learned how to do it, and now he sits on that pot most of the time. Don't ask me why. He rarely eats what's put in front of him unless it's peppermint stick candy. Also in the tent at the moment is Philip/Phil Kittridge, who is sitting on the floor between Mum's bunk bed and my basket bed getting a massage on his slumped shoulders. He is still wearing his ridiculously large cowboy hat, but it now has an arrow hole in it. You might call this the Grieving Tent! Yours truly, the crybaby, is the only one inside the tent who is *not* crying. "Dig your nails in!" Philip keeps telling Mum between sobs, and she obliges, saying, "Yes, Phil" and "I'm doing my best, Phil." She can't rub, squeeze, and dig hard enough to please the sorry skunk. How I wish I had the coordination and strength to help Mum out. I'd really give Philip something to cry about.

But that's not being fair. He is in mourning, just like Grace and Toby. Mum has mostly been in the role of "comforter," but she is so utterly sympathetic to the plight of those around her that she sobs as much as the others. Soldiers, one lanky pale-faced one in particular, often come around to see about Grace. They tell her how strong she is and how good she looks even when she is drowning in tears. Sometimes they also come to comfort the "comforter," in part because Mum is the prettiest person stuck inside this fort and in part because the bluecoats are so isolated and lonely for any kind of female companionship. I've avoided intentionally thinking too much about the horrible trip here from Fort Reno, but I suppose it's best to get it all accurately etched into my head right now for later transcription. Just a second while I turn my head away from blubbering Philip and Mum's nimble but overworked fingers so I can concentrate. Maybe it's something defective in my makeup, but I still can't work up much empathy for the buckskin bastard, if you'll pardon my French, as people say (even people like me who don't even know French). I mostly find him terribly irritating, and I don't think it is something I will grow out of in time.

When we finally got permission to set out from Fort Reno, the Kittridges' spring wagon stood in the middle of a line of pack mules and maybe twenty other wagons, making our party even larger than the Burleson wagon train. There was no reason not to feel safe, even though we didn't have a military escort. We had at least thirty armed men, one of the conditions that had to be met before the Fort Reno commander allowed us to proceed north. Philip Kittridge wanted to be in charge, since he had been on the trail before, but so had a white-bearded Kentuckian named Travis Knapp. The others proclaimed Mr. Knapp wiser because of the whiteness of his facial hair, because of what he had brought along (a map, a compass, and a Bible), and because of what he had not brought along (a handsome woman with a crying baby). And so Travis Knapp became wagon master—his first act was to pray to "Our Lord, Master of the Universe" for safe passage through the "homeland of the heathens"—while Philip continued to be master only of his own spring wagon. As we set out, Philip Kittridge joked (but nobody laughed) that Mr. Knapp knew "south" better than "north" and "Moses" better than "Bozeman" and would, with or without his precious map, lead us right into the middle of Red Cloud's big village. As for the other men in the party, Philip dismissed them all as greenhorns with outdated weapons designed to miss instead of kill and who, in any case, couldn't hit the broad side of a barn.

"Red Cloud don't know that, Phil," said Luther Kittridge, who was driving the spring wagon with his Remington rolling-block rifle within easy reach on the seat. "I don't imagine we look so helpless from afar."

"You're assuming Red Cloud is afar," replied Philip, who was riding his chestnut horse with white spots alongside the wagon, one hand loosely holding the reins, the other resting on the butt of his identical Remington rifle. "He might be breathing down our necks."

Luther slapped at something that landed on the back of his neck, maybe a horse fly, maybe nothing. "You don't figure we'll get much help from these fellas if Red Cloud hits us?" he asked.

"Nope. But if Knapp and the rest of this sorry bunch of men get themselves killed or get nervous feet and run for the hills, that'll leave all the womenfolk for us."

Luther gave that notion some serious thought before sneering, spitting, and saying, "Besides our Lib, I only counted four other females along, and a couple of them, well, I ain't so sure about their sex."

"Them is your two, little brother. I claim the other three, especially that fetchin' Grace woman. She's dreadfully purty."

"She's like that one we already got," said Luther, pointing to Mum in the back of the wagon. "Grace is married with a kid, too. Actually worse—Grace's husband is *visible*."

"He's a greenhorn, a namby-pamby, an odd stick."

"Heard tell he's one of them Quakers. He don't believe in violence."

"That so? Well, little brother, I might have to be the one who beats his wife for him when she gets out of line."

"She don't look like the type to get out of line."

"Shows what you know. When they look like that, they always get out of line sooner or later."

Mum started to say something, but she held her tongue, literally, pinching the tip between her thumb and index finger. She planned to stay silent around the Kittridges, who were mostly big talk. Of course that Philip didn't always stop at just talking, but Mum knew he was unlikely to try anything with the Bible-toting Travis Knapp heading the wagon train and the Quaker Rufus Pennington driving the covered wagon directly behind us. Mr. Pennington had a hard, angular face with a beard but no mustache, quite a contrast to his chubby-cheeked, round-faced son. He talked to his oxen real polite, and the more I studied him from the rear of the Kittridges' spring wagon, the more I thought he looked like Abe Lincoln sitting at his White House desk during the Civil War worrying about how he was going to free the slaves. To me it seemed lucky that Grace Pennington got to ride with a man like that instead of Philip Kittridge. But if Philip worked himself into a state where he did try something, Mum had a backup plan that I heard her mumble fiercely to herself more than once: To take the butt of the Army Colt revolver he lent her and smash it down with all her might between his buckskin legs. I suspect she came up with that plan because some of my thoughts rubbed off on her. I don't know from personal experience, of course, but I heard that kind of thing can cause a fellow major pain.

We were still within full view of Fort Reno (if you looked back, which is all I did from the rear of the spring wagon) when a large band of Indians swept over a ridge as if they planned to thunder down on us. In fact both Kittridges raised their Remingtons before Mr. Knapp and the others even noticed we had company. For some reason the mounted warriors stopped suddenly halfway down the incline. Philip said they were wearing war bonnets and war paint but not much else; it was all he could do to keep from firing first with his long-range rifle. Mum protectively pressed down on the back of my head so that my face was tight against her oversized brown dress, but I naturally (well, naturally for me anyway) saw things out of my mind's eye. These were my first Indians! And the most colorful human beings I had ever seen. At the time, though, I only saw one big red blotch, which must be what a tiny field mouse sees just before a red fox pounces on it. It was hard to tell if I was trembling or if it was just Mum. But I do think the color of fear is red, and I know I was never so afraid in my whole life.

Then, the strangest thing happened. One of the Indians raised his hand toward a cloud (the only one in the sky) over his head and kind of flipped his fingers to the side as if throwing away the pit of a peach. That was all it took to get all the Indians to turn around as one and go back to the top of the ridge and then disappear over the ridgeline. All that was left was that lone cloud over the ridge, and the way the morning sun was reflecting off it, it looked a little reddish. Naturally I wondered if I had seen the great and mighty Red Cloud in action.

"Think they got a glance at our Remingtons and got scared, Phil?" Luther asked.

"Could be," said Philip. "But maybe not—not if they never seen the likes of these fine shooting irons before."

"Then you think it's some dirty redskin trick?"

"Just keep your rifle up, little brother."

"Maybe they want to ambush us when we're farther from the soldiers at the fort."

"Nope. They ain't too worried about soldiers coming out in the open to fight them."

"Not worried about soldiers?" Mum said, unable to contain herself any longer. "Then why don't they just attack us and be done with it?"

"Maybe they got a look at that Colt you're waving," Philip said. "Maybe they figure it's too much to deal with armed white women as well as armed white men." I might have guessed he was joking out of nervousness but his voice was as smooth as a baby's bottom. It was hot out already, but he wasn't even sweating. I figured he was either the bravest man in the world or the stupidest.

Just as Mum gave me a little more breathing room, four mounted figures appeared on the ridgeline. They rode down and kept on coming, at a gallop, directly toward us. Someone from our party fired a shot at them, followed by a second shot, and a third. It was foolishness. Even I could tell the riders were *not* Indians. Two of them had blue trousers with yellow stripes down the legs. None of them wore feathers. Their faces were unpainted and pale.

"Don't shoot!" shouted Rufus Pennington from the wagon behind us. But others in our party must have thought he was just saying that because he was a Quaker, since a fourth and fifth shot followed.

"Hold your fire, men!" wagon master Knapp screamed. "For the love of God! Can't you see they're white!"

"As white as my ass," added Philip Kittridge.

Still, after a delay, a sixth shot came from the wagon right in front of the Kittridges. The shootist turned out to be Asa Coffin, a withered but wiry half-blind, hard-of-hearing veteran of the Second Seminole War in Florida who misheard Mr. Knapp's instruction. What Mr. Coffin had heard before triggering his Model 1842 musket was: "Don't fire until you see the whites of their eyes!"

The Kittridges did not help the situation. They thought it was all a hoot and started cackling at the shooting. Luther joked that the ancient Coffin would send a dozen men to their coffins before somebody finally buried him. But Mr. Coffin missed with his musket shot. In fact, our party did *not* wing any of the riders who had come down from the ridge. The know-it-all Kittridges were at least right in their assessment of our party's weapons and shooting skills. In this instance, we were temporarily grateful, since nobody got hurt. But in the long run, the misses made Mum and I even more unsettled.

"Damn the whole lot of you!" yelled the palest of the incoming riders, who reigned in his horse right in front of the spring wagon. He was bleeding over his right ear—from a knife wound not a bullet wound. "We figured if the Injuns didn't shoot us in the back, the Army would line us up to execute us. But we damn well didn't figure on getting it from a bunch of trigger-happy civilians!"

The frightened men dismounted in a cloud of dust. It turned out that all four were deserters from Fort Reno, two cavalry privates and two scouts. They had skedaddled from the fort in the middle of the night, intent on reaching the Montana gold fields. They hadn't gotten far before the Indians stopped them without a fight. Three of the deserters-turned-captives were shaking in their boots but otherwise unscathed.

"One of the less noble savages started to scalp me alive when some chief stopped him with a Sioux curse," said the palest rider, who was also the tallest, as Grace Pennington applied bandages to his head wound. He was stretched out on his belly in the Pennington wagon bed, and he groaned just enough to make Mrs. Pennington go slower.

"I see," said Travis Knapp, because he was in charge, not because he could *see*. "It's lucky you all got away from the heathens like that."

"We didn't get away. You can escape the Army but you can't escape them bloodthirsty Sioux."

"But you're here, safe and sound. That's the main thing."

"We're only here because the chief let us go. He told us . . ."

"Dear God!" Mr. Knapp interrupted. "Was it Red Cloud?"

"Red Cloud, Black Bear, White Bull, Gray Eagle, Yellow Wolf, Green Lizard—who the hell cares! He gave us our freedom so we could tell the White Chief to take his bluecoats out of this country now or bury them here later. Carrington won't like hearing that, especially from us, but at least we have our scalps. That's the main thing, mister."

His three companions nodded their agreement and then drank from borrowed canteens when Mr. Knapp told them nobody in our party was carrying whiskey. Actually, the Kittridges had several jugs, but the brothers weren't sharing.

"You got a gentle touch," the pale private told Grace Pennington. Clearly no longer feeling any pain, he gazed up into Mrs. Pennington's hazel eyes as she dabbed at his full sideburns with a wet cloth. "And kind eyes."

Grace smiled slightly and continued her nursing work.

The patient smiled back at her, even letting out a brief chuckle. "The fine ends of your beautiful black hair was tickling my nose," he explained, though nobody asked.

"Why have you come to us?" asked Rufus Pennington, who was not smiling. He had a long arm around his saucer-eyed five-year-old son, Toby, and his own narrow eyes on the wounded man. "There are no soldiers here but *you*. We are passing through in peace."

"That reminds me. The chief, whoever he was, also had a warning for you folks in the wagons: Turn back or suffer the consequences."

Toby began to cry as if he could understand the word "consequences," and his father squeezed him closer. It must have been eighty degrees, but a cold shiver ran through our party. Even in Mum's arms I could feel it. Mr. Knapp could see the situation, but he wasn't able to speak—just plucked at his white whiskers as he hissed a little like a frightened pussycat. He crossed his arms against his chest, looked up the trail and back down the trail, and then glanced nervously at the ridgeline. Not seeing anything obviously didn't ease his mind.

"We have a situation here, folks," he admitted. "We should thank the Lord for not allowing those Indians to fall upon us."

"Two of us was supposed to go to the fort, and two of us was supposed to come to you," explained another of the deserters, this one with a jagged scar over his lip and without any yellow stripes on his trousers. "None of us wanted to go to the fort, so we all come here to your wagons. Maybe the Indians won't notice."

"And maybe it will start to snow," the pale private said. "The Sioux ain't easily fooled. They got keen eyes, like you, Miss. Would you mind dabbing a bit with that little cloth on my left side for a while. It feels a mite neglected."

"Your wound is on your right temple, soldier," said Asa Coffin, even though he was thirty feet away and couldn't see so good.

"And she is not a Miss, mister," said Rufus Pennington.

"She's my wife."

"I'm scared, Mommy," Toby said, breaking away from his father and rushing up to the back of the wagon to tug on the hem of his mother's dress. The pale patient turned paler.

Toby was not the only frightened one. In fact, it seemed everybody was immobilized by fear except the Kittridge brothers. They said anybody was welcome to return to Fort Reno but that they were pushing on because they were red-blooded Americans from proud frontier stock and weren't afraid of a few savages. For emphasis, they pointed the barrels of their Remington rifles north.

Mutterings followed and men kept shifting their weight back and forth without actually picking up their heavy feet. Finally Travis Knapp said that we should act as one and that we should take a vote, since we were civilized folks living in a free society. The show of hands twice resulted in a split vote. The mutterings grew louder and angrier. Finally the four deserters, who hadn't previously voted, broke the tie. They said we should be able to make it to Fort Phil Kearny without losing our hair, and we could then reassess the situation. Of course the quartet had deserted from Fort Reno and didn't want to go back there. But nobody mentioned that point, and I of course hadn't learned to talk yet. To my utter surprise, Rufus Pennington practically drooled on his Abe Lincoln–like beard as he voiced his approval for the go-forward plan.

"You can't go forward in life if you keep looking back," Mr. Pennington said. "I'm committed to our chosen path no matter what trials and tribulations lie ahead."

He was a Quaker with an angelic wife and a frightened five-year-old son. If he was willing, so was everyone else. At that point everyone moved. Grace Pennington gave her husband a peck on his cheekbone, the deserters borrowed guns since the Indians had confiscated theirs, Travis Knapp shrunk away in silence, Asa Coffin reloaded his musket, the Kittridges swung their spring wagon (with Mum and I still clutching each other in the bed) to the front of our party, and dozens of wheels creaked as our journey north resumed.

We camped that night at Crazy Woman's Fork, where there was good water and grazing. There was no sign of the crazy woman. Around the campfire that evening Asa Coffin, Philip Kittridge, and three of the deserters told at least five different versions of how this tributary of the Powder River got its name. The crazy woman could have been anyone from a haggard, deranged squaw woman who haunted travelers to a white emigrant woman who went crazy after watching the Indians tomahawk to death her husband and three children. But everyone was worried about more than just an insane lady, so we posted ten guards—nine of them armed with rifles and also Rufus Pennington, armed with his inner light. Before going into the dark to sit on a rock upstream, Mum and I saw him kiss his wife full on the lips. She didn't seem to mind his whiskers.

"What was that for, Rufus?" Grace Pennington asked, running her knuckles gently through his beard. "Do you have to go?"

"To the Virginia City gold fields? Yes. I was getting nowhere toiling in the soil back home. You know that, my wife. We had no meat for the soup, and I could not buy you a hat or even a ribbon for your hair—your beautiful hair, like that soldier you bandaged said. You deserve better. I am not a greedy man, but God has given me a sign. Montana is where I *must go* to make a decent home for you and Toby. I am not putting my faith in gold but in God's personal message to me and in the good earth and in our future happiness."

"Yes, I know that," Mrs. Pennington replied. "I meant do you have to go to the rock?"

"I have to do my part. Lookouts are needed. You heard those

soldiers. The Indians are out there . . . somewhere."

"But you don't even have a gun, my dear husband."

"And so, dear Grace, I won't accidentally shoot myself or anyone else."

That was the last Mum or I or Grace Pennington or Toby Pennington or anyone else heard from Rufus Pennington. Travis Knapp wasn't on guard, but he couldn't sleep. At some point just before morning light he wandered off from his blankets and tripped over something hard, but not as hard as a rock. It was Mr. Pennington, no longer on his lookout rock and no longer sitting. He was on his stomach stark naked with six arrows in his back. Mr. Knapp knelt down because he couldn't see exactly who it was, and even after he knelt, he couldn't tell. The Indians had scalped the lookout of not only his hair but also his Lincoln-like beard. Nausea ambushed Mr. Knapp. He vomited all over the victim before he fired off his old Springfield rifled–musket to alert the others. Indians could have jumped him then before he could reload, but they were off on the other side of camp at that point.

While the other lookouts and most of the other men, including the Kittridges, came running to the sound of the Springfield, the Indians were making off with horses and pack mules. One of the stripped-down raiders, a strapping figure of a man wearing a large-tooth necklace, worked his way on foot to the spring wagon and froze in the last of the slight moonlight. It was as if he knew Mum was there and intended to obtain more than just horseflesh on this night. He worked his way around to the back with a spear raised, as if he intended to thrust it at the first thing that moved. But I couldn't help myself. I tried to hide behind Mum's brown dress. I wasn't ashamed. Almost all babies act more like pussycats than wildcats.

But Mum wasn't going along with my timid act. She had other ideas. She scooped me up and quickly deposited me on a sack of flour or potatoes, which really wasn't very comfortable and did not actually keep me hidden from the painted, spear-carrying intruder. I was as naked and vulnerable as a not-even-two-month-old infant—which, of course, was what I was. And now, as I etch that frightful scene in my heavy skull, I am exactly two months old. That's amazing considering my predicament at Crazy Woman's Creek . . . our predicament. I could see the spear-carrier's gray eyes light up when he saw Mum, and then they lit up even more when he spotted me on the sack. He seemed to bare his teeth at me, although it could have been his idea of a smile. His teeth were not quite as large as the teeth on his necklace. I did not smile back. I didn't do anything. Whatever unusual powers of thought and vision I might possess, they have not been accompanied by any great strength or other extraordinary physical powers. I was as helpless as a baby. I wasn't going to magically pick up the Colt revolver and squeeze off a two-handed shot. It was all up to Mum.

Mum has a gentle grip and she hadn't lifted anything much besides me since we left Missouri in Mr. Gunderson's wagon, but I assumed she at least had the strength to cock the six-shooter and pull the trigger. And if she missed, she still had five more shots available to hit the grinning Indian before he chucked his spear. But Mum didn't go for the Colt, which she surely must have remembered was under the buffalo blanket where she had put it. Instead, she suddenly stood up in the wagon, yanked off her black shawl, and began to make wild sweeping motions with it, as if she were dusting off a shelf. "Shoo! Shoo!" she cried. "Don't bother me. I have so much housework to do." It's hard to tell if the Indian knew any English or not. But he didn't throw his spear and he didn't come any closer. He lost his grin, lowered his weapon, shuffled his feet wildly as if someone had thrown firecrackers in front of him, and then fled. Mum sighed and collapsed back down on the wagon bed with the black shawl over her face. It was another minute before she could catch her breath and retrieve me from atop the sack. Only thing I can figure is that the Indian must have thought the crazy woman of legend had returned to Crazy Woman's Fork.

The Indians left us alone the rest of the night. They had made off with seventeen horses, a dozen mules, and three sacks of flour. The Kittridges' whiskey jugs were undisturbed, thanks to Mum. Peaceable Rufus Pennington was the only casualty but that was enough. Everybody was on edge, especially those who had seen the six arrows sticking in his back. Travis Knapp, who had stumbled over the body and was jumping at shadows till dawn, threatened to turn around and head back to Fort Reno and then to the States. He wanted to lead a retreat. Philip Kittridge told him to shut up or he would shoot him down like a mad dog. Mr. Knapp didn't say another word. He was as afraid of the Kittridges as he was the Indians.

There was no shutting up Grace Pennington or young Toby Pennington. They wailed through half the night as if mourning was their profession. Then Mum stepped up and got them to stop their bawling with reassurances that didn't even ring true to me. The rest of the night, Grace told Mum her life story over and over again, about how she had been raised a Baptist and always thought she would marry an officer like her father, who had been a brevet colonel during the Mexican War and was a lifetime soldier. But while training to be a nurse in Philadelphia, she was swept off her feet by a man with a wise whiskered face, a steady and strong demeanor, and a sprinkling of eloquent sweet talk and kisses too passionate for a Quaker. Her parents disapproved of Rufus Pennington because he refused to fight in the Civil War, but she married him anyway a couple of months before Toby arrived. After the war, nothing changed. Her parents disapproved of Rufus more than ever because he believed the entire South, which had been defeated without any help from him, should be forgiven for trying to destroy the Union. What's more he was poor. They could possibly tolerate their daughter marrying a Quaker, but not one who couldn't give Grace the finer things in life. Grace's father, who held a grudge as tightly as he held his billfold, damned Rufus for eternity. Rufus kept up his chosen occupation, farming, and remained strong and steady, but also poorer than ever. For a while near the end of the war, Grace took young Toby back home to live with her parents. But when her mother died on the day President Lincoln was assassinated, she returned to the pleading Rufus. Her father, now a brigadier general, felt she had deserted him. Soon, he was dying, too.

On his deathbed, the general renewed his damnation for Rufus, and his will stipulated that the hired woman who nursed him at the end (as his only daughter did not) receive his entire fortune. Grace inherited nothing. Poverty hung over Rufus like the grudge-holding ghost of his father-in-law. "I will not stand his presence a moment longer," Rufus told his wife, spreading out the *Philadelphia Inquirer* and slapping it with more violence than he had slapped anything in his life. "See this here," he yelled, looking toward the heavens instead of at Grace. "There are hills full of gold in Montana. And we're going to get our share."

As Grace recalled her late husband's words and their all-to-short time together, her wailing kept threatening to resume. But Mum answered each threat by hugging the widow like a child to quiet her, totally ignoring sniveling sleepyhead Toby and curious wide-awake me. Come morning, Philip Kittridge, totally in charge, ordered Travis Knapp to dig a hole for the unfortunate Mr. Pennington. The one-time wagon master obeyed and then read from the Bible over the body while some of our party listened, some stood guard with rifles, and the rest prepared to break camp. I was one who listened; Mr. Knapp said it was from Isaiah: *The righteous perisheth, and no man layeth it to heart: and merciful men are taken away, none considering that the righteous is taken away from the evil to come. He shall enter into peace: they shall rest in their beds, each one walking in his uprightness.* I can't say it eased my mind much. It scared me. I thought of the evil to come. I told myself *not* to be *too* godly.

Meanwhile, Mr. Knapp moved on to the Book of Psalms: *Yea, though I walk through the valley of the shadow of death, I will fear no evil: for thou art with me; thy rod and thy staff they comfort me.* I could tell he wasn't finished, but Philip Kittridge interrupted him. "Give it a rest now Knapp," the new wagon master said. "We need to hit the trail before the redskins decide to strike us again while we're praying. And don't you worry, Mrs. Pennington. I ain't got any rod or staff, but my Remington will protect and comfort you." The service ended abruptly.

Soon, with barely enough horsepower after the Indian raid, we were on the move north again. Luther Kittridge continued to drive the lead wagon, but Philip Kittridge dropped on horseback back to the Pennington wagon, now being driven by Mum. He ignored Mum, and tipped his ridiculously large cowboy hat to Grace. Maybe he thought he could make Mum jealous, but in any case he selfishly didn't think it was too early to start comforting the recent widow. I was in the back, theoretically being looked after and entertained by Toby, but I knew what was going on—that Grace's red-eyed, tear-stained face made her seem even more pretty and vulnerable to a certain type of man. Like Philip, the pale-faced leader of the deserters was that type of man. He couldn't forget the gentle way Grace had bandaged his temple and soothed his sideburns, and now he wanted to return the favor.

His full name was Private Patrick David Burrows, but he told Grace she could call him "P.D." or better yet "Prairie Dog," a nickname given to him by his fellow soldiers because he was highly sociable, curious, frolicsome, and always popping up to chat or gossip or bark at something an officer had done. The recently widowed woman didn't say much, but she listened to both P.D. and Philip as if they were welcome diversions from her grief. Mum halted the Pennington wagon and tried to shoo both men away, but they weren't as easily discouraged as that Indian intruder. Within a few minutes they were closer to handing out blows to one another than comfort to the widow. Their standoff was making Toby agitated because these two strangers pretending to care were fighting each other instead of avenging his father's death. I didn't blame him, but I didn't appreciate the way Toby kept accidentally or otherwise jabbing me with his elbow.

"Stay there and fight," Mum said, as she climbed back into the driver's seat. "We're rolling on."

But there was to be no rolling on right away. Mum was just about to release the wagon brake when two gunshots from up ahead made her freeze. Philip Kittridge and Private Prairie Dog had exchanged pushes and were working their way up to punches when the shots came. Their fight ended that very second. They instantly recognized the dire situation. The Indians had come and gone at Crazy Woman's Fork, but they hadn't left us for good. Philip Kittridge raced to his horse to get his Remington rifle. Private Prairie Dog didn't go anywhere, but he looked as if he wanted to burrow into a deep hole.

Everything happened quickly I suppose, but I saw most of it clearly in my mind's eye. Four wagon covers were soon filled with arrow holes. The arrows had rained down from an embankment as the head of our wagon train reached Connor's Springs. A woman had screamed and so had a half-dozen men, but it was out of sheer terror, not because any of them had been hit. The attackers apparently did not have firearms. Both of the

fired shots we heard came from Luther Kittridge. His Remington was still smoking when Phil Kittridge got to him, after leaving Prairie Dog behind, along with Mrs. Pennington, Mum,
Toby, and me. Mum naturally got out of the driver's seat and
came back to see about me. The five of us sort of huddled
together. The private deserter said that he would protect us.
Maybe Mrs. Pennington bought it, but not me. None of them
had any idea what was going on in the front of our wagon train.
But my mind's eye was doing its thing; in other words seeing
things too far away for my two regular eyes, or anybody else's
regular eyes, to see. Of course, being a baby, I could not convey
this information to anyone. At that moment I wasn't thinking of
my internal vision as some kind of mysterious gift. I was just
seeing, satisfying my innate curiosity and, as it turned out, scaring myself half to death.

What I *saw* was Luther Kittridge looking as proud as punch
as his older brother examined the arrow holes in the wagon
covers and tried to figure out what had happened while he was
back making time with the Pennington widow. Luther coolly
pointed up to a timbered knoll in the distance, using his
Remington instead of his finger. When he spoke I could hear
him just as if I was physically up at the spring wagon. It was
spooky. "After the arrows flew," he said, his eyes sparkling, "I
seen these two chiefs way up there looking down their red noses
at us. They figured they was out of rifle range. But I lined up a
shot with Remy here and split a twig over their feathered heads.
That was enough to set one of the chiefs a runnin' like a scared
rabbit. The other one, being proud and stubborn, held his
ground. So I lined up another shot, right between his eyes, and
dropped him before he could so much as say 'Hiawatha.' "
Philip tipped back his cowboy hat and scratched his forehead as
he stared off at that timbered knoll. "Man alive!" he said, pat-

ting Luther on the back. "That was one hell of a shot, little brother."

That was about all I saw or heard, because Toby started jabbing me with his elbow again and then grabbing at my patches of hair with his nose-picking fingers, even though I was in Mum's arms. With no more gunshots alarming us, Mrs. Pennington took notice of Toby's strange behavior. An even stranger conversation ensued.

"Stop that, Toby!' Mrs. Pennington said. "Why are you hurting the baby?"

"There was bugs crawling everywhere," the five-year-old said.

"What do you mean? You saw bugs on the baby's head?"

"Inside."

"You aren't making any sense, Toby. Inside what?"

"Inside his head. I saw them."

"Bugs? That's ridiculous."

"Well, they looked like bugs, Ma. They was crawling and jumping around. I wanted to squash them."

"Enough, Toby. You leave the baby alone." Mrs. Pennington apologized to Mum for her son's wild imagination and then said that Toby hadn't been himself since he watched his Daddy being lowered into the shallow grave Mr. Knapp dug. Mum said she understood, but of course she didn't. I didn't understand it myself, but upon reflection, I do believe all those bugs Toby was seeing were actually visions and voices or whatever else I got going on in my active brain. I hate to say it, but even Toby was able to get closer to discovering what kind of a baby I truly am than my own Mum ever has. I think it's a case of her being too close to her subject. She is still clinging to the notion that I am a *normal child*.

Let me just interject here that my mind's eye can't simply go anywhere I want it to go or it wants to go. It has its limits. Some of the limits are definitely distance. For example, I can't see anything going on back in Chicago or up ahead in Virginia City. Nor can I go off and peek in on the Burleson wagon train to see how Old Man Gunderson and his six Georges are doing. There are other limits, too. I have never seen any Indian camps or villages, even though they are definitely out there, some too close for comfort. At that moment at Connor's Springs, I wanted desperately to be able to see if there were any more Indians lurking in the high timber. Like everyone else in our party, though, I couldn't spot a single one, or hear one for that matter. Like the others, I could only imagine. You could say our imaginations were running wild on the Bozeman Trail, except there were two gunshots, and those arrow holes in the wagon covers were very real, as were the arrow holes in the back of poor Mr. Pennington.

We were not out of the woods, as they say, not by a long shot from Luther Kittridge's rolling-block Remington. All the wagons rolled on to the Clear Fork crossing, within a dozen miles of our immediate destination, Fort Phil Kearny. At the crossing, I could see with my regular eyes dozens of warriors emerging from the surrounding timber. Most had bows and arrows or spears, a few had sabers, which they swung in a menacing manner, the sunlight making the blades sparkle. Private Prairie Dog, our self-proclaimed protector, had taken over driving the Pennington wagon, with Grace and Toby sitting with him up front and Mum riding with me in the wagon bed. I had never seen so many Indians in my young life. I expected Mum to scream or to try to hide me in the folds of her dress. Instead, she removed her bonnet and fanned us, as if our biggest worry this day was becoming overheated.

Luther Kittridge stopped the spring wagon, and the wagons behind immediately halted as well. I could hear Toby crying and Mrs. Pennington asking her protector all kinds of silly questions like "They won't hurt women and children will they?" Then I heard Prairie Dog gulp before he drove the wagon ahead until we were parallel and just behind the lead wagon. Maybe the private deserter wanted to satisfy his curiosity. Certainly, like the rest of us, he had nowhere to run.

"Fort Reno don't look so bad right now," Prairie Dog confessed.

"They didn't buy those things," said Philip Kittridge, who was now sitting next to his brother on the front seat of the spring wagon. "They took those sabers off dead soldiers."

"Or slow dying ones," said Luther Kittridge as he lifted his Remington off his buckskinned lap. "You ain't gonna just sit there, are you, Phil? We got a fighting chance. Where's your rifle?"

"There are too many. Don't make any sudden move, little brother."

"We're sitting ducks here. They're going to hack us to pieces."

"Maybe not. They might want to parley."

"Talk! Let's see how many of those varmints we can pick off first."

"No. Ease off that trigger, little brother. They are too close. At this range, our Remingtons are no good. We might only get one apiece. And the way I see it, even Henry repeaters wouldn't help now."

"Well, shit, we don't have a Gatling gun. Look at 'em all. They all look alike, except that one there. He looks strangely familiar."

That Indian wore a full complement of clothes, including an antelope skin shirt with legs and dew claws still attached, over his presumed painted body. He sat proudly on his pony for a moment then slid gracefully off. He lay down his bow and removed the quiver of arrows that was slung over his left shoulder so that he walked toward us unarmed. The war paint on his stone somber face looked dripping wet, and his two long black braids, tied in quillwork strips, hung stiffly in front of his shoulders. Fearlessly he distanced himself from his mounted warriors until he stood directly in front of the Kittridges' spring wagon. He was clearly not a young man but he stood straight as an arrow, handsome, strong, and at least six-foot tall not including his impressive eagle-feathered war bonnet. His steely eyes, scars on his cheeks, and deep worry lines suggested that he was a leader who did his share of thinking but was also as active as a panther.

"I'll do the talking," Philip said, his bravo still going strong but his voice a bit shaky.

"Talk?" Luther said. "He don't look like he can talk American."

I could hear Toby sobbing up on the front seat, but very softly, as if he knew sobbing too loudly would be dangerous. I expected Mrs. Pennington to scream, but she stayed silent, maybe with vocal chords paralyzed by fear or anger. I heard no words of assurance from Private Prairie Dog. I suspected he was regretting his decision to drive the Pennington wagon to the front of the train, not because it put a mother and child in danger but because it put his own life in jeopardy.

"It's him," Private Prairie Dog said, unable to contain himself. "Unbelievable!"

"What the hell you talking about?" said Philip Kittridge.

"That's the very same redskin who seized me and the three other outcasts from Fort Reno. I recognize that headdress and those killer eyes. That's the same war shirt he's wearing. Never did catch his name, but he acted like a chief."

"He's a chief all right."

"He mostly only talks Sioux. He used a translator to tell us he was letting us live but that we must tell the soldiers and you in the wagon train to leave this country. His last words to us, however, were in English and plenty clear. He commanded,

'Go, soldier dogs, go!' And go we did."

"So you wouldn't exactly call him a friend?" said Philip.

"About as much as Colonel Carrington. Never wished to see either again."

"Well, just lay low for now. I'll parley."

"Fine with me. Good luck with that. He's a clever one. He won't understand much except the things he wants to."

"I'll use my hands. I know some sign language."

The chief made the first gesture, actually it was more like a magic trick. He raised two fists high in the air and then opened them, releasing two small fluttering white butterflies. I felt like clapping, but had not yet mastered that skill. Next, the chief pounded his chest over his heart and said something in his own language. Philip tilted his head to the side like a dog trying to understand the words of its master. He gave up quickly, throwing up his hands, palms up.

"He wants you to come down and face him man to man," Private Prairie Dog said.

"Huh? Me? Who says? You don't know Sioux."

"I know he said those same words to me when I first saw him. Don't worry, it doesn't mean you have to fight him or anything."

"I ain't scared of him or any Injun."

Philip started to climb down from the wagon but then thought better of it. From a seated position, he signaled something or else was making the sign of the cross, probably the first time in his life. "We come in peace," he said, holding out his arms as if he meant to embrace the chief, but from a safe distance.

The chief stuck out his chest, made fists again, and banged the fists together three times. I didn't know what he was doing any more than Philip Kittridge did, but every motion this Indian made seemed imposing. When Luther, who obviously knew no sign language, pointed his Remington at the chief's chest, the chief's expression or lack of one didn't change.

"He acts like white man's bullets can't hurt him," Luther said. "Let me blow a hole in him with a .50–70 brass cartridge and see if he changes his tune."

"Shut up, little brother. Put down that rifle and sit tight."

Luther did lay his Remington down on his lap, but it seemed mainly because he wanted to scratch his head with both hands. "You know what, Phil, I recognize him, too."

"What are you talking about?"

"He's one of the two chiefs I saw up on the rise earlier. He was mighty far off, but there's no mistaking all that red rage— it's him. I'd swear to it. When I fired a long-range shot, he held onto his headdress and ran. The other chief stayed. I dropped that one with my second shot."

"So this is the wise one."

"Or the cowardly one."

"He ain't acting like no coward now. Look how he stands there like a stone wall."

"Sure. Why not! He probably thinks that shirt is bulletproof. And he has all those painted devils behind him with bows and arrows and spears and sabers. I don't know who this particular red devil is but he must think he's some kind of red God."

"I got a feeling he also recognizes you, Luther," said Private Prairie Dog. "You a praying man?"

"Let me shoot him, Phil," Luther said. His Remington was now bouncing on his nervous knee.

"Shut up," said Philip. "I think he understands you."

"He'll understand Remy here better when I blast . . ."

"I'll handle him, little brother. You just lay low like Prairie Dog over there."

Philip tried his hand at sign language again while mouthing broken English: "We friends with our red brothers. No shoot.

Make Peace. Not soldiers. Good men. No harm."

The chief raised his hand. "No talk," he said.

"So you savvy English? Great."

"No talk."

"Hold on there a second, chief, I thought you wanted to talk."

"*Blotahunka.*"

"No savvy, your language, chief."

"*Blotahunka.* No talk."

"Your name is Blotahunka? Fine. You understand, Blotahunka, that we don't have any designs on your homeland, don't you? We're just passing through on our way to Montana."

"Road . . . Enemy."

"No, no. It's a free road, open to all—you and us and the soldiers and the buffalo."

"No road. No talk."

Philip Kittridge opened his mouth and pointed to his tongue. Then he made great sweeping motions with his arms as if he wanted to fly, perhaps like a white butterfly. Not even I could understand his sign language.

"No talk." Those seemed to be this chief's favorite words, along with *bloatahunka,* but they weren't getting him anywhere. Without taking his eyes off the Kittridge brothers, the chief reached back over his shoulder and snapped his fingers. A squat Indian with not a single feather in his hair or war paint on his smooth-skinned face, and with no weapon in sight, dismounted with some difficulty and then stepped forward as if his moccasins hurt. The chief pointed to his own tongue and ears and then poked the subordinate in his oversized pink ear.

"I talk for our *bloatahunka,*" the featherless Indian said. "That mean war leader."

"Hey, I know him, too," Prairie Dog said. "Not that we were formally introduced. I think his name is Bull something."

"Great, a translator," said Philip. "All I'm trying to tell your *bloata* . . . Do you mind if I just call him chief? It's so much simpler. Anyway, we don't want war with your chief. We're requesting real polite like that he let us pass in peace to Fort Phil Kearny. By the way, my name is Phil, too, Phil Kittridge. I come in peace. We all come in peace."

The chief and his translator conferred briefly. Then the translator spoke, but with absolutely none of the force of his boss: "With long gun?"

"Oh, so the chief noticed my brother's Remington. Don't mind that. We like to, you know, hunt buffalo like our red brothers. That is to say our *own* buffalo, not the Sioux buffalo."

The translator started to speak in Siouan, but the chief waved him off.

"Go back," the chief said in booming English.

"The chief say go back," said the translator. "He say you already warned."

"Did the chief say that?" said Philip. "Tell him we can't do that. Tell him to give us a break. I'm not crazy about soldiers myself. Just let us go forward in peace to Fort Phil Kearny."

The chief shook his head. He spoke several words in his language, but he also blurted something out in English that sounded like "Fort C.F. Smith." The translator repeated the name of the fort and then added, "You go there next?"

"I suppose so," Philip admitted. "I almost forgot how old Carrington built that third fort on the trail. Soldiers will be soldiers. But we won't stay there long either. We go to Virginia City, far far away from the Sioux. Tell the chief that. Make sure he understands how far."

The chief and the translator talked in their language for what seemed much longer than necessary. Mrs. Pennington and Toby took the opportunity to leave their seats up front with Private Prairie Dog and crawl back to join Mum and me. Once settled in, Toby sobbed louder and buried his head in the folds of his mother's dress. He was a bigger baby than me.

"You go back or die," the translator was now saying. "The chief say this is our land—rich in game. The forts, the soldiers, the wagons, they scare away the game, terrorize our women, frighten our children. The road is our enemy."

"OK," Philip Kittridge replied. "Well, tell the chief, I'm not in love with the road either. But it's the quickest way to Virginia City. The sooner he lets us pass, the quicker we'll go and be out of his hair. Maybe he wants gifts. Ask him that. We got gifts back here for your chief."

I wasn't sure if Philip Kittridge meant Mum and me, Mrs. Pennington and Toby, the sacks of flour, the jugs of whiskey, or the boxes of ammunition. There was practically nothing I couldn't imagine Philip doing or giving away to get himself out of this predicament. Mum seemed to fear the worst. She found the Colt revolver Philip had given her at the beginning of our trip on the Bozeman Trail and pressed it to her bosom, just inches away from me. The barrel was pointed in the opposite direction but that didn't keep me from squirming. I wondered if Mum meant to shoot the chief or Philip. And there was always the possibility if this chief or someone else gave the word to attack that Mum would shoot herself so that she wouldn't fall into savage hands. And would she shoot me too? I mean I knew she loved me more than anything in the whole world, but she could still shoot me out of love to save me from a worse fate. I'm kind of ashamed, but I started making plans to duck (I was getting quite good at moving my head) in case Mum chose that desperate route.

"Chief say no more gifts," the translator was saying. "Chief say tepee already full of trinkets. Chief say your people give too many trinkets, speak too many false words!"

"Is that right?" Philip said, sounding downright annoyed for the first time. "Just who does your big red man think he is anyway, the mighty Chief Red Cloud?"

The translator answered for himself. "Him Red Cloud. Me Little Bull."

"Holy shit!" Philip shouted.

He said other curses, too, that I won't repeat. So did his brother, Luther.

"I should have known," said Private Prairie Dog, who then decided he better talk directly to the most important headman of them all. "It's an honor, sir, Mr. Cloud. Remember me? We met before up on the ridge. You asked me to warn these folks about continuing on the trail. Well, I did. I tried to get them to turn back, like you said, Mr. Cloud, but they were hardheaded. I got nothing against you personally chief, Mr. Cloud. In fact I have the utmost respect for you. Don't be fooled by this uniform I'm wearing. Don't forget I gave up being a soldier. So, if you want to hate those soldiers and attack those forts, it's no business of mine."

"Shut up, Prairie Dog," Philip Kittridge said. "You make me gag!"

Lucky for Mrs. Pennington, she was too busy comforting sobbing Toby to hear their protector's desperate words or the name "Red Cloud." I'm not sure if Mum heard or not who we were dealing with. She was mumbling one of her younger sister's prayers without even realizing how the hammer of the Colt was jabbing me in the ribs. I know it seems strange, but for some reason I wasn't exactly sweating bullets, as they say. I did pee my diaper. Even so, I started to get real thirsty for some breast milk. No, I can't explain it. I was just being an infant, I guess.

Anyway, outside things were taking a turn for the worse. The Indian chief who we now knew was Red Cloud was pointing a finger as if it was a bow and arrow. I thought at first he was pointing at Private Prairie Dog or maybe Philip Kittridge, but that wasn't the case. That accusative finger was directed right between the eyes of Luther Kittridge, who was sweating bullets and more.

"Red Cloud want him," said translator Little Bull. He started to point at Luther with his own finger but then must have realized it wasn't necessary. "Him Long Shot."

"Damnation," said Luther. "He does recognize me."

"Long Shot kill Chief Old Bear," Little Bull continued. "He make long shot with long rifle. He bad medicine. Red Cloud say Long Shot must die."

"Die?" said Luther, raising his Remington again. "You mean me?" He seemed uncertain whether to point the rifle at the chief or the translator. "I can make a short shot, too—a deadly short shot. You tell him that."

The translator conferred with Red Cloud, who reacted by puffing out his chest further without lowering his finger. Little Bull than delivered the chief's response: "Red Cloud say to Big Hat give us Long Shot and he let all else pass free to Fort Phil Kearny but not one step beyond."

"He's my little brother," Philip said. "Tell, Red Cloud, no deal."

Little Bull told Red Cloud nothing and did not wait for Red Cloud to speak. "You, Big Hat," the translator said to Philip. "You must do as Red Cloud say or you all will die. Red Cloud say Long Shot *must* die!"

Philip gave Luther such a long, hard look that Luther turned as pale as Private Prairie Dog and squirmed as if he had red ants crawling inside his buckskin pants. Luther evoked the names of their dearly departed mother and father down on the farm and brought up the time he sucked the poison out of Philip's calf following a rattlesnake bite. It was hard to say if Philip was moved or not; he just kept staring at his younger brother while running his fingers up and down the brim of his cowboy hat.

"No talk," Red Cloud said in English, breaking the silence.

Just then somebody blew a bugle. It could have been an Indian who had stolen a bugle along with a saber. But then we saw a cloud of dust rising from the south and heard someone with mighty welcoming lungs yell "Charge!" That was all Philip needed. He helped raise the barrel of Luther's Remington and said, "Plug him, little brother."

Luther fired. The bullet seemed to pass right through Red Cloud, yet he didn't fall or even lower his enraged fists. What must have happened was the bullet passed through the chief's headdress and struck the torso of the saber-wielding warrior behind him. The saber fell first and then the Indian. But Red Cloud was still standing, more like a red marble pillar than a stone wall. Luther had made the long shot but missed this short one. Little Bull turned and ran like a duck while Philip reached under the spring wagon seat to produce his own Remington rolling-block rifle. Arrows were whistling by the spring wagon and the Pennington wagon, gunfire was coming from behind us, hoofs were pounding, and men and women were screaming. I lost sight of Red Cloud and of Luther Kittridge as well. Philip, with an arrow sticking dramatically but harmlessly through the high crown of his cowboy hat, fired his own Remington at some fleeing form in the timber, then quickly reloaded and fired again. But as he reloaded once more, he noticed that the seat next to him was empty.

"Luther!" he cried, dropping his next bullet to the ground. "Where the hell are you, little brother?"

In the back of the Pennington wagon, Mum managed *not* to pull the trigger of the Colt.

The incessant din lasted only for a few minutes. The relief party of twenty-five wagons and twice that many soldiers was bringing supplies from Fort Reno to Fort Phil Kearny. The soldiers, firing wildly at thin air, apparently didn't hit any of the fleeing Indians. Even the one Indian Luther had accidentally hit had vanished. But none of the soldiers were hit either. Afterward, the lieutenant puffed up his chest, though it was not as large as that of Red Cloud, and kept repeating how he and his men had put the enemy to flight and had saved an endangered emigrant train without a single casualty. He personally shook the hands of the men in the wagons (Private Prairie Dog and the other three deserters managed to avoid the friendly officer, though) and kissed the hands of Mum, Grace Pennington, and the two other ladies who showed themselves.

Philip Kittridge wanted to stay there at the Clear Fork crossing to search for his missing brother, but nobody was willing to stay with him. One by one the covered wagons and the freight wagons passed his idle spring wagon. The lieutenant assigned a sergeant to drive the Pennington wagon for Grace and Toby. But first he transferred Mum and me to the back of another wagon where a half-dozen non-regulation mattresses not only provided comfort but also extra protection in case any stray arrows should come our way. Finally, not wanting to be left behind, Philip plucked the arrow from his hat, cursed the arrow hole, and got his spring wagon rolling at the rear of our enhanced traveling party.

"Not a thing to worry about now, folks," the lieutenant said up and down the line as he and his men escorted us the rest of the way to Fort Phil Kearny.

Just short of the fort walls along Little Piney Creek, we came upon the naked body of a man staked out on his back, with arms and legs stretched out and fastened to pegs. Not a single arrow was sticking out of him, but most of his toes and fingers were missing and much of the flesh had been burned black. That wasn't the worst of it. The gash in his belly was smoldering from a recent intestinal fire. His scalped head, which had been severed from his neck, probably by a saber, was now resting between his thighs where his genitals had once been. One eye had been gouged out. The other seemed to be staring in disbelief at the clear blue sky.

When I think of Luther Kittridge now, I never see him strutting around in his buckskins swinging his Remington to and fro as naturally as if it were another limb on his body. I see him naked, mutilated, dying in agony. I never liked the man, but did he deserve to die like that—I mean any more than his brother or anyone else for that matter? Right now in our tent *poor* Philip Kittridge is receiving Mum's deluxe shoulder rub. "Harder, harder!" he says, half a command, half begging. "I'm trying, Phil, I'm trying," Mum says as if she is to blame for all the sadness and crying going on in here. No doubt the man is sad about what happened, though I doubt he feels guilty that Luther got it instead of him. He can no doubt rationalize that his little brother (who was actually taller than him) was the one who shot Chief Old Bear, thus angering the mighty Red Cloud. Maybe Chief Old Bear didn't deserve to die either.

Certainly Rufus Pennington, a man of peace, didn't deserve to get a half-dozen arrows in his back and then a complete scalping. I can't blame tear-stained, bedridden Grace Pennington for lying there on her stomach unable, despite all the sympathy, to face life inside this tent or inside the fort. And I can't blame young Toby Pennington (well, not so young compared to me) for constantly trying to have a bowel movement in that chamber pot. I never really had a father, even though he is theoretically still alive in that insane asylum, but I can feel Toby's pain. And with all those active bugs crawling around inside my brain, I can feel a lot of other people's pain around here, too.

Right now in my mind's eye I see Colonel Henry Beebee

Carrington in his quarters complaining to his wife, Margaret, about how his superiors are insisting the Bozeman Trail must be open but that he must avoid becoming involved in a general Indian war. "Depredations keep occurring daily, woodcutters scalped, emigrants attacked, horses and mules stolen, outbuildings burned," the colonel mutters. "My forces are spread too thin, with too many green recruits, too few officers, and a lack of modern firearms and ammunition. Meanwhile Red Cloud keeps finding more and more tribal allies in a united front to drive us—that is to say every white man—out of this country. What am I to do, Margaret, what am I to do?"

Margaret Carrington, not as beautiful as Mum but nearly Mrs. Pennington's equal, is as dutiful to her husband as he is to the U.S. Army. She hands her Henry a glass of sherry and strokes the little hairs standing up on the back of his neck.

"And every white woman, too, dear," she reminds her man. "Red Cloud wants all of us gone."

Henry nods and sips.

"The generals don't understand you any more than do the little merchants so safe and comfortable in their Ohio shops," she adds. "They don't understand this place—the isolation, the loneliness, the uncertainties, the danger, the wickedness, the absurd deficiencies in resources. They don't understand *these* Indians, who wait and watch, watch and wait, to gather the scalps of the unwary and ignorant, to decoy and ambush, to enact vengeance fiendish and terrible."

The colonel gulps down the last of his drink. "Fiendish and terrible indeed," he says. "And the men think I should do more, that I should send large commands out to destroy the Sioux. They don't realize how much my hands are tied. Sometimes, and I can only confess this to you, my dear wife, I feel like I am at the mercy of frontier fate."

Mrs. Carrington pours him another drink. The little hairs are smoothed down now. "Let's think nothing more of it tonight, dear," she says, smiling as if she is regarding her own precious child. "For once let's pretend we are not surrounded by red men who have forgotten how to be noble. What do you say, Henry? For once, let's *not* be gloomy."

# NOVEMBER 3, 1866: MORE GLOOM AND ANOTHER STORY

If familiar surroundings and a routine for eating, diaper changing, and sleeping are supposed to be good for a child my age, then I should feel luckier than a hog in a mudhole. After all, it seems like Mum and me, not to mention Grace and Toby Pennington, have been in this Fort Phil Kearny tent for ages. I know every permanent crease in the tent walls, every crack in my cradle, every squeak in the cot springs of Mum and Mrs. Pennington, every beam of sunlight that finds its way through the opening flap or the lone window. I get my breastfeeding every three hours without fail, my diapers never remain soiled for more than fifteen minutes, and my sleep pattern is set—a two-hour morning nap, an hour afternoon nap, an hour and a half evening nap, and almost ten hours at night. That's a lot of sleeping time, and I have no excuse to be cranky.

When not sleeping, eating, or pooping, I mostly roll from side to side and hold a rattle, which Mrs. Pennington, having gone through Toby's questionable development, says is typical. Actually, I can do far more than that, but I'm no show-off. I can roll from my back to my stomach and stomach to my back, I can practically sit up to make faces at Toby, I can reach down and play with my feet (I really get a kick out of my itty bitty toes), and I can grasp the earlobes of Mrs. Pennington and use my drooling mouth to explore them. I can only get away with this because I am a baby and maybe not for much longer, for Grace Pennington is engaged to be married. Oh, yes, and there are some fairly well-developed vocal sounds I can make. Outsiders only think it is babbling. My vocabulary includes, but is not limited to, *Mum-mum, Bee-bee* (which is Colonel Henry Carrington's middle name), *Lobe-lobe* (my pet name for Mrs. Pennington), *Toe-toe* (positive connotations when addressing my toes, negative connotations when addressing Toby), and *wed-wed* (meaning "red," not anything to do with marriage).

Truth is, though, I feel lower than a bowlegged caterpillar. Mostly, it's because Mum is so down. She expected by now to be in Virginia City lounging in the fine Wheelwright house on a big brass bed, reading classic Dickens tales and the latest news in the *Montana Post,* eating poached eggs served by sister Cornelia's maid, and applauding my acrobatic skills on the colorful homespun quilt. Instead it looks as if we will still be stuck in Fort Phil Kearny when the first snow flies, maybe till spring. Indian raids around the fort have increased and resources have dwindled. Thanks to their daily attacks, Red Cloud's warriors have reduced the horses and cattle, ammunition is low, and the soldiers' antiquated weapons are getting older every day. News from the outside, especially from the northwest, is scarce. Aunt Cornelia has always been a prolific writer, but none of her letters from the Montana territorial capital have reached us here. Mum did receive one letter from Aunt Maggie in Chicago a few days ago, but it was not the kind to lift anybody's spirits:

Dear Sister—I imagine you had your baby and that you are both alive. If not both, then hopefully you. Got one letter from Corny asking if you was alive and coming to the gold fields and such. I didn't write back 'cause she didn't send me no money even though she thinks she is the Queen of Virginia City. Also, I worried you might be dead and I've been feeling poorly myself. Blood still makes me faint. Otherwise, I am not such a bad nurse. I nurse Grandma

Duly myself and sometimes Mr. Flowers, who near broke his neck (and would have if it wasn't such a big neck) when some bad-egg German boys pushed him down the cellar steps for being a Negro. He could have crushed those boys but he's too kind, as you know. I don't nurse Grandpa Duly no more on account of he died in the middle of his midday nap a week or two after you left us. Your husband, Abraham, come here once after escaping from the asylum. He was asking about you and Mr. Flowers. I had to tell him a few things on account of he looks like a shaggy mad dog that might bite, but he didn't do nothing to Mr. Flowers except talk crazy to him. He's back at the asylum now.

I think Mr. Gibbs at the corner store likes me cause he keeps giving me certain looks I'm scarcely familiar with and also credit for sugar and canned peaches and such. I know he's a bag of old bones and married, but I ain't no spring chicken. Anyway, I only puckered up to him one time and been praying to the Lord for forgiveness ever since. I pray for you, too. And for poor Grandma Duly. When she dies, I'll be all alone here, unless Mr. Gibbs gets his way with yours truly (fat chance!). Sometimes my prayers even extend to a preacher who moved into the neighborhood but don't have much of a flock yet and poor Mr. Flowers. I can tell that big old black goat misses you something awful 'cause he wanted me to send you a kiss and then tried to kiss me hisself. His eyesight ain't so good—I ain't getting any younger or prettier. But his neck must be better, allowing for his friskiness. Anyway, my fingers hurt from writing. I close with something our dear departed mother underlined in the family Bible: *The Lord is nigh unto all them that call upon him, to all that call upon him in truth.*—Trust in the Lord, Mags P.S. When they caught Abraham, he swore he'd get out again. Hope he don't come back here.

Even with all my time to think, I wasn't thinking much about the Chicago tenement building till Mum got that letter. I was kind of tickled to hear that Papa Duly gave himself a little vacation from the asylum and that a storekeeper was taking more than a passing interest in Maggie, with her pockmarks and all. Of course the man was already married. I felt bad about Mr. Flowers' neck and about Grandpa Duly, even if he was a grouch and was old and sick for a long time. I guess Grandma Duly, being nearly as old and sick herself, will be going next. Out here, of course, people die who aren't old or sick. Sometimes they do leave us other ways, too. I'm happy to say that Philip Kittridge is gone from Mum's life—and mine. It took long enough.

About a month ago, he put aside his aching heart, aching eyes, and aching shoulders and stopped calling on Mum for sympathy. To me that was a good thing. But Mum didn't see it that way. I overheard her telling Mrs. Pennington that she missed having him around, since the new mourning Phil had been so much more appealing than the old brash Philip. She also told *Lobe-lobe* that it seemed impossible that she (and me, of course) would ever get to Virginia City without the man and his spring wagon, that is assuming the trouble with Red Cloud (*Wed Cowed* to me) ever let up enough to allow travel again.

It was inevitable that the mourning Phil could only last so long. The death of his younger brother proved to Philip that Kittridges were as vulnerable as anyone else, even with Remington rolling-block rifles and Colt six-shooters, and he could no longer deny that the Indian hordes had made travel north virtually impossible. He had a great amount of time on his hands, and he wasn't one to stay hid away doing nothing but remembering. One day in mid-September he just got sick and tired of being a weepy lump on a log . . . or in a tent . . . and he up and walked out without a word to Mum. To prove he hadn't turned soft and because he required whiskey money, he hired on as one of Colonel Carrington's civilian workers. Being so splendidly armed, he was desired as an additional escort for the hay-cutting and woodcutting parties that venture out from the fort most days. With his challenging job and his eyes now dry, he lost interest in Mum, who had no doubt further discouraged him by never rubbing any part of his body lower than his shoulder blades. After one paycheck (he complained that the pay was not enough for high-risk work) and one big drunk in early October, Philip lost his job, but there was no returning to the tent to get more of Mum's abundant sympathy. He had moved past that stage.

Instead, Mr. Kittridge began spending his nights three miles away from the fort with Nelson Story's outfit, which arrived some three weeks ago with a herd of Texas Longhorns that they want to sell to hungry Montana miners. The cowboys camped outside the stockade on orders of Colonel Carrington, who wanted them to stay near the post but not so close that their ornery critters would gobble up the nearby grass reserved for Army livestock. Story and his boys were none too happy. They saw only a few mules and the colonel's saddle horse grazing in the restricted meadow, and they were also too far out for the Army to be of much assistance should the Indians attack the cowboy camp. For one thing, it's almost all infantry here right now, with only a few cavalry for support, reconnaissance, escort, and mail delivery. As I've heard more than one commanding officer admit, "Mounted infantry just ain't the same."

Anyway, Philip Kittridge was delighted to be with that unhappy bunch of Texas cowboys because he believed that they had more mettle than the soldier boys and also that he had much in common with the Texans—similar hats, for one thing, restless and brave dispositions for another, and of course the same rapid-fire Remington rolling-block breechloaders. "I'd rather take my chances at night with them boys outside the stockade any day of the week," he told Colonel Carrington after the colonel fired him as an escort for insubordination, drunkenness, and gross negligence.

Speaking of solider boys, Army deserter Private Prairie Dog Burrows acts like a soldier in good standing again. Not only that but he is in good standing and more with the widow Grace Pennington, my dear *Lobe-lobe*. I guess I'll have to stop calling her that before too long. P.D. asked her to marry him three weeks ago, even though her late Quaker husband probably hasn't had time to make peace with his Maker yet. That bold proposition lifted Mrs. Pennington's spirits immeasurably although she said she would not consent to becoming Mrs. Prairie Dog right away, which is what P.D. desperately wanted. Apparently a certain waiting period was in order. I don't know if there are any actual rules about that kind of thing, but Mrs. Pennington was firm in putting P.D. off for one month.

Once in the middle of the night while her cot springs were squeaking from the weight of two bodies, I heard her tell Prairie Dog that going to Virginia City in search of gold had been Mr. Pennington's far-fetched dream not hers. Her dream, also stated in the darkness, is to have forever and a day a strong, responsible man, preferably one in uniform, to look after her and worrisome Toby. It is certainly true that *Toe-toe* has his security and growth issues, but I am happy to report that he has finally become housebroken or tent broken and knows how to find his way to an outhouse by himself.

It doesn't bother Mrs. Pennington a lick that her private not so long ago deserted the Army and now wants to make her his Army bride. She says everyone is entitled to a second chance. She is also under the delusion (funny how I can see it so well) that Prairie Dog protected her nobly the day Philip Kittridge tried to talk to Chief Red Cloud and lost brother Luther. Of course the Army, at least certain Army officers down at Fort Reno, were not so ready to forgive and forget. They made a big stink about what to do about the four deserters, and the quartet was held in the Fort Phil Kearny guardhouse for four days in anticipation of sending them back to Fort Reno for further punishment. But then, Mrs. Pennington spoke with Margaret Carrington, who put in a word with her husband, who outranks all the Reno officers. In the end, Colonel Carrington released them all from the guardhouse because he was shorthanded and Fort Phil Kearny (perhaps even more so than Fort C.F. Smith farther up the Bozeman Trail) has become the center of hostile Indian activity.

While incarcerated, Prairie Dog was of course unable to visit our tent, which didn't bother Mum or me in the slightest. Mrs. Pennington was highly agitated by the turn of events but not enough so to visit her man at the guardhouse. She didn't think it would look right, and Mrs. Pennington is someone who wants anything to do with her to look right. Once released, Prairie Dog again asked Mrs. Pennington to marry him on the spot, but she held to her conviction that he would have to wait until the designated time. In the meantime, she suggested, he should dedicate himself to his duties as a private and even volunteer for special duties. She clearly thought she could make him over into a solid U.S. soldier, if not an officer like her late father. Rufus Pennington had been a man of peace, albeit a man of peace who wanted gold. But that wasn't what Grace Pennington wanted, at least not now.

"So what you're saying, Grace," said Prairie Dog one day in our tent, "is that I am on probation, that I must prove myself to be an upstanding soldier before you will actually say yes."

"No, no, P.D," Mrs. Pennington replied. "I've already said yes to you. You know that I want to become your wife and that I will become your wife. We will definitely go see the fort chaplain when the time is right."

"And now isn't the right time, in your opinion?"

"That's right. I haven't been a widow for very long."

"Sure. And I've been a single man for too long. But I'll soldier on."

"Toby and I thank you. We have our whole future together at the fort."

What future Fort Phil Kearny has was another matter. But I wasn't complaining. Prairie Dog again stayed away from our tent as he went about his duties with something that might be mistaken for diligence, and I found out that despite Mrs. Pennington's moral convictions, her interesting ears remain open to my exploration.

I've probably spent too much time thinking of Philip Kittridge and Prairie Dog Burrows. But like I said, I got the time, just like there's time to think of Mum, Mrs. Pennington, and Toby. And me, of course! After all, I can't spend every waking moment thinking—and worrying—about the Indians, the so-called hostiles. Since our tent is near the officers' quarters and well within the fort walls, there is no reason for us to fear being tomahawked by a Sioux or Cheyenne warrior in the middle of the night. But outside, on the trail, things are so different, and I hear things in here—things so troublesome that they can cause worry at most any hour. I never had much hair to begin with and now it has completely stopped growing. In fact I am shedding hair right and left. They say it happens to the best of us babies. But when I peek at those bald patches in Mum's handheld mirror, I see a little old man looking back at me. I blame it all on the stress of being surrounded by Red Cloud's persistent men of red.

"At least none of *them* will want to scalp you, Dan-Dan," Toby has said at least three times. He's a true sissy whose black hair has grown so long that it sticks out in all directions at once.

He jokes out of fear, for *Toe-toe* has an inviting scalp—that is if the Indians don't mind dealing with lice. He tries to disguise his nervousness, but it shows up in different ways. For instance, after he gobbled up the last of the peppermint candy sticks from the sutler's store, he resorted to chewing his numerous split ends.

Since turning two months old here at Fort Phil Kearny in early September so many "incidents" have occurred in the neighborhood that I don't know if I can remember them all. But I'll give it a shot, since I'm sure many of you dear readers, as they say, are more interested in flying arrows and blazing bullets than in a baby who can't even crawl yet. For starters, on September 8, Indian raiders ran off with Army stock from a corral less than a mile from the fort and then took twenty mules from some civilians who were foolishly out and about. Mounted infantry gave futile chase. In the next few days there were more raids, with one soldier taking an arrow in the hip and another a revolver ball in his side while the warriors escaped into the rugged buttes where Army horses couldn't go. Once, after the opportunistic Sioux seized more than one hundred horses and mules being herded on the trail, Colonel Carrington himself led a party in pursuit, without any luck. What's more, while the colonel was away, Arapahos attacked the herd of a government contractor and made off with a dozen more mules. The bad news was slow in reaching the commander down at Fort Laramie, who, according to what Mrs. Carrington told Mrs. Pennington, had this to say on September 10: "Carrington is doing well. No trouble on Powder River road since July." When Colonel Carrington got wind of it, he told his wife he didn't know whether he should laugh or cry.

The undeclared war heated up in mid-September when several hundred warriors raided an eighty-four-man hay-cutting party, cutting down one man, wrecking a half-dozen mowing machines, destroying the one hundred tons of hay already cut, and surrounding the workmen and their guards until soldiers arrived from the fort to break the siege. The next day there were two more deaths—a mounted guard got too far ahead of a hay train and was killed and scalped; and a soldier who left the fort to go hunting without permission soon became the hunted one. I don't recall if the Indians took the time to scalp that poor fellow, but soon after, just a mile west of the fort, searchers found the body of an impulsive, inquisitive photographer from the East who had been shot, disemboweled, and beheaded. The head, found a few yards away, had been scalped.

All these little incidents did not depress Colonel Carrington, at least not on the surface. He wanted to pretend he was in control, and maybe he even believed it himself on his good days. On September 17, he wrote to a superior in some far safer location to the east that most newspaper reports were exaggerating the danger at Fort Phil Kearny. "No women or children have been captured or injured by Indians in this district since I entered it," he wrote. "No train has passed without being well cared for and protected to their full satisfaction. No post has been besieged or so threatened that could not drive off offensive Indians and at the same time protect itself." The colonel also wrote that more troops were needed at the Bozeman Trail forts, which must have confused his superior. We learned all this from a second lieutenant with more than a passing interest in Mum. The young officer clearly wanted to impress her with how much he knew about the military situation. Unlike Mrs. Pennington, however, Mum has no real attraction to men in uniform.

Much more interesting to her were the men who showed up at the fort in mid-September. There were fifty of them and they were all miners who had managed to come down the Bozeman Trail from Virginia City with the loss of *only* two men to Indian arrows. Mum left her tent to meet with some of them, eager to hear news from the gold fields. They had traveled in such a large group as much for protection against bands of desperados as hostile Indians. Not one of them wanted to discuss the amount of gold dust he had in his saddlebags, but they all knew this Wheely fellow who, as a prominent member of the Virginia City Vigilance Committee, had hanged four road agents in the last year. Mum instinctively grabbed her neck. That wasn't the kind of thing she wanted to hear.

"But doesn't he also own a substantial house on Wallace Street with a large front porch, windowpanes, and flowerpots?" she asked.

"Not that we noticed, ma'am," said one red-faced miner who seemed awestruck by the sight of Mum in a green gingham dress she had borrowed from Mrs. Pennington. "Virginia City has a number of solid, large structures. 'Course not one of us is an architect or even a home buyer."

"But you must have noticed his wife. I'm sure she dresses in fine clothes and . . . well, her name is Mrs. Cornelia Hotchkiss Wheelwright."

"Could be. We wasn't in society, ma'am. We was mostly in the gulches, panning for color. We didn't look at married ladies."

"Well, you're looking at me, mister," Mum said, putting her hands on her hips. "I'm a married lady."

It may have been the first time she had openly stated her marital status without being prodded since we left Chicago. The miner turned even more crimson as he apologized and excused himself. Mum frowned and turned to other miners, but while they all knew Wheely of the Vigilantes, they, too, had no knowledge of the man's bride or the couple's substantial house.

"Mr. Wheelwright hit so much pay dirt up there the road agents just couldn't leave him alone," commented a miner whose smile showcased the gold fillings in his teeth. "I doubt he'll rest easy till he's hung every last one of them sons of bitches!" Realizing his language was unsuitable for a lady, this miner also turned red, apologized, closed his valuable mouth tight, and departed.

As it turned out, these miners hadn't pocketed enough gold in Montana to keep them from seeking work at the fort. Colonel Carrington hired half of them as additional escorts for the hay cutters. So when it came to the soldiers and these miners, I was asking myself who was doing the protecting? The miners, like Mr. Story's cowboys would a little later, slept outside the stockade. On the morning of the 20$^{th}$, a more than substantial Sioux war party showed up and delivered arrows for breakfast at the miners' camp across Piney Creek. The soldiers watched the battle from the fort at first, with the regimental band playing lively numbers to encourage the fighting miners. Finally, Colonel Carrington sent out a detachment, and the warriors disappeared so fast it was hard to tell they were ever there. Despite that small success, the very next day the colonel issued Special Order No. 75, in which he detailed how everyone in the fort should proceed in case of a general alarm. He said there was to be no needless running in haste, and added, "Shouting, tale bearing, and gross perversions of fact by excited men does more mischief than Indians."

Well, perhaps not—I could see that the Indian mischief was spreading like wildfire. Despite the presence of the miners, there never were enough escorts. The Sioux continued to attack hay parties and wood trains, raid stock, and kill and scalp soldiers caught in the open. Carrington responded by sending out relief or pursuit detachments and on occasion by firing his twelve-pound howitzer that the Indians respected far more than the soldiers' old Springfield rifles. According to an Indian named Greasy Nose from Red Cloud's camp at the forks of Tongue River, the big chief kept at least half a dozen war parties watching the Bozeman Trail for desired stock and vulnerable travelers. None other than Private Prairie Dog Burrows managed to get that bit of information out of the English-speaking Greasy Nose, who had been caught by Private Burrows and a Private Adam Gray while skulking about the fort on an apparent spying mission. It was a real coup, as they say, to catch a member of Red Cloud's group, even if this Indian was clearly no warrior and spent most of his time in captivity praying to his own God in his own language. Carrington had intended to thoroughly interrogate the prisoner the next day, but Greasy Nose somehow got loose from his shackles and made his escape sometime between Tattoo at 8 p.m. and Taps at 8:30 p.m. Nobody knew who to blame for Greasy Nose's escape but at least the clever spy had not caused any casualties on his way out. In total for September, Red Cloud's warriors killed three soldiers and at least eighteen civilians, mostly miners and teamsters. That's a lot of graves to dig, a lot of tombs.

Nothing changed when October arrived. On the 5th, the Sioux wounded a woodcutter who later died in the post hospital, and on the 6th the Sioux seemed to focus their attention on the men assigned to guard the woodcutters about six miles from the fort. A relief detachment rushed to the scene, only to find the scalped and mutilated bodies of two of the guards, one of whom was the poor Private Gray. An off-duty civilian guard doing some unauthorized hunting, none other than Philip Kittridge, was found one hundred yards away with his scalp intact. Mr. Kittridge was on his back, alive but semiconscious, in a dense stand of seven-foot-tall big bluestem. He was clutching his Remington rifle the way a baby—but not me—might cling to a favorite toy while dozing. He was proud to show everyone a bump on his head. He claimed that two warriors came at him and that he put a slug from his Remington right in the heart of the bigger, older one. The lithe younger one, who had two small copper feathers in his headband, saw his companion fall and began wailing toward the sky so loudly that Mr. Kittridge didn't have the heart to shoot the little fellow. Then the brave began to dart about like a jackrabbit with a burr under its tail.

"I was too mesmerized to plug him," Mr. Kittridge later told anyone who would listen. "Next thing I knew he was right on top of me in the tall grass, but he didn't have a tomahawk or a bow and arrow or even a knife. He just had this coup stick, see, and he shouted out his name, Two Feathers, before he gave me a hard rap on the noggin and run off like a frightened deer. Two Feathers hadn't wanted to kill me, see, just count coup to show the older warriors and chiefs how brave he was. I could have shot him in the back, but I hesitated on account of he was so damned young and naked and eager to be a man and I was dizzy from the head knockin'. Then I recalled how the savages in his tribe had killed and mutilated my younger brother, Luther, who hadn't been that much older than this fellow. But by the time I was ready to pull the trigger, the fleet little Two Feathers was even out of the range of my Remy. Then I got so dizzy I had to lay myself down in the grass and have a good rest."

Most of the soldiers and miners bought Philip's tale of survival and good fortune, and some even called him a hero. Private Prairie Dog, who believed that any man was capable of being a coward, did not. He suggested that Mr. Kittridge, even if he was hunting on his free time, could have done more to help the men guarding the woodcutters. I thought that was a pretty bold thing for Prairie Dog to say, considering his past record. Colonel Carrington didn't go that far, but he wasn't ready to cite the civilian for bravery because Mr. Kittridge's recollections of the facts were open to question. Nobody else had seen this Two Feathers, and the body of his allegedly dead companion was never found. But other Indians could have dragged the dead brave away, and the colonel didn't bother to have the terrain checked for signs of a scuffle or even for small moccasin prints. Anyway, the colonel recognized that under the circumstances, his soldiers and civilians alike needed a hero. If they wanted to honor Mr. Kittridge instead of mourn two dead soldiers, he wasn't going to stop them. Philip received many free drinks that night, and by midnight every red-faced man around him agreed that the Army should pay such a heroic civilian considerably more money for his dangerous guard work. But when Mr. Kittridge stumbled into Carrington's quarters in the middle of the night to make his salary demand, the sober colonel also became red-faced. After a shouting match, Mr. Kittridge's employment with the Army ended by mutual consent.

"That's Phil," Mum said to Mrs. Pennington the next day. "Always in the middle of things for better or worse."

"Never mind him," said Mrs. Pennington. "What about the two brave soldiers who died out there that day? One of them was Private Gray, who helped my Prairie Dog capture that Indian spy. Wasn't Private Gray a hero?"

"I don't know. Maybe the men didn't want to drink to the dead."

Cattle pioneer Nelson Story and his cowboys arrived a few days later. They were the talk of the fort because they didn't act anything like soldiers or miners or emigrants from the East. They were their own rowdy but loyal breed. They listened to Mr. Kittridge's almost heroic tale and had their own story to tell. Philip was all ears (as was I later when I heard about their story and about Philip's first conversation with the boss cattleman). At Fort Laramie, Mr. Story had wisely purchased a rapid-fire Remington rolling-block breechloader for each of his men. As they headed up the Bozeman Trail, they had seen Indians in the distance eying the Longhorns, but the cowhands had not pulled their prized rifles from their scabbards until Rock Creek. It was there that a small party of Sioux appropriated some of the herd and Mr. Story's outfit gave chase. Never one to back down or give up, Mr. Story led his men right to the Indian camp and opened fire. Two cowboys were wounded in the short fight, but the powerful .50–70 rifle bullets sent every single thief to the happy hunting ground.

"Don't that beat all," said Philip Kittridge, tipping his high-crown cowboy hat to Mr. Story. "What a story, Nelson!"

Philip paused, waiting like some self-proclaimed barroom wit for a response. But Nelson Story didn't laugh or even crack a small smile. He just rubbed his sunburned nose with the back of his calloused hand.

"You don't mind me calling you Nelson, do you, Nelson?" Mr. Kittridge asked. When the cattle boss didn't even bother to shrug, Philip just kept on talking: "I ain't no dude or no deadbeat. I been the whole way on the Bozeman previously. Why, hell, just look at us. We was born to be saddle pards." Mr. Kittridge kept adjusting and readjusting his big-as-Texas hat, but Mr. Story didn't appear to be paying attention.

"That so, Philip?" the cattle boss finally replied, still looking off at his cattle.

"Call me Phil. I'm proud to know you Nel . . . pard . . . Mr. Story."

"You know the difference between a bull and a steer, Philip?"

"Sure. What do you take me for? I also know the difference between a cow chip and buffalo dung."

"That so?"

"And I know the difference between a colonel and a cowboy. When I was out hunting and bagged me that Indian like I told you, Colonel Carrington didn't even appreciate it. I doubt the man's ever personally killed an Indian."

"I wouldn't know." Story finally looked Philip Kittridge over, from big hat to toe of the boot. "It appears to me you got a large hat size, Philip, but that particular hat is still a mite big for you."

"Don't wear them this big down in Texas, Mr. Story?"

"Not me. If I need more shade I just shoot at the sun till I got me a cloud of smoke to sit under."

"With your Remington or your Colt? You notice I got the exact same."

"It appears that way." But Mr. Story was looking at his Longhorns again.

"And we've both plugged redskins."

"That's a fact. They always die game, don't they, Philip?"

"Like the buffalo, just not as big game."

Mr. Story buttoned his coat and then crossed his arms. "Wind sure does blow strong up this way. I ain't aiming to hang around here long."

"Eager to get to Montana, eh? Me, too. Damn Carrington don't want none of us to leave. With all his worrying, he'll lose all his hair without even being scalped."

"Some of his officers don't appear gun-shy."

"That's true, but he's the high muck-a-muck at the fort, and I swear that man's shaking in his spit-and-polish boots."

"Well, real soon me and the colonel will have to sit down for a little powwow."

"You watch his flannel mouth, Mr. Story. Carrington loves to proclaim orders."

"That's why he's an officer. It'll be no hair off his hide if we move on soon. There are some powerfully hungry folks up in Montana and I need to get my herd through."

"You bet. We ain't like the colonel at all, Mr. Story. We're not cut from that same flimsy eastern cloth. Them Sioux don't scare us one bit, not when we're packing our Remington rifles and . . ."

"It's not a matter of being scared," Mr. Story interrupted, as he turned up the collar of his coat. "It's a matter of a man doing what a man has to do."

"Couldn't have put it any better myself, Mr. Story. That's exactly how I feel. Maybe I can tag along with your outfit."

"Anybody willing to ride drag is welcome to tag along, Philip. Now, if you'll pardon me. I'd like to get out of this wind."

After that first conversation with Nelson Story, Philip Kittridge started hanging around the cattle camp three miles from the post. Colonel Carrington wouldn't listen to Mr. Story's simple reasoning. Maybe the miners up in Montana were hungry but they would just have to make do on bread and potatoes for now. His job was to protect lives on the Bozeman Trail, whether Mr. Story liked it or not. And it was his strong belief that Story's outfit did not have the strength to protect the cattle, let alone themselves.

"So exactly how long you want me and the boys to sit still twiddling our thumbs?" Mr. Story asked Colonel Carrington after the first week of thumb twiddling.

"Till I say otherwise," the colonel replied sternly. "If these Indians keep ambushing and raiding, we may be eating those beeves of yours come winter."

There was no room for debate, especially not when the Indians struck twice in mid-October—first attacking woodcutters five miles from the fort, killing two men, wounding another; and then forcing a haying party to abandon their wagons and horses. At the time, less than forty of the horses at Fort Phil Kearny were fit for travel, let alone for galloping after Sioux warriors. The cattleman and the colonel stopped talking to each other.

Colonel Carrington concentrated his energies on something he could accomplish and in fact did by the end of October—completing the construction of the stockade, 2,800 feet around with eleven-foot-long timbers forming tight walls that have port holes every few feet for defensive rifle fire and howitzers ready to deliver their deadly canister from the blockhouses at the east and west corners. Five sturdy guard stands provide twenty-four-hour surveillance, allowing me to nurse, drool, play with my toes, fill my diaper, and sleep without worry day or night. In other words, while there are dangers lurking up and down the trail and all around, Mum and I are reasonably safe and cozy in this tent inside Carrington's great walls. Still, my hair falls out.

I have never seen the colonel more vibrant and jolly than he was on the evening of October 18 when he hosted a hop, for officers and select civilians only, to celebrate moving into his new quarters. The post commander's impressive frame building, built by the regimental band in between concerts, has brick chimneys and a large attached kitchen. It houses the colonel and his wife, Margaret; their sons, nine-year-old Henry and six-year-old Jimmy; and their butler, George. At the hop, Henry and even Jimmy spent most of the evening picking on the younger Toby Pennington, pulling his hair, smacking him on the bottom with wood utensils, and making him flash his bare bottom at several wives of officers. As far as I can tell, their reasons for this incessant bullying were *Toe-toe*'s hair, longer and much wilder than his mother's, and his status as a civilian child whose peace-loving daddy was dead as a doornail while the Carrington boys' own father was commander of this entire frontier world (they certainly gave Red Cloud no respect) and their mother was even more commanding—at least in the kitchen and other rooms of their grand quarters. While even I could see—from the next room where a fat Army laundress in a food-stained dress was babysitting me—that the Carrington boys were behaving like little savages, Toby's mother didn't notice. Grace Pennington spent the entire evening flitting and flirting about the room in a sparkling silver ball gown that she had borrowed from the generous Mrs. Carrington. (Mum borrowed dresses from Mrs. Pennington, and Mrs. Pennington borrowed dresses from the fort commander's wife.)

Mrs. Pennington's dancing partners were all officers, single and married, at the post. You see, *Lobe-lobe* (it's hard to stop calling her that) still intended to marry Private Prairie Dog Burrows in a matter of weeks, but first she was intent on making him jealous. The private wasn't invited, of course, but she figured he would hear plenty of gossip about her dancing and her rubbing elbows with the Carrington crowd. I heard her reveal her strategy to Mum. I can't say it makes much sense to me, but apparently Mrs. Pennington figured that if she made Prairie Dog jealous enough, he would strive to both heroically kill as many hostiles as possible and to nobly protect the lives of women and children. And, according to her calculations, he would be doing this for four excellent reasons—to impress her, to avenge her first husband's murder, to win a Medal of Honor, and to earn a promotion. Poor beautiful *Lobe-lobe* thought all of that was possible out here in this untamed land.

Beautiful Mum didn't think so. She was there at the hop, at least in body if not spirit. Her invitation came because she was a friend of Mrs. Pennington, who had an in with Mrs. Carrington. Mum danced a bit but mostly made excuses to the gentlemen so she could powder her nose and check up on me and the babysitting laundress. Philip Kittridge, of course, was not present. Having been fired by Colonel Carrington and having given up on Mum, he was at the cowboy camp with Nelson Story, who wasn't speaking with the Fort Phil Kearny brass and was plotting his getaway.

Four days later, October 22, there was a somewhat less civilized dance—a dance for the men rather than the officers, and with no officers' wives present, either, of course. The dancing partners for the soldiers were a few wives and sweethearts (some who hired on to do laundry or cook) and a few civilian traveling ladies like Mum who were not attached to any man, at least not any man present. I was allowed to attend but was mostly confined to a pile of blankets in a laundry basket while Toby Pennington, who was assigned to watch me, sucked up his candy payment (there were no more peppermint sticks but one sweet-tooth private had a private stash of sour cherry balls that he donated to Mrs. Pennington) and sometimes pulled my big toes until I hollered. *Toe-toe*'s natural fear seemed to ease off when he was doing little, almost accidental, things to torture me.

The dance took place in a new 100-by-125-foot log building with a shingle roof, the soon-to-be quarters for the much-needed cavalry that was due to arrive at Fort Phil Kearny in a matter of days. (In fact, as I etch this for the record, the cavalry is due to arrive at any moment.) Private Prairie Dog Burrows not only was at this second-tier social gathering but also was the life of the party. His fellow soldiers didn't seem to hold it against him that he once deserted the Army and certainly the ladies present didn't, since he was not only frolicsome and full of gossip but also light on his feet. He kept popping up practically in their arms. Grace Pennington attended this dance as well, but she wore her own gown, which was no match for the sleek one that Mrs. Carrington had lent her for the earlier hop, and no officers were there to make her feel like a real lady. What's more, her strategy as related to Prairie Dog seemed to backfire. Instead of her making him jealous, he made her wish she wasn't there. He danced with her once and then ignored her the rest of the evening as he swung every available partner from Mum to the fat laundress/babysitter. Mum suggested that this was an intentional strategy on the part of the private to get revenge against Mrs. Pennington for having danced with the brass at the earlier hop. Do I get it? Not really. I mean I've come to accept the fact that I must be observant and intelligent to be producing this diary. But I cannot explain why they acted in that fashion when they were already engaged and supposedly in love. The truth is the only kind of love I know about is a child's love for his mother and vice versa. I have plenty of time to learn about *other* affairs of the heart, but frankly, at this moment, I can't imagine loving any other female besides Mum.

When we arrived at the dance, Mum tried to hide her disappointment that Philip Kittridge was not in attendance, or if not him, then Nelson Story. She had heard about Philip befriending Nelson Story and the other cowboys, and she knew exactly where all those boys were bound. She wanted one of them to punch her ticket to Montana. I hate to say this, but Mum had not given up believing in Mr. Kittridge, that is in his ability to do what he sets out to do despite all his easily identified faults as a human being. Yes, he was a cad (actually a rapist, though Mum glosses over such technicalities), but he was strong, bold, reasonably handsome, and had even shown her a gentler side for a while after the death of his younger brother. At the same time, I think that Mr. Story impressed her as a man of action, a leader among men and a true gentleman when in the company of ladies. Of course, there were other men waiting around to be allowed to proceed to the gold fields, but they were a grubby, poor, inexperienced, and uninspiring bunch—a little too desperate to find a quick solution to the monetary and social problems that had plagued them back in civilization. As for me, I didn't think much about Mr. Story one way or another except that his cowboy hat sure did fit him, unlike someone I know. Yes, I was glad that Mr. Kittridge was not at the dance. Not that he ever pulled my toes like Toby or anything. Hardly ever did he pay the slightest bit of attention to me. But the way I saw it, he was plain no good for Mum, and as much as I understood her, I could *not* see how she could tolerate the man.

And then, just like that, Philip Kittridge and a few of Nelson Story's cowboys made a sudden late appearance at the dance, livening things up considerably and stealing Private Prairie Dog's thunder. They had drawn straws to see who would do the waltzing while the rest of them were back with the herd. I raised my head, shook my little fists, and let out a sizable moan when I saw Philip walk through the door, and Toby wasn't even pulling my toes at the time.

"Oh, look! It's the man in the big hat," Toby said.

I moaned again, louder.

"You don't like him hanging around your Mum, do you, Dan-Dan?"

*"BaBa,"* I said, maybe shaking my head a little.

"You saying 'bad-bad'?"

I maybe nodded my head. For a dumb longhaired little sissy, Toby sometimes surprised me with his understanding of certain matters.

"You know something, Dan-Dan?"

I just stared at him. How much talking did *Toe-toe* expect me to do?

"My Mommy wants to marry that Prairie Dog man and live at this fort. I hate him."

In a way I agreed with Toby, but I wouldn't have said so to his face even if I knew how to talk. His mother loved the spry private. While there is no accounting for taste, it was no concern of mine. I mean I had my loving Mum and everything, and it was only *Lobe-lobe*'s unusually shapely earlobes that held any fascination for me.

"And I hate it here," continued Toby, opening up like a total sourpuss to me, because he knew I couldn't stop him. "I hate those Carrington bully boys. I hate the smelly tent. I hate my cot. I hate the food, except this candy. I hate the crappers. I hate this stupid dance. I hate all the guns and cannons. I *really* hate the bows and arrows that killed my daddy. I hate the colonel and Chief Red Cloud and sometimes, Dan-Dan, I even hate you and your Mum." Toby, out of breath and practically in a lather from all his hating, proceeded to tug on my left big toe so hard that I thought it might come off my foot. When I cried out just a tiny bit, he grinned. I had a feeling that given half a chance, *Lobe-lobe*'s kid could torture with the efficiency of the Sioux.

Toby saw some hope in the fact that his mother and Private Prairie Dog were dancing all night but *not* with each other—but that's only because he has even less understanding than me in matters of the heart. I, on the other hand, worked myself into a crying tantrum because Philip Kittridge was dancing every dance with Mum, and his grabby hands and energized buck-skinned body were doing things that shouldn't be done during a waltz. No matter how much I bawled, Mum would not break away to tend to me. Once Mrs. Pennington came over to quiet me down, another time the fat laundress did, and once Toby resorted to feeding me a sour cherry ball that he had already sucked to death.

Nothing was as it appears on that night, however. When Grace Pennington left the dance in the early morning hours, dragging along Toby (who had fallen asleep on the job), she told Prairie Dog Burrows that she would rather go face to face with Red Cloud any day in Powder River Country than to see the philandering private come inside her tent and kiss her rosy red cheek. So what happened at noon? Private Prairie Dog popped into the tent, kissed Mrs. Pennington full on her red lips, and again popped the question: "Will you marry me at the date you desire and stop dancing with graduates of West Point forever?"

Her reply was simple, "You bet, soldier."

And then they *really* kissed, right there on Mrs. Pennington's cot. Toby left without a word, but I knew he was headed to the crapper. Mum smiled at the suddenly re-engaged couple—it went unnoticed by them—before picking me up and carrying me off to the sutler's store to hear the latest news about the Bozeman Trail, Indian activity, and especially Mr. Story's cowboy outfit. Mum was full of new hope. Philip Kittridge's last words to her at the dance were spoken only a few hours before dawn: "You know, Lib, you look like a million dollars, you dance like a dream, and you kiss like a better dream. And you know something else—I don't figure to stay camped with the cowboys outside this fort forever." Those words were followed by the longest dream kiss yet. Putting two and two together, Mum figured that Philip would be back in her tent and her life and that when opportunity finally knocked like a warm breeze, they (and me) would once again be Montana-bound in his spring wagon.

At the sutler's store, though, there was bad news, and everyone there, from the sutler to the customers to the morning social callers, was happy to tell Mum about it. Philip Kittridge and the Texas cowboys who had danced the night away had been in on a Nelson Story plan. They attended the Yankee dance as a smoke screen, and indeed most of the fort's enlisted men were also there instead of on guard duty. Those two factors opened the door for Mr. Story and his other hired hands to move the herd out in the darkness and keep it moving up the Bozeman Trail. "Come morning," said the cattle boss, "we'll be so far north Carrington won't dare send soldiers after us." He was right. By dawn his dancing Texans and Mr. Kittridge had rejoined him on the trail, and the full force of less than thirty men wasn't looking back. They had fooled Colonel Carrington, which I suppose was pretty clever, but now they were daring Red Cloud and most of the Sioux Nation.

It's now been a week and a half since Nelson Story moved on with his herd, and with Philip Kittridge riding drag. I say, or would say if I could talk, "Good riddance to that cad, that rapist liar." But Mum drags about the tent, and sometimes acts as if even lifting me to her bosom is a burden. When I played my rattle like a bugle the other day, she didn't even crack a smile. Sure, Mr. Kittridge let her down again, but what did she expect from the likes of him? Her mood is tough for me to deal with, and yesterday I overreacted and tried to "bite" her nipple with my gums.

Grace Pennington is too preoccupied with her upcoming wedding to try to cheer Mum up or to hold me close enough to get a crack at her earlobes. The nuptials are scheduled to happen on November 6, that is if Private Prairie Dog doesn't get cold feet about that event or about re-enlisting in the Army, two things that seem to be as interconnected as forts and flagpoles. On the last day of October at a dedication ceremony for Fort Phil Kearny, the soldier boys raised a 20-by-36-foot flag on a pole made of two lodge pole pines pinned together, the band played on an octagonal bandstand, and Colonel Carrington spoke of overcoming hardships and tribulations. The upbeat music, Carrington's words, and the flag flapping in the breeze atop the 124-foot flagpole might have lifted the spirits of some folks here but not of Mum.

"As far as I can see, putting that thing up is like waving a red flag in the nose of Red Cloud," she said to Grace Pennington afterward in our tent. "I wonder if Mr. Kittridge made it through to Montana."

"My word, Elizabeth! How can you still care about that man? He deserted you."

"Well, Grace, you should know something about men who desert."

"Private Burrows deserted the Army; he did not desert me. And that's all in the past."

"So he loves the Army again and it's all because of you?"

"It's not *all* because of me. He knows he was wrong. What he did, he did on an immature impulse inspired by a disreputable soldier and two undisciplined scouts."

"Immature impulse?"

"I wish you wouldn't jump to criticize my every word, Elizabeth. It really doesn't matter why he did it. He's now a reformed man, back in good standing with the Army and full of exceptional potential."

"Exceptional potential? To do what?"

"You got a hint of his potential when he caught that Red Cloud spy—Greasy Nose, I believe they call him—sneaking around outside the fort and placed him under custody."

"And who soon got away."

"The spy's escape was not the fault of my Private Burrows. One day P.D. hopes to kill Red Cloud and become a sergeant, maybe even an officer."

"Sure. And I'll be the queen of England someday."

"I won't let you spoil my happiness just because you're jealous that I have a good man. You'd think after all the time we've spent in that tent together you could at least *pretend* to be happy about my marriage."

"You're right, Grace. I apologize. I simply do not wish to be in this place a moment longer. That huge flag pole and flag out there don't make being here any less horrible."

"It's *not* so horrible. Times will get better. The hostiles will be put in their place, and innocent men, women, and children will no longer be murdered in cold blood. This fort or some other fort will be my home for a long time to come. I'm marrying a solider."

"Of course, Grace—to each her own. I apologize again. It's just that I want to leave here with my baby. I want it so badly that it makes my insides ache like when I was pregnant."

"I understand. I'm a mother and a woman, too. We understand the love we have for our children. But what one of us can explain love for a man? I loved Rufus, but he is gone. Now I want to be here with my soldier. So, Elizabeth, if you want to be reunited with Mr. Kittridge in Virginia City, who am I to say it is wrong."

"You misjudge me, Grace. If Mr. Kittridge gets there in good health and I do the same someday, I shall do something very unladylike, like spit in his face or make him eat dirt."

"Let's not talk about such unpleasant things."

"We could talk about the weather. I feel a chill in the air, but it isn't unpleasant yet."

"Have you heard what Margaret Carrington is going to do?"

"Go give Red Cloud a piece of her mind?"

"You're being silly."

"Invite him into the commanding officer's quarters for a glass of sherry?"

"Stop that. Elizabeth."

"I'm sorry. Please tell me. What is Mrs. Carrington going to do?"

"I thought you already knew. I've been telling just about everybody this: Margaret has generously consented to lend me her silk lace wedding dress!"

"Of course," Mum said. "It's practically the talk of the fort."

Since then, moping Mum and busy Mrs. Pennington have not talked much about anything, not even the colder weather. Right now *Lobe-lobe* and *Toe-toe* (hoping for more hard candy no doubt) are checking on the food arrangements for the wedding. At the sutler's store, where the pickings are generally slim and the prices are exorbitant, she might be able to get vegetables and beer and possibly a few oysters if she is lucky. But she will also go to the fat laundress who once babysat for me, since that enterprising woman knows how to make eatable sausages out of any kind of meat and also bakes a delicious peach pie. I mean those are things I've heard. I obviously don't have taste buds for any of that fare yet. I'm still plenty happy with just milk, although Mum's moping has made her a little stingy in that department.

Mum has just taken Aunt Maggie's wrinkled letter out from under her pillow to read it for the thousandth time, even though it is filled with sadness, what with Grandpa Duly having died and Grandma Duly probably set to join him at any time. "Your Aunt Maggie tells me to trust in the Lord," Mum says to me without picking me off the floor, where I have been fluttering about like a landed trout. "How can I do that? Phil leaves me in the middle of the night, I don't hear a word from Cornelia in Montana, and I'm going to be stuck at Fort Phil Kearny forever. And unlike our tent mate, I can't marry a soldier even if I wanted to, on account of I'm already married to your abnormal father. I've called on the Lord repeatedly of late, but when has he ever come through? The Lord is like Phil Kittridge . . . full of promise but completely untrustworthy."

I don't know quite how to react. At least she still has me. I agree with her about Mr. Kittridge, but I would never mention his name in the same breath as the Lord. I pound my fist against the floor and then open the fist and bring my two palms together in a sort of prayerful clap. I'm not really praying, though I do mumble *"gaga,"* which is as close as I can come to saying "God." Mum does glance my way but of course doesn't understand. She sits down at the small writing table and spreads out a sheet of paper she stole from Mrs. Pennington, rather from her late husband. At the top in fancy script are the initials RKP, for Rufus K. Pennington. (I have no idea what the "K" stands for. All I can think of is "Killed," but obviously he got the stationery long before he was killed.) Mum writes to her younger sister, Maggie, in Chicago, for the first time since we were at Ash Hollow, Nebraska.

Dear little sister—Greetings from the frontier. Such a queer thing for me to say, but it is true. The frontier is right here, all around me. I pen this note on the stationery of a dead man. I don't know how much time has passed since he was killed on the trail in a most unpleasant fashion. But it seems like ages ago, and it must be long enough, since his widow is about to marry again. I am *not yet* a dead woman. I am stuck with my son, Daniel, at Fort Phil Kearny, which is somewhere on the Bozeman Trail many, many, many miles from civilization as we know it. Daniel will be four months old tomorrow, the day before the widow takes her second husband, a simple private, but she is desperate! I suppose we are safe enough here, as long as we *never* leave. "Trust in the Lord," I keep hearing you say. But I'm afraid all my trust in the Lord will never get me to Cornelia. Neither will the handsome frontier man I counted on but who coldly deserted me. Not all men are the same, but most share certain faults. Or have you found that out for yourself, little sis? I would write more, Mags, but I have *NO* faith that this letter will ever reach you in Chicago. Mail service is bad in these parts, in part because of the so-called savages all around us who don't even know how to write and rely on smoke signals. That's also why I didn't write you sooner. –Love From the Wilderness, Elizabeth. And hugs and kisses to you, Mr. Flowers, Grandma Duly, your frisky Mr. Gibbs from the store, and even my demented husband, Abe (should he ever show up again). As for poor Grandpa Duly, well, I feel he is in a better place. Poor me.

Mum is on a roll, and takes out another sheet of "RKP" stationery. She writes:

Dear Cornelia—I haven't got any word from you in ages. Don't know if you had stopped writing or letters aren't reaching me. I am now at Fort Phil Kearny and I'm dying to get out of here. I hope Wheely and you are still living like king and queen in Virginia City. I met some miners who came down from there and they knew your husband but not you. That must be because you are truly a one-man woman. If you do meet a man named Philip Kittridge, who might pretend to know me, spit in his eye for me. Don't let him into your beautiful home on Wallace Street. Hope you get this. Hope even more I get there. I, that is we—me and my son Daniel—are eager to . . .

Toby charges into the room, waving a dangerous-looking crooked stick and shouting: "Fetterman is here! Fetterman is here!" His chubby cheeks are flushed. We have no idea what the boy is talking about, but Mum is annoyed at having to stop writing in mid-sentence and I'm annoyed that I can no longer see Mum's written words in my mind's eye. I wonder if this Fetterman fellow is the guy who supplies hard candy to the sutler's store. Mum has misheard the name.

"Did he bring me a letter?" she asks.

"Huh?" says Toby. "Who?"

"The letter man. The letter man. I'm expecting a letter from Montana."

Toby shrugs his narrow little shoulders and his feet fidget the way they do when he wants to be excused to go to the crapper. But something else is going on with him. His eyes are wide with excitement yet he looks terribly confused. They say that happens often when children listen to adults speak.

"Say it again, Toby," says Mum. "Who exactly is here?"

"Fetterman."

"Oh. With an 'F'?"

"Huh?"

"Who is this Mr. Fetterman? I am assuming Fetterman is a man."

"He's Captain William Judd Fetterman—really a brevet lieutenant colonel on account of he was a Civil War hero." Toby beams and begins shooting right and left with his stick gun. I'm convinced one of the imaginary bullets is directed at me. It's obvious that young *Toe-toe* has adapted his mother's love of officers or those she unrealistically sees as potential officers, like her soon-to-be-husband.

"On whose side?"

"Huh?"

"This Fetterman was a hero on which side?"

"Our side. He's a real Civil War hero like General Custer. We met him at the store."

"Custer?"

"No. Captain Fetterman. He kissed Mommy's hand. He kisses all the lady hands. Mommy says he has a gallant tree."

"Gallantry."

"He killed lots of Rebels."

"How gallant of him. What's he doing way out here, just visiting?"

"He come to kill Injuns. He ain't afraid!"

"Good for him."

"Mrs. Carrington says he brings a brave, fighting spirit to the fort."

"Really?" Mum says. "I wish he had brought me a letter instead."

"Mommy says he is bold but polite and full of good conduct."

"I suppose that is unusual in a man," Mum says.

Toby's mother enters the tent, swinging her parasol as if it were a saber. But she doesn't look angry—quite the contrary. She has the same wide eyes as her son and is bubbling all over the way she did when she danced with those officers at the hop. She confirms that Captain Fetterman means business, wanting to "settle accounts" with the Indians who killed so many good men, including the late Mr. Rufus K. Pennington. The captain, she gushes, is certainly not going to sit around like everyone else, paralyzed by fear of Red Cloud. "Margaret Carrington says the colonel is glad to have him and so are all the men," Mrs. Pennington adds, finally exhaling and folding the handle of her parasol. "I'm glad to have him, too!"

"More so than Prairie Dog?" Mum asks.

Mrs. Pennington is starting to look angry, like she wants to stab Mum with the point of her parasol. Now she takes another deep breath. She turns her back on Mum and me and lays the parasol on her pillow. She speaks more softly now, but she can't hide the excitement in her voice: "Of course I've heard so much about Captain Fetterman and his admirable Civil War career. But it's funny what an effect someone like that can have on a body even though you've only just met him. Captain Fetterman is so ambitious, so confident, so alive."

"And so single?" says Mum.

"What? I suppose so. I think it would be good if my Private Burrows could serve under him to see firsthand how an officer should behave and handle himself under pressure. I'm certain Colonel Fetterman will make a tremendous difference here at the fort."

"What can one man do against all those Sioux?" Mum mutters, shaking her head and trying to go back to her letter to Aunt Cornelia.

"Will Fetterman kill Red Cloud?" Toby asks his mother after flopping on her bed.

"Captain Fetterman," she replies. "You must never forget a man's rank. If my Private Burrows, Patrick David, doesn't get around to it, I'm sure Captain Fetterman will, or at least someone from his immediate command."

Mum pushes aside her letter. It's hard for her to write even when words have her full concentration. Her mind is clearly no longer on her older sister in Montana. "The closest any white man came to shooting Red Cloud was Luther Kittridge," she says, nibbling on the end of her pen. "You know, Philip's younger brother. Don't you remember? He was at close range but somehow missed. They say Red Cloud must have had some kind of Indian magic protecting him. And, of course, after that miss, the Indians took care of Luther. May he rest in peace."

"Captain Fetterman is a trained professional soldier who rose from company to battalion commander during the Civil War and was twice brevetted for gallantry. I hardly think he is anything like the Kittridge brothers."

"And hardly anything like your Private Prairie Dog Burrows."

"Oh, dear, you're showing off your jealousy again, Elizabeth. You still resent the fact that your Phil ran out on you while I'm marrying a solider. And by the way he has promised to do away with—or at least *not* encourage others to use—that awful nickname. For now on he will be Patrick David or P.D."

"And that will make him a better man?"

"He's already a good man. But what officer has a nickname like that? How can someone call you 'Prairie Dog' and still respect you?"

"But he can't do away with the fact he is a *private*."

"I'll get him to show more gumption—lots more gumption. They'll have to promote him—to corporal or straight to sergeant and then . . ."

"I don't know about that. The Army brass doesn't have to do anything, except when Red Cloud makes them. But I am glad, Grace, that you are still going ahead with the wedding to Private Burrows, even with Captain Fetterman here at the fort."

"What is that supposed to mean, may I ask? You don't act

like a friend, Elizabeth, not even like someone I should wish to have present at *my* wedding ceremony."

"I'm sorry, Grace. I'm so terribly thoughtless. Will there be oysters?"

"Yes, at least I hope so. I requested them a month ago."

"Reasonably fresh, I hope."

"If at all possible. And much peach pie."

"I'm sure Captain Fetterman loves a good peach pie."

"I wouldn't know."

"You have at least told him about your wedding and the lace dress you are borrowing from Mrs. Carrington?"

"As a matter of fact, I did not. I just met the man. I am not sure he would even be able to attend. I am absolutely certain he will fight the savages without mercy. He instills confidence. I heard him tell Mrs. Carrington, 'A company of regulars could whip a thousand and a regiment could whip the whole array of hostile tribes.' Now, those are the words I love to hear—the words of a brave man."

"Or a braggart perhaps."

"Must you always contradict me, Elizabeth! I don't know what's gotten into you. You should be ever grateful that Captain Fetterman is here to push aside the redskins and open up the Bozeman Trail, which would finally allow you the opportunity to *leave*."

"I will root for our good captain, then," Mum says as she finally comes over to pick me off the floor and hold me tight in her arms. "But I pray to God he doesn't do it all in the next couple days. I'd just die if I had to leave here before the wedding takes place."

★ ★ ★ ★ ★

# PART III: THE WESTERING TOMB

★ ★ ★ ★ ★

# December 6, 1866: Tombs and the Other Side of the Story

There was quite a fight today four miles west of Fort Phil Kearny when the Indians attacked a wood train returning from the mountains. Of course I wasn't there, but Red Cloud was, and soon I will be hearing more about it from several of the participants. I'll let you know as soon as I do. It is getting dark already and right now I hear the low-pitched, echoing *ho-ho-hoo-hoo-hoo* of the great horned owl competing with the frequent howls of a wolf. Some say that the owl is a harbinger of death, but I think that howling is over freshly killed prey. Anyway I figure it, death and doom are in the air, but hopefully not my immediate air. For the past month, Mum has been working hard every day and then half-humming and half-chanting at night to put herself, not me, to sleep. I worry about her, even though I know she is stronger than she thinks and is doing about as well as could be expected under the circumstances. And what circumstances!

You will never guess where I am as I etch this entry in my turned-upside-down skull. It is sure different from the forts and everything else I have been exposed to in my life. Of course, my life hasn't been very long. But it's different than anything Mum has ever been exposed to in her much longer life. It has been often said, though not around here, that where I am is a bad place, full of bad people with bad thoughts. I might have thought so at first, but already I'm thinking it's really more different than bad. You see "bad" is a judgment call and in the eye of whomever is doing the judging, but I'm reserving judgment until I'm a little older and wiser. I am pretty sure that no judgment has been made on this matter by God, or *Ga-ga,* as I'm still saying, though my speech is no longer totally babyish. I've had to grow up pretty fast the last month, partially because of where I am and the company I'm keeping—rather the company that is keeping me. At least Mum is here, too, and while it has been a whole lot tougher on her than me, at least she is surviving and looking after my welfare as best she can. So far it has *not* been a fate worse than death.

Well, was that enough of a hint for you, dear reader? This has to be the biggest event in my life since I was born. I'll just come right out and say it: I AM CAPTURED. At the moment, somewhere near the Tongue River, I am crawling around a buffalo skin blanket in the tepee of Wolf Who Don't Dance, and Wolf's two wives are talking to me in their strange tongue. Or you could say that English is the strange tongue along the Tongue. This is a Sioux tepee.

I pretty much keep my mouth closed these days. The two wives, Pretty Bear and Wounded Eagle, aren't much on baby talk and they discourage any words that sound too much like the ones pronounced by soldiers and emigrants. Mum isn't around right now. She was sent down to the riverbank to give Wolf's breechclouts and leggings and buckskin shirts, as well as the deerskin and elkskin dresses of the two wives, a last good cleaning before the river ices over. Mum is by herself but she knows better than to try to run away—the beatings by Wounded Eagle are particularly harsh—and our hosts know that Mum would never try to make a break for it without me. She is pretty much a slave, doing most of the washing and cleaning and cooking and buffalo hide scraping, but Wolf hardly ever lays a hand on her himself and has expressed his intentions of one day making her his third wife. Telling him that she already has a husband

back in the City of the Big Wind will not put off a man like Wolf
Who Don't Dance forever. I'm not sure how this warrior would
stack up with my Civil War soldier father (before Papa Duly
became mad as a hatter). But it's my humble opinion that Wolf
is more honest, sincere, and thoughtful than Philip Kittridge
ever was and looks more natural in buckskin. Oh, and one other
thing. You don't want to get on the wrong side of Wolf Who
Don't Dance. He's a well-recognized warrior and one of Red
Cloud's favorite young cousins.

As a five-month-old baby, my needs are quite simple, and I
am just as happy crawling around on furs in a tepee at Red
Cloud's village as I would be on the canvas floor of a tent at
Colonel Carrington's fort. And, since pencils and paper are not
necessary or of any use to me for that matter, I can etch things
in my skull (it's not really turned upside down except when
certain caretakers handle me) the same way I could in the white
man's world. However, I am a little worried that if nobody
comes to "rescue" Mum and me and we turn completely Sioux,
I will have to face the fact that few Indians are known to keep
diaries. Right now my desire to one day write down these
personal thoughts and observations is still burning in me like a
sacred fire, but who knows what happens in time when a young
buck is exposed to an alien culture and values. It makes me
wonder all right. If you, dear reader, are indeed reading this at
some later point in time, does that mean I actually put these
words down on paper myself or did I need a translator to listen
to my oral history and then record these words?

But that's enough wondering for now. All I can do is just
keep on doing what I've been doing. I am alive and kicking, as
they say. I should count my lucky stars for that or even thank
*Wakan Tanka,* the Great Spirit. It's funny but Wounded Eagle,
who survived the white man's smallpox a while back but not
without acquiring some pockmarks on her hard face, kind of

reminds me of Aunt Maggie back in Chicago. Certainly Wounded Eagle invokes the name *Wakan Tanka* as much as Maggie mentions the Lord, although Wounded Eagle carries around a medicine bag made of the skin of an eagle rather than a Bible bound in leather. There are bigger differences, too. I can't imagine Maggie ever gnawing on the heart or liver of a buffalo or beating Mum with a horsewhip. Mum seems totally at odds with Wounded Eagle and that's a far cry from Mum's old spat with Mrs. Pennington. In this tepee, poor Mum seems totally overmatched, although the fairly gentle Pretty Bear—and Wolf, when he's around—certainly would never let Wounded Eagle rip Mum's heart out.

Anyway, dear reader, this is no time for me to quit on Mum or myself. Sometimes I think about those captives the freighters told us about—Nancy Morton and Danny Marble. They managed to live through their time with the Indians. Yes, it was the Cheyennes who had them, while the Sioux have us, but it can be done. I hope Mum remembers that. There's no telling what the future holds, but I know one thing: There won't be any future at all for either of us unless we continue to toughen up and adapt.

Speaking of Mum, she has just appeared through the flap of our tepee. I guess she is finally done with the washing at the river and has hung up all the Indian clothes out to dry on the chokeberry shrubs. It's time for her to stir the post-battle soup, past time actually based on Wounded Eagle's ferocious look. Mum mumbles something. Wounded Eagle doesn't like what she hears even if she can't understand Mum. She uses the back of her hand to swat Mum across the mouth. Ouch! Wounded Eagle grunts in satisfaction as Mum stirs double time.

Without resorting to a "woe-is-me" tone or dwelling in self-pity, I shall tell you how Mum and me got to be where we are today. Pretty Bear, whose homemade shimmering bead jewelry utterly fascinates me, is now tickling my bare toes with the white outer tail feathers of a mockingbird. I shall laugh in a moment because it makes her smile and she has a lovely smile. Pretty Bear takes pleasure in the simple things in life, and I guess she sees me as one of those simple things. She has absolutely no idea about all the thoughts that are racing around inside my head and leaving their imprint on my brain, but then neither does Elizabeth Hotchkiss Duly, the white woman who is my birth mother, my poor beautiful Mum.

A month ago, back in our tent at Fort Phil Kearny, Mum and Mrs. Pennington were having their spat, resulting in our own little domestic Civil War. Simply put, the one-time friends could no longer stand each other and no longer even pretended to be civil. They spoke only in fighting words, their weapons being sarcasm, gross exaggerations, and brutal honesty. It was ugly, but at least they weren't slugging or slapping each other. They were too civilized for that, I guess.

Mum and Mrs. Pennington mostly argued about men. Every opinion they had seemed to differ when it came to the cad-like ways of the absent Philip Kittridge, the Quaker lifestyle of the late Rufus K. Pennington, the lack of commitment to anything of Private P.D. Burrows, the effectiveness of commander Colonel Henry Beebee Carrington, the commanding presence of Captain William Judd Fetterman, the killings orchestrated by Chief Red Cloud, and the behavior of Mum's *alleged* husband back in Chicago.

"What man would let his pregnant wife go west without him?" Mrs. Pennington blurted out in the middle of one of their nasty exchanges. "He must be crazy!"

Mum never let on how close Mrs. Pennington was to the truth. Mum dropped the subject of Papa Duly, but Mrs. Pennington didn't know when to stop. Everything wasn't going just perfect with her wedding planning or her molding of her groom,

P.D., into the perfect soldier, so she took it out on Mum. At one point, Mrs. Pennington went so far as to step out of her ladylike façade and hypothesis that Mum had been a woman for sale back in Chicago who got in the family way and decided for once to keep the little bastard—me! Mum, thinking of me, her babies that didn't make it before I was born, and perhaps her crazy husband, came close to boxing Mrs. Pennington's ears (yes, the same ears I used to explore with such innocent delight), but restrained herself. Mrs. Pennington, perhaps thinking of her late husband, said she would never resort to violence herself (even while she was most eager for the men at the fort, particularly Private Burrows and Captain Fetterman, to resort to violence against Red Cloud's people).

Toby, though, resorted to his brand of sissy violence. It wasn't just my toes anymore that he tortured. When he thought nobody was looking he would pull my hair (which has started to grow back), twist my nose, and pinch my little belly. My limited range of motion and lack of coordination made counterpunches and my kicking defense ineffective. Seeing this, Toby became even more daring once when Mrs. Pennington was out for one of her social strolls/visits. The brat actually tried to shove my rattlesnake rattle down my throat. I reacted by regurgitating on the boy. At that point he called me "the stray kitten of a painted cat" (I'm sure he didn't know what he was saying but he must have gotten those words from his Mommy), turned me over onto my belly, and started to shove that same rattle up the tiny opening between my buttocks. I was shocked. All I could do is pass gas—a skunk-like defense. But Mum caught him in the act and chased the screaming *Toe-toe* around the tent with a hairbrush until Mrs. Pennington returned and began screaming even louder than her son. *Lobe-lobe*'s screaming was directed at good Mum, not bad Toby. Mum dropped the hairbrush and lifted me into her arms while I handled the screaming for our side.

As the mini–Civil War raged on, none other than Private Burrows, who Grace Pennington was still scheduled to marry despite some unexpected complications in their relationship, showed up and took our side. That is to say he began to exchange bad words and accusations with his bride-to-be at the flap of our tent. Toby's abuse of me and Mrs. Pennington's intolerance of Mum might have been contributing factors, but the man had his own great cause—Captain Fetterman. The captain was indeed single, and Mrs. Pennington was captivated by the newcomer's presence. In fact, P.D. had just seen his future bride strolling the parade grounds and enjoying a tête-à-tête with the aggressive officer.

There was nothing subtle about Captain Fetterman's behavior. On the very night of his arrival at Fort Phil Kearny, Indians had opened fire on citizens working for a hay contractor, and the captain had wanted to do something about it. He immediately came up with a plan, approved by Colonel Carrington, to hobble some mules as bait near Big Piney Creek that Saturday night while he and an attachment waited in a cottonwood thicket for the Sioux raiders to show up. Captain Fetterman waited all night without anything happening. But as soon as he returned to the fort around nine in the morning, raiders ran off a cattle herd not more than a mile away. That minor failure did not discourage Captain Fetterman. A couple of days later while he was inspecting the woodcutting operation at the pinery, Indians opened fire on him but missed and then retreated. "They have no competence in arms," the brash captain declared to anyone who would listen, and Grace Pennington listened. "The Indians must be summarily punished and not next week or the week after—now!"

Captain Fetterman soon came up with a new, grander plan,

which had the support of two other officers and Mrs. Pennington (he told her about it during a Margaret Carrington tea party). He would take one hundred men, half of them mounted soldiers and half civilians on horseback, on an expedition to the Tongue River and punish Red Cloud in his own camp. Colonel Carrington squashed the plan, saying there were not enough horses, the terrain was too rough and unfamiliar, most of the men were not acquainted with Indian warfare, and there were just too many of the enemy out there. Captain Fetterman kept pressing his argument for aggressive action until the colonel finally dismissed him, essentially sending him to his room. When Mrs. Pennington told her Private Burrows about what happened, he sided with Colonel Carrington, though he had no love of the colonel, and called Captain Fetterman "a damn bloody fool."

The shouting match between Mrs. Pennington and Private Burrows at the flap of our tent came just seventy-two hours before their scheduled wedding. Mrs. Pennington stopped shouting first. She said that he had disgraced her with his tone of voice, if not his actual words. She marched off, perhaps to seek solace from Captain Fetterman. Toby was already off somewhere being teased by the Carrington boys, since his mother thought it was good for the boy to play with the children of officers. The private cursed under his breath for a minute and then came through the flap as if someone had shouted "Charge!" in the opposite direction. I was in my cradle, supposedly sleeping, but who could sleep through shouting like that? Mum was sitting on her bed, engrossed in Charles Dickens' *Great Expectations*, narrated by a character named Pip. I wondered if this Pip kept a diary, too.

"Damn her," Private Burrows said, collapsing on Mrs. Pennington's empty bed and putting a fist into her pillow. "I guess you heard everything."

Mum turned a page without comment.

"She acts like Fetterman won the Civil War all by himself," the private continued. "What about Custer and Sherman and Sheridan and Grant?"

"Not to mention my husband," Mum blurted out. But then she blushed and tried to hide her face behind her book.

"He was another bloody Civil War hero?"

Mum shook her head. "All I meant was that he was in that war, fighting the Confederates—at least that was what he was supposed to be doing."

"Just like we are supposed to be fighting Indians." Private Burrows sat up and stared at a hamper full of my dirty diapers. Mum often procrastinated about going to the laundry. "It's all a bunch of crap."

Mum pressed her book closer to her nose.

"It ain't the same thing, you know?" the private continued. "I don't care how many Rebels Fetterman shot. I figure his first real Indian fight will be his last. Grace can love another dead man. You say your husband was no hero, well, I bet he wasn't such an arrogant bastard, not like Fetterman."

Mum didn't even look up from her book.

"All right we don't need to talk about Fetterman or your husband. What's that you're reading anyway? I once tried to read a brigadier general's book on infantry tactics but it put me to sleep. Am I putting you to sleep, ma'am?"

"I was just reading."

"I noticed. *Great Expectations*, huh? Not in this man's Army."

"I'm sorry." She lowered her book. "You want to talk about Grace?"

"Hell, no. I hope the cussed captain and the rest of them hotheads take the field and get themselves killed."

"That's a strange thing for a solider to say."

"Maybe. But I'm just a private who tried to desert once. I even failed at that. Remember?"

"I remember. It's funny. Grace thinks I'm jealous of you and her. And you are jealous of her and Captain Fetterman."

"I don't want to talk about him. Right about now he's probably bragging to her about what he's going to do to Red Cloud, and all those shiny brass buttons are busting right off his spotless blue coat."

Mum lifted her book and tried to read again. No doubt she hoped he didn't want to talk anymore about anything. But Private P.D. Burrows was just getting started.

"So, you're jealous of Grace and me?" he asked. "You got a secret likin' to me, Miss Elizabeth?" He got off Mrs. Pennington's bed and sat on the edge of Mum's bed.

"It's Mrs. Duly." It was the first time since I was born that I heard Mum call herself Mrs. Duly, but I guess she thought it might keep him at bay.

"Right. Is your husband still with us? I mean are you a widow like Grace?"

"Mr. Duly is alive. And Grace is mistaken. I am not jealous of her and have no interest whatsoever in whether she marries you or not."

"That's plain enough. But a good-looking woman like you needs a man—I mean a man in the immediate vicinity."

"Stay in your own vicinity, Private Burrows. You're soon going to be a married man."

"I don't mean me, honest, Mrs. Duly."

"That's good, Mr. Burrows . . . Private Burrows."

"Call me Prairie Dog. That's what my friends call me, even if she don't. As for that marriage thing, I ain't so sure I want to . . . I mean even if Fetterman gets himself killed. She wants me to be a polished soldier . . . more than that she wishes I was some lick-spittle officer. I'm like you, Mrs. Duly. I hate it here at the fort. I want out."

"You are not like me, Prairie Dog . . . I mean, Private Burrows. The only thing we have in common is that we want to be someplace other than this God-forsaken fort."

"Hey, Mrs. Duly, that's something. And I'm damned glad to hear you say that."

As it turned out, Private P.D. Burrows and Grace Pennington were not ready to patch things up. Just forty-eight hours before their scheduled wedding, Mrs. Pennington went on a picnic with Captain Fetterman in some secluded meadow beyond Big Piney Creek. The day was sunny and unseasonably warm but still not the right season for picnicking in this part of the country. It's not clear if the captain was romantically inclined toward the widow or just wanted to prove to Colonel Carrington that there was no reason to live in immobilizing fear just because Red Cloud's spies were near enough to cough on the fort. The captain proved he could easily eat oysters (wasn't Grace saving them for the wedding?) with his left hand—even feed a few to the dainty mouth of his picnic guest—while pointing a service revolver at the bushes with his right hand.

"I beg your pardon," Mrs. Pennington said to Captain Fetterman, wiping her mouth with a spotless napkin. "I'm afraid I do not eat like a bird."

Captain Fetterman patted her cheek, perhaps even touching one of her irresistible earlobes, and replied, "No need to apologize, birdie dear. You are no longer in your cage."

She smiled and then boldly compared him to an experienced mountain lion that would never go hungry.

Captain Fetterman nodded his approval. "But the birds have nothing to fear from this *lion*," he said cleverly. "Only the men with feathers."

The men with feathers did not disturb the picnic any more than the ants did. As a result, Captain Fetterman became bolder. He at least kissed the widow's bare hand.

Colonel Carrington, who heard about that liaison from his

wife, became slightly perturbed that one of his officers would risk the life of a civilian, and a lady at that. "I do not think our William Judd Fetterman is in the habit of compelling strict obedience in every case to my rules," he told Mrs. Carrington, who told Mrs. Pennington, who told Captain Fetterman, who laughed it all off. "Carrington will recommend me for the Medal of Honor one day," the captain boasted.

Meanwhile, Private Burrows came back to the tent to see Mum and not his intended bride, who was out on a stroll in any case. "I don't mean to marry that damned captain's companion," he said. I'm not sure why he needed to share this information. But he did not act as if he wanted to substitute Mum for Mrs. Pennington. "How eager are you to leave here, Mrs. Duly?" he asked as he stood at attention a safe distance away.

"What do you mean?"

"I think we both could use a change of scenery. But I swear, Mrs. Duly, I have no designs on you myself."

I'm sure Mum was relieved to hear that, but she didn't say so. She didn't bury her nose in a book either. I suspect she was daydreaming about Virginia City.

Captain Fetterman continued to make plans for decisive action against the outside enemy, even though Fort Phil Kearny was undermanned and undersupplied and the officers and men were undertrained. Meanwhile, Grace Pennington, who was no doubt hearing about those plans and wondering if any of the captain's *other* plans concerned her, postponed the wedding two days so that it could better fit into the Carringtons' busy schedule.

"She needs more time to gauge the captain's feelings toward her," Private Prairie Dog said to Mum on another of his uninvited visits to the tent. "Is she ever in for a surprise."

"From Captain Fetterman?"

"From me."

"You will still marry her in two days won't you?"

"I won't spoil the surprise for you, Mrs. Duly."

The private never told his intended bride that the wedding was not just postponed but completely off. However, he showed it with action. He had his own plan, only part of which he told to Mum. On November 7, twenty-four hours before his rescheduled wedding, P.D. scheduled his second desertion in the middle of the night. What he told Mum was that there was a way for her to get safely clear of the fort and not at some undefined time in the fuzzy future but immediately.

"I'm not going to run away with you, Private Burrows," Mum said.

"That's the furthest thing from my mind, ma'am," he replied. "Opportunity is knocking and I'm just going to help you open the door."

"Why would you do that for me?"

"Because I want out and I know you want out. I can get you out, no strings attached."

The private said that there was a large wagon train that was up from Fort Reno and had managed to bypass Fort Phil Kearny as it headed for Fort C.F. Smith and then Virginia City. The wagon train party was making camp less than four miles to the north that very night and would be back rolling along the Bozeman Trail at dawn. Colonel Carrington knew about it and gave the wagon master his reluctant approval. The wagon master had pull with the secretary of war, P.D. insisted.

"But I haven't heard a thing about it," Mum said.

"Of course not. It's Carrington's big secret."

"I don't follow you."

"Carrington doesn't want you citizens to know. He wants to keep you all here. You've been here so long he considers you part of his Fort Phil Kearny family. You are his responsibility, and the colonel, as you know, is overprotective of those close to him. You never see Margaret Carrington dancing with Fetterman."

"Do you really mean to say there is an entire wagon train out there?"

"Yes, just waiting for us. I know Carrington's secret but he doesn't have to know our little secret. We can join that big wagon train. We both can. I know a way out."

Private Burrows did not claim to know the wagon master, but he said he was the bosom friend of a friend of the wagon master. This bosom friend owned two of the wagons, and he was willing to take on three passengers to Virginia City. "We don't even have to ride in the same wagon," P.D. said. "The third passenger would be your tadpole, of course. This is the chance for you to leave here safely with Dan-Dan. Excuse me, I mean Daniel."

The private explained how a soldier who owed him a favor would leave the back gate open, making it possible to easily slip out of the fort sometime after midnight. The obliging soldier would also have a horse waiting for us in the meadow. From there it was only a short ride to where the wagon train was camped for the night.

"I can't believe it," Mum said. "Tonight?"

"Yes, by noon tomorrow the wagon train will be too far away from here."

"And it's a big wagon train?"

"The biggest. Red Cloud wouldn't dare attack it."

"But there must be strings attached—perhaps not yours, but somebody else's."

"No. My friend on the train owes me this favor. It's a free ride, Mrs. Duly, all the way to Virginia City. All I ask is that no matter how long you know me you will never mention the names Grace Pennington and William Fetterman in the same breath, and if possible not even in separate breaths."

Mum wanted to believe it. She was feeling pretty angry with Grace Pennington for all that name calling and decided quickly she owed her no favors. "And you swear you have no wish to make me Mrs. Prairie Dog or anything like that?" Mum said.

"None whatsoever. You are indeed beautiful, Mrs. Duly, but you are already spoken for back in Chicago, and anyway, if there's one thing my time at Fort Phil Kearny has taught me, it's *I don't want to ever get hitched.*"

"And you are certain that my Daniel would be welcome on this wagon train?"

"Like an angel in heaven, ma'am."

"I won't go anywhere without him."

"We know that, Mrs. Duly."

"We? You mean you and your friend on the wagon train?"

"Yes. And everyone else."

Nobody asked me, of course, but it all sounded too good to be true. Being a baby of highly dependent means, I had to go along with the plan. Not that I would have objected if I was able, because I was willing to go anywhere Mum was willing to go. In fact, I could not have even imagined any kind of existence without her.

Mum managed to bring along my green blankie, though there wasn't time for packing. Private Burrows said there were plenty of clothes and everything else where we were going—to a friendly wagon bed. We left with only the clothes on our backs, in Mum's case layers of undergarments under that oversized brown dress Hanna gave her, in my case a cloth diaper and a baggy unfinished wool sweater that Mum was fashioning out of an Army blanket. She didn't even bring any extra diapers. Private Burrows assured her that there were other mothers with babies on the train as well as husbands who were Civil War veterans and armed to the teeth. So Mum wrapped me up in my green blankie topped off by her black shawl and carried her little bundle—me!—along the edges of the parade ground like a thief in the night.

Private Burrows had much to lose if somebody caught him making this second desertion attempt. He acted nervous all right, but not so much that he only thought of himself. He met us on time at the back gate, which was indeed unlocked. Mum was too flushed with excitement to hesitate, and I was calm, practically dozing in her arms. I saw no reason to be alarmed. If the guards caught us, I knew Colonel Carrington wouldn't do much to a mother and her child—we weren't deserters, we were civilians looking for fresh opportunity on the horizon. What was the worst that could happen? If we weren't allowed to go to the wagon train, we would simply end up back in our tent. Nobody was going to lock us in the guardhouse or shoot us at dawn.

The three of us exited the fort and didn't look back. With just enough moonlight to get by, we proceeded to the north meadow, where a tethered animal was waiting for us—a mule, not a horse, but that was a minor detail. The soldier who owed him a favor had come through. We now only had a ride of about three miles to the wagon train, Private Prairie Burrows assured us. Like a gentleman, the private made sure Mum was secure in the saddle and I was secure in her lap before he led the mule on foot. As we crossed Big Piney Creek, we heard hooting that made Mum clutch me tighter to her belly. Private Burrows insisted it really was an owl, not Indians pretending to be owls. He was a cool customer all right. Near Lodge Trail Ridge, he said the wagon train was just ahead but that he needed to rest. He led the mule into a clearing by a boulder with a painted cross on it. He told Mum to dismount and she did so after handing me to him. He allowed her to sip from his canteen and dab water on the corner of my mouth before taking a drink himself. What a gentleman! What a dirty lowdown polecat!

"How curious," Mum said. "Someone has put a cross on this rock."

Just then two Indian men popped out from behind the boulder. One of them seemed like a dark giant for he was larger than any of the Fort Phil Kearny soldiers and his face was plastered with mud. The other one was short but wide. He covered Mum's mouth with one hand and his own mouth with the other hand. Meanwhile, Private Burrows still had me, holding me like a sack of potatoes. Mum knew she was supposed to stay quiet but she couldn't help herself. P.D. might drop me on my head at any second.

"My baby!" Mum cried out, her arms outstretched, trying to reach me. She had her priorities right. If those were the last words I heard her say before they dashed our brains out, I would have died happy. Well, maybe not, but it's easy to say now.

The giant Indian took out a knife. I feared he might slit Mum's throat, but he only cleaned something off the blade that I hoped wasn't blood. Then he tapped his chest, and Prairie Dog Burrows handed me over to Mum, blankie and shawl and all. I thought the giant would now slit the throat of P.D., who after all was a private in the U.S. Army. But the giant ignored the private and reached out for me. He gave my baggy wool pullover sweater a disdainful tug. He must have known it was made from an Army blanket. He then moved his knife higher. He bypassed my throat. I thought he was after the patch of hair on the back of my head. Mum pulled me closer, though, and the giant put away his knife. I don't think he meant to scare me, but what hair I had must have been standing on end.

The giant spoke in his language and the shorter Indian replied. Prairie Dog just stood behind us taking sip after sip from his canteen as if his thirst had been building for days. The water seemed to settle his nerves.

"Didn't I do good?" he asked. "Didn't I deliver like I promised?"

"What?" said Mum. "What's going on? I don't see any wagon train."

"I wasn't talking to you, Mrs. Duly. I'm afraid the wagon train has moved on"

The giant glared at Prairie Dog, who immediately went back to sipping water.

"There is no wagon train," said the shorter Indian in almost perfect English. He rubbed his prominent nose, hooked like the beak of a vulture—ideal for ripping into the belly of a dead buffalo or a live human baby. "Dog is all-fired good liar."

"Coming from you, I take that as a compliment," said Prairie Dog. "It was your idea."

"Hold your tongue, Dog, or Wolf will cut it out. Time to go, Yellow Hair."

Mum let go of me with one hand to rub her fingers through her own hair. "I don't understand."

"Something wrong with my English?" the hook-nosed Indian asked.

"No. You speak very well. I . . . I just don't understand anything. You called me Yellow Hair. You can see the color in the moonlight?"

The Indian shook his head and smiled. "He saw you before. He named you."

"Named me? Who did?"

"Wolf."

"Who's Wolf?"

"Wolf Who Don't Dance. You will learn his name."

"I'm sorry, but . . . did you say 'Who Don't Dance'?"

"Yes. I know it should be Wolf Who Does Not Dance. I did not make the translation."

"Maybe I can just call him Wolf. Where is this Wolf?"

"Yes, Wolf. He's great Sioux warrior. He's cousin of Red Cloud. He's him." The Indian pointed to his larger companion, who had turned his back on us. "We go now. We follow him. You ride."

The giant called Wolf simply walked away into the trees. Private Burrows brought the mule over for Mum, who reluctantly reclaimed her black shawl and handed me over to the hook-nosed Indian. Even without the shawl, the green blankie on top of my sweater was making me too hot, and the Indian somehow sensed it. In any case he removed the blanket and had P.D. stuff it in a saddlebag that already contained at least two bottles. Private Burrows pushed Mum up into the saddle.

"You better not hurt my baby," Mum said. "Give him back."

The Indian did so. "I heal. I do not hurt. I am medicine man."

"And a spy for Red Cloud," commented Prairie Dog.

"What about him?" Mum asked.

"You mean, Dog? He is no worry. He does what he is told. He is Dog."

"No. I meant him." Mum pointed ahead to the broad back of the tall man moving silently through the woods.

"Don't worry. Wolf wants boy baby as much as he wants you, Yellow Hair."

Somehow it didn't feel so great to be wanted, even after I was back in Mum's arms. I was intent on crying, but then I saw the giant Wolf glance back, and I knew I best keep quiet. Maybe he and the hook-nosed, English-speaking Indian were related to those warriors back in Kansas who were known to bash in the heads of infants who squawked. I would not squawk.

"Tarnation," Prairie Dog said, but in a whisper. "Why didn't he bring horses! I thought mighty warriors rode everywhere they went."

"Not everywhere," said the medicine man. "This wasn't a

raid and sometimes Wolf likes to walk."

"But she gets to ride? No need to scold me. I understand. He doesn't want to wear her out before she even gets to his tepee."

Prairie Dog (I sure will stop calling him Private Burrows) led the mule by the reins while Mum held me between herself and the saddle horn. The hook-nosed Indian followed us. We didn't move fast but we moved steady. I didn't know where we were going exactly, but I was certain it would be to a place where the soldiers never dared go. I was worried of course, but not so much that I couldn't ask Mum—in my own way—for some of her milk.

When we finally stopped on the other side of the trees, it was not to rest exactly. Prairie Dog built a small fire but nobody brought out any food. Instead, the hook-nosed Indian made Mum, with me in her arms, stand in front of the flames. Prairie Dog stepped back and stood next to the mule. The one called Wolf turned around to stare at us. I stared back (his bird's-claw earring immediately caught my eye), although out of the corner of my eye I kept seeing those little flames dance. I couldn't help but think there was some other devious purpose for that fire. Mum lowered her eyes as she did with all men who stared too much.

At first Wolf mostly looked at Mum, his hard gray eyes running over her brown dress as if he were judging horseflesh. He didn't touch her, though. After a while he stopped looking like a giant to me—he was big, but not that big. So when he turned his attention to me, I was no longer thinking that he might roast me alive for an early breakfast. I was still glad he kept his distance, though, because the four necklaces around his bull neck were strings of vicious looking teeth. Most of the teeth hung over his breastplate, which was decorated with shiny brass beads. I preferred to look at his earring. But then I noticed something even more fascinating atop his head—a single upright golden eagle feather sticking out of his braided hair.

"Meet Wolf," said the hook-nosed Indian. "Again."

I'm pretty good about remembering faces but I never saw a face with so much mud on it before. He didn't look like the kind of guy anybody dared ask to wash up a bit before presenting himself. His dirty face, dark eyes, square jaw, and jutting cheekbones gave him a passing resemblance to rambunctious George I after a whipping from Old Man Gunderson. But there was someone this Wolf fellow looked like even more who I had seen somewhere along the trail. I just couldn't remember who or where.

When Wolf poked my forehead, I held my tongue, but Mum let out a noticeable gasp. Wolf jerked back his hand. There was no need to, of course, and he bared his teeth at Mum before returning his attention to me. He pulled up my sweater to see everything that was under it. Mum murmured a bit as the big Indian studied my form and then lightly tapped me on the forehead, nose, and chin. With little difficulty he pried open my mouth to eye my tongue and gums (I assume, for I had no teeth yet). I was glad to have no teeth that he might want to put on a fifth necklace. Finally he poked my bare belly.

"*Wankala,*" Wolf said.

"What's he saying about Daniel?" Mum asked, holding me a little tighter.

"Wolf is talking about the boy's belly," the hook-noosed Indian said. "He says it's tender and soft."

"Baby bellies are supposed to be soft," Mum said.

"Not the babies of Lakota."

"Well, he's not a Lakota baby. He's my baby. You tell Wolf that."

"That would not be smart."

"Who says?

"I know Wolf. You don't tell him too many things."

"Well, you should tell him I'm married."

"He knows. Dog got a tongue-lashing for telling him that."

Wolf clearly didn't understand what they were saying and made no response when his name was mentioned in English. He showed no interest in holding me himself, but he didn't want Mum to take me away either. Maybe my belly wasn't much, but something about me pleased him because I saw a twinkle in at least his right eye. Mum seemed to see the twinkle, too, when she glanced at him. He didn't look back at her. I was still the focus of his attention. Finally he adjusted my sweater so that my middle was covered up, but then he wanted me to squeeze his thumbs. After that he sized up my small feet, paying special attention to how large the arches were. He wasn't trying to take me away from Mum or anything, so she just kept holding me up for his inspection, which didn't look like it would end any time soon. She decided to talk to the Indian who knew her language.

"What's your name anyway?" Mum asked.

The hook-nosed Indian squeezed his nostrils together. "You think it's Big Nose, don't you, Yellow Hair?"

"I wasn't thinking anything of the kind."

"Well, it's not Big Nose. Greasy Nose is my name. Yes, Greasy Nose. You think my nose is not clean, don't you?"

"No. I don't think anything about your nose. I . . ."

Greasy Nose laughed through his nose. "I was born on the Greasy Grass in what your people call Montana. That explains my name, in part. And I put my nose in everything. That explains the rest. My mother was one-quarter white. My father took her as his wife from a trader on the Missouri River."

"She did a good job of teaching you English."

"She didn't teach me. She drowned in river."

"Oh. That's too bad."

"When I was young man I take wife from St. Louis. She

teach me good before the Butcher shot her down at Blue Water Creek."

"I'm sorry. This butcher was the one who provided you with meat?"

"General William Harney. We call him the Butcher. He killed many Lakota."

"I really am sorry, eh . . . Mr. Greasy Nose."

"No mister. I am Greasy Nose only. Not a great name, but can't change it now. All the Oglala know it. So do the Brulé and the Hunkpapa, too. All the Lakota Sioux know Greasy Nose. I am Red Cloud's favorite medicine man and, yes, spy."

"And *wintke*," added Prairie Dog.

"What's that?" Mum asked.

"You'd never guess it by looking at him now, but Greasy Nose sometimes wears a dress. He's a would-be woman."

"A better translation," said Greasy Nose, rubbing his nose, "is a two-souls-person."

Mum was about to ask this complex Indian another question, but Wolf cut her off. He was done examining me and was angry about something. He said loud Sioux words to Greasy Nose who chose not to translate. But I think Wolf was sick of hearing English words or so many words without mention of his name. Mum started to back away from him, because she knew something about angry men. He grabbed one of her arms while she continued to hold me with the other one.

"Do what you like to me, but don't harm my baby!" she told him.

I don't think she meant the first part, but it didn't matter. Her words made me feel good. To Wolf her words meant nothing. He gently pinched the flesh of her upper arm and then used his thumb and index finger to measure the size of her wrist. I guess not everything pleased him because he suddenly tossed her hand away like a fisherman would an undersized trout. Mum was just glad to be able to hold me in both arms again. She clutched me to her chest while Wolf continued his examination of her. He poked her in the shoulder first, then the ribs, and finally the belly.

"*Wankala,*" he said.

"I am not soft," she said. "And I didn't say you could touch me."

But she did not protest when he put a meaty claw on her right hip and then moved lower still, lifting the hem of her brown dress briefly to peek at her ankles and calves. He grunted his approval, at least it sounded to me like approval. Then he circled around her for a peek at her backside. I heard another grunt.

When he came around again to her front, Mum dared to look him over, giving him a taste of his own medicine. Wolf allowed it for a while but then rattled several of his tooth necklaces and turned his back on her. He stamped twice on the little fire before lifting each leg in turn to check on the soles of his beaded moccasins. He motioned for Prairie Dog Burrows to finish the job of extinguishing the flames and then walked away as if we had all offended him.

"He looks so familiar," Mum commented. "I don't guess he has ever been to Chicago?"

"No," said Greasy Nose. "Get on the mule."

"Do you really wear a woman's dress?"

"At times. To be as a woman is not all the time. By the way that dress is too big for you?"

"My friend Hanna lent it to me. She was with my first wagon train."

"Quiet yourself now. Wolf says no more talk."

"You do everything he says?"

"Yes. And sometimes he does what I say. I have the Power."

"The what?"

"No more questions. Help her, Dog."

Prairie Dog Burrows threw dirt on the last flickering flame and then boosted Mum into the saddle as she still clutched me. She wasn't about to hand me over again to that two-time deserter and evil liar. He muttered to himself and tugged the reins to get the mule moving again. It looked to me like P.D. had no greater status with Wolf and Greasy Nose than he had back at the fort with Colonel Carrington and Captain Fetterman.

As for what status Mum and me had, that was hard to say. Certainly we were captives, but nobody was threatening us or beating us. Still, we knew better than to try to run away or to squawk too much. This Wolf fellow was clearly someone you didn't want to cross. As our small group continued up and down the nearly naked hills, Greasy Nose hooted behind us like an owl. Maybe he was warning night animals that we were coming or else he was alerting any other Indians out there that we were friendly. He didn't explain. He seemed done talking for the night. Prairie Dog wasn't saying anything either. Wolf no doubt had told both of them to hold their flapping tongues.

Mum leaned forward on the saddle anyway and addressed the horrible ex-private, who was now as lowdown in my eyes as Philip Kittridge. In Mum's eyes, too. "You are a dog, mister," she said. "But calling you a dog isn't fair to the real dogs. You're a snake."

"Yes. Mrs. Duly. No matter what you call me, I've heard worse."

"How can you live with yourself?"

"I ain't exactly. I'm gonna be living with the Sioux now, just like you, ma'am. Of course, it was my choice."

"But why? You were a soldier."

"I *was* a soldier, ma'am. I switched sides."

"That makes you a traitor."

"Yes. A deserter and a traitor and a dog and a snake. But I prefer to think of myself as a white renegade. It has a certain romantic ring to it, don't you think?"

"Romantic ring? I think you're horrible. You walked out on Grace, too!"

"As you did, Mrs. Duly. You left your tent mate without so much as a fare-thee-well."

"How could I? It was our secret. You told me not to say a word to her, which is understandable since you were running out on her."

"No matter. She wasn't true to me."

"How can you even speak of what's true or not?"

"I might lie some, Mrs. Duly, but that don't mean I don't know what's true. Anyway, if you look at it in a particular way, you might say I did Grace a favor. She won't be Mrs. Burrows, of course, but we all know that wouldn't have worked out. She wanted an officer! Well, now she can have Fetterman, if the son of a bitch will have her. Of course, I don't feel like Fetterman has a future in the United States Army. Neither does Greasy Nose. And he should know. He's not only a medicine man and a spy but also our prophet."

"Our prophet?"

"Sure. You know. The prophet for our side—the Lakota, or Sioux."

"I am not on their side and neither are you. Land sakes! We're white."

"You'll get over it in time, Mrs. Duly. As for me, I'd rather face the devil himself than the wrath of Colonel Carrington and Mrs. Pennington."

The conversation came to a halt when Wolf abruptly paused in his walking, looked back, and shouted something that sounded like an imperial command. Prairie Dog knew enough Sioux to understand. He shut up and began pulling the mule along double time.

Riding a mule, with the help of Mum and even Prairie Dog, wasn't much more difficult for me than riding in a wagon bed. It just made my backside a little sorer. Wolf Who Don't Dance obviously enjoyed walking and he expected the rest of us to keep up. When we moved too slowly or otherwise dawdled, he came back to stamp his feet and sometimes to wave a spear. But his spear waving was not particularly threatening. In fact it almost seemed comical because he resembled an oversized child throwing a tantrum. His intention was clearly not to stick that sharp point into the soft bellies of Mum and me. It even amused Greasy Nose, who would snort and slap his knee during the spear waving episodes.

On the fourth such episode, it suddenly hit me—no, not the spear. I remembered where I had seen this large Indian with the dark eyes and tooth necklaces before. He had approached Mum and me with that very same spear while we were huddled in the back of the Kittridge spring wagon on the trail between Forts Reno and Phil Kearny. He had seemed so menacing then, at least at first. Mum remembered, too, at about the same time, because she suddenly shifted me entirely to her left arm and began waving the spear holder away with her right hand. "Shoo, Shoo," she shouted at him, just as she had done the other time.

This time, he held his ground. But he lowered his spear, raised his eyebrows, shook his square jaw, and mumbled a few words in his own language to Greasy Nose. Later, as the five of us proceeded at a brisk pace on the Indian trail toward the Tongue River camp, Greasy Nose translated the words as follows: "Yellow Hair is crazy woman."

Mum fell asleep once or twice on the ride, but Greasy Nose didn't let her fall out of the saddle. Finally we stopped for a rest and a meal. I breastfed as Mum showed her back to the others. Greasy Nose and Prairie Dog gnawed at some pemmican, a mixture of unknown meat and marrow fat that the medicine man stored in a rawhide bag. Wolf chose not to eat any. Instead, he slipped away to hunt for something with his spear.

Mum cut my feeding short because she wanted to take advantage of the absence of Wolf to ask the other two men questions in English. The first thing she wanted to know was what Wolf's intentions were. Prairie Dog obliged with a grin and a quick answer: "To make you his squaw, his No. 3 squaw to be exact." Greasy Nose explained that Wolf already shared his tepee with his first wife, Pretty Bear, and his second wife, Wounded Eagle.

"Land sakes!" Mum said. "He's like a Mormon."

"Or one of those Arab sheiks with his harem," suggested Prairie Dog.

"I won't be his squaw," Mum said.

"Right," said Prairie Dog. "And the Sioux don't like buffalo."

Mum squeezed me tight, a bit too hard. But I understood her fear. She had not rejected Old Man Gunderson and a temple in Salt Lake City so that she could end up with this Wolf and a tepee in the wilderness.

"There are other children in the tepee?" Mum asked.

"No, Yellow Hair," Greasy Nose said. "One wife is too fragile to bear children, the other is barren."

"That's why he wanted a third squaw," said Prairie Dog. "He needs a son."

"You mean my Daniel?"

"For starters."

Mum didn't like Prairie Dog's tone. While Wolf had seen her and me in the back of the Kittridge spring wagon and had apparently liked what he saw, he hadn't gotten us then. The only reason he had us now was because of Prairie Dog's treachery.

"You're a snake," Mum told him once more. "You arranged this whole thing, didn't you?"

"I'm no matchmaker. Greasy Nose was the chief middleman, so to speak. Ain't that right, medicine man, or should I say medicine woman?"

"I saved your life once, Dog, but a word from me and Wolf would cut you from ear to ear. Don't forget that."

"Sure. Sure. Have I ever criticized any of your dresses?"

"That's true. You fear my Power. Do go on and tell Yellow Hair the story."

"Quite a guy, isn't he, Mrs. Duly? He did save my life. Red Cloud favored killing me and my three associates back there on the Bozeman Trail, you know after the four of us left Fort Reno without permission and ran into his warriors. Greasy Nose stepped up and talked the big chief out of it, saying that we would be of more use alive warning others to stay off the trail. I may be a snake, Mrs. Duly, but when a man saves my life I don't forget it. That's why we started working together."

"Working together?"

"Yes, ma'am. But not right away. You see he was doing some spying on Fort Phil Kearny to keep his friend Red Cloud informed about soldier activity. Every now and then a guard would spot him, sometimes even wearing a dress to throw us off, but none of us really tried too hard to catch him. I mean we were in the fort. What could one lone Indian do? Then one day I was on guard duty and I recognized him as Red Cloud's right-hand man, the guy who saved my life. He actually left me a note giving me directions where to meet him. I knew my life wasn't in danger because he had already saved it. And so we met. In fact it was at the boulder with a cross, the same place I took you, Mrs. Duly."

"And you decided just like that to turn traitor and feed him information to pass on to Red Cloud?"

"Well, it wasn't *just* like that. You see, I joined the Army to get out of a little jam I was in after the soldiers came back from the war, but I never was a natural born soldier, and the Indians never done anything to me personally. But then I stopped. Told Greasy Nose I couldn't do it no more. After all, I fell head over heels in love with Grace Pennington, who as you recall had just lost her Quaker husband. And she wanted to marry this poor little private. Hell, I was kind of glad the Indians had killed her husband, but I was prepared to fight the whole bloody Sioux Nation for that widow woman."

"How honorable," said Mum.

"Yes, ma'am, I was right proud of myself. But then along came Fetterman and you already know that whole tale of Grace going behind my back to . . . well, it's all too painful to discuss. In light of her betrayal, I went back to working with Greasy Nose here. I was hoping I could provide the right information, you know information that could get Fetterman killed."

"You would see your fellow soldiers die?"

"Well, mostly just Fetterman. I never kilt nobody—no soldier boy or Sioux boy. Of course during a war such as the one we're in right now, men got to die. I realize that. But I'd just as soon let the other fellows do the killing and the bloodletting."

"Such a noble white renegade!"

"I like to think so. I did almost shed a tear over Adam Gray, because we often shared guard duty. He's the fellow who caught me in a secret parley with Greasy Nose. I had no choice but to help Private Gray capture the spy. Of course I then helped Greasy Nose make his escape from the guardhouse and the fort before Carrington could question him."

"Private Gray was also the one killed while guarding the woodcutters."

"Yes, one of them. We had to target Adam. He knew I didn't really want Greasy Nose caught, that I was really aiding the spy. After Greasy Nose escaped, Adam threatened to spill the beans on me to Carrington unless I gave him most of my Army pay and, well, a few other things I couldn't afford to give up. Greasy Nose is no killer, though, and neither am I. But plenty of young Sioux bucks volunteered for the job. The other dead guard just got in the line of fire and served as target practice."

"You may as well have pulled the trigger yourself."

"The young bucks used bows and arrows."

"You know what I mean. You got him killed."

"Well, Adam shouldn't have been nosing around in my business or become so greedy. Once he was out of the way, I was safe to keep working with Greasy Nose. And because of our working relationship, Greasy Nose was able to devise the plan, fake wagon train and all, to get you and Wolf together. That Wolf must see something in your yellow hair, Mrs. Duly, that just don't do anything for me."

Prairie Dog laughed at what he thought was his cleverness. Mum didn't join in, of course, and neither did Greasy Nose. Prairie Dog had earned Mum's disrespect. I suppose Mum could have also hated Greasy Nose for masterminding the fake wagon train and all, but she wasn't thinking of that just then.

"Land sakes!" Mum blurted out. "I just remembered. That same day Private Gray was killed, Phil Kittridge was out hunting and one of your murdering friends tried to kill him, too."

"That's right, you took a shine to that boy. I assure you, Mrs. Duly, what happened with him was strictly an unplanned sideshow, even if Phil hates Red Cloud's crowd even more than he hates Carrington and the Army."

"The Sioux killed his brother."

"I know, I know. I was with the wagon train at the time, remember? Anyway, Phil was all right. I'm glad he lived through young Two Feathers' counting coup on him and then got the hell out of this dangerous country with them cowboys."

Mum switched my position in her arms. I think her left arm had fallen asleep. She suddenly noticed that her dress was still a little too open to the fresh air on top. She straightened things up. Neither Prairie Dog nor Greasy Nose seemed to notice. They were concentrating on chewing their pemmican.

Mum had one more question. It kind of disappointed me, but I guess she couldn't help herself. "Do you think Phil, Mr. Kittridge, really got away?" she asked.

"Likely," said Prairie Dog with his mouth full. "I told Greasy Nose about how every man in that outfit had at least one powerful Remington and two Colt pistols and knew how to handle them. Greasy Nose in turn told Red Cloud. Now the mighty chief realizes his people on the Tongue and Powder rivers could certainly use the beef, but he wasn't about to send his warriors up against that firepower—at least not between here and Fort C.S. Smith where Story and his men would be expecting them. So maybe, ma'am, if you look at it a particular way, you could say I probably saved your Phil Kittridge's life with my traitorous activity."

"It's no matter to me what happens to him."

"Of course not. Now you have Wolf Who Don't Dance in your life—a mighty warrior, a friend to Greasy Nose, and some kind of cousin of the great Red Cloud. Of course most all of the important Sioux males have brothers and sisters and cousins right and left, not to mention many wives."

Mum looked as if she was ready to ring Prairie Dog's neck. But then out of nowhere came Wolf. He knew how to walk quiet. And he knew how to kill. The point of his spear was still sticking right through a rabbit with the biggest ears I had ever seen in my life. I decided right then and there that I would put off eating meat for as long as I could. Wolf immediately shouted something that made Mum jump even though she didn't know his language.

"I sure hope you can cook a good rabbit, Yellow Hair," Greasy Nose said.

Mum did her best. Wolf was too hungry to complain. After that, we just kept on going until we reached Chief Red Cloud's camp of five hundred lodges on the Tongue River. Wolf washed the mud off his face at the river. Then he pulled Mum off the mule and smeared red paint on her unblemished forehead. Next, he removed one of his tooth necklaces and slipped it over Mum's head, her yellow hair now no longer bunched up on top but mostly falling down to her shoulders. I wasn't sure if Wolf had removed Mum's hairpin or it had fallen out on its own. But Greasy Nose picked the hairpin up and tucked it into his deerskin shirt.

"Does this make me look more like an Indian woman?" Mum asked.

"Not really," said Greasy Nose.

The medicine man explained that the forehead mark and the wolf-tooth necklace would show everyone in the village that Mum belonged to Wolf. Almost as an afterthought, Wolf spread a little red paint on my tiny forehead. Without a doubt, this mighty warrior could do whatever he wanted to Mum and me. We were at his mercy.

After the river, we walked past tepees while Greasy Nose hooted like an owl. That brought other Indians to their tepee flaps and even outside. They greeted us in passing with animal sounds and the yelps of human babies. I thought the men, women, and children we saw were all staring at Mum and me, mostly Mum. Soon we reached a tepee that had a moon and the sun and the seven stars that form the Great Bear star pattern. We went inside, and I knew it belonged to Greasy Nose because I saw many kinds of medicines and good luck charms and at least three deerskin dresses. The medicine man gave Prairie Dog two bottles of what the white men call red-eye—his immediate reward for successfully delivering Mum and me to Wolf. And then Greasy Nose gave Mum some kind of ointment.

"It cures saddle sores," he said. "For the boy, too."

"I suppose I should thank you but . . ."

"No need. A medicine man does what a medicine man must do. I know Wolf is in a hurry. I'll show you my dresses some other time."

As we continued through the village, people came out to watch us at every step. I saw a dozen children point at me as if I had two heads or something. At one point, Wolf sent Prairie Dog and the mule away. Prairie Dog told Mum that he was going to stake down the mule someplace and then go to the outskirts of the village where he was supposed to find his designated tepee—a small, plain bachelor's quarters. Mum remembered to reclaim my green blankie out of the saddlebag. Even in times of stress she can be so thoughtful.

"I'll see you later, Mrs. Duly," Prairie Dog said.

"Why?" Mum asked.

"Well because, believe it or not, Wolf allows me in his tepee at times. I've picked up enough Sioux so that I can do a little translating for him when Greasy Nose or Little Bull aren't around. I mean if he wants you to understand him, he will need a translator. That's assuming he wants to talk to you at all."

Mum turned her back on Prairie Dog, which seemed to keep Wolf from yelling something at her. Wolf motioned her to come quickly. We still had many tepees to go before we reached Wolf's tepee, which was to become *our* tepee. It was bigger than most of the others with a pack of primitive wolves painted near the entrance flap. Wolf led us around a fire pit in the center of the tepee. The green and blue flames looked almost cheerful. He made it clear that it was now time to rest and directed us to a great pile of buffalo hides in the back of the tepee. I sank into the warmth and softness with my green blankie. I hadn't felt so cozy since my early days in the womb. Mum collapsed next to me, only to notice that an Indian woman was sleeping soundly nearby. Only the woman's raven black hair showed over her blankets, but somehow that was enough to tell me that this was Wolf's first wife, Pretty Bear. Mum raised herself to her knees because she heard a noise beyond Pretty Bear. It was the second wife, Wounded Eagle, lying on her back asleep with her mouth open and seemingly one eye open too. In any language, she was snoring.

Mum was too tired to worry about the presence of Wolf's two wives. She lay down and wrapped her black shawl around me as if it could provide some kind of protection. I wiggled until my head was pressed into her nearest armpit. I thought I would dose off right away, but then I heard someone yell. I opened my eyes to see Wounded Eagle standing over us with her hands on her hips and her short dirty brown hair hanging down in front of her face but only partially covering her fiery eyes and some of her many pockmarks. She looked at me as if she wanted to stamp me out like the flames of a campfire. But her look for Mum was worse. She didn't so much resemble a wounded eagle as a bloody-beaked vulture ready to dive into some dead meat. Fortunately Wolf shouted two harsh Sioux words at wife number two and I don't think it was "good night." She grabbed a blanket and left, I assume to sleep under the moon and the stars.

Despite this rude beginning, it didn't take long for Mum to fit into the family life. She didn't have much of a choice. She soon learned how things stood. As a wife-in-waiting, she has little more than slave status as far as the two real wives are concerned. Pretty Bear has first wife status and combs her long black hair instead of butchering or processing meats and hides. She wears a half-dozen necklaces, only one of which has a wolf tooth on it, and spends most of her time fashioning new necklaces from shell beads, animal claws, antlers, horns, and teeth (occasionally using more gentle teeth, such as from an elk). She rarely cooks and she eats daintily, preferring to nibble and crunch on nuts and berries and Indian turnip rather than the parts of a buffalo. She speaks little and smiles often, especially whenever Wolf walks into the tepee. She keeps smiling as she shoos Mum and me out of the tepee every afternoon to be alone with her husband. Otherwise she doesn't give Mum many orders.

Giving orders is the job of the second wife, Wounded Eagle, who is the older sister of Pretty Bear. Smallpox has ruined whatever looks Wounded Eagle once had and that combined with her heavy feet and bad temper kept her from marrying one of the eligible young braves in the village. Finally, Wolf took her as a second wife, apparently mainly to please the first wife. Wounded Eagle was doing most of the butchering, cooking, washing, cleaning, and complaining until Mum came along, so she is no doubt relieved and delighted that Mum is here to be ordered around. Only Wounded Eagle doesn't show it. She yells all the time in a language Mum can't understand and then blames Mum for not following her orders fast enough. To prod Mum along or to punish her, she will strike out at Mum with anything handy—a horn spoon or ladle, a bone shovel or hoe, Wolf's war club or spear, a moccasin or bracelet, buffalo parts or buffalo dung, even me! More than once, Wounded Eagle has manipulated my feet so that it seems like I am kicking Mum about the chest and belly. She could have given the brat Toby Pennington lessons.

Still, I must admit, Wounded Eagle generally lets me do as I please on her watch. Pretty Bear is the same way. In the warm tepee I crawl around naked (Mum is back to wearing the black shawl again), with pretty much free rein of the place. They don't believe in giving a baby a lot of silly rules and discipline. On occasion one or the other bundles me up, sticks me in a cradleboard, and takes me out so that I can watch Mum slave away at some chore or just so they can show me off to the other women in the village. What Greasy Nose said about them is true—neither Pretty Bear nor Wounded Eagle has been able to bear a child for Wolf Who Don't Dance. Sometimes each of the Indian wives acts as if I am her own baby boy, although it is rare that I forget who is my actual mother. I mean Mum is the one who holds me the way I'm used to being held and the one I rely on for breast milk. I have no real desire to taste Indian food yet. I still call her Mum-mum. Wounded Eagle is "Wo-Wo." Pretty Bear is "Be-Be." Thankfully, the wives don't call me "White Face" or "Red Bottom." To them, I am *"Wanbli-cikala-mato,"* which translates to "Little Eagle Bear." Not wanting me to forget my roots, Mum recites memorized passages from Charles Dickens and Henry Wadsworth Longfellow and calls me "Daniel," but usually in a whisper when the others aren't listening too closely.

As for the patriarch of the tepee, he spends most of his time away from home, sometimes hunting, sometimes on vision quests, sometimes smoking tobacco with his fellow warriors, sometimes conferring with Greasy Nose, sometimes visiting with his cousin Red Cloud, sometimes ambushing soldiers from Fort Phil Kearny. When he is home and not sharing blankets with the smiling Pretty Bear and not pretending to listen to the frowning Wounded Eagle, he likes to sit cross-legged across from Mum and watch her play with me. He has brought Mum ten assorted feathers (but no Eagle feather yet) for tickling my toes and has brought me three different kinds of rattles, which I usually put in my mouth when nobody is looking but shake wildly when he is around looking for entertainment. I tug Mum's wolf-tooth necklace and Wolf's necklaces but never too hard. I know my own strength and don't want to break a necklace, which would upset him and cause more work for Pretty Bear. He calls Mum "Yellow Hair," the name that he came up with when he first saw her in the back of the Kittridge spring wagon. Of course, it didn't take much imagination to come up with that name. I'm sure Wolf wants to share his blankets with Mum, too, but he is not at all forceful about it the way the so-called civilized Philip Kittridge used to be. One day, if things go according to Wolf's plans, Yellow Hair will officially become his third wife and bear him many sons. But until that time comes, I have a unique and special status around this family tepee. Anyway, I'm not complaining.

I don't get out much and Mum only gets out for certain kinds of labor, so we don't have much contact with other villagers. But they all seem reasonably happy. Winter is fast approaching, but there are plenty of hides and blankets, thanks mostly to the buffalo. None of Red Cloud's Oglala Sioux are starving, again thanks mostly to the buffalo but also to the elk, deer, and occasional dog, along with a few civilized cows acquired in raids. In fact, many Minneconjou Sioux have moved in nearby, their lodges full of warriors eager to participate in Red Cloud's War. No man, woman, or child seems worried that the soldiers will venture out from behind the walls of Fort Phil Kearny and attack this camp or one of the other Indian camps in the Powder River Country. I'm not sure Red Cloud even puts out guards regularly. Colonel Carrington's reluctance to commit troops to the offensive is well known and it actually makes sense—his soldiers are hopelessly outnumbered. Sometimes I forget that there is a war going on between the white men and the red men. I mean it's much easier to forget here than it was back at the fort. I see men tossing bone dice by hand and women doing the same in a basket or bowl. They are gambling for twigs and sticks or perhaps more. I see boys and young men shooting arrows or throwing spears through spiderweb-style hoops that are made of rawhide, bark, and beads. I see ball kicking, stone throwing, top spinning, sledding on buffalo ribs, catching deer bones with a needle, rattling of turtle shells and gourds, whistling, singing, and dancing. There are spirit songs and dances and medicine songs and more dances.

Almost all the Indians here dance, as naturally as I crawl. But not Wolf Who Don't Dance. He lives up to his name. While he on rare occasion sings in a low voice a brief personal song about love or war, he does not do dancing of any kind. Greasy Nose contends that early in life his friend, at the time called Bean Shooter, had two left feet and could not follow the rhythm of the drum. His name was changed to Left Feet. When still a young man, he took part in a ceremonial dance in which he wore the pelt of a wolf, the animal that had chosen to be his spirit guide in a dream. It did not go well. The elders could not help but notice that Left Feet danced with his legs like a white man instead of with his individual muscles like a red man. And then he tripped over his own feet, stumbled past a line of young giggling girls, and fell off a cliff. Left Feet lay on his back for many months tended to by dozen of healers, each with his or her own medicine bag full of roots, bark, animal substances, fetishes, charms, and herbs. Lying there with his own thoughts and prayers for so long, he vowed to do two things if he recovered and could once more walk and run and ride: (1) Never try to dance again; and (2) Take as a wife the one girl who had not laughed at him—Pretty Bear. His recovery happened because of the good medicine of Greasy Nose. Pretty Bear immediately consented to marry him. And Wolf Who Don't Dance, as he was now known, became a great Oglala warrior. And still he does not dance.

Greasy Nose has many stories to tell, but he does not come by the family tepee often because Wounded Eagle treats him like an outsider. She believes that he is an evil *wintke* who is trying to steal away her husband and all her nice three-skin dresses. Greasy Nose says that Wolf's second wife does not understand his nature and that he has no interest in anybody's husband or wife.

"Double Face Woman came into my mother's vision when I was in the womb and blessed me with a Power that is supernatural," Greasy Nose told Mum on one of his rare but welcome visits. "She said it was the wish of the Great Spirit, *Wakan Tanka,* for me to be a *wintke,* and so I crawled out of the womb to be that which I am. Today I am held in awe and reference by all the Oglalas for my Power includes the gift of healing and of prophecy. The thing is it is not all the time that I want to be as a woman. And that is a good thing, Yellow Hair, because with a name and a nose like mine it is hard to be accepted as a woman, no matter how pretty the dress."

Greasy Nose continues to do some spying for Red Cloud, too. He says that he often wears a dress while on his spy missions near the fort. He feels that the soldiers, should they catch him again, would not be so hard on him if he does not look like a fierce warrior—which he certainly is not.

Prairie Dog, unfortunately, comes around more often. Since he can't show his face around Fort Phil Kearny anymore, he can no longer serve as "eyes" for the Sioux and is of no use to Red Cloud. But Wolf Who Don't Dance is of course grateful that P.D. brought him Mum and also finds the former private of use (just because he is a white man) at interpreting the moods of Mum and relaying them to him. The traitor/deserter/snake knows just enough Sioux words to make a few translations and also is counted on (again because of his pale face) to make Yellow Hair (Mum) and even Little Eagle Bear (me) feel more at home in the tepee. In truth, he mostly makes things up instead of translating accurately, and Mum and I detest him.

And then there is the great Red Cloud. He has been the honored guest at the family tepee only one time because he is a busy man, what with trying to plot the destruction of the forts on the Bozeman Trail and that kind of thing. Even Wounded Eagle was at her best behavior that time the Oglala headman came over for some buffalo tongue and testicles. He stands about six feet tall, slightly shorter than Wolf Who Don't Dance but with a more commanding presence, which is saying something since Wolf is a mighty warrior in his own right. Nobody would giggle at Red Cloud if he happened to dance badly. He has proved himself to be an exceptional *blotahunka,* or war leader, and all the pale faces (yes, like mine) know his name.

When he spoke that night in our tepee, everybody listened, including Mum and I, and we didn't understand a word he said. But he didn't *need* to say much. He was surprisingly quiet during the meal, chewing his food thoroughly and only responding to questions. Prairie Dog was not invited of course, but he did provide a bottle of whiskey he had stolen from the post surgeon on the night he broke out of the fort with Mum and me. Red Cloud licked the cork but did not otherwise take a drink. Red Cloud did appreciate a nice face, though. While he didn't stare openly at Pretty Bear, he clearly appreciated her smile, whether it was for him or her husband. And he appreciated Mum's appearance, several times gesturing at her yellow hair, and upon getting an understanding smile from Mum, actually laid a hand on her head for a good half minute. After the meal, Red Cloud stood over me for even longer than that as I lay on a buffalo blanket. I shook one of my rattles at him, but then offered him my best little smile to show him it was all in fun; I didn't want him to think I was simulating the rattling of a saber or anything like that.

"*Anho,*" he said, poking me in the not-so-soft-anymore belly with a surprisingly sharp fingernail but then half smiling, showing me it was not like getting speared to death. Mum and me never let on that we were there that day on the Bozeman Trail when Red Cloud boldly stepped in front of the emigrant wagons to converse (through interpreter Little Bull) with self-appointed wagon master Philip Kittridge. That talk, of course, had turned into a fight, during which Luther Kittridge somehow fell into Sioux hands and ended up a mutilated mess. It didn't seem like proper dinner conversation and anyway Mum didn't know his language and I spoke my own baby language. The next day, when Prairie Dog showed up at the tepee to see if all his whiskey had been drunk up, Mum asked him about that word *Anho*. She had been wondering about it all night. "Not sure on an exact translation," admitted Prairie Dog. "But as best I can figure it, ma'am, Chief Red Cloud counted coup on your baby boy last night."

That was three, maybe four, days ago. Today Red Cloud was fighting or at least directing his warriors in something that was more than the typical skirmish. Tongues are flapping about it already here at his Tongue River village, based on rumors and several firsthand observations. Now I hear the beating of hooves and a few whoops. The warriors have returned from what must have been only a modest victory. When they have many scalps to wave at the women, old men, and children, they tend to howl like wolves. Right outside this tepee the great Red Cloud is talking with a deep, steady voice to his men. He sounds proud of what they did today, although the couple other times I heard Red Cloud say something, he also seemed proud. The war party is breaking up now, and the men are going their separate ways to share news of battle deeds with their families. I'm not sure exactly what they are saying as they part company, but none of their words translate to "goodbye"—it isn't in the Sioux vocabulary because, as Greasy Nose says, if they actually said "goodbye" that would break the love connection. Instead they say "see you soon" or "see you later." Of course that concept of a love connection among warriors takes some getting used to, not unlike most everything else around here.

Pretty Bear has spent most of the day trying not to look worried while working on a bead necklace. She has had to start over on the necklace a dozen times and there seem to be only three beads strung together even though it is already dark. Her mind has been on her man, Wolf Who Don't Dance, and she keeps looking up in the hope of seeing his tall, strong figure fill the flap opening. Wounded Eagle on the other hand has her back to the opening (I believe she is superstitious about her sitting, standing, and most everything else) and is watching Mum stir a gigantic pot of soup containing all the eatable parts of a buffalo, with some prairie dog thrown in just in case guests arrive for the post-battle feast. If Wounded Eagle is worried about Wolf Who Don't Dance not making it back to the tepee alive, she is trying not to show it. But I've noticed the way she occasionally mouths *"Wakan Tanka"* and grips her medicine bag made from the skin of an eagle. Of course, Mum doesn't look worried, even though the death of the man of the tepee would probably mean her own death, since nobody else seems to have much use for her. Within hours of Wolf Who Don't Dance's death, Wounded Eagle would probably cut Mum up into little pieces and throw them into the pot to make the soup last for a week or more. What thoughts I have! But I know that most captivity tales don't turn out as well as the story of Nancy Morton and Danny Marble. And I also know how totally unforgiving this frontier world can be.

Wait. Hold it. The flap is opening. And it is . . . Red Cloud. Holy Cow. I didn't expect the head chief to appear at the family tepee again so soon. Where is Wolf Who Don't Dance? I don't think anything bad has happened to him. Red Cloud is smiling (to my surprise—I didn't think he knew how to do that) and flashing around little mirrors. He hands one to Pretty Bear first and the chief's smile widens as he sees her look at her beautiful face and raven black hair in the mirror. Then he hands one to Mum and with a wave of his hand tells her to stop stirring and have a look. Mum obeys. It might be the first time since we were brought to this camp that she has looked at her own lovely face and yellow hair in a mirror (though perhaps she has seen her reflection while washing clothes in the Tongue River). Wounded Eagle, who is anything but beautiful, gets the third mirror offered by Red Cloud. If her husband should ever put the white captive ahead of her, she would attack him like a wildcat. But this is Red Cloud. *"Pilamaya, pilamaya,"* she says, bowing her head but *not* even glancing into the mirror. I think that word means "thank you." Just a guess. I might be ahead of the curve for babies in some areas of comprehension, but not when it comes to picking up foreign languages.

Now comes another figure into our tepee. He enters nose first and there is no mistaking that nose. But the nose is soon forgotten. The red dress he is wearing is spectacular. It has bright beads on the edges and polished shells up and down its full length, front and back.

"My war outfit," Greasy Nose says to Mum, when he sees her staring at him. Then he says something in Sioux, and the two Indian ladies nod their heads many times. He quickly translates for Mum: "Red Cloud Was Brilliant Today." Red Cloud has lost his smile to return to his usual stoic look, but his chest is expanded and I can tell he is listening to every word and watching the reaction of the three women.

Greasy Nose goes off in his own language again. The tip of his nose twitches when he is excited and he rubs it hard with the back of his hand. And the nose tip keeps twitching and he keeps rubbing when he returns to English. "The old trick is still the best trick—have some brave men act as decoys to lure the bluecoats out of the fort to an ambush. Red Cloud positioned himself along the ridge top, using mirrors and flags to signal the

soldiers' movements to the decoys. But I must say Carrington
finally got a little smarter. He sent out a detachment led by
Captain Fetterman to help the wood party get out from under
our siege but also came out with his own detachment to catch
us in a pincer movement. But their timing was off. They didn't
have anyone on a ridge directing the way our Red Cloud did. It
was a double ambush, but Red Cloud did it better than the
Army. We trapped some soldiers and it was their sabers against
our spears. The decoy ploy worked again. Prairie Dog says we
killed Lieutenant Bingham of Fetterman's command. We killed
a sergeant, too, and a private. We wounded many bluecoats.
Carrington blamed the dead Bingham. Fetterman blamed
Carrington. It was beautiful to watch."

Mum listens politely, but I can tell she is uncomfortable
hearing an Indian speak in perfect English about recently killed
soldiers, even if she didn't know the late Lieutenant Bingham. I
must admit that some of Greasy Nose's excitement is rubbing
off on me, yet I am also disappointed in him. He is a medicine
man in a dress, not a warrior in a war shirt, but he somehow
can revel in the deaths of his enemies.

When Greasy Nose is through talking, Red Cloud embraces
him. I couldn't imagine Colonel Carrington embracing one of
his men dressed up like a woman. Red Cloud says a few words
and walks out, no doubt to hear others speak more good words
about his brilliance. He didn't even try the soup.

Greasy Nose sips soup from a wooden bowl as he waits with
us for the master of the tepee to return. Now we hear steps.
Wolf Who Don't Dance is not walking quietly. Wounded Eagle
and Pretty Bear, both full of anticipation, are on their knees.
Mum drops her large wooden spoon into the pot of soup. I
raise my head from my green blankie, which is serving as my
pillow. When Wolf comes through the flap, he stands proudly at
the entrance in his buffalo horn headdress, with his favorite

wolf-tooth necklace dangling over his poncho-style war shirt that is made of deerskin hide and has on it horse hair, quills, woodpecker feathers, pigment, and I suspect human blood. His hands are behind his back, his chest looks just as puffed out as Red Cloud's, and the flush of victory fills out his face where there isn't war paint. Greasy Nose hails him in two languages.

"You all should be proud of your husband," the medicine man says in English, even though Mum is the only one of the three women in the tepee who knows that language. "You are looking at a truly great Sioux warrior." With that, Greasy Nose pats Wolf three times on the shoulder, twice on the back, and once on the breechclout before departing. He obviously wants to leave the stage entirely to the man of the tepee.

I manage to flip over onto my belly and then crawl across a buffalo robe toward Wolf. Yes, I am against warfare and killing, but I am caught up in the moment. I speak without being spoken to: *"Wuf-Wuf,"* I say, which is as close as I can get to "Wolf" at this stage of my talking life. I don't see any wounds on him. I sigh with a child's relief. The blood on him must have come from some other human being. I hope so. He is our captor but it's not like I wish him harm. I'm not sure Mum feels the same way. I glance over at her and see her head lowered. She seems to be watching the buffalo and prairie dog parts bobbing in the soup.

Pretty Bear can restrain herself no longer. She springs up from her knees and rushes to her man, pressing against him as if they have been separated for many moons. Wounded Eagle waits her turn but not with much patience. Now she rises from her knees and goes to her man (the same man of course). Pretty Bear steps aside, but not too far aside. Wounded Eagle touches Wolf on his bloody war shirt and then on his painted forehead. I have a gut feeling that she is trying to read what truth lies in his heart and in his head. She likes what she reads and wraps her arms around his middle.

He steps back and she lets him go. They talk in Sioux. She pokes at one of his shoulders. Pretty Bear steps up and pokes at the other shoulder. Wolf keeps a straight face. Like a magician, he will dramatically reveal what he has been keeping hidden behind his back. First he shows a closed fist, which he wiggles about before he opens it. Nothing is there. His eyes open wide, as if he is as surprised as the women. They keep poking his shoulders. Now they try to get around him to look at what's in his other hand. He takes a step back. Wounded Eagle stamps her foot. Wolf is having trouble keeping his face straight now. He gives in and shows his other hand. He is holding a short stick with a scalp, a bloody scalp, dangling from the other end. Both wives touch the scalp, then they touch their husband again, and finally, though hardly the best of friends, they touch each other. Wolf revels in this for only so long. I think he must smell the soup because he walks to the gigantic pot, looks into it, and sniffs.

Mum has stepped back from the pot. She is staring at her bare feet. Wolf reaches out and shakes her chin from side to side. At last she lifts her head. He immediately wiggles his stick in front of her eyes so that the scalp swishes like a horse's tail back and forth across her nose. He says something to her. The only word I understand is *Hinziwin,* which is Mum's name in Sioux—yellow hair woman. Mum tries to look away but Wolf won't take the scalp out of her face. She won't give him the pleasure of screaming.

"Lieutenant Bingham," Wolf says in pretty good English. He must have been practicing on the way to the tepee.

Finally Wolf lowers the stick. He walks over to me and says my name *Wanbli-cikala-mato,* which is too much for my tongue. Of course the translation "Little Eagle Bear" is also too much for my tongue. I guess I still think of myself as Daniel Duly.

Not that it matters. Now, look what Wolf is doing! What a dad! He's holding the stick over my head and wiggling the scalp in my face like it's a furry toy. Now Mum screams. She can't help herself. Wolf shrugs and tosses the scalp down. It lands right on my blankie. Wolf turns his attention to the soup. He doesn't wait for Mum or one of his Indian wives to serve him. He dips a ladle into the pot and takes his soup that way, directly.

Prairie Dog now shows up, just in time for dinner. He says some words in Sioux, or something passing as Sioux, to Wolf, who nods his head. Prairie Dog fills up a bowl and begins slurping the soup. He gets more on his hide shirt, which has finally replaced his woolen Army shirt, than in his greedy mouth. When his bowl is empty, he fills up another bowl. Wolf motions the guest to sit down then calls the women to the pot. Only Pretty Bear and Wounded Eagle listen to him. Mum slips over to me to rescue my blankie from the lieutenant's scalp.

Pretty Bear sips her soup like an officer's wife. Wounded Eagle takes in far more soup, but she is careful not to spill a drop, as if that might dishonor any Sioux who has ever gone through a starving winter. Prairie Dog goes back to slurping. Wolf Who Don't Dance finally sits down next to them but without a bowl. Pretty Bear jumps up and brings him soup in the biggest bowl. Mum should really eat something to keep up her strength. But she never enjoys her own cooking in the tepee. Now she turns her back on the others and invites me to breastfeed. I'm in her arms now and heading for the target. Darn. Here comes Prairie Dog for a look. Mum covers up and delays my immediate gratification.

"Nice scalp, huh?" he said. "I never really got to know Lieutenant Bingham and I guess I never will. He was all eager like Fetterman. Too bad Wolf didn't take the hair of the captain instead. Damn that Fetterman. He got clean away. But tomorrow is another day."

"I don't want to hear about it," Mum said. "What do you want?"

"Your husband wanted me to tell you that he likes the soup."

"Wolf is not my husband."

"Well, I'm sure not going to tell him that. I'll just tell him you were glad to cook for such an outstanding Sioux warrior."

"I didn't say that."

"Just trying to help you out, Mrs. Wolf. I mean Mrs. Duly. An honest mistake."

"Leave me alone."

"He also wanted me to tell you to come over and have some soup with your family."

"I hate him. I hate all of you, especially you."

"Keep your voice down. He wasn't exactly asking you to come over. He was telling you. Let's not make Wolf mad. People in this village love the guy, you know, almost as much as Red Cloud. I bet Greasy Nose told you how the two of them helped whip the bluecoats. Well, you want to hear the other side of the story?"

"No. It was awful."

"I just thought that you being white and all, you'd like me to set the record straight. At least twenty of Red Cloud's warriors bit the bullet today and maybe ten of them died. Sure a few arrows felled a few soldiers, but Carrington and Fetterman didn't suffer as much as a scratch. Doesn't sound like much of a Sioux victory to me."

Mum looks at Prairie Dog like he is a snake. "Why tell me? It's all so horrible. And I thought you were on the Indians' side."

"Sure. Sure. I'm here, not back there, aren't I? I'm now a true blue white renegade."

"True blue?"

"Look, ma'am. This is Indian country, and the soldier boys

should just vamoose. Don't think for a minute I want all those boys dead. Mostly just Captain William Fucking Fetterman!"

Mum pulls away as if Prairie Dog has slapped her. She just doesn't like bad language. Wolf doesn't like what he sees and hears (even if he can't understand a word) either. He pushes his soup bowl aside and yells something. Prairie Dog shakes his head and tries desperately to put together the right Sioux words. Whatever P.D. has come up with, I don't doubt it's another lie.

"I better get back to the soup and you better come along yourself, Mrs. Duly. Pronto. I just told Wolf you were as hungry as a horse . . . I think."

# DECEMBER 25, 1866:
## TOMBS OF CAPTAIN
## FETTERMAN'S COMMAND

For nearly five days now, Prairie Dog has been the happiest man alive—Captain Fetterman got it good, and the Army private–turned–white renegade had a ringside seat. I suppose mastermind Red Cloud, warrior extraordinaire Wolf Who Don't Dance, and noncombatant prophet Greasy Nose are close behind in their delight—they all helped give it good to poor Fetterman and his command of eighty men. But none of them, except the vengeful Prairie Dog, has been rejoicing much since the victory dance on the 22$^{nd}$. While they taught the white soldiers a lesson on how costly it would be to maintain a presence in the Powder River Country and to keep the Bozeman Trail open, they know the long winter is just beginning and the Army will keep sending replacements to the fort. Wounded Eagle thinks the soldiers might strike back during this powerfully cold time because that's what she would do in their shoes. Greasy Nose has had no vision of soldiers falling out of the sky like grasshoppers onto our tepee tops, but that doesn't matter to her or to my other Indian mother. Pretty Bear has twice told Prairie Dog to warn me not to crawl too far away from our tepee or the *Wasichus* will get me. Now *Wasichus* are "white people," and I am one of those, so why should I be frightened? I guess Pretty Bear already sees me as one of her people, albeit a very little one, and in my baby buffalo robe after dusk I could easily be mistaken for a redskin infant. The soldiers, both my Indian mothers insist, must be so angry now that if they found me crawling in their direction, they would slice me with their sabers like a ripe tomato or squash me with their rifle butts like a bug.

I can certainly imagine the Fort Phil Kearny soldiers, especially Colonel Carrington, ready to burst at the seams with rage after that awful battle that they are calling an Indian massacre. At the same time, I can also imagine most of them shaking in their boots, and not just from the breath-stealing temperatures. There is no way to sugarcoat it. The bluecoats took a licking four days ago. I was there or at least near enough—far closer than the colonel himself—to get a taste of the battle and the gruesome aftermath. What horrors I didn't actually see with my own two eyes, I saw in my mind's eye. But I'm trying not to think about it. After all, despite my living in Wolf's tepee in the village of Red Cloud, I am a pacifist at this stage in my life, and this is Christmas Day. The snow has been falling since morning and now six inches cover the ground. Can all this heavenly whiteness cover up the blood and gore of battle and man's inhumanity to man? That's a question for another day—and perhaps for someone older and wiser than me. Like I said, it's Christmas—my first ever!

With my increasing fine motor skills, I can not only see my gifts but also reach out and grab them and taste them. And I'm not just talking about Mum's breasts here. I see each drop of refreshing rain, each snowflake, each rainbow as another gift to me from the Lord or the Great Spirit—the kind of thinking that would surely meet the approval of Aunt Maggie and Wounded Eagle. In other words, I do count my blessings, which is a good thing because so many other things that happen make me want to curse or cry.

As you dear readers know by now, the Almighty (whatever name you use) has given me certain gifts—the ability to etch things in my mind long before I will learn how to write, the ability to think (but not necessarily act) far beyond my years, and the ability to see things in my mind's eyes that are out of the range of my two regular eyes. You might say I am blessed to have these abilities. But sometimes I'm not so sure. They can be a curse, too. Dwelling on past events, often terribly disturbing events, is necessary for the etching process to work. I forget almost nothing. That can hurt my head. Thinking beyond my years destroys a certain innocence a baby should possess. That makes me feel old before my time. My extra vision can be the biggest curse of all. It might sound good in theory, and I suppose it is comparable to the supernatural Power that the medicine man/prophet/spy/*wintke* Greasy Nose holds so sacred and dear. But I've seen things that no man, let alone a baby, should see. And it's hard to think of my extra vision as a Power. I mean no matter how much I see, I am still powerless to do anything about what I see. I'm sorry to complain, dear readers, but I doubt you've seen what I've seen. Take the Fetterman Fight. And I wish somebody would because it bothers my little brain to no end. I saw too much of that clash between soldiers I once knew and Indians I know now, and the unimaginable pictures are locked inside my head like, well, like brain-eating termites, if there are such things—and in this frontier world, I can't imagine there aren't.

Forget about Captain Fetterman. Forget about his command. That is what I wish I could do, especially on a day that should be festive. They say—and by "they" I don't mean the Sioux—that Jesus Christ was born today. It makes me wonder about his Power. I don't believe he was just some innocent babe born in the manger any more than I was just some innocent babe born on the Oregon Trail. Jesus Christ! Have I begun to compare myself to him? Maybe that makes me like Papa Duly—you know, insane. I refuse to think about it. I shall concentrate on the blessed snowflakes instead. I am sitting outside the tepee right now, bundled up in an appropriately small buffalo robe instead of my pullover sweater or my green blankie—both of which Wounded Eagle burned because she thought they reminded me of the white world (and she didn't mean snow). I am tilting back my head. I am catching the big wet flakes with my tongue, sometimes with my nose and chin. It soothes me on the outside and also inside my skull. Mum is bundled up even more than I am. She would prefer to be inside, but Pretty Bear shooed us out the front flap, not out of meanness but because she still insists, as the number one wife, on having time alone with Wolf Who Don't Dance every afternoon. I, however, thrive on being out here in the fresh air. The cold doesn't bother me like it does Mum, who has wrapped her black shawl around her sore throat. She says she is feeling mighty poorly today. But the truth is she has been sickly ever since the Fetterman Fight.

Every once in a while she will sneeze, and each time I turn my head to her and pretend to be startled even though I know another sneeze is coming. We will smile at each other. She will say "Ha-choo" and I will respond with "Ah-goo." We make these sounds back and forth. They aren't English and they aren't Sioux, but it's like we are having an important conversation in our own language. It's a way of coping with our life in Red Cloud's village. There she goes: *Ha-choo.* Here I go: *Ah-goo. Ha-choo. Ah-goo. Ha-choo. Ah-goo. Ha-choo, Ah-goo.* I could go on like this all night, but my funny bone is more easily tickled than hers. Her bones are mostly tired and cold and her funny bone is hanging by a thread. She slips back into her own thoughts. Mum coughs. That's not part of our game. So much change, so much to worry about.

I long for Mum, even with her cold hands, to let her fingers wander over my no longer soft belly while she repeats in the most delightful fashion "gitchee-gitchee-goo." She started saying that two weeks ago. At first I thought she had picked up on a funny Sioux word that Pretty Bear (certainly not Wounded Eagle) might have used. But it turns out it's white American adult baby talk. Don't ask me to figure it out. Language, as you know by now, isn't my strong suit. Mum just isn't in the mood for sneezing or tickling games. Catching the falling snowflakes with my tongue is the best thing I can do.

"I hope those two finish soon," Mum says to me, her teeth chattering. "We need to get in that tepee and warm up, Daniel."

She only calls me Daniel when she is absolutely certain nobody else is around, because Wounded Eagle will slap her in the mouth for saying my English name. I snuggle up closer to Mum. I don't know if I feel more like a Daniel than a Little Eagle Bear, but whenever Mum whispers my English name it causes a tingle in my brain. She turns her head away to cough again. I love when she sneezes for fun, hate it when she coughs for real. It's really only she who needs to get inside. I could catch snowflakes out here for another couple hours. But maybe I can provide a tad of body warmth for poor Mum.

"Here I am all worried about catching a piddling cold," continues Mum. "And just a few days ago one hundred good men lay dead on the frozen ground."

I know. I saw many of them myself, although I didn't count bodies. Some say one hundred, some say eighty-one—either way that's a lot of bluecoats turning red. I see a tear falling slowly from Mum's eye. I think it might form a miniature icicle.

Mum coughs once more and scolds herself for being alive and cold.

*Stop it, Mum! Please! It's Christmas!* That's what I want to yell, but nothing comes out but some nonsense word, half-English, half-Sioux, that I can't even recognize myself. I wonder how I can get her to change the subject. I could laugh, but that doesn't seem appropriate. I could cry, but that might encourage her to continue in the same sad vein. I can't think of any other options.

I do nothing, but Mum continues anyway. "I wonder if they pushed away the snow and tried to bury Captain Fetterman and his soldiers?" she asks as she rubs my hands in hers. "Wouldn't the earth be too hard? How many tears do you think have been shed at the fort? Can they even manage a holiday feast? Do you think Grace Pennington will ever get over the loss of her officer on top of the loss of Rufus Pennington and of Private P.D. Burrows? Of course, Prairie Dog is alive, and wouldn't you say he is no loss at all?"

It is as if Mum half expects me to answer all her questions. All I can do is mumble *"Lobe-lobe."* She wipes a wet spot off my upper lip with a corner of her black shawl and now wraps the shawl more tightly around her neck. She turns silent, maybe to protect her throat, or maybe because she can't bear to talk about life and death at Fort Phil Kearny. She looks like a woman in mourning.

I close my mouth and lower my chin. I suddenly feel guilty. Instead of catching snowflakes, I really should be crying almost like a baby! No, that won't do any good. But there is something I should be doing. In fact, it is my duty to do it. My ability to remember the past, however painful, and etch it into my skull for the future is a gift. How else can I view it on this day— Christmas Day, the day Jesus Christ was born? I cannot waste my gift!

So here I go. I etch for you, dear readers, what has been going on since the day my Indian "dad" brought home a lieutenant's scalp and Chief Red Cloud passed out little mirrors to my two Indian mothers and even to my original Mum. Already that skirmish from earlier this month seems like it occurred many moons ago. I suppose a full-blown, one-sided fight like the one

I recently witnessed simply takes hold of time and refuses to let go.

The slippery Sioux medicine man and spy Greasy Nose, who even in a red dress finds a way to make himself invisible to the soldiers, got close enough to the fort cemetery on December 9 to witness the burial of Lieutenant Bingham. Afterward, he reported to our tepee. My Indian dad and my two Indian mothers showed no interest in the event. But Prairie Dog was all ears. He was there because Wolf wanted him to interpret and monitor Mum's mood. All morning Mum had been singing a spiritual slave song she had learned from Hanna, and Wolf was worried it might be her death song. Anyway, Greasy Nose said the lieutenant was buried with full Masonic honors, which seemed to involve covering a Holy Bible, a square, and compasses with black crepe, mourners wearing aprons and a chaplain pronouncing, "The will of God is accomplished." Prairie Dog didn't appear to understand Masonic honors any more than I did. He guessed right, though, that it was a closed coffin, which was a good thing since Wolf Who Don't Dance had scalped the late lieutenant. Greasy Nose, who always had an eye for detail, added that the coffin was lined with metal to protect Bingham's corpse from wolves. Considering who killed the lieutenant, I consider that ironic—if I am using that word correctly.

I was glad not to have been at the funeral. I didn't know Lieutenant Bingham but I know I would have cried anyway. I did not, however, escape such mourning matters for long. That next morning, when Pretty Bear took me on an outing to the river, I witnessed most of a Sioux funeral service. I didn't know those three dead warriors, either, but I still became teary eyed. The body of each was painted red and wrapped inside a buffalo robe, with a packet of food near the head. None of those fellows was lowered into the ground. Instead, they were raised into trees and laid to rest on natural platforms formed by various tree limbs. All their heads pointed north. Below, a small fire was crackling and some of the men who had touched the deceased were purifying themselves with cedar smoke. I supposed these were full Sioux honors and they didn't seem any stranger to me than full Masonic honors. I also supposed that babies that died, either in forts or Indian villages, did not receive such honors. I mumbled a vow *not* to die anytime soon and accidentally tugged two hard on one of Pretty Bear's pretty necklaces, sending two beads flying to the ground. My grasp has been steadily getting stronger. Maybe it is just natural development, but perhaps my new environment has toughened me up. I'm not sure.

Pretty Bear did not grow sad at the Sioux funeral. And she kept smiling at me when I accidentally pulled those two beads off her necklace. In her eyes, I could do no wrong. Had I punched her in the nose, I believe she would have kept smiling. But of course I would never do anything like that to her. I hadn't even punched Wounded Eagle in the nose for mistreating Mum or Prairie Dog for being himself. Sensing my mood, Pretty Bear wiped away my tears and then tapped me gently on my nose with one pretty finger. *"Tuki,"* she said, which is her favorite thing to say whenever I mumble an English word or so much as burp in her presence. Prairie Dog told Mum it means "So what!" But Greasy Nose said the correct translation is "Is that so?" and that only women say it.

As she walked away from the burial tree, Pretty Bear began rocking me in her arms and talking in a prayerful voice. *"Yad-alanh Yunke-lo,"* she said when we went over a hillock and approached the river. I hadn't heard that one before and guessed it meant "Time for a bath." I wasn't close. Later I heard the two words used separately and eventually put two and two together. Pretty Bear was saying, "Farewell death."

Death did go on a vacation, but it was a short one. I think

both Colonel Carrington's bluecoats and Chief Red Cloud's red men (my skin is turning redder all the time, by the way) needed to lick their wounds for a while. The soldiers, according to reports from Greasy Nose, were also vigorously drilling in the cold so that they could be better prepared to fight Indians in the future. The fort was on constant alert, with at least fifty horses kept saddled from dawn to dusk in case they were needed for quick action against the enemy. Back at the tepees, we were mostly just trying to stay warm, but I was eager to show off my new mobility and was ready to crawl at any time. Wounded Eagle, who most of the time has a half-angry, half-hurt look on her scarred face, surprised Mum and me by fashioning a miniature buffalo robe for me to wear outside as temperatures dropped to zero degrees. Maybe she felt guilty about burning my sweater and blankie. Inside I was still mostly going around stark naked, which is what the Sioux boys do around here, at least in warm weather, until the age of ten. Yes, it's true. I am a diaper-free baby.

Although potty matters might seem irrelevant in time of war, they are still important to me and Mum and the others who live in this tepee. None of us want to have me urinating or defecating in our living area. I have been told that some of the babies around here wear animal skin wrapping with moss or dried grass placed in strategic areas to trap body waste. Mum was leaning in that direction but was overruled by my Indian mothers, Pretty Bear and Wounded Knee, who both believe in the more traditional practice of elimination communication. They are attuned to my innate body rhythms and I have quickly developed a degree of self-control. Timing is very important.

Here's how it works. I can go an hour without urinating, so every hour or so I give them a signal—usually a nose scrunch combined with a full body squirm—that they pick up on. They then take me outside or place me on a sheet of moss near the backside of the tepee to do my business. Defecation is less frequent and less regular but I have learned to hold my bowel movement until one of my caretakers holds me in a particular squat position. It was during the lull after the December 6 fight that I began to use the Sioux word *"maka"* when it was time for any kind of elimination. In my naivety and because Prairie Dog makes things up when translating, I thought the word meant "make," as in "make a little gift," but it turns out it means "skunk." Still, Pretty Bear and Wounded Eagle catch my drift, and it's less trouble saying *maka* than squirming like an earthworm on a hook.

For the most part Mum is not privy to this elimination communication. She is far too busy laboring on behalf of the two Indian women and Wolf Who Don't Dance to have time to communicate with me over potty matters. I can tell that being left out of this important developmental element of my life makes her sad and jealous because she wants to be my one and only mother. Still, she no longer has to change me or wash cloth diapers—and how can she complain about that! Also the breast-feeding remains her exclusive department. And I still love it! But sometimes Mum is not available. Also in early December, my lips and tongue started to work together so that I was able to accept some solid food put in my mouth by my Indian mothers and even once by Wolf Who Don't Dance. I do enjoy the plainer soups, the mashed potatoes, and the squash, but I turn my nose up at and spit out something they call *timpsila,* a prairie turnip. Pemmican, which requires some serious chewing, is of course out. Consuming some solids has made my defecation schedule even more erratic, but something tells me that most of you dear readers have heard enough about such infantile matters. So back to the violence, the blood, guts, torture and death, of this war on the frontier.

The December 6 skirmish, as Prairie Dog said, might not

have been a total Lakota victory. The soldiers rode into an ambush but escaped annihilation. And I saw for myself a number of casualties on our side—whoops, did I say *our side*? Am I really one of them now, a Lakota baby? Well, I was with them that day in spirit if not body. I can't say, though, I was rooting for the Indians. I wasn't rooting for the soldiers either, even if Mum was—at least she was rooting to be saved by the soldiers. Not me. I am not unhappy where I am. It is the fighting that makes me unhappy. I consider myself a total pacifist, which when you think about it is about all most babies can be. I am against war, particularly any war that might reach our—that is to say Red Cloud's—village and endanger the lives of innocent women and children, especially babies!

As I started to mention, the December 6 skirmish was an indecisive action (my favorite kind, I reckon) but it bolstered the confidence of Red Cloud and the other Indian leaders. Wolf Who Don't Dance said it himself one night, interrupting a game of peek-a-boo I was playing with Pretty Bear and Wounded Eagle: "I tell you, my wives, if we can lure a large group of soldiers out of the fort, a thousand Indians armed with only bows and arrows could kill them to the last man." Anyway, that's how Prairie Dog, who was in the tepee trying to trade tobacco for pemmican, later translated it for Mum. For once, P.D. got it right. Amazingly, the following night, when Prairie Dog was not present, Wolf Who Don't Dance came back from a tribal meeting and said enough words I knew and made enough motions with his hands for me to understand that the Lakotas had a plan: After the coming of the next full moon, they would spring a deadly trap on the soldiers of Little White Chief, which is what Colonel Carrington is called around here.

Our camp on the Tongue River grew during December with the arrival of more allies. In case I forgot to mention it in one of my earlier entries, dear readers, I should tell you that Red

Cloud, Wolf Who Don't Dance, Greasy Nose, the interpreter Little Bull, the young warrior Two Feathers, and the strange fighting man Crazy Horse all belong to the Sioux sub tribe called the Oglalas. That means "to scatter one's own," which doesn't sound like an inspiring name, but the Oglalas are nevertheless plenty inspired and plenty tough. I'm kind of proud to be an adopted Oglala, even though the only things I've scattered so far are my own feces. We have been joined by many Minneconjous, which means "planters beside the stream." But the chiefs of that sub tribe, like White Hollow Horn, Makes Room, and Brave Bear, are here to plant only one thing—the bodies of bluecoats. The number of fighting men further swelled with the arrival of Northern Cheyennes and some Arapahos. This one Cheyenne called Crazy Mule seemed like he was out of his head. He would stand right out in the open and let his friends shoot at him with bullets. Yet nothing happened to him. Everyone wanted to follow bulletproof Crazy Mule into battle.

Red Cloud and the rest of the Oglalas think they have more than a match for Crazy Mule in the aforementioned Crazy Horse. A year or so ago, Crazy Horse became a "Shirt Wearer" for having killed so many traditional enemies, such as the Crows, Pawnees, and Shawnees. He grew to detest Fort Phil Kearny as much as anyone, and some folks around here consider him the ultimate bluecoat killer. He doesn't exactly look the part, maybe because his skin is so pale for an Indian and his hair is light and curly. I saw him on several occasions walking past our tepee without looking up from the ground. Apparently that's not unusual for him. He is known to bump into things, such as other people, trees, and tepees. Two Feathers, who once counted coup on Philip Kittridge and considers Crazy Horse a friend (along with Red Cloud, Wolf, and every other famous Oglala), has an explanation for these little accidents. He says that Crazy Horse has his head in another world, one full of the spirit of all things and more real than our own world, where everything we see is just a shadow from Crazy Horse's world. In his world, he rides on a black-and-white horse that floats and dances and supplies him with great Power that allows him to pass through anything without getting hurt. He got his name from that vision.

Greasy Nose says that with his own Power he can see Crazy Horse's Power, but that Crazy Horse's Power is more unpredictable and, while often quite effective, it will not keep him from dying an early violent death. And I don't think Greasy Nose is just saying that out of jealousy, although the sometime impudent Two Feathers brought up that possibility to the medicine man himself. Greasy Nose of course has no wish to be a great warrior like Crazy Horse or Wolf Who Don't Dance. He is content being a medicine man and a prophet in a red dress.

Two Feathers was carrying on for weeks earlier this December, sounding as if he was the Sioux's answer to Captain Fetterman. "With Crazy Mule, Crazy Horse, and me leading our people in battle, we can not know defeat!" he boasted, according to Greasy Nose's translation. "All the long knives will leave this land without their hair." Crazy Horse said nothing. He was apparently more concerned about his frequent visions and trying to find a wife, although he rarely shares his thoughts with anyone. Two Feathers' words did cause a certain amount of snickering in Red Cloud's village—not because the older warriors thought they could lose but because they thought Two Feathers was too big for his buckskin leggings.

*"Dho!"* said Wolf Who Don't Dance right to the bold young brave's face. *"Wonunicun."* Wolf apparently was telling the boastful one that a mistake had been made. Wolf then lifted me off the ground and high into the air so that my bare bottom was tickling the two wild turkey feathers that stuck up high over Two Feathers' big head but still only reached my Indian dad's

271

forehead. Wolf called out my Sioux name, *Wanbli-cikala-mato,* while making a pronouncement that Greasy Nose later translated for Mum as "I'd rather follow into battle Little Eagle Bear, who can only crawl, than you, Two Feathers, who can only talk!"

As it was, when a great war party left our village on the Tongue River, some of the women and children followed, including Wounded Eagle with me in a cradleboard on her back and her eagle-skin medicine bag hanging around her neck. While he might have considered Two Feathers too boastful, Wolf Who Don't Dance was so confident of victory over the soldiers that he believed we could witness his brave warrior deeds without being in harm's way. Pretty Bear wanted to go, too, maybe to collect the teeth of dead soldiers for her necklaces, but somebody had to stay back at the tepee to keep an eye on Mum.

The idea of bloody battle was revolting to poor Mum, and the prospect of the merciless Wounded Eagle taking me close enough to the battlefield to taste the blood sent her over the edge. She became hysterical, tearing at her hair, throwing pemmican, screeching like an owl, clawing at the painted body of Wolf Who Don't Dance. He showed her the back of his hand but did not strike her; he wasn't nearly as ferocious as he looked. But Wounded Eagle produced a knife and was ready to cut out Mum's tongue if given the nod from her husband. Wolf Who Don't Dance waved her off and turned to his first wife. He gripped both of Pretty Bear's shoulders as he talked sternly to her, then planted a kiss on her forehead and walked out of the tepee. Mum interrupted her screeching for a moment after he was gone, but then started up again louder than ever when she saw Wounded Eagle following him. Mum gave chase, wanting desperately to reclaim me from Wounded Eagle. "No *sicaho-waya!*" Wounded Eagle shouted, pushing Mum away. I needed no translation; she was telling Mum to stop screaming. Mum didn't listen. Like a small dog, she nipped at Wounded Eagle's ankles, but she didn't have a chance of reaching me. I was safe and secure attached to the formidable Wounded Eagle's back. When Wounded Knee displayed her knife again, Mum, oblivious to the danger, kept up her desperate pursuit. Pretty Bear came out of the tepee and chased after Mum. I saw black hair and yellow hair flapping in the wind.

I closed my eyes and did my best to cover my aching ears. I didn't like the horrors of war any more than Mum did, but at that moment the horrors I knew were coming seemed less bothersome than her screaming. I'm not proud of it, but I wanted Mum to shut up and go home, that is go back to our tepee with Pretty Bear. Of course I immediately felt ashamed of treating Mum that way, if only in my thoughts. And I felt even worse a moment later when Wounded Eagle turned around to confront Mum not with the knife but with a war club that Wolf had forgotten. It looked like nothing more than a love tap, but the blow Wounded Eagle delivered knocked Mum out cold.

*"Awayaye!"* Wounded Eagle yelled to Pretty Bear. And from having so many Sioux mothers and babysitters, I knew what that word meant—Watch! Indeed Pretty Bear knelt down over Mum and watched her lie there. There was nothing I could do. I saw Mum stir before she was out of range of my regular eyes, which was good, because my mind's eye did not go back even one time to check on her. My mind's eye was looking ahead with a warrior's sense of anticipation. And so it was that I went to war in a cradleboard.

On December 20, the warriors rode to a meadow near the frozen water of Peno Creek. The followers, including Wounded Eagle and me, reached a rise overlooking the meadow in the afternoon. We watched as the warriors chanted and raised their arms to the sky, part of their ceremonial preparation for the next day's attack. Greasy Nose, in high-topped, buffalo-fur moccasins, suddenly stepped out from the middle of the line leading a sorrel horse. He was wearing his red dress, which looked a little too tight at the waist and hips, but that was overshadowed by his headdress, which was made out of wolf skin and complete with a tail, but no paws or claws. A few bald spots and scars on the body of the wolf indicated that it had been a true fighter. There were no feathers, quills, bells, or shells to clutter up the headdress and interfere with whatever medicine it could bring to Greasy Nose. I could see the wolf's spirit shining through its amber eyes and Greasy Nose's Power pouring out of its mouth past the sharp, slightly curved fangs.

"I seen him in a coyote headdress before but never a wolf one," commented Prairie Dog, who had come up behind us, trailing not only the warriors but also the warriors wives and female followers, not to mention at least one baby. Unless he was speaking to me, I guess he was talking to himself, since I was the only other one around who knew much English. Wounded Eagle gave him a quick glance of disdain and then turned back to the impressive sight of a stout wolf in a red dress addressing a line of colorful (if war paint can make one colorful) fighting men. "Maybe that dead wolf is helping him obtain some kind of Goddamned vision," said Prairie Dog. "Greasy Nose has outdone himself!"

I caught a glimpse of the human wolf, my Indian father: Wolf Who Don't Dance. He was stripped to his breechclout despite the bitter cold (I imagine that war paint must be warm) and wearing only his usual single eagle feather in his hair. His pony, which seemed too short for Wolf's long legs, wouldn't stop sniggering or trying to get out of line. I knew that Wolf, unlike most of his fellow warriors, preferred to fight on foot rather than horseback. His preference wasn't something that he liked to talk about much in a horseback society like the Sioux, but he once admitted something to cousin Red Cloud that Prairie Dog translated as "You can lead a horse into a battle but you can't make him participate."

I didn't watch my Indian father for long because it was Greasy Nose's show at the moment, and all eyes were on him. As the medicine man mounted his sorrel, the warriors hailed him as if he had climbed onto the back of a grizzly bear. Wounded Eagle, watching with fire in her eyes, raised the war club and, with a great show of strength, moved it for several seconds as if it were a mere flyswatter. Even though I was pretty much immobilized on her back, I felt agitated, as if her bubbly aggression was seeping through the cradleboard into my bundled body.

Greasy Nose was now zigzagging bareback on his horse in front of the line of men as if either he or his mount had drunk too much firewater. The sorrel stopped in the middle of the line in front of Red Cloud, who sat atop a paint that had red circles around its eyes and red hand marks on its white spots. Greasy Nose held up a fist and then opened it, showing his palm first to the head red man and then to all the others.

"*Zapatan,*" Greasy Nose shouted, which means "five." I had recently learned my Lakota numbers from one to ten because of the merciless instruction of Wounded Eagle. Greasy Nose then opened his other fist and repeated "*Zapatan.*" His sorrel snorted and reared. Greasy Nose adjusted his wolf-skin head-dress and called out "*Wikcemna,*" which means "ten." Greasy Nose said many other words that I did not understand. Yes, *zapatan* plus *zapatan* equals *wikcemna*. In a vision, Greasy Nose had learned to do addition? There had to be more to it than that.

The warriors and chiefs up and down the line suddenly shook their heads vigorously as if trying to loosen lice from their hair. Their horses shook their heads, too. Wolf Who Don't Dance's pony shook its head hardest of all. Wolf hung on with some difficulty because he was using only one hand. His other hand was clutching, no doubt for good luck, the favorite wolf-tooth necklace Pretty Bear had made for him. Three riders down from Wolf I spotted Two Feathers, who looked small on his large horse. As Two Feathers shook his big head, his two turkey feathers, sticking out from his hair at strange angles, began to dance. I did not see Crazy Horse. Considering his reputation, I guessed he might have been off somewhere on his floating black-and-white horse having a vision of his own.

Greasy Nose again began to ride his sorrel in zigzag fashion. Red Cloud and his warriors followed his every movement in absolute silence, showing admirable patience with their medicine man and prophet. Finally, the sorrel reared and turned as if a rattlesnake or perhaps a spirit had frightened it. Greasy Nose bounced on its back, seemingly with no control, as the sorrel galloped its way right to where Red Cloud sat on his mount. At that point, Greasy Nose held two fists in the air and then went flying, bucked off by the spirited sorrel. Red Cloud shook all over, and his neck recoiled so violently that it knocked his flowing headdress askew. The great Oglala leader had to grip his horse's mane with both hands to stay aboard. Other riders and their mounts had similar reactions up and down the line, but nobody fell or lost control of his horse, not even Wolf Who Don't Dance. All these man had been riding since they were knee high to a jackrabbit. But they all saw something or sensed something, and their wonderment showed right through their war paint. I wasn't sure what was happening. I'm used to seeing more than I should, but I couldn't see what they saw. I was dumbfounded (something not usually associated with babies). Greasy Nose picked himself off the ground and smoothed out his red dress. The men and horses became still once more. This *wintke* had such Power that some of the greatest mounted warriors in the world, including Red Cloud himself, were waiting further word from him before daring to take military action.

Greasy Nose suddenly dropped to his knees and raised one fist high over his wolf-skin headdress. He opened and closed the fist again and again as he repeated the word *"zapatan."* Red Cloud repeated the word each time. They were counting together by fives. Finally, at the same time, Red Cloud and his medicine man shouted *"Opawige!"* If it was another number, it wasn't one I knew. And then Greasy Nose spoke other words in his language that caused Red Cloud to rise up on his horse and thrust a fist toward the cold blue sky. *"Tanka,"* he shouted, which is the same word Pretty Bear often uses when I squat outside in the right place and have a successful bowel movement. The word means "great."

*"Tanka,"* repeated Wounded Eagle, talking to me over her left shoulder as she kept her eyes glued on Red Cloud. *"Tanka,"* said some of the other women and girls and boys around us who were straining to see the warriors' ceremony. From my cradleboard pointed the wrong way, I naturally could not see anything directly (a problem that did not seem to concern Wounded Eagle), but my curious mind's eye wasn't missing much. Still, I was missing something—the ghostly human or animal spirits that the Indians apparently were seeing but that didn't show up in my mind's eye. I felt inadequate. All the Power that I was born with and that made me stand out in my own mind could not grasp this ceremony. I noticed out of the corner of my actual left eye that Prairie Dog was rubbing his pale chin and looking on with at least as much confusion as me. That was small comfort.

Most of the warriors jumped off their horses at this point and dropped to their knees or on all fours, becoming one with the earth, just like Greasy Nose. They beat the ground with their coup sticks, spears, and war clubs so hard and so long that I finally remembered to worry about Mum back at the tepee. I hoped that she had recovered from Wounded Eagle's clubbing and that Pretty Bear was looking after her. I felt bad about selfishly not thinking about Mum for so many hours.

Prairie Dog interrupted my contemplation with his peculiar mutterings. He was muttering in English but using some words I had never heard before. I suspected they were curse words, for Prairie Dog had a large vocabulary when it came to such words. He was muttering to himself and had no idea anyone on the rise could understand him. He did throw in one Sioux word—*opawige*—at least three times.

"One hundred," Prairie Dog said loudly, as if reading my mind. "Five dead soldiers aren't enough. Ten aren't enough. Not fifteen, twenty-five, or ninety-five, either. One hundred soldiers are going to die. He saw one hundred in his hand. Hard to believe! Wonder if that old woman-man knows what the hell he is talking about. This don't figure to be some run-of-the-mill skirmish. One hundred dead soldiers! Can you imagine that, Daniel boy?"

I could not imagine that—a few scattered dead bodies were too many for me. But I could not imagine Greasy Nose saying something he didn't believe was going to happen. He had his solid reputation as a prophet to uphold. I could only hope that Prairie Dog had not translated Greasy Nose's final number correctly. But I had heard both Greasy Nose and Red Cloud pronounce that same number—*opawige*. A stream of cold sweat started to run down Prairie Dog's brow, and he mopped it up with his shirtsleeve. Then he borrowed some war paint from a long-haired boy, too young to fight but not to dream of glory on the battlefield. Wounded Eagle turned away from the proceedings to scowl at Prairie Dog as he liberally applied the paint to his forehead, cheeks, and chin. I guess he didn't want anyone to mistake him for a paleface.

We spent that night camped separately from the warriors.

Wounded Eagle did manage to sneak over to the warriors' camp to give her husband his favorite war club and a quick kiss on his war paint. Nobody complained about the cold. Most everyone wore a buffalo robe, some with the hair turned in, or else wrapped themselves in trade blankets. We slept in a ring of shelters made of willow poles and covered with brush and horse blankets. In the middle was a fire that blazed as if made by the devil. I wondered if the Carringtons, Captain Fetterman, Mrs. Pennington, Toby, and the others back at Fort Phil Kearny could see the smoke rising over the distant treetops. It was no matter to Red Cloud and his warriors. Greasy Nose's vision had done wonders for them. Not that they hadn't been confident before, but now they were dead certain that the enemy would meet disaster. No doubt they figured that the white eyes—or long knives or bluecoats or whatever you want to call them—would not be able to see what lay ahead whether or not a screen of smoke rose in the hills.

I thought I might be up all night worrying about something—perhaps all the soldiers who had white faces like me and were predicted to die or maybe Wolf Who Don't Dance, who could be among the Sioux casualties. I mean I figured there had to be plenty of Sioux deaths, too, if one hundred soldiers were going to fall. Well, I did worry for a while about those things and then I started to worry about how much Mum must be worrying back at our tepee. But it didn't last. I drank some sweetened water and sucked on dried chokecherries and then fell right to sleep in the blankets I shared with Wounded Eagle. It happened so fast I didn't have time to even miss Mum's breast milk.

December 21, the winter solstice, dawned frigid but sunny. It was a day to remember, in infamy by the U.S. Army and with a certain pride by Sioux, Cheyennes, and Arapahos. Red Cloud, wrapped in a red blanket, positioned himself behind a wind-blown snowdrift on a ridge where he could observe the soldiers at the fort. He already had more than his share of war honors and he would leave it to the younger warriors, such as Crazy Horse, Wolf Who Don't Dance, and even Two Feathers, to achieve glory on this day. In all there were close to two thousand warriors, mostly armed with bows and arrows, lances, and clubs—not quite enough firepower to attack the fort but plenty to pull off an ambush.

At about 9 a.m., a few young warriors with some knowledge of English swear words (possibly learned from Prairie Dog) rode onto the bluffs about a mile from the fort and challenged the soldiers to come out and fight. Soon after, other warriors attacked the garrison herd of horses and cattle and chased after a surgeon's orderly who was out looking for his cow. None of this was unusual. Red Cloud and friends wanted to make it seem like a typical day at Fort Phil Kearny. Colonel Carrington had his men fire the twelve-pound howitzer, driving off about twenty Indians from a ravine and killing one of their ponies. No doubt he considered it a job well done and that the rest of the day would be more peaceful. Perhaps he and Margaret might even share a glass of sherry that evening and discuss something pleasant, like their time together before either of them had heard of the Bozeman Trail or Red Cloud.

While it was cold, the snow wasn't too deep, and Colonel Carrington saw no reason to alter his plans for the day. At ten o'clock he sent the wood train to the pinery, as still more firewood was needed to make it through the long winter. A mile and a half out, maybe forty warriors attacked, forcing the colonel's men to corral their wagons with the stock inside. An hour later, Colonel Carrington sent out a relief column of forty-nine infantrymen headed by Captain Fetterman. A cavalry column then set out from the post and joined Fetterman's force, for a total of eighty-one men. Red Cloud and other Sioux observers saw this development. It pleased them—everything was going according to plan.

It also pleased Wounded Eagle and Prairie Dog, who got word of the situation through the Sioux grapevine. Prairie Dog muttered how Fetterman had stolen the lovely Quaker girl he had intended to marry and deserved to be turned into a pincushion. Only I understood him as usual, but that was no matter to him. The only thing on his mind was revenge, even if he didn't dare to carry it out personally and even though some of his other soldier acquaintances might have to pay the ultimate price.

"Die, Fetterman, die!" Prairie Dog suddenly yelled.

Wounded Eagle turned to him but not with displeasure. "Yes, *wacicu*, die!" she yelled. There were certain English words she could understand.

I shivered in my cradleboard. Death brought sadness to so many, but I mostly was thinking of Grace Pennington. If Captain Fetterman was indeed Grace Pennington's man, she surely didn't need to lose him. The Indians had already made her a widow by killing her Quaker husband, Rufus. And Toby, even though he had been annoying and even cruel to me at times, didn't deserve to lose another father figure. Of course I didn't know for sure that Captain Fetterman was any kind of father figure. I realized how out of touch I was with everything back at Fort Phil Kearny. These days, Greasy Nose, Red Cloud, and other Sioux knew far more about the fort's goings-on than I did.

For some reason, while Prairie Dog and Wounded Eagle were sharing their anti-Fetterman moment, I blurted out *"Lobe-lobe"* and *"Toe-toe."* Neither the white renegade or my second Indian mother seemed to hear me. But then I said *"Fet-fet"* for perhaps the first time ever, and they both turned to me with what might have passed for looks of wonderment.

"Yes, *Fet-fet* die!" Wounded Eagle shouted as she reached

back to pat me on the shoulder.

"It's unanimous then," Prairie Dog roared, pounding his chest. "Nothing would please me more than to see Fetterman's scalp on a stick."

Captain Fetterman was supposed to help the wood train, but once he had crossed Piney Creek, he realized it was no longer necessary. The attackers fled and some other Indians appeared out of the leafless brush on the creek banks to divert his attention. They looked like an easy target for Fetterman, which was by design. These were the decoys. Crazy Horse was said to be among them, but I never saw him in my mind's eye and it was never confirmed. Two Feathers, though, was in the thick of this clever Sioux ruse, and his blood was boiling for battle. The danger and the cold did not concern this firebrand. He galloped right toward the troops, then pulled to a sudden halt and taunted them by standing up on his pony and showing them his bare rear end. The soldiers opened fire, and Two Feathers ducked down low on one side of his horse as he turned the animal and took flight. No matter what he was, he was no coward.

Captain Fetterman took the bait and signaled his command to pursue. When the decoy party got too far ahead, Two Feathers or one of the others would ride back to show the soldiers the way by turning in fast circles on the Bozeman Trail. The captain's determined pursuit continued to the top of Lodge Trail Ridge and then over the other side—just where Colonel Carrington had told him not to go and just where Red Cloud and his followers wanted him to go. Actually, according to my Indian sources, it was Lieutenant George W. Grummond and his cavalry who galloped ahead of Fetterman's command and sprang the trap. In any case, hiding in gullies on the other side of the ridge were Wolf Who Don't Dance and perhaps 1,999 other Minneconjous, Oglalas, and Cheyennes—the main ambush force.

The arrows flew so thick that they looked like a plaque of locusts. The cavalry, in the lead, got it first, but some of the troopers were able to pull back and take up a position one hundred yards above Captain Fetterman and the infantry, who retreated to a defensive position behind an array of large rocks. And so the infantry and cavalrymen fought separately, but it didn't take long for both elements to be destroyed, maybe forty minutes. I could not watch in my mind's eye after ten minutes. Some of the women and Prairie Dog moved in closer when it became clear the soldiers had no escape. The surviving soldiers made it back to the ridge for their last stand. Prairie Dog was close enough to identify one of the survivors as the hated captain.

"Get him!" Prairie Dog yelled, pointing from behind a boulder. "That's Fetterman!"

I couldn't help but look again. The captain was firing his rifle as if there was still hope. So were the other bluecoats. As they continued to shoot, they became half-hidden in the powder smoke. A direct assault proved costly to a few Indians, so most of the others dismounted and began crawling up the ravines. Not being content with his role as a decoy, the young brave Two Feathers reappeared and was now determined to count coup on the captain of the bluecoats. He did not believe in crawling. He scrambled up the slope directly toward Captain Fetterman and got halfway there before he slipped on a patch of icy snow and fell hard on his side. Immediately he took a bullet in his exposed arm. I saw blood flow from his elbow and freeze before it reached his wrist.

"It's up to you, Wolf!" shouted Prairie Dog, pounding a fist too hard against his boulder and crying out in pain. In the heat of the moment he couldn't come up with any Sioux words of encouragement.

*"Hokay hey—Le anpetu kin mate kin waste ktelo!"* cried many warriors, including Wolf Who Don't Dance, and even the soldiers knew what that meant—"This is a good day to die!"

In a matter of minutes, the Indians overran Captain Fetterman's impossible position. One warrior rode at a gallop into the fray, and his amazingly cooperative horse knocked down the distraught captain. That same warrior then employed his war club to smash in Fetterman's skull before using his knife to slash Fetterman's throat. No, the warrior's name was not Crazy Horse. Another Oglala, American Horse, claimed he was the slayer, but Prairie Dog insisted he had seen Wolf Who Don't Dance slash Captain Fetterman before other warriors moved in for the after-kill. None of them had the slightest respect for the captain, and they—no big surprise—mutilated the body.

Captain William Fetterman's death, unfortunately (at least as far as eyewitness history is concerned), was a blur to me because at the time Wounded Eagle was in another part of the battlefield cutting off the top of a dead cavalryman's skull and removing his brains. My mind's eye was seeing that horror—just one of many that day. Soldier brains weren't the only things cut out or severed and then laid on the windswept rocks—so were other internal organs, as well as eyeballs, noses, ears, teeth, hands, feet, and private parts. Never before had I wanted to close my mind's eye so desperately.

It turned out that Prairie Dog, the former soldier who saw many of the bluecoats die, had a stomach for blood as long as it wasn't his own. Wolf and the other warriors at the battle scene wouldn't let the renegade white man have a piece of the late Captain Fetterman. The best Prairie Dog could do was show up at our tepee after the battle waving the curly beard and mutton chops of a bossy sergeant he had disliked.

Wolf Who Don't Dance was a proud warrior, but my Indian dad did not talk about killing Fetterman or anybody else in the battle, at least not in the presence of Mum or I. Greasy Nose had worn a wolf-skin headdress at the warriors' ceremony before the battle, and Wolf had gone on not only to escape the battlefield unscathed but also to slay the boastful enemy leader. Coincidence? I could only wonder about it.

Wolf did bring back to the tepee some human teeth that others had carved out of the mouths of dead or dying soldiers. He wanted Pretty Bear to make him another tooth necklace and she, as always, was obliging. Prairie Dog and Wounded Eagle had done some of the mutilating at the site of the one-sided fight, and afterward they did most of the talking. On the day of the victory dance, Prairie Dog tried to tickle Mum with the sergeant's curly beard as he told her once again about how Captain Fetterman had looked with his head smashed in and his throat cut.

"Stop," Mum told him. "Don't touch me, Dog. Don't talk to me about it. Not ever. I'll tell Wolf."

"No need to tell Wolf, ma'am. He's the one who done Fetterman justice. Too bad somebody else made off with the Fetterman scalp, though. It would look good hanging . . ."

"Shut up!"

"Oh, please. It's time for celebration. I guess Wolf won't be taking part in the victory dance. The man just can't dance. He should be proud as punch, though. I could kiss him myself for doing Fetterman that way."

"How can you talk that way? He was a captain in the U.S. Army."

"Officers are a dime a dozen. And that one had the nerve to try to steal my fiancée away from me. What happened to him, he rightly deserved."

"Grace Pennington must be in such pain. Maybe she admired the captain's boldness, but she was still set to marry you, not him. You deserted her and your command, and I was fool enough to go along with you."

"Well, look at me now. And look at Fetterman. I'm alive and happy and tickling you with a sergeant's beard, and Fetterman is naked and dead with all that excessive pride cut right out of him."

I was curled up in the back of the tepee trying not to throw up. Pretty Bear had her back to me and wasn't even trying to understand what Prairie Dog and Mum were saying. She was already working on a soldier-tooth necklace. It wasn't that she was happy over the bloodshed, but making the necklace kept her hands and mind occupied. And she always wanted to do something that pleased her Wolf.

When somebody entered the tepee, Pretty Bear didn't even look up from her work. Prairie Dog, though, stopped tickling Mum. It was Wounded Eagle holding a string of muscles that had been stripped from various white arms, chests, backs, thighs, and calves. She greeted Prairie Dog of all people. They seemed to understand each other. Both had enjoyed witnessing the fight or massacre, whatever you want to call it, but they were not warriors and were not allowed to fully participate in the victory dance.

Wounded Eagle dangled the muscles in Mum's face and then tossed them in my direction. Mum gagged and so did I. Wounded Eagle laughed and so did Prairie Dog. She went through a mock demonstration, elaborate and crude, of how she had driven a spear shaft through—and there is no delicate way to say this—the poop hole of Captain Fetterman's friend Frederick Brown, the erstwhile post quartermaster. Prairie Dog and Wounded Eagle then had a short conversation, partly in English, partly in Sioux, partly in sign language. At some point Mum fainted and I crawled over to her. When Wounded Eagle doused Mum's face with cold water, some of it spilled on to me. As soon as Mum awoke, she cried "Ha-choo," but I was in no mood to respond with an "Ah-goo."

"I was just asking Wounded Eagle here why she didn't shove the shaft up Fetterman instead of Brown," Prairie Dog told Mum. "The gist of her answer was that Brown was a lousy soldier who didn't know his ass from a hole in the ground while Fetterman was known to be too bold for his own good and a total asshole. Or at least that's how I interpreted it."

Mum fainted again. Nobody bothered to douse her this time. Pretty Bear interrupted her necklace-making to take me outside for my regular bowel movement. I couldn't go. Not the next day either, or the day after that.

But today is Christmas, and I managed to leave a little gift in the snow for Wounded Eagle this morning. And now in the late afternoon I have slipped outside again to catch snowflakes with my tongue. But Pretty Bear is at the entrance now. Her alone time with Wolf is finished. She motions Mum and me inside. Mum can't get inside fast enough, but it's not because she considers our tepee a real home. She's just so very cold, and the snow shows no sign of letting up. I crawl inside, too, at my own sweet pace. I hadn't minded sitting out there with those snowbanks all around me. It was kind of comforting, like being in a womb. Not that any womb could be that cold.

Now Wounded Eagle shows up. Her cheeks are flush, perhaps from running into the chilling wind. I have seen similar cheeks on Mrs. Pennington, who I never saw running with or against the wind. I believe Wounded Eagle was visiting at Prairie Dog's single man's tepee to borrow some tobacco. Wolf is a hero in her eyes, but she knows he doesn't let his women smoke and that she will forever stand in the pretty shadow of her younger sister. Not that I am trying to spread any rumors. She is a married lady, even if she is the number two wife in our tepee.

Mum is now lying on the buffalo robes. She is curled up in a womb-like position. She is coughing and moaning. I'm afraid she is mighty sick, maybe even sicker than she was when she was pregnant with me on the trail. I crawl toward her. I stop. I hear a noise. It sounds familiar. It's coming from the fort. Boom! I see Wolf and his two Indian wives chattering away in their language. They only seem to hear each other.

Boom! There goes another one. I know what it is—artillerymen are firing the mountain howitzer at Fort Phil Kearny. Again no reaction from the three Oglalas, and Mum's moaning is so loud she can't hear anything except herself. I'm sure the gun wasn't fired as part of any confrontation. I don't think any Indians are even skulking around the fort—it's too darn cold for skulking. Prairie Dog says that Greasy Nose might not bother spying anymore himself. It's understandable. Red Cloud doesn't want to risk the life of his people's great prophet. Boom! That's the third one. My family in the tepee is oblivious, so oblivious that I suspect I am only hearing the howitzer go off in my mind's eye, or I guess I should call it my mind's ear. I really can't explain my Power any more than I can explain Greasy Nose's Power.

I wait for another boom. It doesn't come. I hear nothing with my two actual ears, and I hear nothing in my mind's ear. But I think I have the booms figured out. It's a three-gun salute to commemorate Christmas, the day that Jesus Christ was born and four days after Captain Fetterman and his command all fell. I would like to maybe see the fort in my mind's eye. But my mind's eye is dark and fuzzy, totally uncooperative. I wonder how much the Carringtons, Mrs. Pennington, and Toby are actually commemorating. I can't see any of them. Still, a three-gun salute is something. The Fetterman Fight, a full-blown bloody Indian massacre, is not the end to all things.

# FEBRUARY 4, 1867:
## ANTICIPATING MORE TOMBS

Today I am a month into the second half of my first year—my seven-month birthday, if you prefer. But who's counting? Only me, I think. My Sioux family has no idea today is any different than yesterday or the day before. I guess they must figure my age in moons, full or otherwise, since I was captured. Mum hasn't had the time or the strength to note this occasion, not that it calls for a celebration or commemoration in most circles. But in my small circle, occupied by me and me alone, it is special. I mean every day I am still alive is special, since I am in captivity and this has been the harshest winter in the memory of our great leader, Red Cloud. The Moon of the Terrible— that's what the Sioux call January—is finally over. But now we are in Moon When There Is Frost Inside the Lodge, and it is no better. How frigid has it been? Well, we're in the middle of a war but nobody is fighting. The Army and the Indians are both static, except when it is necessary to move to stay warm. In other words, it has become a war of survival, which isn't such a bad thing when you think about it. There are relatively few casualties—several folks frozen stiff but mostly just coughing fits and frostbitten fingers, toes, and earlobes.

As an infant I am supposedly at greater risk, but I don't curl up in a ball and worry about the weather—and I still can't talk about it. I'm so active with my crawling and sitting up and tumbling, both inside and outside the tepee, that I'm now called "Snow That Drifts" far more than "Little Eagle Bear." Yes, my

Indian family uses English for my name, but never uses my actual given American name and otherwise has little interest in the language. They mostly stick to Sioux words and leave the translations to the bilingual Greasy Nose and the renegade white man Prairie Dog, who lies well in both languages. Mum (nobody expects me to call her "Yellow Hair" yet) still sometimes whispers my white name, Daniel, but not too often, because she has felt the back of Wounded Eagle's hard left hand too many times.

Once in the middle of the night, when I believe she was sleeping and having a rare good dream, Mum called out "Angel Lamb." I had almost forgotten her old nickname for me. Although still an infant, of course, I don't feel anything like an Angel Lamb anymore; I don't think anyone with such a label would survive in this place, which can be hard and unforgiving. Thing is, though, this place is feeling more and more like home. Unlike Mum, I never actually set foot in our Chicago tenement building. My earlier "homes" have been nothing but covered wagons and frontier forts. Mum dreams of sleeping again in a bed, preferably a soft one with two or three down pillows at the fancy Wheelwright house in Virginia City. As for me, I can't imagine any bed as being as comfy as the fur blankets in our tepee. Why, these days, I scarcely even miss my green blankie.

I must say, though, that I have not been satisfied with my names. I guess everybody needs something to complain about. I enjoy being outside in any season (though I haven't actually been outside in spring yet) and I like the taste of fresh snow, but the name "Snow That Drifts" leaves me cold. It doesn't flow from anyone's tongue, and my tongue certainly can't handle it. Also I don't drift. I crawl with a purpose. Furthermore, I don't plan on becoming a drifter. I like having a home, even if it is shaped like a cone instead of a square or a rectangle. "Little Eagle Bear" is not any better. I mean what is an eagle bear anyway? My two Indian mothers just wanted parts of their names in my name so they made the creature up. Pretty Bear already seems to have a connection with the male Elk spirit *He-haka,* who apparently watches out for her and even pleases her—I guess as sort of a backup to her human Wolf. And there are other animistic spirits hanging around, such as the Beaver, the Hawk, the Fish, and the Frog. I'm not positive, but I believe Wounded Eagle's connection is with the Snake (and I don't necessarily mean the human Prairie Dog). But not even in this crazy world are there flying bears.

I guess what I feel like more than anything—though I have never actually seen one—is a white fox. Yes, a white fox, crawling around on his own exploring his half-cozy, half-icy environment. Wolves are tougher than foxes, but there is already a Wolf in the family and anyway, in case you haven't figured it out yet, I'm not so tough. Naturally, it will be some time before I am able to let anyone around here know that I want to be named White Fox. No, I haven't forgotten the name "Daniel." It sounds natural enough coming out of my Mum's mouth, and Daniel Boone is quite the frontiersman according to the standards of the white world. But I don't feel like I am a Daniel. I'm not a total baby, though—I'm no "Dan-Dan." I'd say "Danny" sounds about right.

I am *not* an unhappy child despite the captivity, my silly Indian names, the severe winter, Mom's persistent cough, Wounded Eagle's temper, Wolf Dad's moodiness, and all the faces around me that remain various shades of red whether it is winter, summer, or fall. I am *surviving*! That's the main thing. With the fire always going in the middle of the tepee, I can become too hot crawling around in the little buffalo robe coverall—a Wounded Eagle original. Naked is still best at times.

Like I said, every day is special here, not that every day wouldn't be special some other place. But this is where I am. I am adaptable. I figure the way my leg and torso muscles are developing I'll be walking instead of crawling in another month or so. That will be when I'm eight months old. But seven months on this earth is right now, and I'm content crawling up a storm! The day is special because it is *now*. I plan to celebrate by eating a few snow pies, by making eagle impressions in the snow, by building forts and tepees with my arrowhead collection, by recreating the comfort I had in the womb, by looking back on the scary but beautiful day I was born in Ash Hollow, Nebraska, by etching for the future, by accepting anything that might appear in my mind's eye, and by grinning real silly at everyone I happen to see with my two actual eyes.

If you can't be with the one you love, love the one you are with. That has been my philosophy out of necessity while living with the Sioux and being separated from my working, sickly Mum for long stretches most days. Her hacking coughs have become too real for her to play the sneezing game with me. I think I've outgrown it, in any case. She still nurses me when she can, but the nursing times seem shorter and shorter even though I latch on better than ever and am a growing boy. I get enough to eat, though, from other sources. I don't cry about it. Mum is doing the best she can.

My caretakers have included not only my two Indian mothers, Pretty Bear and Wounded Eagle, but also my Indian dad, Wolf Who Don't Dance, and some of his friends and acquaintances—including the medicine man prophet Greasy Nose, the white renegade Prairie Dog, Red Cloud's interpreter Little Bull, the young warrior Two Feathers, and Two Feathers' recent love interest, Yellow Crowfeather. Red Cloud himself is too busy for babies but feels I am almost family, so every once in a while he sends his interpreter to teach me Red Cloud words of wisdom. Two examples: "The Great Spirit raised both the white man and the Indian. I think he raised the Indian first. He raised me in this land; it belongs to me. The white man was raised over the great waters, and his land is over there" and "They made us many promises, more than I can remember, but they never kept but one; they promised to take our land, and they did." Little Bull, a short, jumpy fellow who doesn't like to bend down to my level, speaks the words of his boss in a monotonous tone broken up only by a squeak at the end of every other sentence. But Red Cloud's messages still come through.

With all the others, I can smile and interact at various levels. I've already told you about Wounded Eagle and Pretty Bear. One is kind of loud and bossy and tough but she appreciates good bowel movements and any Sioux word I might utter, however babyish. The other is kind of quiet and gentle but just as tough in her own way. I mean Pretty Bear has to be tough to maintain her number one wife status in the face of her aggressive older sister, Wounded Eagle, and my beautiful Mum. With me, neither of my Indian mothers is overprotective. They let me crawl around to my heart's content most of the time unless they are taking me somewhere in a cradleboard, at which times I'm as safe and secure as a bug in a rug. Of course I'm sure Pretty Bear would never carry me off in a cradleboard to watch Indians ambush soldiers. Wounded Eagle, on the other hand, thought that was a good experience for me. She can't have a child of her own so she wants me raised right, which is her way. She doesn't want me to be a sissy; she wants me to be *all warrior.*

I think the thinking of Wolf Who Don't Dance is the same. I have been told that he shows far more interest in me than most Sioux fathers do for their infant sons. He says, through one of the translators, that as soon as I am able to walk, he will have Greasy Nose pierce my right ear with a sharp stick during a Sun Dance so that I can wear a bird's-claw earring like him. And he talks of teaching me how to use a bow and arrow to hunt—I assume small game, not white soldiers, but who knows.

When I cry, my Indian mothers will often sing to me, cuddle with me, or hug me. Wolf Dad isn't big on those things. Usually he will hand me off to someone else. But when nobody else is around and my crying is too persistent, he will pour water into my nose until I am too uncomfortable to even cry.

Prairie Dog might do his caring for me only to stay in the good graces of Wolf, but it's nice to hear him talk to me in English (even if he mostly talks to hear his own voice) and he makes funny faces. The left side of his upper lip is nearly twice as thick as the right side, so when he curls that lip, intentionally or not, it covers one nostril but not the other. He also can stare at the tip of his pug nose until his eyes become crossed. Those kinds of things still make me laugh. With Greasy Nose, I have developed an appreciation for a slightly more sophisticated humor. He shapes his hands and fingers and makes them or their shadows hoot like owls, howl like wolves, growl like bears, and soar like eagles. He can also imitate a buffalo breaking wind, which I suppose isn't quite so sophisticated. Greasy Nose's visits are infrequent, though, and he never shows up in a dress (red or other) or tries to foresee my future in the tribe.

Two Feathers talks to me in the Sioux language, but I'm quite sure he is mostly talking about himself. I get the same feeling even when his young woman (not future bride quite yet), Yellow Crowfeather, is with him. Apparently she got that name as a little girl when her father single-handedly drove away four Crow Indian raiders and she claimed a yellow feather one of them left behind. She hardly says a word in our tepee, just listens to Two Feathers. Once I swear he was telling me about the time he counted coup on Philip Kittridge, but I can't be certain because he has nearly a dozen coup-counting tales. Each story seems to impress Yellow Crowfeather. Two Feathers can make me laugh, but rather uncomfortably. Twice he showed up when he knew Wolf was napping and woke the older warrior up by blasting a few off-key notes from a battered bugle taken from the Fetterman Fight. Both times Wolf sprang up to reach for his war club while his feet become hopelessly tangled in his blankets. By the way, nobody here—in this tepee or in any of the tepees for miles around, except in Prairie Dog's puny little one-man tepee—calls it the Fetterman Fight or any kind of massacre. More on that in a bit.

Despite his impudence, Two Feathers does believe Wolf killed Fetterman and in any case thinks Wolf is the greatest warrior this side of Crazy Horse, who apparently is much less accessible. That's why Two Feathers has kept coming around our tepee, with or without Yellow Crowfeather, since last year's one-sided battle. Two Feathers, according to Greasy Nose, hopes some of Wolf's Power and invincibleness will rub off on him. Two Feathers admitted as much himself one day last January when he and Greasy Nose came to our tepee—Greasy Nose to bring some herbs to sickly Mum, and Two Feathers to observe.

"Sure I have counted many coup, but I must learn to kill like the great ones," he said to Greasy Nose in their language. "I killed no one in the battle. I only got a soldier's bullet in the arm. But someday I will be the greatest warrior who ever lived— greater than Wolf Who Don't Dance, greater than Crazy Horse, greater even than Red Cloud once was." Greasy Nose made the translation for Mum, because Mum was concerned about the way Two Feathers was constantly staring at her and constantly picking me up with his one good arm and making faces at me.

"Silly woman," Greasy Nose told Mum after Two Feathers had finally gone for the day because he was supposed to meet Yellow Crowfeather's father. "Two Feathers has Yellow Crowfeather to bring him many Lakota babies. He only looks at you because you belong to his hero, Wolf."

"Why doesn't he look at Wolf, then?" Mum asked.

"He is not like me, not a *winkte* or *berdache*."

"But you are also a great medicine man, I think. Will your herbs cure my cough?"

"Hard to say."

"But they say you can foresee the future."

"I saw the bluecoats falling in my hands, but I am not Two Feathers' hero. I didn't actually kill anyone, either."

"There is too much killing," Mum said, coughing.

"Not enough for Two Feathers. He wants to be like Wolf, who has raw Power and possesses the innate qualities of a wolf that make him so formidable in battle. You cannot stare directly at one with such Power. You would only crumble at his feet. Do you understand?"

"Not really. I refuse to crumble at Wolf's feet."

"It is different between wife and husband."

"I'm his captive, not his wife."

"That too shall crumble, Yellow Hair."

"Maybe not. He has Pretty Bear for his . . . his beastly pleasures."

"Only you can bring him another son, Yellow Hair. My medicine has not helped Pretty Bear or Wounded Eagle to carry his child. Snow That Drifts is a fine son. But Wolf wants many sons like his Snow Drift."

"His Snow Drift? Danny is mine!"

"If you feel that way, then why not give him other sons?"

"You need to ask . . ." Mum cut herself off with a well-timed coughing fit. She had not lost her spirit or her motherly pride, but saying too much to Greasy Nose was not wise. The medicine man told his friend Wolf everything.

"You cannot keep a Wolf at bay forever," Greasy Nose said as he packed up his medicine bag. "I'll return tomorrow to see if you need more of my medicine."

Since that mid-January day little has changed. Mum, with the help of her sickness, keeps putting off Wolf Who Don't Dance.

Two Feathers keeps coming around to pick me up (now with two hands since his wounded arm is better) and make his faces. He is trying to teach me things, at least the one thing he knows best—counting coup. He has gotten me to count coup not only on a lazy mule but also on a skittish horse, on a hungry mouse, and on a horsefly. And let me tell you that counting coup on any living creature is not easy when you can only crawl. I think he is trying to impress or at least influence Wolf, who does not seem to want to teach Two Feathers anything about secret warrior Powers or killing bluecoats.

What stays the same here more than anything else is the cold, which Mum calls bitter and deathly and I call challenging and stimulating (though I haven't been able to convey that thought to her in words yet). Day after day the snow falls and drifts; the icy wind blows and chills the bones. None of that bothers me. The sun still shines. There is no shortage of blankets. The tepee fire keeps burning bright. And there are three Indian mothers who are usually willing to share their body heat with me. If you must know, not only do I like the taste of snow, but I like the way the snow "cleanses" my bottom after a bowel movement (which have become regular again, by the way). I am as fit as an arrow to a bowstring, as happy as a bear cub in its winter sleeping cave.

Of course Mum's health is a worry. Greasy Nose never shows up these days without his medicine bag full of roots, barks, herbs, plants, animal substances, and various inanimate charms. He has applied heated smooth stones and heated oil, scented and unscented, to all parts of her body—none of which Greasy Nose is interested in except from the standpoint of a healer. It's more than just a series of colds plaguing Mum. No matter how much he makes her sweat or expectorate mucus, she soon reverts to her coughing, sneezing, and listlessness. Greasy Nose says she is suffering from spirit sickness, a severe reduction in spirit caused by dwelling on evil thoughts, such as wanting to break out of captivity and return to the white world and refusing to accept Wolf Who Don't Dance as her legitimate husband.

When Mum in self-defense speaks of her white husband, Abraham Duly, back in Chicago, Wolf scoffs at the notion, much as Philip Kittridge used to do when he still had an interest in Mum. Greasy Nose says that if Mum doesn't fulfill all her duties of a Sioux wife soon she will only get much sicker no matter how often he opens up his medicine bag. But of course he is Wolf's good friend. Greasy Nose's bedside manner is starting to make Mum angry. Meanwhile Wounded Eagle, who never misses a beat when it comes to tormenting Mum, repeatedly insults Mum's womanhood in elaborate sign language and choice words that Greasy Nose and Prairie Dog duly translate. I shall repeat none of this because it serves no purpose. Besides it bothers me, even though I have nothing against the naked body. If it wasn't so cold, I'd be naked all the time. It's just that someone my age, seven months, isn't supposed to know yet about the facts of life and the ugly ways people stretch, bend, and twist those facts.

Truth is I only know enough of those "facts" to make me uncomfortable. I know that Mum had relations with other men besides absent husband Abe during the Civil War years (the miscarriages and short-lived children don't lie) and that the awful Phil Kittridge forced himself upon her at least once. A few times I have caught Mum, when she isn't feeling so sick, staring at Wolf when he isn't looking, such as when he is busy putting on his leggings or is engaged in under-the-blankets activity with his number one wife, Pretty Bear. Of course, far more times I have caught Wolf staring at Mum, with Mum pretending not to notice. He doesn't even try to hide it anymore. His eyes get all big, he growls a bit (like a hungry wolf, I suppose), and sometimes his tongue hangs out. In that regard, he and Mr.

Kittridge (long gone to Montana with Nelson Story, thank goodness) have much in common. But I'm not going to talk about it.

It's early February and the cold shows no sign of letting up. How much longer can it last? This is my first winter outside the womb so I really don't know. I do have this lingering feeling way down in my small gut that Wolf Who Don't Dance will at any moment suddenly turn to Mum Who Don't Act Like a Wife, sick or not, and go to her like a wild animal desperate for warmth and more. Enough said.

But you know something, dear readers, that wouldn't be the end of the world—that is looking at it all from my self-centered, childish point of view. I kind of like the idea of having a half-Sioux blood brother down the road, even if Mum has to go through another difficult pregnancy. Sure there would be a certain amount of jealousy on my part, but I'm convinced that I would benefit from such young companionship and that I—in fact, all of us—could handle such a new development in our tepee.

"We can never have enough young blood in the tribe," Greasy Nose often says, sometimes quoting himself, sometimes quoting Wolf, sometimes quoting Red Cloud, sometimes quoting Yellow Crowfeather, and sometimes quoting Oglalas whose names I've never heard before. I guess it's just one of those things every Sioux man or woman says. It's understandable. Life is hard on the Plains, what with sickness, accidents, and war. Death is always lurking on the horizon like a black storm in summer or a white storm in winter. Apparently not enough babies are being made or there are not enough male babies or at least not enough male babies who survive childhood to become warriors or too many young warriors who die trying to count coup or whatever. I hear all kinds of things like that. I know for a fact that despite the victory celebration after last year's big fight on December

21, many Sioux women slashed their arms and legs in mourning because their husbands or sons died that day. The white man call it the Fetterman Massacre, but Prairie Dog says that is only because Red Cloud was too clever for Captain Fetterman and his followers and the soldiers *lost*. Prairie Dog prefers to call it "Fetterman's Day of Reckoning."

Like I mentioned earlier, the Sioux and the Cheyenne nations have another name for it—the Battle of Hundred in the Hand or the Battle Where a Hundred Soldiers Were Killed. And you know who is responsible for those names? Hint: It isn't Red Cloud or Crazy Horse or Wolf Who Don't Dance or any other warrior or war leader. The credit goes to Wolf's friend and Mum's doctor, Greasy Nose. In the warriors' ceremony before the fighting, as I witnessed, he saw in his hands one hundred soldiers dying, and that's what happened, even if the whites say that only Fetterman and eighty others fell that day, including two men who were civilians. Maybe the one hundred dead also includes the Indians who were killed outright in the fight or who died later in the cold from their wounds. In any case, Greasy Nose was close enough to the correct number of slain enemy to now be considered a great prophet in the eyes of Red Cloud's people.

Somehow, though, I have trouble thinking of Greasy Nose as a great anything, especially when he makes those buffalo breaking wind noises and can't even cure Mum's spiritual sickness. At the same time I often have trouble thinking of my Indian dad (who I now prefer to think of as Wolf Dad!) as a great Sioux fighting man, even if he did kill Captain Fetterman in the Battle of Hundred in the Hand. I guess they are both just too familiar to me, and Wolf never even spanks me. Personally, despite my white blood, I don't call the fight a "massacre," and wouldn't even if I could pronounce the word. For one thing, I hate the word and all its connotations. I don't even like the word "battle." I guess killing is something I'll have to grow into if I survive to become a warrior in the moccasin steps of Wolf Dad. The name I happen to like best for what happened last December 21 is "Hundred in the Hand" because I prefer to think of the fallen men as not being dead but just sleeping in the giant hand of *Wakan Tanka* (God) waiting to be awakened far from the dangerous frontier.

I can't stress enough, though, that I *am not* miserable on this dangerous frontier at the seven-month point in my life. The people here and over at Fort Phil Kearny are all just like me now—not fighting or even thinking about fighting anyone, rather just trying to survive the cold winter. The Bozeman Trail is dead, no movement at all in either direction, according to Prairie Dog, who heard it from Red Cloud's scouts. He also heard that Colonel Carrington was one of the scapegoats for what happened to Captain Fetterman's command (since the captain was dead) and was forced to leave the fort he built, departing with family and staff on a January day when the temperature hovered at thirty-eight degrees below zero. Prairie Dog found it amusing that Colonel Carrington's replacement as post commander, a lieutenant colonel named Weasels or Whistles or something like that, did nothing but twiddle his thumbs—and only did that to keep his thumbs from getting frostbite.

"Carrington's lucky he ain't still at Fort Phil Kearny and so are you, ma'am," Prairie Dog told Mum even though she had not asked his opinion about anything. "There ain't no place to wash clothes or take a bath until spring. Colonel Weasels has no contact with the other forts and can't get no supplies. Half the soldiers got scurvy and are living on the mules' corn while the starving mules are eating holes through the logs in their stables. I swear if Red Cloud showed up at the fort tomorrow the soldiers would gladly surrender the damned place for the hump meat of a bison and the scurvy-curing herbs of Greasy Nose."

Red Cloud obviously didn't agree with the white renegade. The soldiers at the fort still had cannons, there were no travelers on the trail to ambush, and many of his warriors had scattered to their winter camps to obtain food reserves and warmth. When the weather improved, the attacks on supply trains, woodcutting details, and hay-cutting crews would resume. Red Cloud wasn't pressing his war this winter, but he wasn't worried. He knew come March he would still have the upper hand and could send into battle thousands of well-rested Sioux, Cheyenne, and Arapaho warriors intent on completing his stated mission—to drive from the Powder River Country all the bluecoats and all the white-eye travelers they were futilely trying to protect.

The fact that nobody is fighting right now makes me want to jump for joy. Of course I can't jump for anything at this stage of my development, but that's beside the point. The cleansing snow is falling gently outside the tepee flap at this very moment. Wolf Who Don't Dance is off with the boys having a smoke in one of the lodges or something like that. He smokes a lot to ease the boredom of the peaceful season. Mum and Wounded Eagle are somewhere outside, Mum using a U.S. Army shovel (borrowed from the former private Prairie Dog Burrows) to keep the paths in the snow clear while Wounded Eagle supervises her hard labor. Pretty Bear is the only one inside the tepee with me. She is sitting in the corner, barely watching me. She knows I have the good sense not to do anything crazy. Her back is to me and she is keeping her hands busy. She is trying not to let me see what she is doing, but that is a hard thing for her or anyone else to do, at least when my mind's eye is active. I know that she has interrupted her necklace making to fashion matching bird's-claw earrings for her Indian husband and her adopted white son. I find it rather touching but pretend I have no interest in her work. I know I have several months to wait before my ear is pierced and me and the earring are ready to be joined at the earlobe. I adjust my buffalo robe coverall and crawl away to the other side of the tepee where I keep my rattlesnake rattle under my favorite blanket.

I shake the rattle and hum a merry tune that is stuck in my head, though I am not sure if I first heard the tune on a white man's piano or a Sioux drum. I remember how Mum told me that her sister in Montana, Cornelia the "Queen of Virginia City," has a grand piano in the fancy house she shares with her rich miner husband. No doubt I shall never hear that piano or see that house or wrap my little fingers around a gold nugget. Not that a gold nugget sounds any better than my rattlesnake rattle. All these thoughts about what will never be don't make me sad, though, at least not for myself. But I know how Mum has dreamed of the piano, the home, and the gold. And I think how sick she always is and how she could die outside shoveling snow in this Indian village. I consider crying, and I consider crawling through the flap and through the snow to find Mum. I do neither. I cannot change the way things are. And so I just sit here, rattling and humming.

What's this? Where did all this drool come from? I am drooling like a mad dog. Something isn't right with my mouth. I wipe saliva from my chin. My lower gum is hurting, not real bad but enough to make me wonder what the heck is going on. I've never felt such a sensation in my mouth. Breast milk might help, but I'm not sure. Anyway, it is not immediately available. I pull up one corner of my favorite blanket and stick it between my lips. I don't just suck on it, either. I chew, naturally, like any living human or beast who has a set of teeth.

I try to forget that anything unusual is happening, even as I chew. But Pretty Bear has noticed—sometimes I think she has eyes in the back of her head—and has come over to me on all fours. She strokes my cheeks and says my name softly, "Snow That Drifts." The English words don't come easy for her. I say nothing, just revel in her touch. She moves smoothly into Sioux baby talk. I am soothed. Now she pinches my nostrils shut until I need to breathe out of my mouth and let the blanket fall out. She rubs my jaw and then pokes my lower gum with her pinky.

"*Hi*," she says.

I am confused, but I play along thinking it's some kind of Sioux children's word game. "Hewoo," I reply.

"*Hi*," she repeats, but it doesn't sound like a greeting this time.

I don't know what to say so I give her my oversized toothless grin. Pretty Bear smiles back and places two fingers on her two upper front teeth. Then she wets a strip of cloth and puts it in my mouth. I chew on that for a while and my lower gum feels better.

"*Hi*," she says for a third time. She touches my gum with her left pinky again and then taps one of her lower teeth with a finger from her right hand. I get the message, no translation necessary. My first tooth is breaking out.

"*Hi*," I say, reaching out toward Pretty Bear's mouthful of teeth, strung more beautifully than any necklace. I'm not the sharpest arrow in the quiver, but give me enough time and I'll master this Sioux language yet.

My first-tooth moment is spoiled. Prairie Dog Burrows comes barreling through the front flap of the tepee. His hair is sprinkled with snow as if he has the worst case of dandruff in history, his face is beefy red instead of pale, and he is panting like a Sioux dog. He has been running, which accounts for some of the redness, but he is also bleeding slightly from the nose and the left ear. He looks like he has seen a ghost, a ghost who can fight and also bite. There are teeth marks on his left earlobe.

Some semi-Sioux words gush from his swollen lips. I have no idea what he is saying and it is clear that Pretty Bear doesn't know either. Prairie Dog shakes his head. "I ain't got time to explain nothing!" he shouts in English. He ignores Pretty Bear and comes right at me. I know it isn't to make funny faces with his lopsided upper lip or his crossing eyes. I think he wants to stomp on me with his menacing boots, so I scramble away as fast as I can. I'm not one to brag, but I can scoot on the ground like a horned lizard escaping a bird of prey. I'm behind Pretty Bear now, but that is small protection. Prairie Dog puts his heavy hands on her shoulders, something he would never dare do in front of Wolf Who Don't Dance.

"I need the little drooler!" Prairie Dog says, pushing Pretty Bear away with one hand while trying to scoop me up with the other.

Pretty Bear is yelling a lot of things in her own language that don't sound so pretty.

"Shut your bone box, squaw!" he says, not even trying to speak Sioux. "I ain't asking you. I can't afford to be nice. Not no more!"

I can't believe how Prairie Dog is acting, even with the man of the tepee off smoking somewhere. Isn't he afraid that Pretty Bear will tell Wolf about this rough treatment? I squirm out of his grasp and try to sink my one tooth, which is still mostly in my gum, into his ankle. It does no damage. I am under-armed. Oh, no. He has me now, holding me under his left armpit like a squealing piglet. He goes for the tepee flap. Pretty Bear steps in his path. He slaps her face, forces her to the ground. She gets back up on her knees and takes wild swings at him with both arms. Even Pretty Bear can be a fighter if she has to, but she is trying not to accidentally strike me. That's all the advantage Prairie Dog needs. He yanks her by the arm. I hear a horrendous popping sound. Pretty Bear reaches for her shoulder as she slumps into a sitting position. The brute has pulled her shoulder out of its socket. She hasn't given up, though. She is bouncing along on the seat of her fur-lined skirt, trying to grab me with her good arm. She is screaming as she bounces. I am screaming as I squirm.

Prairie Dog curses both of us in two languages. He tries to tell Pretty Bear something in her language but soon gives up in frustration. He is frantic. "I ain't got no choice, squaw," he yells. "Me and the drooler got to get out of here pronto. They got Wolf, your husband. Yes, Wolf. Dead. *Kte. Kte.* Dead. Dead. Understand?"

*"Kte?"* Pretty Bear says. She is no longer bouncing, no longer reaching out for me, no longer screaming. A darkness falls across her face like nighttime. She suddenly looks almost ugly. She howls, like a bear or a wolf perhaps, but not like one of this earth. *"Sumanitu Taka! Sumanitu Taka!"* she cries, which I know means "Wolf," though I never heard her say it quite that way before. And now she is silent as stone. She looks up toward the smoke hole at the high point of our tepee. Her eyes are glassy, as if she sees into the clouds and even beyond the clouds. I stop squirming and screaming, too, to listen in case the Great Spirit says something or gives a sign. Even Prairie Dog has stopped halfway in and halfway out of the tepee as if he expects to be struck down by lightning if he takes one more step. But nothing happens. There's no sound, until Pretty Bear screams again, this time even louder than when the brute dislocated her shoulder.

I can't believe it. Wolf Dad dead? I heard no pounding hooves of Army horses in camp, maybe because of the snow cover. But I heard no bullets or bugles either. Were this new thumb-twiddling commander's men actually capable of a silent winter ambush? I try to see something in my mind's eye, but all I get is a white blur—as if I can't see past the rapidly falling snow. Maybe it is because Prairie Dog is practically holding me upside down now, but I get no mind picture at all. I feel so helpless in his hairy brute arms. I have so many questions to ask—if I could only speak.

"Woof-woof?" I manage to blurt out, but Prairie Dog pays no attention to me. He seems frozen in place. His eyes are fixed on Pretty Bear. She has a knife out. He thinks it's meant for him. His eyes grow wider than the Tongue River. *Watch it, you fool!* No, I don't care if she knifes him, but he is about to carelessly drop me on my head. Now, he sighs deeply. He sees Pretty Bear's real intent. She uses the knife to slash twice at her own arm, the one disconnected from her shoulder.

"Hell, I guess you really did love him," Prairie Dog says as he roughly flips me up so that he can get a better grip on my flanks. I feel like I am a sack of potatoes. He still doesn't leave. "But it ain't my fault, squaw," he adds, as if trying to convince himself. "Wolf was my friend, too, one of my only friends around here or anywhere. I don't think Red Cloud even likes me much. I sure don't have any friends back at Fort Phil Kearny. I ain't glad that he's dead. No, sir! But Wolf knew the dangers. He is— rather was—a warrior. Sioux warriors die just like Army soldiers. That's the way things work. And it ain't safe around here for me without my *only* warrior friend."

Pretty Bear stands up, not even wincing from her self-inflicted cuts or the dislocated shoulder. She says one word, almost calmly, *"Silaada?"*

"Huh? You mean 'soldiers'? No, it wasn't soldiers."

That was one of my questions, too. But if not done in by soldiers, who did it? Who killed Wolf Dad? Unfortunately, Pretty Bear has no follow-up question. She gives her arm a third slash. It pains me to see it.

"No matter to me what you do to yourself," he tells her as he swipes with his hand a trickle of blood running from nostril to fat lip. "A squaw's got to do what a squaw's got to do. As for me, I got to go. They got the little drooler's *real* mama."

Ouch! Prairie Dog might as well have pulled both my shoulders out of their sockets, wrung my neck, and beaten me to an inch of my life. The spirit and soul sag right out of me. I am limp, like a rag doll. I am big on personal survival, but if he wants to drop me on my head now, I am ready to go. I won't put up a fight. *Put me out of my misery, fool!* But dropping me is not his intention.

"I know you people don't like to say goodbye, so I won't say it," Prairie Dog says to Pretty Bear, who is now standing still as a scarecrow. Prairie Dog isn't moving either. "Hell, I don't even know how to say it in Sioux anyway."

I regain my bearings. *"Kte?"* I ask, repeating Pretty Bear's earlier question.

This time Prairie Dog hears me. He seems stunned. He holds me up close to his face and stares into my eyes. No longer a rag doll, I become stiff as a cradleboard. I stare back at his bloody nose, determined not to cry. Maybe his eyes become cross-eyed but neither of us is laughing. He has completely forgotten that he is in a rush to take me somewhere.

"Did you just say what I thought you said? I didn't even know you could speak, Sioux or American. Naw, it must have been just one of those accidental things . . . coincidences."

I try to translate for him. *"De. De,"* I say, but I can't make it sound like "dead." So I go back to Sioux. *"Kte?"* I ask again.

"Bloody hell!" Prairie Dog says. He takes a few small steps so that all of him is back inside the tepee. "Yes, Wolf is dead. Shot."

"Mum-mum?" I say frantically. "Mum?"

He is at a temporary loss for words.

"Mum. *Kte?*" I wish I could make it plainer for the fool, but I can't.

"I must be loco," he says, his eyeballs bulging. "If you're asking me if your mama's dead, little drooler, she ain't. They got her. That is to say they got her away from Wounded Eagle. There was quite a scuffle, and I got a little bloodied. Wounded Eagle bit my ear by mistake. They took her to Greasy Nose's tepee, where Wolf now lies dead."

Whooosh! I catch my breath. I'm so relieved to hear that Mum is alive that I have a sudden urge to plant a kiss on Prairie Dog's forehead. But the urge passes quickly. He continues talking. Amazingly the man is speaking to me. The only other person in the tepee, poor mourning Pretty Bear, doesn't know English and is just standing there bleeding all over herself from her slash wounds. My ears perk up. I don't so much as blink.

"The son of a bitch shot Wolf, who was there at Greasy Nose's tepee having a smoke," Prairie Dog says. He kind of whispers these words in my ear, as if doesn't want Pretty Bear to hear. Despite his basic cruelness, I think he feels sorry enough for Pretty Bear not to want to harm her any further. "And now they are holding Greasy Nose hostage because some of the hotheaded young warriors like Two Feathers have come there," he continues much louder, but with his voice quivering as if he is afraid of his own words. "My tepee's right next door. It's natural I would be coming back there. I'm hoping I can get you inside Greasy Nose's tepee without too much trouble and, like I said, that is what they want me to do—actually they are demanding it. I want to live. Look what they already did to Wolf? I don't have a choice. Do you understand?"

I understand about survival and about Wolf dying. But my head is light. I can't feel too bad about his death because I'm so happy that Mum is *not* dead. Still, I don't understand who "they" is, and that annoys me. I want to scream out: "Don't you know how to tell a story, you idiot! How can you tell a story using *they* when the listener has no idea who *they* might be."

Prairie Dog rolls his eyes, shakes his head, and answers his own question. "Of course, you can't understand me," he says. "You're not even knee-high to a short-legged rabbit. But I swear you look like you're listening and catching my drift. You, see, little drooler, that's what those fellas came all the way from Montana for—for her. And for you. Yeah, you! If I don't bring you to them pronto, they aim to shoot my mule, butcher my dog, take my goods, burn my tepee, and scalp Greasy Nose alive. Now, I can live with all that mind you, but I ain't as dumb as I look. With no more Wolf to stand up for me in this here village and with those three crazy bastards around who shot that genuine Sioux war hero and who are holding the great medicine man hostage . . . well, I figure I'll lose my white renegade status before the sun goes down and be considered just another *wasicu* who needs to part with his long hair. The thing is that unless they get you back safely, little drooler, that bloodthirsty trio aims to let me go with them only as far as the Bozeman Trail, at which point they promise to give me the full Fetterman treatment! That is if we can even get away from Two Feathers and the others. Damn crazy white folks are scarier than the Sioux! What am I telling you all this for? Living with the Injuns has got me talking to myself and, worse, talking to a little drooler. You ain't much more than a tadpole." His voice trembles and fades. He wipes blood from his ear. Maybe he is having trouble deciding if he really wants to take me to where he *must go*.

I keep staring back at him with a blank expression. If I really were a tadpole, things would be so much simpler. His lopsided upper lip curls instinctively, but I don't find it funny now. I don't know how to begin to ask who these three "crazy bastard fellas" are who killed my Wolf Dad and want Mum and me for purposes unknown. Prairie Dog said they have come all the way from Montana Territory. Could Aunt Cornelia and husband, Wheely, in Virginia City have sent out a three-man posse of vigilantes to save us? That's my childish wishful thinking. How could Aunt Cornelia even know we are captives? Of course, Fort C.F. Smith, just eighty miles away, is also in Montana Territory. Is it a trio of soldiers? Well-armed civilian volunteers? Good Samaritans? I assume they aren't literally bastards. Maybe the Army has posted a reward for our return. But that doesn't make sense. Colonel Carrington might have cared about us, but the new brass at Fort Phil Kearny doesn't even know who we are. Anyway, the soldiers there are having enough trouble just trying to survive the winter.

My imagination is running wild. Prairie Dog called the trio "bloodthirsty," too, and he never actually said that these fellas were white men. Maybe they are more Indians! Couldn't Indians be fellas, too? The Sioux don't only battle U.S. Army soldiers or attack only white folks in wagons. They have other enemies. The Crow tribe in Montana, for one, is the traditional enemy of the Sioux. Such is Red Cloud's Power and influence that some Crows became his allies. It could be, though, our Sioux camp has been invaded by three young Crows who don't want to save Mum and me but want to turn us into their own captives so they can gain status as warriors and cause Red Cloud and his Sioux to lose face. Or the invaders could be three Pawnees. I heard that because they hate Sioux and Cheyennes so much, Pawnee warriors are becoming scouts for the U.S. Army. The possibilities are many; alliances on the frontier are complicated. I've been thinking too much. Ouch! All this thinking and all this staring into Prairie Dog's eyes has given me a powerful headache. He snorts, curls that lip, and then lowers me, seemingly giving me my wish. I guess he doesn't want to look at me anymore either.

"It don't all make sense to me," he admits. Then he looks back at poor Pretty Bear, who is sitting down again in a little pool of her own blood. She hasn't resumed slashing herself but is tearing apart one of her pretty necklaces. "Those fellas want the kid and I'm a dead man unless I deliver him. I'm probably a dead man even if I do, but . . . say something!"

Pretty Bear isn't even trying to understand his English. Teeth and beads scatter all around her. She looks for another necklace to break.

"Don't worry, squaw," says Prairie Dog. "You'll heal up in time and you ain't hard on the eyes, not even cut up that way. I know any number of young bucks around here who'd jump at the chance to take you for his wife." Then he throws in a few Sioux words, but still Pretty Bear makes no response.

For a man in a rush it has been a long, long goodbye. But Prairie Dog pulls me against his hip and finally leaves the tepee. Pretty Bear doesn't try to follow us. She has so many necklaces she could be inside there tearing them apart for a week.

Another human being confronts us in the pathway between two walls of hard snow. It isn't a warrior but still someone for-midable—my other Indian mother! But Wounded Eagle isn't herself. She staggers toward us. She is actually wounded. Blood pours from her head, a fountain of blood that outdoes Pretty Bear's blood puddle. Her eyes blaze like prairie fires. She makes a grab for me with a hand but only manages to wipe blood on the buffalo robe coverall from my neck to my buttocks. I notice an unnatural dent on the side of her head. Prairie Dog backs away from her as if he has seen a ghost from his past. Her strength is gone, which is lucky for Prairie Dog, who is not a fighter. She collapses at his feet, forming a mound in our path. He hesitates, and I squirm, trying to get down to go to Wounded Eagle. But Prairie Dog grips me with both hands and gingerly steps over the body. Whatever kind of relationship the two of them had, it doesn't count for much now.

"I . . . I got to go," Prairie Dog says to the body. But he freezes when Wounded Eagle stirs and half opens one eye.

I need to say something. She is lying there in the snow like a dying bird. Wounded Eagle can be cruel, especially to Mum, but I know she cares for me, physically and deep down to her *woniya,* or soul. She wants me to make her proud by becoming a tough little warrior. She loves me without babying me.

"*Luta!*" I shout, pointing down at her. "*Luta!*"

"Huh?" says Prairie Dog, but then he nods his head.

We both know this word because Red Cloud's name in Sioux is "Makhpiya-luta."

"Yes, you are right, little drooler," Prairie Dog says. "Wounded Eagle is red all over. But it wasn't me who done it. I'd never make her bleed that way. It was my shovel though. That Injun hating bastard used my shovel!"

"Who-who," I manage to get out, probably from listening to owls and Greasy Nose's owl sounds.

"Huh?" he says. "You're a tadpole. How can you be asking me questions?"

"Who-who," I repeat.

"It's Kittridge who's to blame."

Of course I don't believe him. I have only known two Kittridges in my life, the brothers on the trail who both wanted to marry Mum. The younger one, Luther, is dead, killed and disassembled by Indians. The older one, Philip, took off with Nelson Story's cowboys, bound for Montana.

"Kit-Kit," I say, because Kittridge is a long word.

"Damn. You ain't no normal tadpole."

I squirm out of Prairie Dog's arms and get on the ground. I crawl to Wounded Eagle and cling to her shoulder. Both her eyes are closed. I forgive her for being so mean to Mum. I ask her to please not die.

"She wanted to stop them from taking your mother," says Prairie Dog. "Wounded Eagle was kicking and punching like it was a saloon brawl. Kittridge picked up the shovel and . . . You understand?"

"Mum-mum," I say.

"That's right. Nothing we can do for Wounded Eagle now." Prairie Dog tears me away from Wounded Eagle's shoulder and stuffs me under his right armpit. He scurries away but only takes a few steps before he trips. Underfoot is the bloody U.S. Army shovel that Mum used to clear snow and Philip Kittridge used to win a brawl in the snow with Wounded Eagle. Prairie Dog stares at the shovel as if it is somebody's severed limbs. The snowbanks on both sides are disturbed. Tracks are all over, some too large to be human. I wonder what kind of beast could have made them and whether the beast is from this world or the spirit world.

"*Luta,*" I say again, because it's easier for me to say than "red" and because I can't say "shovel" and don't know its Sioux equivalent.

"Yup, little drooler, red snow," Prairie Dog agrees. He starts to trot away, but I squirm and point to the ground. It's Mum's black shawl. He picks it up and sniffs it. "She must have dropped it when they came for her on their snowshoes," he comments.

I can hardly contain my frustration. *Who is they?* I shout, but all that comes out is "Huh?"

"Snowshoes, for walking on snow. They came by sled pulled by dogs and two of them had snowshoes—that is the men, not the dogs. They caught me and I had to tell them where your mother was. They forced me to show them the way. There was three of them. What choice did I have?"

"Mum-mum," I say.

"Right, Mum-mum. After they got her away from Wounded Eagle, they took her and me to Greasy Nose's tepee where Wolf was. I don't know if it was to get vengeance or to get hostages. Anyway, when Kittridge went in, Wolf shot an arrow. Kittridge shot back with a gun. Kittridge plugged him right in the chest.

Wolf died game, though, like a good Sioux warrior should! Damn, what a dirty rotten shame. What's going to happen to me now?"

"Die-die," I say.

"Huh?" Prairie Dog says. He is so stunned he drops me. Ouch. Good thing he wasn't holding me too high. And good thing there is all this snow on the ground. I am OK. Well, maybe my knee is bruised. But I'm not going to cry.

"Die-die," I say from the ground.

"Are you saying 'die,' tadpole? I sure as hell hope not. Those three bastards got me into this mess. They better get me out of it."

"Mum—huh?" I say.

"Mum-huh? Oh, you're asking about your mother? Well, she was there, too. Didn't I tell you that already? The one who looks like a black bear swiped your Mum up off her feet just like she was bee's honey while Kittridge fought off Wounded Eagle and I got caught in the middle of it. That's one hard-nosed squaw! She put up one hell of a fight. He had to use the shovel. And the third fella, the tall one, just stood there watching. He was the one without the snowshoes."

"Mum?"

"Your Mum is fine. Nobody used a shovel on her. They didn't come all this way to hurt her. Like I've been telling you, they want her and they want you."

"Who-who?" I say. I'm still desperate to know who "they" is.

"Who do you think—the three bastards who came here from Montana."

"Die-die," I say again.

"Yeah, maybe they'll die. Maybe we'll all die. How the hell should I know! I swear it ain't easy talking to you, tadpole."

*The feeling is mutual, Prairie Dog. How do you expect a seven-month-old boy to be easy to talk to? And I don't like being called "little drooler." "Tadpole"* isn't much better. *Let's go find Mum. Pronto.* Those are the things I would say to him if I could. I want to see across the village into Greasy Nose's tepee to make sure Mum really is alive and well. But my mind's eye still is not cooperating. All I see is blowing snow and flowing blood. It's become downright useless! Am I losing my Power? Will I even be able to one day put down in writing all these things I've been etching in my skull?

"Come on, you," Prairie Dog says, lifting me into his arms again. "Unless you have any other questions?"

I should be grateful we can communicate at all and that he is telling me things. But I am not satisfied. *Now tell me more! More! Can't you understand, you fool. More!* My words don't come out as I think them out in my head. All that emerges from my lips is "Mo. Mo. Mo Mum. Mo Mum."

"Huh?" he says.

"Mum-huh. Mum-mo."

"Yes, we're going to see your mother," Prairie Dog says, wiping his brow with Mum's shawl. First he puts me under his left armpit but soon switches me to his stronger right. He runs down the snow trail for maybe ten seconds, then stops. "You're damn heavy for a tadpole," he complains. But he runs again.

Now we are both panting. I see both our breaths forming miniature ice clouds. Neither of us can say anything. But questions are running wild inside my aching head. What in the frontier world is Philip Kittridge—if it is indeed him, and it is more likely him than his late brother—doing back in the Powder River Country? And who are the two other fellas—the man who looks like a black bear and the tall one who watches? Did they really come all the way from Montana just to see Mum and me? How did they dare invade Red Cloud's winter camp when there are just three of them? My mind's eye does not give me a glimpse of these strangers. Instead of seeing snow and blood, I see smoke. A smoky mind's eye is frightening—different from seeing Fetterman getting massacred but frightening just the same. It makes me feel as if I am going blind.

But I do see smoke, with my two regular eyes. And I smell the burning wood, too. The smoke is rising from the tops of all the tepees we are passing. Maybe some of it is getting to my mind's eye through my nostrils. I snort and sniff and cough. Prairie Dog keeps running, stumbling here and there but never falling and never dropping me. I know I could be in better hands, but babies can't be choosy. At least we are headed toward Mum—I can only hope!

The pathways through the snow become wider and packed down better. We are at the center of the village. There is Red Cloud's tepee. It is painted blue at the top for the sky, and there is not a cloud in the painted sky. Smoke rises from the hole on top toward the real sky, which is cloudy and turning gray. No other tepee has so much smoke rising from it. Even I know that means there is a big fire going inside with big talk going on. Four rainbows run down the sides of the tepee all the way to the green border at the bottom that represents earth. A glaring red buffalo painted over the entrance flap suggests that visitors shall never go hungry or else should bring bison delicacies, such as tongue and testicles, for the host.

I am not expecting anything from my mind's eye. But it has something to show again—the inside of the important tepee. I see a ring of men. Red Cloud sits in the middle wearing his flowing headdress. The others are all trying to bend Red Cloud's ear. I can't hear their words, but I wouldn't be able to understand them anyway. The great chief blows his nose into a blue neckerchief and all talking stops. I hope to see more but smoke forms a screen inside my head. Everything is blacked out. I must rely on my two outside eyes again. My mind's eye was only teasing me.

I realize two guards are standing outside the entrance flap of the important tepee. They are silent and look as stiff as the war clubs they each hold. One of them peers at us as if he has his own vision problems. The other, though, points a finger in our direction. The widest, clearest pathway leads straight to them, but Prairie Dog quickly darts left onto a much less traveled path. His boots sink so deep into the snow that he must slow down. He plows through the snow like a sick buffalo. I'm slipping out of his grasp! He's about to drop me. I'm falling, head first. I'm . . . well . . . I'm all right. The snow, like a stack of pillows, cushions my head. I don't even say "Ouch!"

The guard who is pointing takes a step forward and shouts something at us. Prairie Dog waves Mum's black shawl as if that somehow explains what he is doing with me. The guard comes toward us. Prairie Dog curls his lip and tries to pick me up, but his fingers must be numb and I slip out of his grasp. I instinctively try to jump—and for the first time in my life it works. I get high enough off the ground to latch on to Prairie Dog's right arm. We're moving again—Prairie Dog fighting through the snow, me clinging to his elbow for dear life. The guard has no bow and arrow, so the most he can do is shake his war club at us. Now he is hopping around in a circle on one leg. I catch a glimpse of a bare foot. He must have lost a moccasin in the snow. There is no pursuit, but Prairie Dog does not look back or slow down.

We continue on a winding path that lengthens our trip but avoids many of the other tepees. Prairie Dog is panting. When he stops in his tracks I think it is because he is exhausted. But something else has stopped him—a ghastly sight. Some kind of white man's sled is there, overturned with the runners sticking in the air. It looks like a turtle I once saw on its back near a creek crossing on the Oregon Trail. One of the George Gunderson boys had done that. But this was no innocent mischief.

Lines of rope extend from the sled in several directions. Attached to the other ends of these lines are eight dogs, lying still on the ground, but they aren't napping. Each is caked in frozen blood, each full of arrows. I make noises like I need to throw up. To me this scene looks as bad as the aftermath of the Fetterman Fight. Not that I like dogs better than people, but these furry friends of man seem more innocent than soldiers. What had the dogs done so wrong to deserve this? I'm sure they were unwilling or unable to fight back. I quickly label this scene: the Sled Dog Massacre. At least the Sioux didn't scalp the dogs.

"Damn!" Prairie Dog says. "It's their sled, the one those three fellas came in on. Don't look like they will be leaving by sled. And whoever killed the dogs knows the white men are near. Getting into Red Cloud's village is one thing. Getting out is another. How they going to get away now? How am I going to get away? I feel sick."

Prairie Dog sniffs and holds his nose. I do, too. Death by arrow is ugly and doesn't smell so good, either.

"Woof-Woof," I say, which is my word for dogs as well as wolves.

"The Injuns could've at least eaten the dogs. They must not be hungry enough yet."

Prairie Dog makes a noise like he might throw up. I think it's called gagging, and he gags a lot like me. It surprises me that he would gag. Maybe it's because of his nickname. But I don't know. Prairie dogs aren't really dogs. I know he didn't gag over Captain Fetterman. He must think more highly of those dead dogs than he did of the late captain.

"Let's get the hell out of here," he says, even though I can't go anywhere unless he goes first. He switches me to his other side, the one away from the dogs, and sidesteps the poor beasts without looking directly at any of them.

In a roundabout fashion, Prairie Dog works his way to his

small tepee—plain and dull brown and slightly lopsided with no smoke rising from it. But instead of going there he slips behind it and, walking in a crouch, works his way to the back of Greasy Nose's tepee, decorated with the moon, the sun, and the stars of the Great Bear. Smoke pours out of the top as if this is just another family tepee in Red Cloud's camp. I know better. We slip behind a nearby cottonwood, which is sacred to the Sioux because it is the tree that taught the people how to make their first tepee. The branches are now bare. But in September Pretty Bear brought me to this place to show me how the wind makes the heart-shaped leaves twist and turn on their stems so that they glimmer like silver stars.

"You can feel the Great Spirit here," she told me in her language, and though I couldn't understand her at the time, I felt something I could not explain. But now I feel only sadness. Seeing those dogs didn't help. The sacred tree looks dead and the mourning Pretty Bear is back at the late Wolf Who Don't Dance's tepee bleeding from self-inflicted wounds while breaking her own carefully created necklaces. I almost forgot—Wounded Eagle, my other Indian mother, is also back there, suffering from a serious head wound. My sadness is so large that I have room for all of them, plus the Fetterman command, Rufus Pennington, Luther Kittridge, Grandpa Duly, and even that long-ago turtle put on its back by a George. Wolf Dad was shot down inside this very tepee. I want to see inside but the smoke has turned my mind's eye into a pile of black soot. I groan so loudly that Prairie Dog covers my mouth.

"Look past the tree, past Greasy Nose's tepee," he whispers.

For a moment I have a strange thought. I think the white renegade of all people knows I have a powerful mind's eye. But that makes no sense. Nobody knows. Anyway my mind's eye appears as broken as an overworked plow horse. With my two normal eyes I can make out parts of various bows, arrows, legs, arms, and feathers on the far side of the tepee. I'm not a great counter like Greasy Nose. It's hard to figure out how many warriors belong to all those parts. But by anybody's guess there are more than enough fighting men ready to fight. The enemy this time apparently consists of a mere three men from Montana. Even if one of them really is Philip Kittridge with his powerful Remington rolling-block rifle, they don't seem to have one chance in a million of getting out of Greasy Nose's tepee alive.

"Now look over there," Prairie Dog says, pointing behind the tepee. I look and don't see a single warrior, not anyone at all. "The coast is clear."

*Sure, Prairie Dog, sure. But tepees don't have back doors.* That's what I think.

"By now the whole cussed tribe must know what's going on," Prairie Dog says, looking me straight in the eye. He actually waits for me to speak.

"Mum-mum," I say.

"That's right. Your mother is holed up in there with the dead Wolf, the hostage Greasy Nose, and those three crazy bastards from Montana. I must be crazy too to want to bring you in there. All those Sioux braves are *not* standing out front because they want to see the medicine man about their winter sniffles."

I sniffle a little. I have enough sense not to start bawling. Those warriors would surely hear me. I actually bury my face against Prairie Dog's ribs. He isn't very soft, but a baby has to make do with whatever adult is holding him. I want to see Mum something awful but I can imagine myself full of arrows, like one of those sled-pulling dogs. Now that would really be something awful!

"I could leave you under the cottonwood and get my white ass out of this village. No need to give me the dirty look, tadpole. I wouldn't get far on foot. It'll be dark before I know it and I still don't know my way around this wretched country. There's all that snow out there, too. Plus, I'm too damned tired already."

I have nothing to say. I'm not going to pat him on the back or anything.

"So, here we are, little drooler," Prairie Dog continues, pinching my cheek a bit too hard, even though I think he is trying to be friendly. "The question is: How the hell we going to get inside that tepee?"

I shrug one of my little shoulders—rather one of my little shoulders shrugs itself, for I didn't even think about it. Prairie Dog responds with a double shoulder shrug.

We wait. The longer I wait, the more I worry. But the worries change in my head. Instead of worrying so much about those Sioux arrows piercing my flesh, my worries are for the health of Mum. She's my real flesh and blood mother. She *must* be all right. Wolf Dad is dead. Greasy Nose has his Power (not only more powerful than my Power but also more reliable) to protect him, and besides nobody wants to hurt him. I can't imagine Philip Kittridge having come back here because he missed my Mum. Not for any other reason, for that matter. And he shot down my Wolf Dad. I'm sure not going to worry about that man's health and well-being.

My mind's eye remains blacked out. It's aggravating, but I tell myself I don't care. I don't want to see Mum in my mind's eye. What I need to do is *really* see Mum, to have her hold me . . . and then what? She can't hold me forever. I'm not sure of the exact intentions of the men who invaded the camp, except they killed my Indian dad, bashed in the head of one of my Indian mothers and have the disreputable Prairie Dog doing their bidding. And I don't know the intentions of these warriors standing in the front of Greasy Nose's tepee, but I know they aren't inclined to be peace-minded. I suspect Red Cloud will make his intent known soon. No doubt he is back at his own tepee wrapping up his strategic talks and preparing to take action. His Sioux are experienced at killing and mutilating palefaces. Getting into the tepee is one troubling thing. But another more troubling thing is how can Mum and I get out of this alive?

Prairie Dog is still shrugging his shoulders and mumbling to himself. He has stopped trying to converse with me, no doubt figuring I don't have any bright ideas. I'm sure the last thing he wants to do is fight anyone. We have that in common.

"I suppose I could stand here until hell freezes over," he tells himself.

He notices me staring up at him from his own arms and looks surprised. Maybe he forgot that I was still here. He sets me down under the cottonwood. He turns in a circle, looking at the Indians in front of the tepee, the emptiness in back of the tepee, and the snowy terrain at our rear. He wipes his face with Mum's black shawl once more, then puts it over his fur cap and ties the shawl down under his chin. I wonder if he thinks it will be safer to resemble, at least from a distance, a woman. But unlike Greasy Nose, he has no dress.

"Don't worry, tadpole," he says. "I ain't going to bolt and get hunted down like a wounded mule deer."

I nod my head, expecting him to explain what he is going to do. Then it's my turn to be surprised. He reaches down under his pant leg and comes out with a knife that looks as long as my arm. I never saw him carrying a weapon after he gave up his Army rifle. Had he always carried this concealed weapon? Would he have used it if Pretty Bear had come after him with her much smaller knife? He tests the blade against the top of a bush. It cuts through the wood real easy. I'm a little nervous. He doesn't look like the type to start slashing his own arms. And I hope he isn't the type to slash babies. I lose my composure. I'm drooling all over myself. And drool can turn to ice just like water. I gulp, then I howl, maybe a little bit like a wolf but probably more like a dog that's taken an arrow to the gut. Prairie Dog immediately pounces on me. But he has good intent. He only wants to cover my loud mouth.

"What's got into you, little drooler?" he asks. "You want to get us killed. You want to die-die?"

I try to shake my head, even though it's already shaking.

Prairie Dog finally takes his hand away from my mouth. "I got me a plan," he says. "You're going to have to do some serious crawling, but I've seen you crawl. You're good, very good. First I'm going to crawl and then when I give you the signal you crawl after me. Got it?"

I am totally confused. But he's right. I'm a heck of a crawler.

"Yup," I say, for the first time in my life.

Prairie Dog tightens the black shawl, grips the big knife with his teeth, and plunges ahead, crawling through the snow toward the back of the tepee. I watch in a trance, like I'm seeing it in my mind's eye. But I'm actually seeing it. When he waves for me to follow, I snap out of it. I crawl after him as fast as my little limbs will move. All my crawling practice has paid off, and because I don't weigh much, I don't sink much into the snow. The snow is cold at first against my hands, but I keep going. As long as my fingers keep moving, I'm all right. I catch up to him in no time. In fact, I scoot right past him. His mumbling doesn't slow me down. I get to the tepee way ahead of him. And I can't wait. I press my mouth to the hide. I gum it a little, with the help of my lone tooth. "Mum-mum," I whisper. "Mum-mum." My whisper isn't half as loud as an adult's whisper, but I'm afraid to talk louder. Not surprisingly, I get no answer from anyone inside. I wait for Prairie Dog to catch up.

"You're a damn show-off, tadpole," he says when he finally works his way next to me. The knife falls out of his mouth as he speaks. He's panting again but trying to keep it down. "Give me room now and let a man work."

I already gave him room, as soon as that knife fell. He picks it up and wipes it off on Mum's shawl. I give him more room. He blows on one hand then the other.

"Here goes," he says as he stabs the back of the tepee. He stabs again. Now he slashes, again and again.

I think of Pretty Bear and her knife, used to slash herself in mourning, and Wolf and his knife, used to take the scalp of Lieutenant Bingham and slit the throat of Captain Fetterman in battle. A gunshot! Prairie Dog drops his knife and accidentally cuts the tip of a finger on the other hand. Fortunately he has been cutting low and I am even lower than that. The bullet passes through the hide over his head.

"Damn you Kittridge, it's me!" Prairie Dog snaps. "You 'bout made me wet my buckskins. Hold your cussed fire. It's me, Burrows—Prairie Dog. I got the tadpole. You hear me? I got the little drooler, the kid."

"This some trick, Dog?" says a voice from inside, a familiar and unpleasant one that agitates my eardrums. "Who else is out there?"

"Nobody. Coast is clear back here . . . at least for now. Would you kindly put down your rifle and let me finish cutting a hole before those guys in front catch on."

"Those guys in front are your friends, you traitor. I know where you are now. I could put the next shot from my Remy right between your red eyes."

"This ain't no time for joking. You know I'm on your side."

"You swear on Fetterman's grave?"

"Look, I came back, didn't I? And I brought the kid like I promised." Prairie Dog nudges me. "Say something, tadpole!"

"Huh?" I say.

Prairie Dog curses. "Call your mother. Hurry! Don't start *not* understanding me now. Say 'Mum'!"

"Mum-mum," I say too softly. He gives me a sharp elbow. "Mum!" I shout.

"It's Angel Lamb!" Mum calls out. "Let my baby in here, Philip Kittridge. Right now!"

Two hands poke out of the messy little hole Prairie Dog has made. The gnarled, hairy knuckles and the sheer size of the thumbs tell me they aren't Mum's hands. But there is no time to be fussy. I jump—my second successful jump ever—into the hands! They pull me through head first, with my behind only getting hung up for a second. I flash back to the moment I emerged from the womb. And here I am—temporarily safe and secure in the hands of Philip Kittridge, although he has not let go of his Remington. I look into his eyes but he only glances at me to make sure I'm in one piece. I see he's wearing a fur cap with earflaps instead of his cowboy hat—it must be too cold for him to maintain the Texas look.

"Mum," I say, wanting to be in her far more tender arms.

"Shit," he says. "It talks now."

The slashing resumes behind me. And the cursing. The hole needs to be plenty bigger to admit Prairie Dog. He slashes like there is no tomorrow.

Mum relieves Mr. Kittridge of his little burden—me. I am in Mum's arms again. It hasn't really been that long since she went out to shovel under the supervision of Wounded Eagle, but it seems like weeks ago. She feels the same way. She squeezes me tight and rubs my little cold hands, creating great friction and then warmth.

"Praise the Lord," Mum says. "I never thought you'd get here."

I want to say something clever—to show her how well my speech and my brain have developed at seven months—but I am suddenly speechless. For some reason, one of my shoulders shrugs as if it has a mind of its own.

"We couldn't leave without you," she says. "Couldn't go without my darling Angel Lamb. I'd rather die."

I wonder who "we" is, but I bury my face against her neck instead of looking around the tepee. I'm glad to be an Angel Lamb again, if only temporarily, instead of a Snow That Drifts or even a Daniel. I feel some warmth on my backside from the tepee fire. Is there anything in the world more wonderful than having a toasty behind? Not at the moment. But I'm beginning to wonder how much fuel wood is left. I wonder what happens when the fire dies. While I am wondering, I hear someone groaning but don't raise my head. I prefer not to break contact with Mum's neck. I only want to listen to Mum breathing and maybe start humming. Yes, she has begun to hum the way she used to do to lull me to sleep. What's more she isn't coughing. Maybe I have brought her good medicine. Maybe seeing me alive and well has helped ease her spiritual sickness.

But there is no time to sleep or to settle in and become content, let alone to go for something even more soothing—like breast milk. Prairie Dog screams like a tortured soul. "I've been hit!" he yells as his hands, the ones that carried me to this place, suddenly appear through the hole. They are clawing at the air inside the tepee. Philip grabs a wrist and someone else, a bulky fellow bundled in a black overcoat, takes the other wrist. Prairie Dog is pulled through on his belly, his right side coming through first because the bulky fellow is tugging harder than Mr. Kittridge. Prairie Dog is something to see lying there on his belly. His lips are curling and uncurling as if they belong to a fish out of water, both his hands are bloody from hasty and careless slashing, and he has a Sioux arrow in his left buttock.

"You brought my shawl, too," Mum says.

"Get it out, get it out!" Prairie Dog cries, reaching back to where the pain is centered. "They shot all your sled dogs. Now, they've shot Prairie Dog!"

The bulky fella unties the black shawl from Prairie Dog's fur cap, and presents the shawl to an appreciative Mum. She sniffs the shawl. Even I can smell the blood and the stench of Prairie Dog on it. She spreads it out at her feet to air out. No doubt she hopes to wash it before she puts it over her shoulders or her yellow hair. The bulky fella observes her closely but finally goes back to Prairie Dog's troubled backside. He easily snaps off most of the arrow shaft but doesn't try to yank out the arrowhead. "Don't want to make the wound worse," he says, wiping his dark brow. It's zero degrees outside but he is sweating in here.

"That's supposed to help?" Prairie Dog shouts.

"It's more than I'd do for you," says Mr. Kittridge, who is leaning against his Remington rifle.

"Just don't try to sit down, Mr. Dog," says the bulky fella. He is totally black—his coat, his boots, his face, his hands. In my seven months since leaving the womb, I have seen many palefaces and more than my share of what is generally called red skin, but the only other black face belonged to Hanna, the Burlesons' maidservant. This man is even darker than Hanna.

"That all you got to say, Plowers?" Prairie Dog says to the black man.

"Flowers. Yes, sir, Mr. Dog."

"Don't call me that. My name is . . . Gawd! I'm in some pain here."

"Yes, sir, Mr. Dog."

Prairie Dog squirms about belly down, the way I used to before I had the skills for turning over.

"You got something for the hurt, Flowers?" Prairie Dog asks.

"You know I'm no doctor, Mr. Dog. I'm a handyman from Chicago."

The name "Flowers" sounds familiar, and so does that title—

"handyman." I'm not sure what a handyman is, but it sounds important, maybe one step below a medicine man. And of course, I've heard of Chicago, a crowded, civilized place with dirty rivers and tall, square buildings where they slaughter animals (but not dogs) instead of human beings. Mum is from there. I am, too, you might say, before I emerged from the womb. I am most curious.

Right on cue, the black man strolls over to Mum, takes my right hand, and shakes it with his thumb and one finger. "Glad to meet you, Daniel," he says with a smile that makes his black cheeks shine. I don't see all that many teeth there. I'm just getting my teeth, while it looks like this fella has been losing his for some time. But it's a good smile just the same. "My name is Flowers. Leon P. Flowers. I'm an old friend of your mother's. I hear you call her Mum. That's a right fine name. And you're near cute as a button."

I smile back. Prairie Dog says the man looks like a black bear, but I can't imagine a black bear smiling like this or being so altogether gentle. He uses the tip of one finger to stroke what little hair I have on my head. He is more like a black pussycat.

"You ain't got your Mum's yellow hair but you got her nose and eyes and . . ."

"And his daddy's chin," Mum interrupts.

"Why, yes, there are the makings of two dimples there." The man traces the tiny holes with his fingertips. "I hear tell, Daniel, you've been helping your mother get through your ordeal with the heathens. All of us from Chicago is mighty proud of you."

I want to scream out something to Mr. Flowers, but of course I can't. I want to scream *How the hell did you ever get here from Chicago?* Whoops. Mum wouldn't like me using such language or even etching it in my skull for later use. I guess I've spent too much time hanging out with the cussing Prairie Dog. Still, Mr. Flowers' presence is a mystery, at least for my young brain.

When Mum packed her bag and left the tenement building with me in her womb last May, Mr. Flowers was still down there in the basement being a handyman. And if he arrived here with Mr. Kittridge, that means my question should really be modified to *How the hell did you ever get here from Chicago via Montana?* What's more, Prairie Dog mentioned a third man from Montana. Where was this third man?

"Holy smoke!" Mr. Flowers continues. "This sure be a long way from Chicago and brother am I ever out of my element! We all is. But don't you cry, Daniel. We is here to bring you back to civilization." Mr. Flowers glances over at the suffering Prairie Dog. "I want to thank you, Mr. Dog, for reuniting Daniel with his loving mama."

"No need to thank the redskin-loving deserter," says Mr. Kittridge. "He just did what he was told for once, knowing I'd give him the Fetterman treatment if he didn't. He ain't nothing much. Don't forget he's the one who handed Lib over to the savages."

"Everyone makes mistakes," Prairie Dog says. "Give me a break, would you? I'm hurting real bad over here."

"You deserve worse," Mr. Kittridge says.

"Like you're always perfect, Kittridge. Shooting Wolf down like that was a bad mistake. He's a big man in this village with a ton of influential friends, including Red Cloud."

"He shot an arrow. What was I supposed to do?"

"He shot an arrow at somebody else, and to wound, not kill."

"I guess you know just about everything that goes on in the minds of these savages, Prairie Dog."

"All I'm saying is we all make mistakes. Didn't you make a few that day your brother, Luther, got himself killed?"

"Shut up, traitor! Don't you dare mention Luther's name again as long as you live. And that might not be too long."

"Now, gentlemen, let's not bicker," says Mr. Flowers. "We

have Elizabeth and Daniel all safe and sound." He smiles at me a little longer, then redirects his smile toward Mum.

"Yeah, that's right Flowers. We have them safe and sound in the Sioux medicine men's tepee with God knows how many Sioux devils standing right outside."

"I see your point, Mr. Kittridge. If this tepee had a door, I'd surely lock it."

"Speaking of that medicine man, where the hell is Greasy Nose?" Prairie Dog shouts. "I got an arrowhead digging in me. I need some medical attention."

"Greasy Nose—not my idea of a good name for a physician," comments Mr. Flowers, now smiling at Prairie Dog. "Of course at home when I busted my back bowing to too many non-colored folks, the only physician who would tend to my kind was a Doc Whitehead. Names sure is funny that way. Nobody would mistake me for a pretty flower, now would they?"

"I would," says Mum. "An old black rose."

"Yes, Elizabeth. Old is right. And black is for certain."

"Well, don't you two sound real chummy," Mr. Kittridge says. "Don't often see that between a colored man who resembles a full-grow'd black bear and a yellow-haired white woman with a husband."

"He's an old friend," Mum says. "And I'm a squaw."

"No, Elizabeth Duly," says Mr. Flowers. "Not no more. We're here to rescue you."

"Damn, damn, damn," mutters Prairie Dog. "Somebody fetch Greasy Nose quick."

"He be right by the fire, Mr. Dog," Mr. Flowers says. "But he's tending to the other Indian gentleman."

"What other Indian?"

"The one called Wolf something . . ."

"Wolf Who Don't Dance? What the hell are you talking about, Flowers? When did Greasy Nose start resurrecting the dead?

Wolf is dead ain't he?"

"Apparently not."

Prairie Dog curses as usual, but it's hard to tell if he is pleased, disappointed, or just surprised by the news. "I saw him get shot in the chest. If he pulls through, I'm going to have to start calling him the Wolf Who Don't Die." He chuckles at his own cleverness. It doesn't last long. Apparently chuckling doesn't help his condition. He pounds a fist on the ground and calls for immediate medical attention.

I can't work up much sympathy for him. I'm smiling inside at the news that Wolf Dad is still among the living. I try to locate him. Mr. Kittridge sticks his Remington rifle out the back hole of the tepee and without warning fires off a shot. Mum jumps like it was fired at her, then presses my head to her thumping heartbeat.

"Must you do that, Philip?" Mum says.

"Don't worry your pretty head about it, Lib," Mr. Kittridge replies. "I'm only making sure the savages don't get the idea of executing a rear attack. Ain't that good U.S. Army tactics, Prairie Dog?"

Prairie Dog does what he does best—curses. Mr. Kittridge curses back using many words I've already learned from Prairie Dog. I think of them as two of a kind.

Mum holds me tighter. I could suffocate from her tenderness. But I don't complain. I never will. Mr. Flowers pats me on the bottom and Mom on the arm.

"I love a good reunion," he says.

I'm not so sure he's talking about the mother and son reunion. I mean Mum and me were not even apart for a full day. On the other hand, Mr. Flowers and Mum separated in Chicago some nine months ago.

A howl from the middle of the tepee makes Mum jump again. I've heard Wolf Dad howl before but never in pain. I pull my face away from Mum's neck to finally get a peek at Wolf. Through the flames rising from the central fire pit, I see him lying on his back next to a sizable buffalo skull and three or four open medicine bags. Greasy Nose stands over him, dropping herbs and powders on Wolf's chest wound with one hand and throwing other herbs and powders into the air with the other. The medicine man is in a dress, but not his red one. It's green with fur trimmings and too short to cover up his thick calves. His lips are moving and I can tell he is chanting intensely, but I can't make out a sound. He is using his soft healing voice. He has much experience as a healer. He knows it is not necessary to speak loudly to get the ear of *Wakan Tanka*.

"Ain't he dead yet, medicine woman?" Mr. Kittridge calls out.

Greasy Nose ignores him, continuing to work his medicine.

"He'll die for sure," Mr. Kittridge tells the rest of us. "I put the bullet in his chest just where I intended it."

"I wouldn't bet your life on it, Kittridge," Prairie Dog says. "Greasy Nose ain't no Army doctor."

"He's unconventional," Mum says. "But I believe his medicine is finally starting to rid me of my cough." She touches her throat and immediately coughs. "Anyway, maybe he can save Wolf."

"And what about me? Aren't we friends, Greasy Nose? I know you hear me. Can't you take a break from Wolf's chest to work a miracle on my white ass?"

Greasy Nose ignores Prairie Dog, too.

Philip Kittridge laughs. "You think all those warriors out there care if you heal or not, Prairie Dog? Likely we'll all be dead before this is over. I ain't bowing out, though, till I make damn sure Wolf and that medicine woman bite the dust."

"You better watch it, Kittridge. Greasy Nose knows what you're saying. He talks American better than you."

Mr. Kittridge starts to argue the point, but a new voice rings out: "To want to kill and to brag about it shows allegiance to the Devil!" At least this voice is new to me or almost new for there is a trace of familiarity to it. I'm not sure where it's coming from. I think maybe heaven. So I look up to where the smoke is pouring out the hole at the top of this tepee. Of course nobody is up there. My second choice is my mind's ear, the companion to my mind's eye. But it can't be that. Mr. Kittridge has heard the voice, too.

"Tell it to the warriors outside, noble white man!" Mr. Kittridge replies. "They want to kill us, and they'll brag about it later, too. We're surrounded by red devils!"

This other fellow, who must be the third man from Montana, shows no inclination to argue the point. He was so silent I hadn't known he was there and now he is silent again. He's clear on the other side of the tepee with his back to us. He's tall enough but made taller still by his stovepipe hat—the kind I've seen the late President Lincoln wearing in pictures. With his long back and his narrow shoulders he is definitely an all-over vertical person. His coat collar is turned up so I can't see the back of his neck. I figure his skin isn't red, but I'm not sure if it is really white like Mr. Kittridge or black like Mr. Flowers. I'm not sure why he is standing so dangerously close to the opening flap.

"You really are loco if you think those red devils are going to let us walk out of here," Mr. Kittridge shouts across the tepee. "The one in here, this dying Wolf, already put an arrow in your leg, friend. If I hadn't shot him, he'd of put the next one in your crazy heart."

"The Wolf man thought I meant him harm," the third man says, keeping his back to all of us. "I mean nobody harm."

"Well, he meant you harm."

"He had only one arrow."

"Look, I saved your damned life. You should be thanking me."

"I will heal."

"He snatched Lib, for Christ's sake!"

"I bless all men, all beasts, every tree, every blade of grass."

"So you keep saying. How you bless anything with that killer stick of yours is beyond me. Of course, I understand how you might be confused."

"That's enough, Philip," Mum says. "Leave him alone."

"Don't worry, Lib. I made it all the way from Virginia City without shooting him, didn't I?"

The third man still doesn't turn. I'm not sure what his killer stick is. He tips his stovepipe hat, but it's not to Mum or anyone else in the tepee. He's tipping his hat to one of the warriors outside. Most of his weight seems to be on his right leg. Now I see why. There is an arrow sticking into the calf of his left leg. The shaft has not been broken. Unlike Prairie Dog, the third man does not whimper or complain.

*"Who-who?"* I say to Mum.

"Yes, Angel Lamb, you are my baby owl," she replies instinctively.

I think about asking Prairie Dog to translate for me. But then I see something else rather strange. The third man is now waving something at the warriors. It's a large, heavy object. This must be the killer stick. It has a hammer face on one side and a blade face on the other. It's like having a war club and a big-bladed knife all in one weapon. The thing is, the man isn't waving it aggressively. He may as well be fanning himself on a hot summer's day.

"I wonder how many of those savages you could silence with that killer stick before they filled you with arrows, friend?" Mr. Kittridge shouts.

"Silence!" Greasy Nose calls out. It's the first thing he's said since I've been here. "This is my home. It is a place of healing." He lifts the buffalo skull high in the air. "All the four-legged animal people, like the two-legged animal people, need to be honored and respected," he says, watching the smoke rise through the hole at the point of the tepee.

"My, my," says Mr. Kittridge. "He does speak good American for a savage."

"You show no respect. I am a Sioux medicine man."

"You're a medicine woman as far as I can see. And let me tell you, you don't look so good in a green dress. How soon till the Wolf stops howling?"

"You show Wolf Who Don't Dance no respect or honor. He is a great Sioux warrior."

"And I'm the one who shot the son of a bitch."

"Philip Kittridge respects nobody," Mum says.

"I shot the savage who captured you and did you wrong. Is that the thanks I get?"

"You came here to kill."

"I came here to save you. And the nipper, too. All the way from Montana. You ain't got no call, Lib, to look at me like I'm brother to a rattlesnake. It wasn't so long ago you was ready to do anything short of selling the nipper to get to Virginia City."

"No call to talk to Mrs. Duly like that," says Mr. Flowers. "If we can't make peace with each other, how we going to make peace with the Sioux Nation?"

"We ain't," says Mr. Kittridge. "Nobody's smoking a peace pipe around here. Those savages out there hate us. And they figure that their great medicine man has so much powerful medicine, he can *not* be killed by bullets or the killer stick. Ain't that right, redskin lover?"

Prairie Dog only groans.

Mr. Kittridge casually points his rifle at the prone Wolf. "As soon as that medicine man tells them that Wolf is dead, you can count on one thing—them rushing this tepee in an all-out frontal assault. And they aren't going to take the time to bless us or pray for us or honor us before they cut us to little pieces."

"No call for that kind of talk neither," says Mr. Flowers. "Elizabeth don't need to hear that."

"Like she don't know what's in store, what these red devils are capable of. That Wolf made her his squaw!"

"You best button your lip, Mr. Kittridge."

"Sure, noble black man. I'm done talking." He pats the butt of his Henry rifle, then kisses the end of the barrel.

It doesn't seem like Philip Kittridge has changed much, except he is back here in Red Cloud Country instead of being in Montana acting like a cowboy or trying to find gold. I'm not sure why.

Wolf lets out another howl that drowns out Prairie Dog's moaning. Mum pushes my head down so that my face is against her chest. If she had more hands she would try to cover my ears, too.

"He's not going to go easy," says Prairie Dog, during a pause in his groans. "If Wolf don't die, he'll watch my back, he'll put in a good word for me. I translate for him and run errands for him. I thanked him for getting Fetterman. He likes me."

It's like he needs to convince himself he has a chance to survive. I understand that.

"That's not all," Prairie Dog continues. I watch out for the tadpole sometimes and I look out for his wives . . . Damn!"

I can tell Prairie Dog is remembering what he did to Pretty Bear to get me away from her back at our tepee. Wolf won't like that. If Wolf Dad lives, he might cut out Prairie Dog's heart. Prairie Dog has nothing more to say. He goes back to groaning and squirming on his belly. He isn't even trying to change his position.

"If the entire U.S. cavalry arrived at this very instant, we wouldn't be saved," says Phil Kittridge. "Not even if all those bluecoats had Remys like me. Hell, even Nelson Story and his Texas cowboys couldn't get us out alive. We're sitting ducks in a shooting gallery—a bows and arrows shooting gallery."

"You led us here, Mr. Kittridge," Mr. Flowers says, "of your own free will."

"For money."

"Not much money. It wasn't greed that made you do it. No, sir. You have more heart than you think, mister."

"Actually, it was for a gold claim."

"One you knew you might never see."

"Yeah, well, maybe I have more heart than brains. And maybe I have more belly than heart. I've had a belly full of these savages. They murdered my brother." He fires another shot out the hole in back, without aiming or looking. "Eat my lead!" he shouts out the hole, but it's like spitting in the wind.

"And you done it for her," says Mr. Flowers, nodding his head toward Mum.

"Her? Why would I risk my neck for her!" He tips his Remington so that it is pointed for a moment at Mum's head. "Lib ain't even halfway glad to see me."

Mum doesn't dispute that. But she doesn't ignore him. She gets up. Holding me kind of loose, she walks right up to Philip Kittridge and plants a kiss on his forehead. Mr. Kittridge looks at her as if she has just slapped him, which I would have done.

"What was that for?" he asks.

"A last kiss—to thank you for bringing my old friend to me."

Before Mr. Kittridge can say or do anything foolish, Mum turns her attention to that old friend, Mr. Flowers. She plants a kiss on his forehead, which is dark yet rosy.

"And that's to thank you for coming to get me, Leon," Mum says.

"My pleasure," he says, giving her that almost toothless grin.

"I sure hope that wasn't a last kiss, Elizabeth," he quickly adds. His smile flickers but holds up. "I'll get you and Daniel out of here. Somehow." He pats me real gentle on the head.

Mum isn't done. She carries me to the center of the tepee where Greasy Nose is back to chanting. She pauses by the fire, not for warmth but to take a closer look at the wounded Wolf Who Don't Dance. Greasy Nose steps back to give her room.

Wolf's face is wet with sweat. His lips have turned white. He stays perfectly still on his back. And he doesn't howl again. Whatever pain he has, he is not going to show it to her. His chest barely rises and falls. But when he looks up at her, I see something flash in his eyes, more like moonlight than firelight. It's the same look he had when we first saw his face months ago and Mum shooed him away from the wagon. Mum bends down over him and I'm not sure what she's going to do. Would you look at that? She gives him a quick peck on the forehead. He doesn't so much as twitch a facial muscle. But his chest rises higher.

"*Ano,*" she tells him.

I am familiar with that word, as the young warrior Two Feathers employs it frequently when talking about himself. It means "to count coup."

Wolf closes his eyes.

Mum looks up at Greasy Nose. She asks a question with her eyes.

"I don't know," the medicine man answers.

She has kissed three men on the forehead but does not make Greasy Nose the fourth. She nod her heads and walks away, allowing him to further administer to Wolf Dad.

Mum continues across the tepee and stands directly behind the tall man in the stovepipe hat. She glances down at the arrow in his leg and winces. No doubt she is like me in wondering how this fellow doesn't crumble in pain. He is looking through a small opening between the entrance flaps. I raise up in Mum's arms and take a peek. Of all the things I might see, my eyes land right on a pair of turkey feathers atop a short warrior. I know it must be Two Feathers, out in front ready to make a bold move to prove himself.

Mum puts a hand on the small of the tall man's back. I forget about Two Feathers and wait for the man to turn. He does not.

"Does it hurt?" she asks.

"To be touched by you, Elizabeth," he says. "Never."

"I meant that arrow in your leg. It must hurt."

"I feel no pain."

"I can understand you not wanting to look at me, but don't you want to at least look at him."

Her hand moves down to the seat of his britches. She gives him a good smack.

The man puts aside that killer stick he is carrying and makes a slow turn. I see his face for the first time. It is as long as the rest of him. His skin is taut and white with red blotches. He looks at my face, but only for an instant. His head turns away. If he can still see me it is out of the corner of his eye. His ears stick out like the wings of a sparrow, and the one closest to me wiggles. His lips quiver, maybe from the strain of keeping his mouth closed. My eyes roam over his unfamiliar profile.

"You came all this way," Mum says. "I don't mind if you look. His name is Daniel Duly."

The man swivels his head enough to look down at me over his left shoulder. My eyes fasten on his chin. It's not long like the rest of him, rather small in fact, but what fascinates me are the two large indentations that make me think that a fanged animal, perhaps a dog or a wolf, once bit him there when he was a small child like me.

"Danny," he says.

"Well, I call him Daniel," says Mum.

"He's Danny. I'll call him that."

"If you like. Does he look like you expected?"

His stovepipe hat nods a half-dozen times as if it has a mind of its own. Then the man abruptly, even rudely you might say, turns his back on us. He picks up his killer stick and again looks between the flaps at the warriors growing restless outside.

"You didn't get much of a look," Mum tells him.

"I am still looking at them," the man replies. "The Indians are tantalizing."

"Not them. I mean Daniel . . . Danny."

"I have seen him ten thousand times."

Mum works her way around the arrow sticking out of the man's leg and fills up the narrow space between him and the entrance. She stands on the tips of her moccasins to kiss him, but not on his forehead and not just once. She kisses him twice on the chin, once for each dimple. The man does not try to kiss her back. I'm not sure what Mum would do if he did.

"Ten thousand times, huh?" Mum says to him. "In your imagination?"

The tall wounded man shakes his head. "In my mind's eye."

# MARCH 16, 1867: PUTTING
# TOMBS ON HOLD

Here I am back where I was before Mum and I fell into captivity. Well, not exactly—the location is slightly different, but the situation is exactly the same. We have been here for well over a month. We wait, day after day, surrounded by tall walls and distressed men in blue coats. Our goal is still the same as it was in pre-captivity when we were waiting back at Fort Phil Kearny—to get moving again on the Bozeman Trail. Yes, the trail is still closed off by bad weather, bad communications, and bad Indians. Of course we recently resided with those *bad* Indians, some of whom weren't so bad at all. I admit I sometimes think back at those times—crawling around on all those comforting buffalo robes in our tepee, riding securely in a cradleboard on Wounded Eagle's strong back, and having Pretty Bear's nimble fingers rub my temples or explore my gums for my first tooth. I no doubt miss my life among the Sioux more than Mum, who had it a lot rougher in Red Cloud's village than I did. Even so, once or twice in the middle of the night I've heard her call out the name "Wolf." Of course I've also heard her, while in her dreamy state, say—in this order of frequency—the names Abraham, Leon, Philip, and George. The last is probably a reference to Old Man Gunderson, the Mormon widower who I'm guessing has two or three wives in Salt Lake City by now. Of course George Gunderson had six almost-grown sons also named George traveling with him on the Oregon Trail. Could Mum have been thinking of one of the younger Georges instead? Anything is possible in dreams. Not that it matters. Why should I care how many men's names Mum mentions at night. The main thing is that all through the day, the name she says by far the most is "Danny." That's me! She agrees that it does fit me better than Daniel. I still do like that name White Fox I picked out to replace 'Little Bear Eagle" and "Snow That Drifts." But this isn't the place anyone wants to have any kind of Indian-sounding name.

I write this from our shared quarters at Fort C.F. Smith, which is in Montana Territory, ninety-one miles northwest of Fort Phil Kearny and 281 miles from Virginia City. Crow Indian scouts say that Red Cloud's village of 1,800 lodges, with an average of three warriors per lodge, is thirty-five miles away. It worries the soldiers here, but doesn't really surprise anyone. Red Cloud does get around. It's a whole lot easier picking up tepees and moving them to a new spot than it is to relocate a fort or a town. I'm sure most of the soldiers wish they could move. They carry antiquated weapons, are weakened by scurvy, and eat mostly baked commissary beans, desiccated potatoes, and hard bread. I'm not complaining though. I'm still mostly getting my nourishment from Mum's breast milk. Yum. Yum. Can't get enough of that. I can sense that some of the soldier boys are jealous.

Mum and I had a room for just the two of us until a few weeks ago when a party consisting mostly of pack mules and armed military escorts finally made it from Fort Phil Kearny to Fort C.F. Smith. The escorts brought with them the widow Grace Pennington and her chubby-cheeked son Toby. Actually Toby looks thinner all around these days. He turned six and rarely got any candy treats while I was with the Sioux. Times are desperate and Lieutenant Colonel Henry Wessells, the post commander at Fort Phil Kearny, decided that since it was absolutely necessary to bring supplies to the northern post, they might as well risk bringing the Penningtons as well. It would be best for the poor lady's mental health. Since hearing the tragic news about Captain William Fetterman, whom she had not known for long but had envisioned marrying in a grand fort ceremony, Grace Pennington had gone into a deep depression. Twice she nearly killed herself with an overdose of laudanum and almost daily she suggested that the savages might as well carry her and Toby off as they had done to Elizabeth Duly and her infant.

When news reached Fort Phil Kearny that Mum and I had been saved from a fate worse than death and were now situated at Fort C.F. Smith, Mrs. Pennington called it a pack of lies, adding, "I won't believe it until I see her holding her baby in her arms." So they brought her to us, along with Toby, of course. Mrs. Pennington seems to be doing better here, although she still breaks into tears at random moments. At night, I've heard her mostly call out the full name "Captain William Judd Fetterman," including the rank. But several times she has mentioned "Rufus," the name of her civilian husband who had been killed earlier by the Sioux, and once or twice she has cried "P.D.," which can only stand for Prairie Dog, the man who jilted her to run off with the enemy Indians. Because of Mrs. Pennington's still delicate condition, Mum makes no mention of having lived in the same village as the Fetterman-hating Prairie Dog and in the same tepee as Wolf Who Don't Dance, the man who by some accounts killed Captain Fetterman.

I have outgrown my desire to play with her earlobes. Frankly, her bare ears can't stand up to the memory of the jeweled ears of Pretty Bear, not to mention Pretty Bear's neck, always draped by at least one shiny necklace. Toby hasn't changed much. He still calls me "Dan-Dan," still whimpers, still wets his bed on his bad nights, and still wonders how come I act like I see and know so much. We all aren't created equal *Toe-toe*.

"How come you can walk already?" was one of the first things he said to me at our reunion. "Is it 'cause you turned Injun?"

I just grinned, showing him my three teeth. But if I could say the words I can think, I'd have told him, "That's right, *wasicu*, and I know how to scalp, too."

Lately, when talking to his mother, he has started referring to me as "the squaw's papoose." He thinks it's an insult. I don't, but I still might bite his leg when I get a few more teeth in my mouth.

Some of the soldiers around here seem nearly as scared, if not as excitable, as Grace Pennington. They know—instinctively, if not from their commanding officers or the friendly Crows— that only the deep snow and severe temperatures have kept the Sioux from committing depredations. The Crow scouts have reported that Red Cloud sent the peace pipe to the Piegans, Bloods, and Gros Ventres and that they had all accepted. That means that those tribes are now in league with the Sioux and the Cheyennes against the white soldiers. The bluecoats at Fort C.F. Smith, like those at Fort Phil Kearny, have reason to be scared. They don't need me to tell them (I suppose I would if I could, but I'm not sure) that as soon as the weather permits, Red Cloud and his allies will vigorously renew their brand of warfare.

Mum talks about older sister, Cornelia, and Virginia City on occasion with Leon P. Flowers, since he stopped there briefly with Papa Duly and visited Cornelia and her rich husband before coming to our rescue. Whenever we do continue our journey on the Bozeman Trail, whether in the spring or the summer, Mr. Flowers will be coming with us. He is devoted to Mum, loves my childlike spirit, and has the approval of his friend Papa Duly.

"Look after her, Leon," my father told him. "And Danny, too. Remember, I'll be watching."

"You know I won't let nothing happen to mother or child."

"Good. And I will ask the Great Spirit to watch over all of you."

Papa Duly was here with Mum and me for only a few weeks last month before he decided he must leave rather than wait at the fort with us or even travel the trail with us in the future. It wasn't an easy decision for him, not after reuniting with Mum and me, but there was somewhere else his heart told him to go. He didn't say so—but I knew—that he was seeing that place in his mind's eye. I don't believe Papa Duly is crazy, but he does possess a large heart and extended vision. Right now, although my own mind's eye has been malfunctioning more often than not, I can see him quite clearly in his new home, the tepee of Greasy Nose. He is wearing his stovepipe hat and making great circles with his famous heeling poleax while the Sioux medicine man, in a new beaded blue dress, throws assorted curing powders in the air. They are administering to the injured head of a sitting patient who looks a lot like my second Indian mother, Wounded Eagle.

I sometimes grow anxious thinking about how Papa Duly will react when Red Cloud resumes his war with the likely approval of Greasy Nose, who after all is the one who foresaw the results of the Fetterman Fight and dubbed it "Hundred in the Hand." Papa Duly believes in peace even more than me. But I don't over worry. Papa Duly did say he would one day see Mum and me again, in Virginia City or wherever we might be. He said don't worry, he would find us. Although nobody back in Chicago would believe it, Papa Duly can take care of himself, even in a place where few Chicagoans would be expected to last long—Red Cloud's Powder River Country. For now, I am just glad I can see him in my mind's eye. I know he can see me.

Before Papa Duly left, he found mild amusement in asking soldiers at their posts or in their quarters what the "C.F." in

Fort C.F. Smith stood for. Half of them didn't know or had forgotten. But Papa Duly knew. Charles Ferguson Smith was a Civil War general who injured a leg jumping into a rowboat in Tennessee and died when it became infected in April 1862. It is not common knowledge, Papa Duly noted to those who didn't tell him to get lost, that Smith was also suffering from chronic dysentery at the time. The soldiers didn't want to hear any more about it. Most, at some point, did tell him to get lost. They didn't appreciate—or else were afraid to adapt—the message Papa Duly brought with him wherever he went: Talk peace with the Sioux for they are not so different from you or me; be kind not only to each of your fellow human beings but also to horses and mules and the beasts of the forests and prairies; and, if you eat meat, bless and honor the animals that sacrificed themselves to keep you alive.

He told none of these soldiers, but he did tell Mum, why he knew so much about General C.F. Smith's dysentery. It seems Papa Duly was suffering from his own case of "loose bowels" in April 1864 when he skedaddled in the middle of a battle in Virginia. He told me that dysentery, not the Rebels, made him run. It was just two days after we got to Fort C.F. Smith that I developed a bad case of diarrhea. Papa Duly showed up at my cot side and this not-so-strange man, who had hardly talked to me directly since I met him for the first time in Greasy Nose's tepee, unleashed words that he had kept bottled up for too long. I didn't mind. I believe my attention span is superior to most babies my age. At first I don't think he believed I could understand him. But that changed the more he talked, because I sat up, perked my ears, rubbed my double-dimpled chin, nodded my slightly oversized head, made little sighing noises, and offered an occasional "Huh?" or "Who?" Anyway, this is what he said to me or at least what I etched inside my skull at the time:

"More soldiers died from bowel disorders than battle. Nobody tells you those things. Soon as I joined my regiment in Virginia I developed a bad case of what the doctor called 'alvine flux,' with more blood in my stool than I had seen in battle up to that point. I never knew such misery. And this alvine flux, or dysentery, got worse. The Union doctors tried everything to cure me—castor oil, whiskey, quinine, opium, turpentine, calomel, lead acetate, silver nitrate, and ipecac. Cauterization of my anal opening was the last straw, and I took to running. It wasn't a lack of grit, Danny, it was too much bloody shit. I found me a drier climate where I could breathe pure mountain air and bathe in a pure mountain stream and drink pure mountain whiskey. Once I was better I hightailed it back to my unit and went back to fighting, or pretending I was fighting. My gun always jammed or fired high. It was all too real, and the killing sucked the life out of me. You talk of your Fetterman massacre, but I saw men on both sides slaughtered like you wouldn't believe, over and over again. No scalping or mutilating bodies, though. We were too civilized for that. But streaming blood and mounds of gore just the same. It took over all five of my senses—the killing. I saw, smelled, heard, tasted, and touched death. Do you understand? It didn't just touch me, it climbed inside of me—up here inside my head. That's when I started to see maiming and killing at all the other battlefields, even when I was hundreds of miles away standing guard duty on the Potomac. Nobody else could see like I could, but I saw too much. The horrors of that awful war were lodged inside me, and they turned my brain inside out.

"So, you ask, or would if you could: 'Did the Civil War make Abraham Duly plum crazy?' That's what they say—'they' being everyone who knew me or thought they did. But I had my good days and my bad days wandering the countryside after the so-called peace at Appomattox, and this continued after I finally

348

made it back to my home in Chicago. On one excellent day, I stayed in bed all day and helped your Mum make you. Most days were bad, though, because I worked at the slaughterhouse. I hated it. They were four-legged animals not two-legged men, but there was more blood and gore than I saw in the war. I found no peace. It was my job to beat these creatures senseless. Every day at work was a battle, a Civil War inside my brain. Sometimes I felt like turning my poleax on my own head. On one of my especially bad days, I came home feeling slaughtered on the inside. And though I was home with Mum and her sisters and my old parents, I was still able to see those animals being stunned and sliced at the slaughterhouse. Senseless! Senseless! Unlike men at war, they could not fight back. Leon Flowers happened to come up from the basement to fix something in our stove that evening. I mistook him for John Wilkes Booth, who I hated for having assassinated that other Abe—Mr. Lincoln. I don't know why. I was out of my senses. They don't look anything alike. Mr. Flowers, as you know, is midnight black, not any kind of actor and not even from the South. Anyway, it was a bad day, the worst of my life, and I acted crazy. He was much larger than me, but I was strengthened by my righteous anger. I put my hands around his neck and tried to avenge President Lincoln. Yes, I assume you've heard differently. But I swear to you, Danny, I always knew I was Abe Duly, not the late president. Fortunately, your Mum struck me over the head with a frying pan. It was the only violent act I ever knew her to do, and it saved Mr. Flowers' life. The judge just misunderstood me when I told him my name was Abraham, and the only reason I bit those two vicious police officers who beat down our door is because they had my arms and legs restrained.

"Maybe I deserved to go to the bughouse, maybe not. On my good days, I didn't think so. In my heart—and most of the time in my head, too—I was against all violence. I wanted to get away from all those lunatics and go back to your Mum. I kept seeing her. You know, up here. Nobody would believe me at the asylum, so I stopped talking crazy. But I kept watching her as she went about her housework, cared for my parents, spoke to her sisters, hummed to the baby in her belly, and went to Mr. Flowers for help and advice. Do you know that when she packed her bags and left Chicago, I saw her kiss Leon and leave our building? It made me cry. Even more amazing, I saw her in the state of Missouri trying to catch on with a wagon train. That's when she disappeared from view. But even though I wasn't talking crazy and wasn't seeing things no more, the authorities still stuck me in a padded closet without any hooks because they thought I'd try to kill myself. The point is, Danny, as bad as things can get at the bottom end of you, everything's much worse if things go bad at the top end of you—your head."

I guess I already knew that, but I was glad to take any words of wisdom away from the man who fathered me. For what it's worth, my diarrhea went away the next day, and though it has come back periodically since, I do not complain. Nor do I complain that Papa Duly also went away. I know he cares about me and will return some day. And, like I said, we see each other in our mind's eye. It's true he was declared insane, and that was from *seeing too much,* but I'm not worried about what other people think. Maybe they'll think I'm insane, too, when I grow up and they read what I have written. For now, it is my good fortune to be able to still etch everything into my skull, so that I can get it down on paper later. Sometimes I wonder if Papa Duly had this same unusual ability when he was a child, but I doubt it. He has never written anything about himself and never even writes letters. I was amazed when he made that long cotside speech to me. It might have been one of those once in a lifetime occurrences, though I hope not. For the first seven months of my life I was convinced I would never actually meet my real father, seeing as he was in a madhouse back in Chicago and Mum and me were en route to a new life in Virginia City. Luckily, he and Mr. Flowers came west and found us. No matter what happens from here on out, I'm glad Papa Duly and me got acquainted.

As for Mum and me, there are worse things than just waiting around to get on with our lives. At least we are alive. And she hasn't coughed for some time. I'm confident now it won't take a third miracle to get us to Virginia City. There have been two of those already. It was a miracle that Papa Duly, along with Mr. Flowers and Mr. Kittridge, made it to Red Cloud's village last month, and it was another miracle that we all got out of Red Cloud's village safely—well, most of us anyway. Allow me to explain.

I need to go back to Greasy Nose's tepee. Actually, and bear with me on this, I should go back for a moment to Chicago. Like me, you are probably wondering how Papa Duly ever teamed up with Leon P. Flowers, who might easily have seen each other as foes or rivals for Mum's affection. Papa Duly never talked about it to me, but Mr. Flowers did. The handyman had no intention of ever leaving his basement in our tenement building. For one thing he had promised Mum to go upstairs regularly to keep an eye on younger sister, Maggie, along with Grandpa Duly and Grandma Duly. But then Grandpa Duly died in his sleep and soon after Grandma Duly, who missed her husband's snoring most of all, died of loneliness combined with her persistent cough. By then Maggie was being saved from her married grocer and everlasting misery by a traveling preacher. He said it was God's will that she join him in holy matrimony, so she left the tenement rooms behind and rolled south out of Chicago in her preacher husband's Humble Wagon of Harmony and Faith (it said so in big red letters on the side).

After Maggie was gone, Mr. Flowers didn't feel obliged to

stay in the basement, especially when many of the other residents in the tenement building looked down on him. But he stayed anyway, like a bat in the only cave it ever knew. Then change was forced upon him. The building got a new owner who wanted to cast out everything old, even the old and true. He said that anyone who looked like a snorting black bull (I guess the new owner had seen more bulls than bears) was bad for business.

"I been here since before the war, sir, and I ain't heard no complaints," Mr. Flowers argued.

"Don't be uppity," the new owner replied. "The complaints have all come after the war. You've been scaring off the decent folks. They're all afraid of you after that row you had with one of our residences, Mr. Duly."

Mr. Flowers tried to explain that he had done nothing in the "row" except get choked near to death for somehow resembling John Wilkes Booth and that this Mr. Duly was now a resident of the Dunning asylum for the insane. Nevertheless, the new owner told him to vacate the premises within two weeks.

"For the next six days I sat on the banks of Bubbly Creek watching the dirty water trickle along while I contemplated ending my long, dark days not just back in the basement but also on this here planet," Mr. Flowers told me. "I even contemplated praying like a sinner should. Things wasn't the same no more anyway, not since the day your lovely pregnant Mum departed, westbound!"

On the seventh day along the Bubbly, Mr. Flowers had turned to praying when who should show up but Abraham Duly, recently escaped for the fifth time from Dunning. A goodbye letter from Mum had inspired Papa Duly's fourth breakout, but Mum had already hit the trail, and Maggie and three city police-men were waiting for him at the tenement house. His fifth breakout came in the middle of the night and took everyone by surprise. But there was only more bad news waiting for him on the outside. His parents were both dead and Maggie informed him she herself would be leaving soon, not to see God quite yet but to live "till death do us part" with a man of the cloth. She refused to tell him where her sister Elizabeth had gone but promised to pray for his salvation, to forgive all his sins, and to wait five minutes before screaming for the police. All that bad news brought Papa Duly to the Bubbly, not to think about taking his own life but to think about invading his old workplace, the slaughterhouse, and freeing as many four-legged animals as he could before the police arrived or one of his former coworkers took a poleax to him. When Papa Duly saw Mr. Flowers praying by the creek, he did not for a minute mistake the handyman for John Wilkes Booth or a black bear or a black bull.

"Hello, there," Papa Duly said. "You praying for the Confederacy to rise again?"

Mr. Flowers didn't jump in the creek or run for his life or otherwise panic. Maybe he added a new prayer, though. "No, sir," he replied. "Never been a slave, never want to be one neither. My skin is black, free black. Can you see that, sir? I hope so. You can bet your bottom dollar that Mr. Booth was a white man. You come back from the dead, eh . . . Mr. Lincoln is it?"

Papa Duly rubbed his chin and tried to see their reflections in the dark water. "You look more like Booth than I look like Lincoln," he said. "I ain't so crazy today. I been to my place. It ain't my place no more."

Mr. Flowers nodded. "Ain't my place neither, Mr. Duly."

"You can call me Abe. My name ain't Lincoln, but it is Abraham."

"I know that. Have a seat. Can't offer you a chair, Abe, but there's plenty of room."

And so Papa Duly sat and after a long silence, he said, "You praying for yourself or you praying for her?"

He didn't even have to mention her name. Mr. Flowers nodded again and handed Papa Duly most of what was left of a green apple. Papa Duly chewed thoughtfully. Next thing you know, they were discussing Mum—nothing about what she had done in the past, only about her future. Mr. Flowers knew where Mum was going—to sister Cornelia's golden dream house in Virginia City, Montana Territory.

No sooner did Papa Duly process that information than he asked, "How we get there, Leon?"

Mr. Flowers didn't think it was a crazy question at all. He picked up a pebble and tossed it into the stagnant water of Bubbly Creek. "That way is west," he said, pointing across the creek. "You ever hear of the Missouri River, Mr. Duly?"

The next day, they rode the rails to St. Louis after picking up a bit of traveling money from Maggie's preacher-husband (who had obtained money from his flock and had not yet targeted it for the Lord's work) and from the new owner of the old tenement house (who had obtained money through dishonorable real estate deals and gave some of it up, though most reluctantly). They didn't stay long. St. Louis, as it had been for so many adventurous souls before them, was just their gateway to the West. Without enough money to buy passage on a Missouri steamer carrying forty paying passengers and two-hundred tons of freight to Fort Benton at the edge of gold country, they earned their passage by lifting and hauling freight and luggage for fifty-seven watery days and nights. Once they stopped moving for a couple days because the riverboat got stuck on a sandbar. Compare that to all the waiting Mum and I had to do on our overland route. Also, a boat on a river made for a smoother ride than a wagon on the prairie. Of course Mum couldn't have been lifting and hauling freight or done much else because of her pregnancy, but she might have thrown herself on the kindness of some riverboat captain to gain passage.

There was some potential danger on the river from accidental collisions and boiler explosions, plus the chance of falling overboard and drowning. Mr. Flowers said that neither he nor Papa Duly was a strong swimmer and that each fell into the river once, only to be saved by the other throwing him a rope. And since Mum can't swim at all, she might have drowned if she had tried to reach Montana by steamer. But, far more likely she would have been lying down inside somewhere the entire trip, and I would have been born on the Missouri River. What's more, Mum and me would have made it to Montana without ever having spent a single day in Fort Phil Kearny or Red Cloud's village. Imagine that!

Mr. Flowers said that by the time he and Papa Duly stepped onto dry Montana land at the town of Fort Benton, they were tired, wet, and sore but closer than brothers. They still had to travel 250 miles overland to reach Virginia City, and since they couldn't afford to take a stagecoach, they worked their way as wagon freighters. Mr. Flowers did not detail that part of the trip because he said there was nothing to tell. They encountered no Indians, hostile or otherwise. Mum told him she was envious and full of great regret that she had gone west by way of the Oregon and Bozeman trails. She wanted to hear all about Virginia City, of course, because she and me are still trying to get there.

Virginia City didn't prove to be as different from Chicago as Mr. Flowers thought. He later told Mum that both are gritty, busy places full of rich people looking to get richer, poor people trying to survive if not save a few dollars, and disreputable people doing most anything for the price of a drink or two. Virginia City is much smaller than Chicago, of course, but all the action is more concentrated. The bustling mining town has been the capital of the territory for more than a year. Most of the commercial buildings are now actual wood and stone buildings instead of tents or brush shacks, and business transactions are made with gold dust, at $18 an ounce. Mr. Flowers even noted that they already have a public school in Virginia City, which kind of made me cringe although I have a long way to go (geographically and chronologically) before I must sit in any classroom. Although the town has its rough edges, including far more saloons than places of worship, many of its hard cases have been banished or hanged, thanks to the Montana Vigilantes.

Not being nearly as spread out as Chicago, Virginia City was easy for Mr. Flowers and Papa Duly to navigate on foot. They seemed to make people nervous, though. While many residents wore gun belts or carried rifles, none went around town clutching a poleax the way Papa Duly did. When the two strangers asked questions, people were generally closed-mouthed except for the few who believed Papa Duly's claim (seemingly backed up by that poleax) to be related to the Wheelwrights. The duo bathed in a horse trough before showing up at the three-story, wood-frame Wheelwright house, said to be the largest residence in town outside of the home of acting territorial governor Thomas Francis Meagher. A flustered housekeeper reluctantly admitted them to the hallway but she insisted Papa Duly leave his poleax outside. The former Vigilante captain Wheely (apparently the only name he went by) brought them into the parlor but was not in a listening mood and he almost turned them away before they could get in a word edgewise. But curiosity brought Cornelia Hotchkiss Wheelwright out of her music room to look over the two strangers, who turned out not to be strangers at all. When she saw Papa Duly and Mr. Flowers standing there seemingly larger than life, Aunt Cornelia fainted on the spot from the shock of recognizing them. In falling to the floor, it was her misfortune to hit her head on a marble table that came all the way there from the Orient via San Francisco and Salt Lake City—a present from Wheely.

Fortunately, Virginia City has several good physicians, but she was unable to talk to them or anyone else for days (I can imagine her frustration). Wheely told the two visitors from Chicago that neither he nor his wife had heard a thing from Elizabeth Duly and that Cornelia had been rather frantic because of all the Indian trouble and lack of movement on the Bozeman Trail. He also told them to wash up in the creek out back, saying they could keep any gold dust they found. It was a local joke—the creek was practically dry and every last ounce of dust had been removed long ago. The guests were not amused, but what could they do. Wheely wielded power in this frontier community and, anyway, they partly blamed themselves—almost as much as Wheely did—for Cornelia's unfortunate condition. Wheely was a rich man who did not act like it with other rich men but who lorded over the poor and men of questionable character. He allowed the two Chicago men to sleep in his big house for one night and then assigned them to an outbuilding with his chickens. His leanings had been toward the South (especially old Virginny) like many others in town and he was not comfortable having a colored man sleeping in one of his guest rooms, and even less so giving comfort to his wife's sister's potentially dangerous husband. He could not forget a letter his dear Corny received from the youngest sister back in Chicago. The young lady stated that Abraham Duly's "complete madness" kept him in an asylum instead of the penitentiary.

While Cornelia was still fuzzy in the head and being attended to by three physicians, the two Chicagoans by chance ran into Philip Kittridge, who had had a serious falling out (at least two Remington rolling-block rifles were pointed) with cattleman Nelson Story over salary, had found all the gold claims in Alder Gulch already taken, and was working part-time in a Wallace

Street butcher shop of all places. At some point after arriving in the bustling Montana capital, he had contacted Cornelia himself and mentioned having seen her sister Lib at Fort Phil Kearny. Cornelia was naturally intrigued and asked the stranger many questions. But Mr. Kittridge told lies to disguise the extent of his relationship with Mum and things went sour fast when he tried to jump one of Wheely's gold claims (and possibly the very much married Cornelia as well).

Philip Kittridge was no doubt fortunate that Wheely and his associates didn't run him out of Virginia City or even make him dance from a rope. But Mr. Kittridge didn't see it that way. He kept wearing his cowboy hat, even inside the butcher shop, and strutted about town with his Remington rolling-block rifle in hand. At work, he often treated customers like unwanted guests, but his boss didn't dare fire him. His evenings were spent in the saloons of Virginia City and nearby Nevada City, where his relentless whiskey drinking led to endless boasting about his exploits among savages and soiled doves. He wasn't fooling anyone about his lowly status, but his Remington had a way of making people treat him as if he were royalty. Wheely told his wife he wouldn't be surprised if "that worthless weasel turned out to be a road agent."

Mr. Wheelwright made no mention of Mr. Kittridge to visitors Papa Duly and Mr. Flowers, but while going about town in search of nourishment (since Wheely was as stingy with his food as he was with his fine spring beds), the Chicagoans visited the butcher shop on Wallace Street. Papa Duly had left his poleax behind one of Wheely's chicken coops as it seemed to frighten everyone, including some of those men who toted firearms. Virginia City's citizens didn't understand that it was not a weapon but a special walking stick that he believed had the Power to keep him safe. Of course not even Mr. Flowers understood that. Anyway, Mr. Flowers told the man behind the counter that Papa Duly, who was holding his stomach as if in pain, had once worked in a slaughterhouse but could no longer stand the sight of cow or hog blood or the flesh of dead animals.

"So why'd he come in here?" the butcher's assistant replied.

Mr. Flowers tried to explain, but the rude man cut him off: "And you don't look like you have any gold even if you wanted to buy a pound of meat, so why the hell have you come to Stoneman's Butcher Shop and Meat Market?"

Mr. Flowers, who was so hungry he had wanted to kill one of Wheely's chickens and risk the wrath of the old vigilante (Papa Duly had protected the chickens), explained that they were staying at the Wheelwright house and were under the impression that Mr. Wheelwright had credit at the shop.

"We deal only in gold here, friend," the butcher shop employee replied. "Show me the gold dust."

Papa Duly started to walk out; he couldn't stand the smell of the place. But Mr. Flowers was not so easily put off. "I'll have you know, sir, that Cornelia Wheelwright, the wife of one of the most prominent men in your little burg, is related to that man you have offended," he said.

"I don't cotton to the lucky rich or the prominent, who are often one in the same," the employee countered. "And for another thing, friend, the folks around here don't much cotton to having coloreds hanging about looking for our gold."

"I'm not looking for gold, *friend*. I'm helping my friend here find his wife."

"You're a big one all right, but I got a rifle under the counter."

"I'm not looking for trouble either, just Mrs. Duly."

"Man alive!" said the man behind the counter, tilting back his broad-brimmed hat. "Did you say Duly?"

"Cornelia Wheelwright has a sister named Elizabeth Duly, who is missing," Mr. Flowers explained. "She was due here long ago on the Bozeman Trail."

"Damn. You don't say."

"I do say. And I'm telling you that the man over there who you offended happens to be Abraham Duly, the brother-in-law of Cornelia and . . ."

At that point, according to the story that Mr. Flowers told, the rude man removed his cowboy hat, smacked it against a countertop stained in animal blood, and shouted: "Honest injun? By thunder, Lib really does have a husband after all!"

The Chicagoans were startled and confused until the worker explained that he was Philip Kittridge, twice a veteran of the Bozeman Trail and once a good friend to Mum and her nipper. What a joke. I mean there was some truth to it, but Mr. Kittridge was never a friend of mine.

When Cornelia finally got her bearings straight again, she sent word that Papa Duly and Mr. Flowers should report to her in the big house at once. This time she was already sitting down at the parlor's marble table when they arrived smelling of chickens. While she didn't shake the hands of these old acquaintances (her excuse was she didn't want to break her long fingernails), she fed them well and then peppered them with questions. At last she was satisfied that they had both really come all the way from Chicago for the sole purpose of finding her dear sister, rather than to find gold or to get free handouts. But there was one other important question to ask: "And what are your intentions toward Elizabeth?"

That question seemed to baffle Papa Duly and his eyes practically fell back into his head as he became tongue-tied and then lost in his own thoughts.

"A husband's place is by his wife's side," Mr. Flowers suggested.

Cornelia considered that notion and at first, perhaps thinking of her Wheely, smiled at Mr. Flowers. But when she turned toward Papa Duly, the smile vanished. A frown formed and deepened into a scowl the longer she studied his skull-like head, sunken eyes, wildly straggly eyebrows, and unusual double-dimpled chin.

"Don't worry, Mrs. Wheelwright," Mr. Flowers said. "He ain't violent no more or anything like that. Quite the opposite, in fact. He just wants to see his wife."

"How nice."

"And you know that even though I was just the colored handyman in the basement, she became my best friend back at our building," Mr. Flowers continued. "I care for Elizabeth deeply, Mrs. Wheelwright. I swear I do."

Cornelia took a long sip of her gray tea, imported from England and brought to Virginia City by ocean liner, train, paddle-wheeler, and freight wagon. "That's what I'm afraid of, Mr. Flowers," she admitted. "Don't forget that I was there when it happened."

She wasn't talking about the formation of a friendship, and it nearly spoiled Mr. Flowers' appetite. Of course he knew that she knew about the war baby that he and Mum had produced but that had never made it out of the womb. He had not, however, expected Cornelia to bring up the subject, especially in the company of Mum's husband, who had *not* been there.

No doubt war veteran Papa Duly had found out about it when he finally returned from the war and his wanderings, alive but not exactly himself. In fact, hearing that piece of information about the overly friendly handyman might have aggravated Papa Duly's delicate condition at the time. Why else would a man who hated to harm Rebels or cows or houseflies have mistaken Mr. Flowers, a burly black man from the North, for John Wilkes Booth? It wasn't something the two men had spoken about while making plans at Bubbly Creek in Chicago or during the long journey to Virginia City. But it wasn't something that had kept them from becoming boon traveling companions.

Papa Duly snapped out of his daze. He smiled at both of them and sipped a little tea, like a sensible civilized man. When he spoke, he sounded fairly rational.

"No need for any undue worry," he announced. "I never drank much of this stuff back in Chicago. Don't recall you did either, Cornelia. You were partial to whiskey like your old man. They didn't call him Whiskey Man Dan Hotchkiss for nothing."

"You trying to get my goat, Abraham Duly?" she asked.

"Not at all. I don't want your goat or your chickens either. I'm just saying this tea ain't half bad."

"Wheely and I like it. We were talking about my sister."

"Yes, my wife."

"I only want what's best for Elizabeth. Her intention is to live here."

"So I've heard. When we find Elizabeth, we'll just let her decide, OK? She can choose Mr. Flowers, who is dark as sin but not unlikable, or me her husband, who has come to his true senses. On the other hand, she might elect not to be with him or me. She might have her heart set on being with you and Wheely in this fine home."

"Yes, I'm sure that will be her choice."

"None of us can see into the future. But no matter what, I ain't going back to Chicago where they think I'm buggy and I ain't going to stay in Virginia City where most everyone and everything appears buggy to me."

"Me included, I suppose?"

"Folks here are gold crazy, Cornelia. They'll do anything to get it, including shooting their neighbors. I need to find me—and Elizabeth, too, if she is willing—a better place to rest my bones, maybe somewhere along a more peaceable creek away from all the hurry-scurry. But that's putting the cart ahead of the mule. The main thing to do right now is to find Elizabeth, so she can have the chance to choose. Pass me another sugar lump, would you please, Cornelia."

Mr. Wheelwright may have been the stingiest rich man in Virginia City when it came to giving away anything to the less fortunate (those who hadn't hit pay dirt), but he could not say no to his wife. He had built the big house, with its marble tables, cushioned chairs, and spring beds, for her. He promised to build her a garden gazebo, a church, and a music hall, not necessarily in that order. He was as gold crazy as all the rest of them who had risked everything to come to the territory, but having all the riches in the world wouldn't mean a thing to him without Cornelia at his side. She made him prove it to her by insisting that he spare no expenses to outfit a Bozeman Trail expedition to locate her sister. Communication between Virginia City and the three forts along the trail was practically nonexistent much of the winter, and the town was virtually cut off from the outside world in all directions. The last supply wagon to make it up from Salt Lake City was before Christmas. The snow was still so deep that all the gravestones on boot hill were buried. But no, she said, the expedition could not wait for spring and fair weather. She knew of at least one miner who owned a dog sled, several who owned snowshoes, and a handful who had stashed away more than enough canned and dried goods to get them through the cold months. Everything was available for a price, she said, and her Wheely agreed to pay the price each time.

The expedition was to be co-commanded by Papa Duly and Leon Flowers, but though most residents in Virginia City were bored while waiting until spring for things to thaw, none wanted to venture on what sounded like a fool's mission at best, and most likely a suicide mission. "If the snow don't bury you, Red Cloud will," the miners said. "Don't you know that's Red Cloud Country." In fact, the two Chicagoans did not know. Papa Duly hadn't even heard of Red Cloud, but he was intrigued, telling

Mr. Flowers and even strangers, "His name fills my head with visions of sunrises I saw over Lake Michigan when I was a boy." Everybody and his brother was happy to tell the newcomers about how white blood spilled wherever Red Cloud went, before or after sunrise.

Through questionable Indian sources and the testimony of several worn-out Christian travelers, Virginia City did learn in mid-January about the unthinkable massacre near Fort Phil Kearny. Whether rumor or fact mattered not—every man, woman, and school child had digested the information (often to the point of being sick to the stomach). All Papa Duly wanted to know was whether any women or babies were killed in the massacre. Nobody knew for sure, but everyone in town *knew* that Red Cloud was more than capable of massacring innocent women and children alike. The good citizens, and the bad ones as well, decided they had all better stay home and protect their mining claims and town from the bloody savages. Undeterred, Papa Duly said he would go alone into Red Cloud Country if necessary. Mr. Flowers said that wouldn't be necessary—he was going, too.

"Let's go, then," Papa Duly said.

"It's not like finding your way from Dunning back to the old tenement house," Mr. Flowers told his friend. "We need a guide."

That's where Philip Kittridge came back into the picture. Cornelia Wheelwright and everyone else in town knew that Mr. Kittridge had safely traveled the trail on several occasions (coming to Montana, returning to the States, and coming back to Montana)—because he boasted about it to everyone he met.

"Sure I did it with Nelson Story and his well-armed men last time," he told whatever audience he could muster. "But who needs them? Traveling with the cow pushers and their half-tamed Texas Longhorns was like waving a red flag in Red

Cloud's face. I would've been better off without them."

But when Cornelia asked him if he would lead Elizabeth's husband and friend from Virginia City to Fort Phil Kearny, he laughed in her face and said he wouldn't make that trip again until hell was as frozen over as Montana Territory.

"She's my flesh and blood, my sister—one of them anyway," Cornelia told him. "I love her dearly. And I have a hunch that she was more than a passing acquaintance to you, Mr. Kittridge. Am I wrong? Well, you don't deny it."

"No, ma'am," he said.

"Isn't finding her the right thing to do?"

"No, ma'am."

"Don't you want to prove you are an honorable man?"

"No, ma'am."

"What about a brave man, the bravest man in Virginia City?"

He hesitated now and carefully adjusted his cowboy hat. "Can't kill no redskins working in a butcher shop," he admitted. "I ain't afraid of them. My guess, though, is that your sister is still sitting pretty inside Fort Phil Kearny."

"But there was a massacre."

"Maybe. But it was outside the fort. I'm sure enough bluecoats remain inside to watch over Lib. Hell, I bet she's dancing with the soldier boys all night and playing peek-a-boo with her nipper all day."

Mum had mentioned me in a letter she wrote from Fort Phil Kearny, but that letter probably never made it up the Bozeman Trail. Still, Cornelia knew about me from Maggie's earlier letters, and Mr. Kittridge may have referenced me when he first met the Wheelwrights. My existence apparently had not registered in Cornelia's head.

"Nipper? Oh, yes, Mr. Kittridge, the child, too. You *must* find her and the child!"

"I ain't said I'm going."

"And after you find them, you must bring them both to Virginia City, no matter what her husband or friend say—that is if she still wants to join me here, and I don't see any possible reason she would change her mind about that."

What Phil Kittridge said next made sense, even to me when I heard about it later from Mr. Flowers: "If she and the nipper are in Fort Kearny, they don't need to be found. If they somehow made it up to Fort C.F. Smith, they don't need to be found. Either place, they're under the Army's protection and will come along in the spring when the trail opens up and things start moving again. If they are anywhere else on the trail, we'd find their bones at best—more likely them bones is buried in snow or been carried off by starving wolves. I ain't no coward, Mrs. Wheelwright, but I know that country. Anybody who goes looking for her, for them, will end up buried in the snow his own self."

Mr. Kittridge's argument made no sense to Papa Duly of course, but he was her husband and had been declared a lunatic. It didn't hold water with Mr. Flowers either. Some of Papa Duly's abnormal behavior must have rubbed off on him or maybe he loved Mum that much, too. They both wanted Mum to be safe, and they weren't about to just wait for her to show up. Not that the notion of her capture (or mine) by the Indians entered their minds. They hadn't heard captivity stories aboard the Missouri riverboat the way Mum and I had while traveling the overland trails.

Of course, with so few women and babies actually on the Bozeman Trail during this time of war and winter, Red Cloud's people had few opportunities to seize any victims even if they wanted to keep doing that kind of thing. That's why even a frontier veteran like Mr. Kittridge didn't even consider the possibility that Mum and me were in the hands of the Sioux. Our capture was indeed a rare thing, made possible only because a mighty warrior sought a fertile blond woman for his third wife; a spy/medicine man friend with supernatural Power devised a devilish plan; and a no-account Army private helped carry that plan out.

Cornelia didn't care whether Mr. Kittridge's argument made sense or not. She wanted her sister found or, barring that, to get some word about her sister's health and whereabouts. She certainly had strong reservations about the fitness of Papa Duly as a husband. I'm guessing that the idea of her sister living in holy matrimony with a man in war paint wouldn't have sounded much worse. No doubt, she also had doubts about Mr. Flowers' fitness to be a friend of Mum. Papa Duly and Mr. Flowers couldn't be counted on to bring Mum to Virginia City even if they managed to locate her. Cornelia had no choice but to put all her eggs in one basket—one Philip Kittridge. Of course, that is all speculation on my part based on things Mr. Flowers told me. I haven't even met Cornelia Hotchkiss Wheelwright yet. What Cornelia in fact did was make it too hard for Philip Kittridge to say no.

She again turned to her husband, instructing him to give Mr. Kittridge whatever he wanted to guide the expedition to Fort Phil Kearny. What Mr. Kittridge wanted was one of Wheely's high-paying mining claims, preferably the one he had tried to jump earlier. He got it—rather he would get it when he returned to Virginia City with Mum and me in tow or at least with substantiated news about us. In the meantime, he had to settle for a dog sled, snowshoes, three-weeks' supply of food for three, a new fur cap and coat, and all the ammunition he wanted for his dear Remy. Wheely even threw in a stovepipe hat that had belonged to one of the Yankee hard cases he had hung. Mr. Kittridge had no use for such a hat, but Papa Duly strapped it on his already high head.

"I hope this don't mean you got some notion of becoming

the next Abraham Lincoln," said Mr. Flowers. "I was kind of liking you as Abraham Duly."

"No, sir," said Papa Duly. "I don't got a decent hat. And this feels like a good fit."

"Sure is. Just as long as you don't commence to splitting rails with your poleax."

As much as I never could stand Philip Kittridge's behavior toward Mum, I must admit he came to know the Bozeman Trail about as well as founder John M. Bozeman, who first marked out his namesake path four winters ago. The sledding and snow-shoeing was slow going at first for the three members of the expedition, but by the time they were on the east side of the Bozeman Pass, Mr. Kittridge was driving the sled smoother than his old spring wagon and Mr. Flowers had mastered his snowshoes and was master and friend to the eight dogs. Papa Duly mostly went along for the ride, talking to both animate and inanimate objects along the way and keeping a firm grip on his poleax—not because he wanted to smash man or beast with it but because he had grown abnormally attached to it and thought the sight of the former slaughterhouse instrument would scare off evil spirits.

"You mean like animal evil spirits?" Mr. Flowers asked him.

"Whatever evil spirits they got out here," Papa Duly replied.

Nobody disturbed the unusual winter travelers until they had passed around the northernmost spurs of the Big Horn Mountains and were stopped in their tracks by a hunting party of Crow Indians. Mr. Kittridge wanted to put his Remington rifle into action, but Mr. Flowers said that made about as much sense as shooting the sled dogs and then shooting each other in the foot. The hunting party consisted of at least twenty men, mostly carrying bows and arrows but a few armed with cavalry carbines. Mr. Kittridge was ready to shoot anyway because he couldn't believe that Indians out in the middle of nowhere could possibly be friendly. Papa Duly brought Mr. Kittridge to his senses by threatening to use the poleax to smash Remy into splinters.

"They look like people, not crows," Papa Duly noted. "But either way, we mean them no harm."

Such was Red Cloud's Power and influence that certain Crow bands wished to form an alliance with him. Others tried to stay neutral, which irritated both the Sioux and the Montanans. But these particular Crows had a village near the trail and were friendly to the white men. Some of them had even served as scouts and couriers at Fort C.F. Smith. They were a curious bunch. Half of the party studied and touched Mr. Flowers' skin for they had only seen one old mountain man who was that dark. But they were even more fascinated by Papa Duly, for my blood father had the idea of keeping beat with his poleax while singing a song that he had learned as a youngster in church or perhaps later from Mum's younger sister, Maggie: "O Jesus, I have promised to serve Thee to the end; Be though forever near me, my Master and my Friend; I shall not fear the battle if Thou art by my side, Nor wander from the pathway if Thou wilt be my Guide."

One of the Crows who knew English and had heard of Jesus translated the words to his fellow hunters, and they asked many questions. They proved to be comfortable with the concept of a man dying and coming to life again. Papa Duly, in turn, inquired about the supernatural guardian helpers that the Crows acquired in dreams or during vision quests. The Indians were in no hurry to remount their ponies, and Papa Duly was suddenly in no hurry to find Mum.

"So you can have all these different visions and still not be considered a mad man," Papa Duly said. "Is that the same with the Sioux?"

"We share visions, yes," the English-speaking Crow said.

"They see us falling out of the sky without eyes. We see them lying in the red snow without hair."

"Why do you fight the Sioux? You are all Indians."

"Do not white men kill each other?"

"Yes. I saw much of that in the battlefields of the Civil War. No men should fight."

"We should leave it to our women?"

"No people should fight. I do not carry a gun."

"But you carry a great fighting weapon."

"No, no. This is a poleax. It was once used to kill animals. Now, I carry it in the name of peace. I do not want to fight anyone."

"That is good. You want to trade poleax for turquoise beads?"

Although a dozen of the Crows had their eyes on Papa Duly's poleax, he would not trade it for beads, a war club, a cavalry carbine, two hunting medicine bundles, or even a pony stolen from the Sioux. The Crows grunted and muttered to each other or themselves but did not try to take the poleax from him. Ten of them kissed the hammer face as if the object used in the slaughter of domestic animals was a special totem. Then they graciously pointed out where there were Sioux Indians camps to avoid, said goodbye in two languages, and rode off on their rested mounts in search of the buffalo.

"Jesus go with you, Tall Man with Big Stick," the Crow who spoke good English said to Papa Duly.

Not until the hunters had disappeared into the whiteness of the horizon did Mr. Kittridge finally put down his Remington rifle. Papa Duly sat back down on the sled and signaled with his poleax for the journey to continue. He mostly sat with the cargo because he had trouble managing the snowshoes and was an erratic driver.

"By thunder nobody got shot," said Mr. Kittridge as he stepped onto the floorboards of the sled and picked up the reigns. The eight white mush dogs were ready to go as usual, always preferring to run than to sit and ever eager to see what was around the next corner. "Whoa," he said to the dogs. "Whoa. Easy. Whoa."

"Some of them Crows looked hungry enough to eat our dogs," said Mr. Flowers as he shook snow off his snowshoes.

"They prefer buffalo, but I was ready for them nonetheless," said Mr. Kittridge. "My trigger finger got a powerful itch. Must have been my Remy that discouraged them redskins from their thieving ways."

"They were friendly," Papa Duly said. "I hope all the Indians we meet are that way."

"Not likely, Duly," Mr. Kittridge said. "Those were the tame ones. You better hope you never see the wild Sioux. You climbing aboard, Flowers?"

"I'll start on the big shoes," Mr. Flowers said, "and give the dogs a break."

Despite his heft, Mr. Flowers proved adept on the snowshoes, which were made of white ash with a rounded triangular frame and a tail behind to keep him going straight. He would swing his arms with vigor and gaily sing "When Johnny Comes Marching Home" as he maintained a surprising gait. Nevertheless, he would inevitably fall far behind and run out of steam, at which point he would have to join Papa Duly on the sled. The dogs never complained about the added weight, but whenever the sledding party stopped to rest, Mr. Flowers would beg the dogs' pardon. He also praised them as if they were the children he never had and fed them breadcrumbs and the bones of the small game that Mr. Kittridge shot.

Many miles after the meeting with the Crows, the sledding trio stopped to eat and let the dogs rest where a rock overhang provided a break from the wind and blowing snow. Papa Duly sucked on one of the onions Aunt Cornelia had packed for him.

The other two ate beans and jerky.

"I'd starve to death before I'd eat me a dog," Papa Duly commented.

"Amen to that," said Mr. Flowers. "Never cared much for the mongrels in Chicago. But these mush dogs is different."

"Can't blame the Crows, though. Killing cause you're hungry ain't the same as slaughtering cows and hogs."

"You still thinking of *those* Injuns, Duly?" said Mr. Kittridge. "We're in Sioux country now. Red Cloud's crowd would just as soon skin you alive as look at you."

"I was thinking about that one Crow myself," admitted Mr. Flowers. "He talked good English and had a passing knowledge of Jesus Christ."

"Maybe that's why he didn't scalp your curly hair, Flowers. But I'd rather put my trust in Remy."

"That's a crying shame, Mr. Kittridge."

"Is Jesus your guiding light, Flowers?"

"On occasion. I got a feeling he's guiding me now through this snowy wilderness to find Elizabeth. You see, Mr. Kittridge, I heard tell our savior is dark skinned."

"A Negro? Why the hell not." Mr. Kittridge laughed so hard that even the dogs looked at him. "At least we know our savior ain't no redskin, Flowers. We better get a move on while there's still daylight."

"Fine by me. The dogs are rested. It's this way to Smith's fort, correct?"

"Wrong. You're all turned around in your head, Flowers. That way will get us lost in the mountains. Fort C.F. Smith is over that-away."

"If you say so. This all-over whiteness must have blinded me for a spell. Just point us in the right direction, Mr. Kittridge."

"Sure will, Flowers. God bless the guides—Jesus and me!"

The three travelers were indeed blessed enough to arrive

safely at Fort C.F. Smith (which is where I am now), about five hundred yards from the east bank of the Bighorn River. The soldiers here learned about the Fetterman fiasco from a party of Crows who visited the post on December 28, 1866. The Crows had heard that Red Cloud and three thousand warriors would next attack Fort C.F. Smith, but it never happened. As a resident of Red Cloud's village on the Tongue River for almost three months, I know why—the Sioux were too busy trying to stay warm and keeping an eye on the movements of the buffalo herds. It's hard to fight when you are cold and hungry and facing howitzers tucked behind a 125-foot stockade built of bluff adobe and hefty logs. The men at Fort C.F. Smith heard little substantial news from the U.S. Army or anyone with pale skin. Twice in January detachments of infantry and cavalry from Fort Phil Kearny tried to reach the northern Bozeman Trail post but had to turn back because of impenetrable snow drifts. The soldiers clearly had no dog sleds or snowshoes.

Rumors started that the Sioux had burned Fort Phil Kearny to the ground, but friendly Crows reported that it wasn't true. They did say that another rumor was indeed true—that a beautiful white woman with yellow hair and a mostly hairless baby boy with big pink ears were living in Red Cloud's camp in the tepee of Wolf Who Don't Dance, the man who had killed the white-eye captain named Fetterman. Most of the officers and soldiers at Fort C.F. Smith did not believe the captivity story, partially because these Sioux were known for killing whites, not seizing them, but mostly because the undermanned, desperate garrison was not about to attempt the rescue of anybody.

It was all up to the peculiar civilian trio—the burly black man who looked like a bear and came to this dangerous country unarmed; the tall, gaunt white man who didn't eat meat and carried a strange primitive weapon that he insisted was no longer a killing stick; and the guide who talked to his Remington rolling-block rifle and said that even though he owned a gold mine in Virginia City he was willing to die for a cause, just like Jesus Christ. The officers forbade the three men from continuing on the mission (perhaps because it might make the U.S. Army look bad if they died or if they succeeded), but it was easy enough for the trio to bribe a few guards and slip away, even with eight mush dogs. Two Crow Indians went along far enough to point out Red Cloud's village before returning to their camp near Fort C.F. Smith. Mr. Flowers wondered how they would ever find the tepee of Wolf Who Don't Dance. He had never seen so many tepees in his life; in fact he had never seen a single tepee in his life.

Mr. Flowers froze in his snowshoes. "We can't just go amongst them like we were out-of-town guests," he said. "We wasn't invited."

"I ain't going to just sit here," Papa Duly stated, but he didn't get off the sled. "I'm going to go down to that first tepee and ask directions to Wolf's place."

"If you wanted to die quick you could have done it back in Chicago," said Mr. Kittridge.

"Nobody in Chicago would know where Wolf's place is."

"Could be Elizabeth will come out for an afternoon stroll," suggested Mr. Flowers. "And maybe she'll be carrying her baby."

"And maybe the U.S. cavalry will ride out and rescue us," said Mr. Kittridge.

Although the other two were the co-commanders of the expedition, Mr. Kittridge knew that they would never have gotten here without his sense of direction and that his companions from Chicago were totally helpless now that they were within spitting distance of the village. He was a guide with frontier savvy and he possessed the only gun. He told them to shut up and listen to him. Amazingly, they both did. The only problem was he didn't have any kind of plan. They waited for ten minutes before Mr. Kittridge decided they should rest and feed the dogs. Mr. Flowers liked that idea and began whispering to the dogs. Papa Duly began whispering to his poleax in a similar voice.

"I'm going to scout around," Mr. Kittridge finally told them. "Stay put. I'll be back. And if not, I don't care what the hell you do."

He lashed the leather lacings of his snowshoes to his feet and began to move slowly around the perimeter of the village. It was noontime and so cold that he wiggled his trigger finger to keep it from going numb. He smelled the smoke of inside fires and of meat cooking. Almost all the residents were in their tepees, staying warm and feeding their bellies as best they could—but not everyone. While catching his icy breath behind some cottonwoods, Mr. Kittridge saw a lone figure trudging along a path to bring a bag of feed to a string of braying mules. It was a man who walked with a slouch and with loud heavy steps that crunched the snow almost angrily. He was no Indian.

When the man cursed the mules in English, Mr. Kittridge identified him. They had spent time together back at Fort Phil Kearny. The man had been a private with a hankering for whiskey and Mrs. Grace Pennington. Mr. Kittridge fashioned a quick snowball and hurled it, striking the man in the seat of his buckskin pants.

"Get your red ass over here Prairie Dog," Mr. Kittridge called out, "unless you want to be hit by a .50–70 rifle bullet in the same location."

"Jesus!" said Prairie Dog. "That can't be you. You went to Virginia City."

"Jesus never went to Virginia City. But I did. Now I'm back and there's going to be hell to pay, P.D., unless you get me Elizabeth and her nipper."

"You couldn't forget her, Kittridge? She's Yellow Hair now."

"I don't have to explain nothing to you, redskin lover."

It was a most fortuitous meeting. Mr. Kittridge kept his Remington pointed at Prairie dog's chest while threatening in many imaginative ways both the body and the property of the private turned white renegade. Prairie Dog was soon ready to fully cooperate. Yes, he knew where Mum and her tadpole (me!) likely were but said that was on the other side of the village. He pointed out his small tepee directly below, along with the neighboring much larger and more colorful tepee of the medicine man, Greasy Nose.

"What the hell do I care where you live, you traitor," Mr. Kittridge said. "And I don't care about the medicine man. I want Wolf Who Dances . . ."

"Actually, it's Wolf Who Don't Dance," Prairie Dog said.

"Whatever. He's the Wolf who snatched Lib, right?"

"Eh . . . sure. But Wolf ain't home. Down there is where Wolf be at this very moment. He and Greasy Nose been smoking the funny pipe. The other smokers all went home. It's just the two of them in there now, Kittridge."

"You want me to shoot Wolf?"

"No. No. He's not so bad, I mean for an Injun."

"Friend of yours, huh?"

"No. But . . . I mean sort of. He killed Fetterman, you know?"

"You really have sided with the savages, Prairie Dog, or should I say Prairie Chicken?"

"No. I . . . I'm my own man. Really. I'm just trying to help you out, Phil. Wolf can lead you to Yellow Hair, I mean Mrs. Duly. He can be useful to you alive, you know like a hostage."

"I'd rather shoot him. You can lead me to Lib yourself, Prairie Dog. And you will, too, if you know what's good for you."

"Honestly, I don't know what's good for me anymore. Let's talk this thing over, Phil, and figure out the best thing to do . . . for both of us."

"I ain't concerned about your well-being, P.D."

"So you do care that much about Mrs. Duly?"

"I'm doing a job, P.D, and I'm going to see it through. You wouldn't understand about that. Anyway I'm not here alone. Mrs. Duly's white husband and a colored man are with the dogs. Our mission is to bring her and her nipper back to Virginia City, not kill her redskin lover. I ain't getting paid for that. So let's go find Lib."

"How about if I just give you good directions?"

Mr. Kittridge answered by pointing his rifle barrel between Prairie Dog's eyes and making more threats. Prairie Dog went along peacefully to the sled. There was hardly time for introductions. Papa Duly and Mr. Flowers didn't care about Wolf. They wanted Mum. And they only cared about Prairie Dog because he could show them the way to her.

Keeping their distance from the nearest tepees, the four men traveled by sled and snowshoes, circling around until they spotted Mum shoveling a pathway in the snow under the stern watch of Wounded Eagle. They were maybe sixty yards from Wolf's tepee (which had become my home, too) where Pretty Bear was watching over me. Of course I didn't know this at the time. My mind's eye was not working.

The four men left the dogs and the sled behind to move in quietly on Mum. They didn't see any other villagers around, and didn't anticipate much trouble from the lone Indian woman. I don't know exactly what happened next except that the Indian woman, Wounded Eagle, acted like a wildcat. She punched and kicked, landing blows on three of them. Prairie Dog, like Mum, was trying to stay out of the fray. But when one of the others pushed Wounded Eagle in his direction, my second Indian mother treated him no differently than the rest. She socked him in the nose and bit him in the ear. At some point, Mr. Kittridge picked up the shovel Mum had dropped and whacked the fighting Wounded Eagle on the side of the head. She went down but not out and not silent. She howled in pain. Mr. Kittridge saw how much she was bleeding and gave her a gentler second whack to keep her quiet if not to put her out of her misery.

The plan was to go to Wolf's tepee next and fetch me, but Wounded Eagle's howls had not gone unnoticed. Tepee flaps opened and Indian faces appeared. Men began emerging from their homes. They looked bewildered but were armed with bows and arrows or knives and were potentially dangerous if they could make sense of what was happening. Philip Kittridge determined that there was no way for his rescue party to reach me in Wolf's tepee without him shooting someone. As appealing as that might have been to him, he knew that a shot would only bring out more angry Indians.

"Change in plan!" Mr. Kittridge said. "Back to the sled everyone."

"We're going to make a run for it on the sled?" Prairie Dog asked.

"No. We're going back to your original plan, P.D."

"Huh? My plan?"

"That's right. Things are too worked up on this side of the village. We're going back to that medicine man's tepee and get ourselves a hostage or two."

"My baby!" Mum screamed. "I'm not going any place without my baby."

Her motherly and very understandable request fell on deaf ears. Prairie Dog and Mr. Kittridge were running, not listening. Mr. Flowers scooped Mum up as if she were a mere baby herself and, even as he apologized, raced with her in his arms back to the sled. At that point I'm not even sure she knew who was carrying her or that her white husband, escaped from the Chicago asylum and now running loose on the frontier, was right behind her with his trusty poleax.

Nobody gave chase as the eager-as-ever dogs pulled the overcrowded sled. The warriors who had stepped out of their tepees either didn't see what was happening or were too confused to make sense of it. Left behind was Wounded Eagle, lying flat in the now bloody passageway Mum had shoveled out and no longer making a peep. The other Indians certainly didn't see her. They must have decided there was no real danger and returned to their warm tepees.

The entire rescue party made it back to the other side of the village, where all was quiet. Mr. Kittridge parked the sled behind some trees. Mr. Flowers wanted to stay by the sled with the dogs and Mum. He had to keep his big hand over her mouth because she was hysterical, still screaming for her baby. Mr. Kittridge, though, insisted everyone come with him to the medicine man's tepee and he had the rifle, so Mr. Flowers said a few reassuring words to the sled dogs and dragged Mum along as gently as he could.

"That includes you Prairie Dog," Mr. Kittridge yelled. "Once we are in there and have our hostages, then we can demand the nipper and safe passage out of this hellhole."

Nobody had to force Papa Duly to come along. "I want to go inside a tepee," he declared. "I've never been." He had already found a well-cleared pathway through the snow and was walking fast using his poleax as a push-off pole to maintain his momentum.

And so they all descended on the tepee, which lacked windows, of course, and had a tightly closed entrance. Inside, Wolf and Greasy Nose were preoccupied with sharing their pipe, a good medicine pipe not a peace pipe. Even with his Power to foresee many things, the medicine man had no idea that his home was about to be invaded.

When he realized there was no warrior opposition to contend

with outside the tepee, Mr. Kittridge again modified his plan. He said that he could handle this situation without Prairie Dog's help. He ordered the white renegade to go all the way back to Wolf's tepee and get me.

"What?" Prairie Dog said. "Why now? And why me?"

"Cause I just thought of it now and it's damn hard to do all the thinking for everybody. Only you can get the nipper, P.D. You can just walk right through the village and fetch him. You're one of them, ain't you! If anybody questions you, just tell them that you're bringing the white kid to his Indian father."

"But one of the warriors back there might have seen me with you."

"I'll chance it. Get moving."

"You mean you want *me* to chance it. Listen here, Kittridge."

"I ain't listening to no traitor. You do like I say or I swear I'll plug you where you stand. And don't try to run off on me or I'll tell the whole Sioux Nation how you helped us, and that will get you kilt just as dead."

Prairie Dog didn't move right away. None of his options were particularly inviting. He caught a break. Mr. Kittridge was otherwise distracted. Papa Duly had reached Greasy Nose's tepee and was now poking at the entrance with his poleax.

"You fool!" Mr. Kittridge said. "Wait for me, Duly. I got the gun."

"Don't shoot anyone, Kittridge," Prairie Dog called out. "I'll get the tadpole. Just don't shoot anyone or we're all doomed."

Of course, Mr. Kittridge did not listen. He caught up with Papa Duly, and they pushed their way through the entrance flaps together. Wolf Who Don't Dance was not exactly ready for them, but he was a warrior who could act fast in an emergency. He dropped the medicine pipe, grabbed his bow, and fitted his only available arrow to the bowstring. It is uncertain which one of the two white men he was firing at or what body part he had targeted. Maybe the sight of the poleax scared him more than the rifle. In any case, he unleashed an arrow that found Papa Duly's calf. About the same time a bullet fired from Mr. Kittridge's rolling-block Remington lodged in Wolf's chest.

Prairie Dog saw this horror unfold through the flap opening. As soon as he witnessed Wolf clutching himself somewhere near the heart and falling backward, the white renegade turned and ran as hard as he could, convinced that his Indian benefactor was dead. Exactly where he intended on going at that moment is debatable, but he did eventually end up working his way back to Wolf's tepee and using force (out of character for him, but he was only dealing with the gentlest of Wolf's two Indian wives) to tear me away from Pretty Bear. But you already know about that from the previous diary entry I etched into my skull.

Of course at Greasy Nose's tepee all heck broke loose (this would seemingly call for a "hell" but Mum's distaste for rude language is ingrained in my head). Warriors within hearing distance of the gunshot came running to the scene. Mr. Flowers quickly carried Mum inside before any of them could confront him. The medicine man rolled up the sleeves of his green dress and began to attend to his badly wounded warrior friend next to the pit fire at the center of the tepee. Mum was sobbing too much about my absence to show much interest in the serious bullet wound of my Wolf Dad or the lesser arrow wound of my Chicago Papa. Mr. Kittridge kept the warriors outside at bay with several shots from his Remington and then forced Greasy Nose to apprise them of the situation inside: Wolf was shot and being cared for but would be instantly dispatched, along with the medicine man, should the warriors charge the tepee. Papa Duly, ignoring the arrow sticking out of his calf, Wolf's physical pain, and Mum's psychological anguish, walked to the flaps of the tepee where he could look out upon all the colorful characters wearing moccasins and feathers.

That was the situation when Prairie Dog, true to his word for once, delivered me to the tepee and cut a hole in the back so that I could crawl into Mum's arms. Prairie Dog, as I've mentioned, also managed to get inside after expanding the hole, but the price he paid was an arrow to the buttocks. I suppose Prairie Dog could have just forgotten about me and taken off for the hills alone. But he was a deserter from the Army and didn't dare show up at one of the forts. Anyway, the Sioux probably would have tracked him down or the cold dropped him in his tracks before he even reached the bluecoats. Trying to remain on the good side of the Sioux after Wolf's demise and continuing to live in the village would have been impossible. Prairie Dog knew that all the others, from Red Cloud to Two Feathers, would assume that he had reverted to his true colors and changed sides again.

I am, of course, only guessing about what Prairie Dog's thinking was, because I never could get a good read on a man so full of insincerity and deceit. He was at his most insincere and deceitful worst that day in early December that he led Mum and me out of Fort Phil Kearny and into the clutches of Wolf Who Don't Dance. And all the while he was carrying me to Greasy Nose's tepee and even inside the tepee, I felt he was planning more deceit but wasn't sure what form it would take. As it turned out all he could think about was the pain in his backside. He had a very low threshold for pain, like some babies you might say.

I must confess that not only Prairie Dog could confuse and baffle me. Even more responsible men and women—like Wolf, Wounded Eagle, and Leon Flowers—are hard for me to read at times. No matter what unusual talents I possess for one my age, I am lacking an essential ingredient for true comprehension—experience. It takes experience to understand what motivates people to do the things they do. But I'm not sure even the most experienced human being in the world could truly grasp what goes on in the heads of unusual and often contrary thinkers such as Prairie Dog, Greasy Nose, or Papa Duly—not that I like to lump that trio in one category.

But back to Greasy Nose's tepee. Once I was in Mum's arms, my happiness could only last so long. It was a tense time, what with the place surrounded by warriors just waiting for word from Red Cloud on how to proceed. Mum was holding me tight, praying awkwardly for the two of us (at least I never heard her mention the names Wolf or Abe or Leon) and at least twice wishing that she, instead of younger sister, Maggie, possessed the Hotchkiss family Bible. Mum's going around the tepee kissing all the men except Prairie Dog and Greasy Nose was a one-time thing, but she repeatedly smothered me with kisses (no complaints from me) and whispered sweet things in my ear. Papa Duly was leaning on his poleax watching the Indians as if it was a paying job, though on several occasions I caught him glancing back at Mum and me. Mr. Kittridge was firing random shots out either the front entrance or the hole in back. Wolf was barely hanging onto life. Prairie Dog was moaning about his wound and bemoaning his inevitable doom. Greasy Nose was alternating between attending to Wolf and telling those warriors outside that the Great Spirit did not wish for them to rush the tepee and cause more death. We all knew, of course, that Red Cloud might have a different interpretation of what the Great Spirit wanted.

When Mum's arms finally began shaking from holding me so tight, she put me on the ground. To stretch out a leg that had fallen asleep, I crawled around, just in a circle though as not to alarm her. I wanted to see what was going on outside, so I closed my two regular eyes to try to trigger something in my mind's eye. It didn't work. It was still all smoky in there. Next thing I knew, my head bumped into something hard. To my surprise it turned out to be Papa Duly's shinbone. He had deserted his post and was standing over me with that poleax raised in the air. I felt no fear, but Mum got the impression that he might want to do me harm for some crazy reason only known to him.

"Don't do it, Abe!" she screamed, as she tried to grab him from behind. "He is your son."

But even as Mum grabbed, Abe did what he wanted to do, which was to wave the poleax in circles over my head while saying "Danny be blessed" at least thirty times. By the tenth time, Mum stopped grabbing and gasping and let him finish in peace.

"No harm will come to you, Danny," Papa Duly said to me when he was through making the circles in the air. He tipped his stovepipe hat to me. "You are blessed."

He never touched me. As soon as he walked away, Mum quickly scooped me up and held me tighter than before.

"Lord knows what he thinks that thing has become," Mum muttered. "He used to kill cows with it."

"Ain't that the truth," said Mr. Flowers. "Abraham has come a long way."

From Mum's arms, I noticed that Papa Duly did not return to his post to continue observing the warriors outside. Instead he carried his poleax to where Greasy Nose was throwing magical herbs and powder on Wolf's chest and chanting Sioux words that sounded no different than the ones he used when trying to rid Mum of her cough. Papa Duly stared so intently at what Greasy Nose was doing that he broke the great medicine man's concentration. Greasy Nose threw up his hands, which were now empty. I thought he might get angry and tell Papa Duly to leave before the Great Spirit also got angry. Instead Greasy Nose reached out and touched the hammer face of the poleax.

"It is hard but has strong medicine," Greasy Nose noted.

"I feel no pain in my leg," Papa Duly said, raising the leg to better show the medicine man the arrow sticking into the calf. Papa Duly held his poleax over the arrow and then made circles around it without touching either the feathers or the shaft.

Greasy Nose rubbed his hooked nose and watched, mesmerized in just seconds. After less than a minute, the arrow plopped out, point and all, and fell harmlessly to the ground. I could see no blood on the arrow or on Papa Duly's calf. The medicine man did not act surprised, but I uttered in amazement some word I made up for the occasion and I heard Mum gasp twice as if she was short of breath.

"It is a healing stick, then?" Greasy Nose asked.

"And a blessing stick," Papa Duly replied. "Two sticks in one."

Greasy Nose nodded as if he had heard of such a thing before. "I have much Power, but I am all out of medicine and still Wolf Who Don't Dance is not well," he said. "You think you can help Wolf, do you?"

"I don't know how much medicine is in here," Papa Duly admitted as he lifted the poleax and pressed it to his forehead.

"Generally I do not trust the white man's medicine, but you are not a doctor. What are you?"

"Once I was a killer of domestic animals. When I stopped wanting to kill, they called me crazy. Now, I am a man of peace."

"And do they still call you crazy?"

"It doesn't matter what they call me. I only want to bless and heal."

"You don't act like any white man I've ever met. Not that there's anything wrong with that. But why would you want to help Wolf? I know you are Yellow Hair's pale-faced husband."

"I don't want to bless this man, only to heal him, if I can."

"Well, I've done all I can. I fear Wolf will die now. You can't do him any harm. Do as you like."

Greasy Nose stepped back to give the white man room, and

Papa Duly raised his poleax over Wolf's body. At first he cut wide circles through the smoky air from above the toes of Wolf's moccasins to directly above his bare head. Then he minimized the circles and concentrated his effort over Wolf's wounded chest, which was covered with herbs, powders, and blood and, as far as I could tell, not even rising and falling.

"Wolf be healed," Papa Duly said. And he kept saying those three words, one hundred times by my count. Greasy Nose had his "Hundred in Hand." Papa Duly had his "Hundred in Poleax."

The blade side never touched flesh. I was glad Papa Duly was not trying to dig the bullet out. The poleax was no surgical instrument. It seemed too bulky to be a magic wand. But I had seen with my own two eyes the arrowhead fall out of his calf earlier so I half expected to see the .50-caliber slug pop out of Wolf's chest. But it must have been too powerful a bullet and had penetrated too far or else Papa Duly didn't have enough Power going for him.

"He does not stir," Greasy Nose said. "Do you have other words to say for him?"

Papa Duly shook his head almost violently. His stovepipe hat fell to the ground, but he did not bother to retrieve it. His dirty brown hair danced in all directions, one strand seeming to attach itself to his nose. Sweat poured down his reddening face, filling up the two dimples in his chin and then overflowing. I believe he was tearing up and drooling, too—a baby can tell about those things. His eyes were naturally sunken, but now they seemed to fall back inside his head. Quite frankly, he looked like a madman.

"Never mind," continued Greasy Nose. "They would just be English words anyway. But don't stop. Something is happening. He isn't stirring. He is just lying there. But he must be healing inside."

"You can feel it?" Papa Duly asked as he kept making the circles in the air.

"No. I can see it. That is I can see Wolf back on his feet, and it is not in the past."

"Oh? I see things myself, but never things that haven't happened yet."

"You're a healer, not a prophet. Keep going. Even if your arms are tired, keep going. All circles now! No squares! No triangles! Just nice circles! That's it—the circles of life."

Tremendous hoots and yelps from the outside of the tepee threatened to disrupt this peculiar healing process. But Greasy Nose told Papa Duly to stick to it and then went to the tepee entrance to see what was happening. Mum, with me in her arms, followed. And Mr. Flowers followed us. Mr. Kittridge was already there, sometimes using the sights of his rifle to see his potential targets. Only Prairie Dog hung back, still on his belly as if he feared the arrow in his backside would somehow sink in deeper and strike a vital organ if he so much as wiggled.

"As I thought," Greasy Nose said as he stood in the opening, knowing that nobody on the outside would shoot him. "Red Cloud has arrived. He's out there somewhere."

If I had learned anything in my time in captivity, it was that the Sioux warriors were independent types, each with his own vision, spirit guide, and plan of action, but that when push came to shove, only one opinion mattered. This was Red Cloud's camp—his *country* in fact—and he could pretty much do as he pleased. What he did first was send out his nervous translator. Little Bull, wearing a derby hat and carrying a stick with a white cloth at one end, took up an exposed position thirty feet in front of Greasy Nose's tepee. He quickly raised the stick and made the white cloth dance to show he was no threat. Mr. Kittridge promptly shot the hat clear off his head. Little Bull dropped the stick and ran for cover.

From behind one of the other tepees, we heard Little Bull speak, but just barely, for his voice was small with much squeak to it: "Red Cloud says, 'No talk till I see the gun that never stops firing thrown into the snow.'"

Greasy Nose made a reply in Sioux, which upset Mr. Kittridge. "Only talk American medicine man," he said, "or I put the next bullet in your red hide. I don't trust a word you say, and this gun ain't coming out of my hands."

"We need to talk in English," Greasy Nose called out to his fellow tribesmen. "So show yourself Little Bull. And don't speak like you have glass beads in your mouth. Tell us what the great Red Cloud has to stay."

"I don't want to be shot!" Little Bull screamed. "That's what I say."

"The rifle will not be thrown in the snow," Greasy Nose replied. "But it will not be fired as long as we talk. You have my word."

Greasy Nose gave Mr. Kittridge a hard look. I don't doubt that Mr. Kittridge would have liked to plug the medicine man. But even he knew that you didn't shoot your only standing hostage, at least not yet. He nodded his head and pulled the barrel of his Remington back inside the tepee.

Little Bull showed himself again, but did not come as close as before. He stayed well behind the grounded derby hat with the hole in it. He cleared the glass beads or mice or whatever was in his throat and spoke in a somewhat louder and steadier voice: "Red Cloud says, 'You are brave men, as brave as Fetterman. But you need not die like Fetterman. If Wolf Who Don't Dance lives and you send him out unharmed with his yellow-haired wife, his hairless son, and our much good medicine man, then . . .'"

"No deal!" yelled Mr. Kittridge. "Tell Red Cloud we are taking the woman and the nipper out of here and if we don't get safe passage I'll shoot his medicine man just like I shot his great warrior."

"Go ahead and tell Red Cloud," Greasy Nose shouted to Little Bull. "Also tell him that Greasy Nose wishes for no more killing. Tell him I am willing to go with the white eyes until they are safe away."

Little Bull scurried back to wherever Red Cloud was hiding. On the return he was not moving so fast, and he again stopped short of his previous mark.

"Red Cloud says that your Power and Wolf's war shirt will protect you from the white man's bullets," Little Bull said, but he didn't sound like he believed that himself. "He says that his warriors would attack at once but he does not want to put Yellow Hair or Little Eagle Bear in harm's way. He says to send them both to safety and to let the men fight."

"Easy for him to say with hundreds of warriors backing him," said Mr. Kittridge. "Well, you tell the chief that we don't like them odds. You tell him to step out here and face me like a real man."

Little Bull just stood there like a scared rabbit surrounded by hungry foxes. Mr. Kittridge prepared to fire his Remington again, but Greasy Nose pushed the barrel aside and stepped in front of him.

"Remind Red Cloud that the white eyes have only come here because of the woman and the child," the medicine man called out to Little Bull. "They want to take them away from here. They do *not* want to fight."

"I'll fight Red Cloud any day of the week," Mr. Kittridge proclaimed.

"You're not helping the situation, Mr. Kittridge," Mr. Flowers said.

"And you can, Flowers? It's bad enough I have to listen to the redskins, let alone to a black-skinned fool who comes west without a gun and with a plum crazy white man who thinks he's some kind of medicine man!"

Instead of arguing the point, Mr. Flowers stunned us all by barging his way between Greasy Nose and Philip Kittridge and walking out into the open waving a white handkerchief. When nobody shot him from the front or from behind, he continued walking. He picked up Little Bull's stick and derby and held them out until Little Bull got his orders from Red Cloud and ventured forward to reclaim them. Little Bull then got nervous feet and backed away until he was parallel to the most advanced warriors.

"I am Leon P. Flowers from Chicago, Illinois, and I got some things to say. You can start now, Mr. Translator. Commence! Translate my words for Mr. Cloud."

Little Bull did as he was instructed, and Mr. Flowers talked on. Except for their contrasting voices (one high-pitched and nasal, the other husky and a little horse), there was no other sound to be heard. Not even an Indian dog barked. The warriors were all staring at Mr. Flowers, perhaps impressed with his size and no doubt as fascinated by his dark skin as that Crow hunting party had been.

"This war you got going with the soldiers holed up in those forts ain't our war at all," Mr. Flowers said. "I got a friend inside who is the rightful, legitimate, genuine husband of the one you call Yellow Hair, and the one you call Little Eagle Bear is rightfully called Danny and is the rightful, legitimate, genuine son of that happily reunited couple from Chicago."

Mr. Flowers waited for Little Bull to finish the translation and then continued speaking, sounding like a preacher at a pulpit or one of those orators back in the U.S. Congress (that's according to Mum—I never heard either type). His voice boomed except those times he respectfully lowered it to talk of Wolf's grave condition.

"It sorrows me to see your mighty warrior lying in that tepee. It is unfortunate that Wolf was shot. But, I tell you he shot an arrow first, and he hit my friend, the husband of Yellow Hair and the father of Little Eagle Bear. Wolf is *not* either of those things. Only one of us came to your village with a gun, and he only shot Wolf to defend the rest of us. He is as sorry as the rest of us for what had to be done. And even as I speak, our medicine man, the same friend of mine who is the husband of Yellow Hair and the father of Little Eagle Bear, is working hard to save the life of Wolf, the very man who stole his wife and son. My friend's name is Abraham, which is the same name of the Great White Chief in Washington who freed the slaves and who was shot by a very bad man named John Wilkes Booth. But you don't need to know that, I suppose. All you need to know is that Abraham is not only a friend to me but also a friend to Wolf and to the great Red Cloud and to all his people and that there is nothing in the world he would rather do than heal the mighty warrior who lies inside that tepee even as I . . ."

"Talk too fast!" Little Bull shouted. "Stop. I lost you at that man Booth."

"Never mind, I'm finished—that is I'm finished talking. And in conclusion, Mr. Cloud must know that all I say is the truth and spoken in true friendship. White men might tell him lies, but not this man of color. And if for some reason he doubts me, he can just ask his own medicine man. Mr. Nose can vouch for my every word! Oh, and one other thing. I heard you fellas killed our sled dogs. I wish you hadn't done that. They was good dogs. But dogs is dogs. And bygones be bygones. No reason for any more killing, and I know my good friend Abraham feels exactly the same way on this subject."

After Little Bull finally got done with the translating there was plenty of mutterings and stirrings among the warriors, and I began to fear for Mr. Flowers' safety. The only words I made

out were *"Matosapa, Matosapa!"* Mr. Flowers didn't like the
sound of that and retreated until his back was up against Greasy
Nose's tepee. He was shaking all over and needed to steady his
big body.

"That's a tough crowd," Mr. Flowers admitted, wiping his
broad brow. "I think them fellas is calling me some mighty bad
names."

"Not so," said Greasy Nose. *"Matosapa* means 'black bear.'
That's a show of respect."

"That right? But you Sioux shoot bears, don't you?"

"Naturally. But we respect them."

"Right. Only time I was this scared was back in '60 when I
showed up at the Wigwam in Chicago at the corner of Lake and
Market streets where they was having the Republican National
Convention. I don't know what got into me then either. I was
but a simple handyman of color, but I started to tell them bigwig
white-faced politicians about the evils of slavery. Some listened,
some didn't. I got escorted out of the Wigwam faster than you
can say Jack Robinson. But you know something, those boys
went ahead and nominated Mr. Lincoln for the presidency of
the United States."

At that point I did something that amazed me even more
than what Mr. Flowers had done. I stood up on my own two
feet so I could get a better look at the goings-on outside, and
for the first time in my life, I walked. It wasn't a long walk. I
took three and a half steps before falling softly onto a deer hide.
But it counts! Nobody noticed, not even Mum. It's understandable, I suppose, because something else pretty big was happening. Red Cloud appeared. If he had ever been in hiding, he sure
wasn't now. He walked straight for the tepee, wearing a blue
Army coat and a non-matching headdress with horns. He was
not armed. Two Feathers, the young coup counter, followed
him, carrying not a coup stick but a rocking chair. After Two

Feathers set the chair down about thirty feet from the entrance, Red Cloud dismissed him with a wave of the hand. Two Feathers could only demonstrate his bravery by walking away slowly and wiggling his fanny at us.

"He no doubt stole that rocker after murdering a family in a covered wagon," Mr. Kittridge muttered. "He has a lot of nerve."

"That he does," said Greasy Nose.

There wasn't much of a breeze that afternoon, but I swear that chair started to rock back and forth on its own. After a while, Red Cloud settled into the seat like he was a retired gentleman and this was his front porch. He rocked slowly and waved to someone. At first I thought it was to his friend Greasy Nose, but the medicine man told Mr. Flowers he should wave back. Mr. Flowers did.

The chief motioned for Little Bull, and the translator scurried forward to take up a kneeling position behind the rocker. Red Cloud spoke and Little Bull had no trouble keeping up with the translation because the chief's speech was loud and deliberate and full of dramatic pauses and gestures: 'Hear my words. *Matosapa* speaks much truth. We are the people who use the bow and arrow. You are the people who wear hats and garments and are paler than us but sometimes darker. The Great Sprit protects both of us. It is true all across this land we are melting like snow on the hillside, while you are growing like spring grass. But you who have come to our island of lodges are few in number. You are uninvited guests. You are at our mercy. Whether you live or die will be decided in time. I, Red Cloud, will decide. But first, Red Cloud will have more talk with *Matosapa*.'

Mr. Flowers, with the encouragement of Greasy Nose, began walking toward the chief. His legs wobbled but his knees did not buckle.

"What the hell!" Mr. Kittridge said. "He wants to talk to the colored man?"

"You should just be happy he still wants to talk, Phil," Prairie Dog called out from the back of the tepee. "When he stops, that's when we're sure to lose our scalps."

"This is too good a shot to pass up," said Mr. Kittridge, as he started to raise his Remington. "The Army will give me a medal for shooting Red Cloud. And my brother will be avenged. Come on, Flowers, You're right in my line of fire. Get out of the way, you Goddamned . . ."

Mum slapped Mr. Kittridge on the cheek and told him to watch his language. Then she told him she would slap him again if he didn't put away his rifle. Mr. Kittridge didn't take it well. He looked as if he'd just as soon shoot her. But he restrained himself.

"This might be a dirty redskin trick," he said, as he threw the Remington over his shoulder and turned his back to her. "They could be getting ready to storm us from the other side. I'd better check the back hole."

"It's still there," Prairie Dog told him. "But there ain't no escape."

Mr. Flowers advanced to within six feet of the rocker before finally stopping.

"Hair like buffalo," Red Cloud said in English.

"Yes, sir, I imagine so. To be honest with you, I ain't never seen a buffalo close up. I am starting to lose my head of hair naturally, you know with age. But I ain't complaining. I won't mind at all if this somewhat slower removal process continues."

Red Cloud listened to the translation and smiled. "Yes, *Matosapa*," he said. "You talk."

What followed was a lengthy exchange between the two of them, with Little Bull, though often looking confused, translating and the rest of us listening as best we could. While Red Cloud rocked away, Mr. Flowers told him about Chicago—the tenement building, the stockyards, the slaughterhouses, the Chicago River, Bubbly Creek, the dozen railroad lines now reaching the city, the one-hundred-thousand people, the nomination of President Lincoln at the 1860 Republican Convention, and how he wasn't going back home because there were too many pale faces. That last remark, which lost nothing in translation, cracked up Red Cloud, and he nearly fell out of the chair laughing. When he recovered, the chief said it would be a good idea if the bluecoats tore down their three forts on the Bozeman Trail and carried them off to Chicago.

"I understand, Mr. Cloud," Mr. Flowers said. "My friends and I would only be too happy to go to the soldiers at the forts right now and tell them you wish for them to move to Chicago. We just need your OK, OK?"

The translation only inspired Red Cloud to proudly name four other American cities he knew about—St. Louis, Washington, New York, and Sioux City, Iowa.

"Sure," agreed Mr. Flowers. "When we leave here, first thing we'll do is tell the soldiers you want them to move not just to Chicago but to all them other places as well—and just as soon as humanly possible."

Little Bull provided Red Cloud's terse response: "I think they already know."

The chief had become stern, as if to balance his emotions. He stopped rocking. He held his stomach as if he had been gut shot. And his eyes narrowed suspiciously, as if he were talking to a peace commissioner sent from Washington.

"Something bothering you, Mr. Cloud?" Mr. Flowers asked.

"No talk," the chief shouted in English. He motioned Mr. Flowers to go back to the tepee, and Mr. Flowers obliged, without ever showing his full back to the Indians. Maybe Red Cloud had become bored with all the idle chatter. Maybe he didn't think it helped his image with his warriors to be smiling so much to the enemy, black or white.

The chief began shouting out words in his language that Little Bull did not even try to translate. Greasy Nose, talking Sioux, responded. I had no clue what they were saying. Red Cloud did signal his medicine man to come closer, but Greasy Nose could not oblige. Mr. Kittridge had returned to the front of the tepee and was pointing his Remington against the small of Greasy Nose's back.

"You're our hostage," Mr. Kittridge reminded Greasy Nose and maybe himself as well. "You stay put. Tell Red Cloud to let us go and no harm will come to you."

"No need. He understands the whole picture now. He isn't worried about me. He has made a demand—that Wolf come out."

"What did you tell him?"

"I told him the truth, that Wolf could not come out. That I had done everything in my power but that Wolf had already sung his death song and . . ."

"I really should kill you," shouted Mr. Kittridge. "Hostage or no hostage. He'll kill us anyway if Wolf is dead. Isn't that right?"

"I can't speak for Red Cloud."

"Well, you go back inside and see about Wolf, medicine man. Then you come back here in no more than half a minute and, whether Wolf is dead or not, you tell Red Cloud that Wolf is doing fine—and you tell him in American. That will at least buy us some time."

"He will know I am lying. He must see Wolf and hear his words."

"We both know that's impossible, so we die, is that it? Well, then I'll just have to shoot him out of his chair. His warriors will scalp me and mutilate me like they did my little brother, but am I afraid? Hell, no! I know the Army will hear of my great deed and honor me just like U.S. Grant for a thousand years. Why I bet they'll put up a statue of me holding Remy in Washington, D.C. And on the base of the statue it will say 'In fond memory of Philip Kittridge, the fearless civilian who sent Red Cloud to his well-deserved Hell and saved the Bozeman Trail!' "

Mr. Kittridge made me so mad. And it looked like this time he really would put his Remington to bad use. To distract him, I stood up to my full height and tried to shake both my fists at him. When I lifted my arms, though, it threw off my balance and I plopped back down on my bottom. He didn't notice. Nobody did. But it didn't matter. There was a much bigger distraction. Something happened—no easier for me to explain than a double rainbow or a man walking on water or a red cloud forming in the blue sky.

"My God!" cried Mum.

*"Wakan Tanka!"* cried Greasy Nose.

"Holy shit!" cried Prairie Dog.

This is what happened. Papa Duly made a few thousand circles with his poleax over the chest of Wolf Who Don't Dance and issued nearly as many repetitions of "Wolf be healed!" Then his trembling arms gave out. He could hold the poleax not one second longer. The blade face struck the ground, only inches from Wolf's left ear—a near tragic accident. Papa Duly's legs gave out next. He collapsed in a heap, drained of his energy, his tongue hanging out. He curled up in a tight ball as if there was nothing left to do but return to the womb. He was temporarily removed from this world. He did not notice when Wolf rose off his back and walked without a grimace or a smile to the front of the tepee.

Wolf brushed past Mum, stepped over me, and snatched the Remington rolling-block rifle out of the hands of Mr. Kittridge, who was too stunned to resist. Greasy Nose and Mr. Flowers gave Wolf plenty of room at the tepee opening. Wolf spun around with the rifle in both hands and, as he completed his full circle, he unleashed the rifle into the air. It was a mighty heave, but the rifle did not go as far as an arrow. Remy landed six feet short of the rocking chair. Red Cloud watched the flight without flinching, and then nodded his approval. When Wolf followed the rifle out of the tepee, the chief lowered his buffalo horns and sprang out of the rocker to greet his friend. First Red Cloud poked Wolf's shoulder. Then he clasped his arm. And finally he gave him an unrestrained embrace, but it didn't last long because the chief suddenly stepped back and examined Wolf's bare chest.

Red Cloud said just one word, *"Akisni!"*

Little Bull, speaking with enthusiasm for a change, made the translation: "Healed!"

Most of the warriors were already raising their bows and arrows to the sky and roaring their approval. Some chanted Wolf's name, some sang an honoring song for the man who had risen from the dead. Indian women and children soon joined them. I saw Pretty Bear and Wounded Eagle, my two Indian mothers, standing in the crowd with their arms interlocked, supporting each other. Both looked to be in a daze, but that didn't keep them both from smiling as they waited their turn to touch their living husband again.

Two Feathers took the opportunity to rush forward. I thought it might be to celebrate the surprise appearance of one of his warrior heroes, but he ran past Wolf without delivering so much as a pat on the back. Instead, he touched Mr. Flowers' relatively small black nose and then pulled back his hand as if he had burned a finger on a live coal.

*"Anho!"* he yelled.

But that wasn't enough for the young warrior. He ran ahead to the still stunned Mr. Kittridge and knocked him flat on the back with a manful punch to the nose.

"*Anho! Anho!*" he yelled. It was the second time in the young warrior's life he had counted coup on Philip Kittridge.

As the celebration continued outside, Greasy Nose reentered the tepee to pull Papa Duly out of his womb-like ball. It wasn't easy. It took most of the Indian medicine man's Power to get the physically and mentally exhausted white medicine man to his feet. It took Papa Duly even longer to realize that the first patient (besides himself) he had treated with his unusual healing stick was not only alive but also walking among his people again. Greasy Nose restored the stovepipe hat to Papa Duly's head and led the white medicine man out of the tepee. Their appearance caused the warriors' cheering to rich new heights. It made my ears hurt, but I did not cover them. Papa Duly had barely enough strength left to raise his poleax over his head. Mum, leaving me behind in a rare forgetful moment (I didn't mind at all), found an opening in the crowd and came up to him from behind. She wrapped her arms around his tall body, her hands clasping together at his chest as if she wanted to keep his pounding heart from bursting.

I've admitted to you, dear readers, that I don't understand adults all that well, not even Mum at times. I know just then that she saw something in her husband that had been lost since his return from the Civil War. Exactly what she saw, I can't say, but I hope to figure it out some day when I acquire more experience.

I held back because I didn't want to be stepped on by a happy moccasin. But I felt I was missing too much, so I left the tepee, and I wasn't about to come out crawling. I walked out straight and tall, or as tall as a baby my age can get. I guess I was trying to reach Mum and Papa Duly. But I didn't quite make it. I was good for twelve steps. When I started to go down, one of the adults reached out and caught me from behind. Not that I was in any danger—a baby is used to falling right and left, almost always without injuring himself. But I still considered it a nice gesture. I figured the adult who grabbed me must be Mr. Flowers, the great black bear orator, since he had done so much for me already. It wasn't. I caught a glimpse of him off to my right—half a dozen curious Indian children had him surrounded. The hands that held me were red and strong. When the man raised me high enough, I could see the horns on his head and his amused face. I looked him straight in the eye.

"Tanks, Wed Cowed," I said.

Well, that's about it—the whole story of my captivity and release. Wolf and Red Cloud did indeed let Mum and me go free, along with Papa Duly and Mr. Flowers. Prairie Dog Burrows and Philip Kittridge were not so lucky. Both men had done Mum and me wrong, so I wasn't about to shed a tear over them . . . at least not at the moment we left them behind to their fate. I was not without sympathy, though. After all, I had communicated with them both, in my own fashion, and they had occasionally done some good, no matter what their motives. Certainly if the Sioux killed them, I hope the pair got to keep their hair and most of their body parts.

Leaving the village wasn't as easy as you might think. My two Indians mothers said they would never forget their Little Eagle Bear and added a few other things in Sioux that made me ache inside even though I didn't understand them. Pretty Bear gave me a new wolf's-tooth necklace to protect me, and Wounded Eagle found my favorite rattlesnake rattle, which I have not yet outgrown. I tried not to shed a tear as I parted company with them (you know, to show what a tough little Sioux infant I was), but I cannot say I was totally successful. Wolf didn't have any parting gift for me, except for one tear that started rolling down from his right eye before he hurried off to hunt a buffalo or something. Greasy Nose merely said to us, "Till we meet again."

We didn't have the sled or mush dogs, of course, or much sense of direction, and none of the Sioux had horses or mules to spare. But we were not turned out to walk in the deep snow with no guidance. Red Cloud generously provided us with two travois pulled by Indian dogs (Mum and I and the supplies rested on one travois, and Mr. Flowers, Papa Duly, and the healing poleax on the other) and directed Two Feathers and some of the other young bucks to lead us through the winter wonderland to the Bozeman Trail and then up it until we were safely within range of the Fort C.F. Smith guns. It wasn't such a long trip, but even so, when it was over, both Mr. Flowers and Papa Duly were sad to have to say goodbye to the dogs. They expressed the wish that the winter would be over soon and that the Sioux would not grow hungry enough to make a meal of the dogs.

Ever since, Mr. Flowers, Mum, and I have been waiting here at the fort. Papa Duly eventually made his difficult decision to take his poleax back to Greasy Nose's tent—a decision that Mum and I both understand and respect even though it is beyond the comprehension of all the soldiers here, as well as comfort-loving civilians like Grace and Toby Pennington. I imagine most people still think Papa Duly is crazy, but I don't care what they think. When my mind's eye isn't acting up, I can catch glimpses of him looking at me with his own mind's eye, listening to Greasy Nose, healing folks, sharing creation stories, going on vision quests, blessing beasts and eatable plants, and trying to stomach a little buffalo meat. On rare occasion I also see him interacting with Wolf Dad and my two Indian mothers, who clearly are grateful to him for saving Wolf but have no idea what makes him tick. Oh, and one more thing I've seen— another miracle you might say. Both Pretty Bear and Wounded Eagle are pregnant. All I can say is good luck with all that.

That concludes my etching on the skull for now. I am about

etched out. I wonder how many words my head can hold and how many I will be able to transfer onto paper when I learn how to write. Well, I guess if you're reading this now, it must have worked out fairly well. I have a feeling that most of you out there, whether on the frontier or not, just love a good captivity story, especially one with a happy ending like this one. At least I think the ending to this story will be happy, although I am convinced Red Cloud and his fighting Sioux will be back on the warpath as soon as the snow melts.

I won't worry about that now. It's time to walk over to Mum and spring into her arms and maybe show her my new third tooth. Walking and jumping a little and growing a third tooth might not sound like much—and I'm not one to boast or call too much attention to myself—but just remember dear readers that I won't even turn nine months for another two weeks. No matter what happens on the frontier in the future, whether or not Mum and I ever make it up the Bozeman Trail all the way to Virginia City, I think you'll agree with me on one thing—I've come a mighty long way since venturing out from the exquisite warmth and security of the womb.

# ABOUT THE AUTHOR

**Gregory J. Lalire** majored in history at the University of New Mexico and was a newspaperman in New Mexico, Montana, New York, and Virginia for sixteen years. *The Red Sweater,* his children's book set in the Rockies, was published in 1982. In 1990 he became copy editor and staff writer for ten history magazines published in Leesburg, Virginia. His article "Custer's Art Stand" in the April 1994 *Wild West* magazine was a Western Writers of America (WWA) Spur Finalist. Since 1995 he has been the editor of *Wild West* [www.WildWestMag.com], which chronicles frontier history and is part of the Weider History Group. He is a member of both the WWA and the Wild West History Association. Much of his spare time is spent writing fiction.